THE CURSE OF THE SUNDERED WINGS

M.P. HILL

All rights reserved. This book or any portion thereof may not be reproduced or used in any manner whatsoever without the express written permission of the publisher except for the use of brief quotations in a book review.

This book is a work of fiction. Any references to historical events, real people, and real places are used fictitiously. Other names, characters, places, and events are products of the author's imagination. Any resemblances to actual events or places or persons, living or dead, is entirely coincidental.

eBook ISBN: 979-8-9921261-1-2

Paperback ISBN: 979-8-9921261-0-5

Hardcover ISBN: 979-8-9921261-2-9

Original Cover Art by Lydia Faye Hill

Copyright © 2025 by M.P. Hill

Published by Frostglen Publishing, LLC

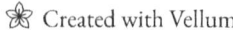 Created with Vellum

To all who have braved the unknown in search of a better life.

CONTENTS

Prologue	1
1. Missing, Presumed Dead	5
2. It's Called Theorizing	21
3. Dinner with Mr. Blackstone	31
4. Moonlight Machinations	43
5. A Fortuitous Discovery	55
6. Nothing Worthwhile is Safe	67
7. Hidden and Heartfelt	85
8. Murder in the Lounge	99
9. Destiny	115
10. A Question of Trust	133
11. Close Your Eyes	153
12. Sermon in the Saloon	165
13. The Engine Room	179
14. In the Shadows	193
15. Facing Judgment	209
16. Mr. Harlowe's Tale	219
17. Deadline	231
18. The Man at the Center of the Universe	241
19. Emily's Gambit	253
20. The Wing of Light	271
21. Knife's Edge	283
22. Together at Last	297
23. The Curse of the Sundered Wings	317
24. Return of the Sun	329
Afterword	343
Acknowledgments	345
About the Author	347
Also by M.P. Hill	349

PROLOGUE

Lieutenant Marvin Morgan tried one last time to flex his deadened fingers. They remained frustratingly still. At this point, the only color left in his hand came from his silver wedding band. He grimaced and turned the withered limb over, studying it with a detached sort of sorrow. The curse was spreading faster than he'd expected.

One whispered promise. One moment of weakness. That was all it had taken to seal his fate.

The guilty objects lay upon his desk. Their golden surfaces, ever greedy, drank in what little sunlight remained in his stateroom. They were insatiable. Cursed. The sort of artifacts that dangled a man's dreams before him, only to drop the terrors of the night into his outstretched palms. How easy it had been to fall prey to their temptations! To lose all sense of restraint!

Morgan's lone consolation was that he would soon, gladly, be rid of the bedeviled things.

Of course, no matter how quickly that happy moment arrived, it would be too late for him. One only needed to look around his stateroom to see that. He had tried not to notice the strange shadows climbing the walls. Done his best to ignore their creeping presence. But it was no use; these illusory creatures, his silent tormentors, had been hounding him all afternoon. Were they manifestations of the curse? Hallucinations? It was growing difficult to tell the difference. Frankly, Morgan wasn't sure there was one anymore.

This tension was joined by the thrumming of the RMS *Olympic's* mighty engines beneath his feet. The ship was now an hour removed from Cherbourg, racing the sunset on her way to the vast expanse of the open ocean. Morgan had been at sea enough times to know that her masters were opening up her boilers and stoking them for speed. They had no reason not to do so. Those men were unaware of the evil their ship bore as cargo. Ignorant of the ancient powers that had already been unleashed on board.

They would have reconsidered their passage if they'd known. A part of Morgan wished they still could.

One of the shadows dashed between his nose and his hands. He waved it away, only to flinch when the returning light of his desk lamp cast its glow upon a photograph.

The message on its back was brief:

Mitternacht. Bootsdeck. Komm alleine.

Midnight. Boat deck. Come alone.

He had discovered this ominous message waiting for him in his stateroom. Morgan had his suspicions about who might be behind it. If he was right, he was facing an enemy far more ruthless than he'd encountered in South Africa. An adversary who held no fear of the curse. Someone who would stop at nothing to possess the Wings of Amun-Ra. The same enemy who had stalked him from the shores of Egypt on through the fields of France. *The things that madman could do with power like this...*

His arm spasmed. The curse had reached his wrist now, spreading its decay further with every beat of his heart. A wraith with ram's horns darted around his desk, its maw gaping wide, just as footsteps passed by his door. Morgan held his breath until they faded. They weren't his enemy's footsteps, not yet, but they were a reminder that his time was short. He rushed to pack the artifacts away.

The first stars appeared beyond his porthole. Night had fallen. It was time to move.

Morgan checked the corridor outside. Empty. He slipped out into the darkness. If all went well this evening, his midnight contact would be flushed out of hiding, the Wings of Amun-Ra would be separated, and England would be safe once more.

And if all went poorly—well, such a thing didn't bear considering. After all, there was no going back. Not now. Morgan had made his choice.

He could only pray it was the right one.

I

MISSING, PRESUMED DEAD

Once you have the facts, I'm sure you'll agree that everything I'm about to tell you was Oliver Wentworth's fault.

Just... don't ask him about it. With no small amount of exuberance, my best friend will insist that his twin sister, Emily, is to blame; he's charming, so you might even believe him. If you ask her, Emily might fault me, James Kelly, just to keep things fair. But let's be honest: no one looking at the facts objectively would hold me accountable for the mess we got tangled up in on that fateful Atlantic crossing.

On second thought, perhaps I should tell you what happened and let you decide for yourself. That seems the fairest way to settle the matter.

Our story begins aboard the RMS *Olympic*, sister ship to the now-infamous *Titanic*. We were heading home after spending the summer of 1913 in Paris. For the twins and me, it had been a season of celebration, our reward for finishing high school in the spring. For Dr. Wentworth, the twins' father, it had been an opportunity to network abroad. For Mrs. Wentworth, the twins' mother, it had been months of visits with yet another medical specialist. Her health had long been fragile. Trips like these were nothing new. Neither was my presence on them. Since losing my parents, I'd become a constant fixture at the Wentworths' side. It was only their kindness that had saved me from living my life on a dingy factory floor.

We boarded the *Olympic* on a Wednesday. If all had gone according to plan, we would have been back home in New York the following Wednesday night, perhaps even in time to watch the sunset from the Wentworths' front porch. Things started off well enough. The first day of our trip was blissfully uneventful. It was the second day of our journey, just after lunch on Thursday, when things went awry.

The sun was out in force on that autumn afternoon, its waning brilliance still strong enough to ward off the chill of the ocean air. Rays of light sparkled on the rolling sea. A breeze waltzed alongside them, its gentle steps sufficient to bring the flags to life, but not so strong as to be uncomfortable. The aroma of sea salt was thick enough I could taste it on my tongue. Were it not for the steady hum of the *Olympic's* engines, one would never suspect that we were traveling on an ocean liner and not vacationing at a coastal villa. Such was the grandeur of our floating hotel.

Everything would have been perfect if I hadn't been losing to Oliver at a deck game called quoits. There are precious few things in the world worse than losing to Oliver Wentworth in a game of skill. You'll find this out for yourself, but I'll warn you now that my friend is a bit of a talker. He chirps even more than usual when he's winning. Unfortunately, he was winning that afternoon.

"Had enough, Jimmy?" Oliver crowed.

I shot him a glare fierce enough to wilt the hairs of his

meticulously groomed beard. "You won't be asking me that after this toss," I said with more confidence than I felt. "This'll be a comeback for the ages."

Oliver tucked his hands into the pockets of his tailored suit, his smugness so palpable he could have bottled and sold it. My best friend is the suave sort: tall, cheeky, and effortlessly handsome, seasoned with a dash of that devil-may-care charisma girls swoon for. His smile that afternoon was wide enough to flash every one of his brilliantly white teeth.

"Prove it."

I turned away and gripped my quoit, sizing up my next toss. Oliver and I were taking turns throwing them at a spindle affixed to a wooden board. Nothing but a perfect throw could help me catch up to him. I had two chances left.

"Here goes!" I spun and released the quoit.

It arced through the air, flying over the gathered crowd of onlookers... over the spindle... and just past it. My wayward quoit rolled to rest right in front of Oliver's sister, Emily. She tipped her straw hat at me and smiled in a bright, cheery sort of way before winking mischievously.

"Take care, Apollo," she said, laughing. "I am not suited to the role of Hyacinth."

I laughed along, though I wasn't entirely certain why. There was a story about Apollo killing someone with an errant discus. At least, I think there was. *Had that been Hyacinth?*

The nuance of her reference may have been lost on me, but I can remember precisely what Emily looked like when she made it. She was sitting primly on a deck chair with a book clasped in her hands, looking far more composed than anyone our age had a right to look. Her auburn hair, loose strands blowing in the breeze like wisps of flame, framed her heart-shaped face and matched the flowing lines of her colorful, calf-length skirt. Like Oliver, Emily had natural charisma. She was magnetic.

I could have watched her for hours.

Oliver stepped up next to me, his last quoit in hand, blocking Emily from my view. "Bad luck, that. Speaking of unfortunate turns—you've heard about the man who went overboard last night, haven't you?"

The breeze swept over us, colder than before. Flags snapped back and forth overhead. I raised an eyebrow at Oliver, who was waiting for a response, though I hadn't any idea why he was asking me this. Everyone had heard about Lieutenant Morgan. The Boer War veteran had been a second-class passenger, just like us, until he'd fallen from the boat deck after we left port in Cherbourg. The ship stopped to search for him, but he never resurfaced. "Missing, presumed dead," one of the masters-at-arms, William Harlowe, had said. It was a tragedy. There were all manner of rumors swirling about his fall.

I suppressed a shudder. Despite the magnificent weather, I couldn't keep the image of the dark, churning water below the ship's hull out of my mind. Drowning in the Atlantic would be an awful way to lose one's life. It wasn't something I wanted to think about when we were surrounded by an endless horizon of open ocean. That felt a bit too much like tempting fate.

"Indeed, I have," I said. "But what does that have to do with our game?"

"I'm simply reminding you that your loss will only be the second most tragic thing to happen on this voyage. It's good for one to maintain a sense of proportion."

"Is that a joke you should make in public? It hardly seems respectful of the dead."

Oliver shrugged before he let his quoit fly. It spun off to the right, barely missing the spindle before rolling to the side. "Perhaps not," he replied, frowning at the final resting place of his throw. "But since when have we been concerned with politeness?"

I chuckled as I squared up to make my last toss. "Well, it's not just us here, is it?"

It was a rhetorical question. A small crowd surrounded us to spectate the end of our game.

Mrs. Henderson worked her knitting needles from the deck chair beside Emily. A retired governess, she tutted whenever Oliver made a cheeky remark, something that occurred at an industrious rate. I confess I found her behavior tiresome. Evidently, Emily and I agreed on this point; despite her proximity to Mrs. Henderson, Oliver's sister resolutely avoided conversation with the oft-offended woman, preferring to keep her face buried in Wilkie Collins's *The Woman in White*.

Next to them stood the thin, slight, and twitchy Mr. Clarke, a bespectacled journalist from Sweden whose fraying tweed jacket had seen better days. To hear him tell it, he'd had a rather decorated field career, though I'd never heard of him or his work before this voyage. Perhaps he was bigger in Sweden than he was in New York. Regardless, today, the fastidious man had been assigned as our scorekeeper. He tallied each point we made on a slate board.

At the edge of our group, an elderly gentleman with a silver mustache, known to all of us only as Captain Dinsmore, entertained a couple of wide-eyed children with tales of his seafaring days. His voice boomed as he regaled the youngsters with a story about whales that I was almost certain couldn't be true. Of course, given his fondness for whiskey—there was, even now, a well-nursed bottle peeking out from his oversized boots—it's quite possible that Captain Dinsmore didn't know the truth of his tale, either.

"I suppose we do have something of an audience," Oliver admitted, having taken a moment to look around at the crowd. "But setting my joke aside, you must admit it is tragic this chap emerged from the Boer War a hero, only to pitch himself off an ocean liner. One struggles to make sense of it."

We must have been talking louder than we'd realized. Mrs. Henderson's knitting needles paused mid-click, and she trained her sharp, watery eyes on us, her lips pursed in disapproval. Emily lowered her book to peer at us over the top of its well-worn cover. Captain Dinsmore waved the children off and took a swig of his whiskey before turning to face us from the edge of his chair.

Mr. Clarke adjusted his wire-rimmed glasses and tucked the scoring slate under his arm. He was a man possessed of a brisk manner, and when he stepped closer to where Oliver and I were standing, we stopped our game to listen to him speak. "I have heard the most remarkable rumors surrounding your Lieutenant Morgan's demise," the journalist said. His voice was high and reedy. "Tales of a smuggling ring, deals gone wrong, and a pair of remarkable Egyptian artifacts. Some even say that an ancient curse claimed his life."

"A what?" Oliver asked.

Mr. Clarke repeated himself.

"An ancient curse, you say?" Oliver winked at me. "I know some choice phrases in Latin, Mr. Clarke, but I daresay they couldn't kill a man."

"I fear I am not referring to curse words." He adjusted his glasses once again. "No, this is something much more unusual. I am referring to a pair of cursed artifacts known as the Wings of Amun-Ra. Are you familiar with them?"

Oliver and I exchanged a confused glance. My best friend shrugged.

Mrs. Henderson saved us from responding. "Oh yes, Mr. Clarke," she began, her tone as sharp as her sewing needles, "I have heard talk of Marvin Morgan bringing—or perhaps smuggling—those accursed things on board. To do so is to tempt bad luck, I say."

"Ah! Mrs. Henderson. Who, might I ask, were you talking to when you learned of them? A member of the crew, perhaps?"

Mrs. Henderson raised her wrinkled chin. "My nephew, Reginald Blackstone, of course! Reginald is an expert on Egyptian history. And an expert on curses, of course, though I would prefer not to ponder such blasphemous things."

"Curses?" Emily closed her book with a snap before rising to her feet. "Really, Mrs. Henderson, I should have thought you would know better than to indulge in such fancies. Lieutenant Morgan's death was nothing but an unfortunate mishap. An accident."

Mr. Clarke frowned. "I have heard differently. Do you know of anyone who witnessed Lieutenant Morgan's fall? There has been much speculation about this supposed accident, but not a word from anyone who saw it happen."

"A steward told me that passengers on both A-deck and B-deck heard him screaming on the way down," claimed Captain Dinsmore, who now seemed to be just as invested in this macabre conversation as Mr. Clarke. "He was shouting something about Anubis. Most unusual!"

I had no idea whether or not he should be believed. I glanced at Oliver, who looked as befuddled as I was.

"Be that as it may," Mr. Clarke said, folding his hands behind his back, "I believe that a dangerous plot is afoot, and there is not an excess of time to uncover it. The *Olympic* will dock in New York on Wednesday morning. After that, any chance we have to learn the truth will be gone."

"You mean to investigate Marvin's death?" Captain Dinsmore asked.

"I have already begun. The idea of a veteran being so unjustly slandered by his peers is galling. The world deserves the truth."

I turned my last quoit over in my hands. "And you're serious about this curse?"

"Supposed curse," Emily muttered, while Mr. Clarke said, "Yes, Mr. Kelly. I have a duty to follow any lead."

"Clearing Lieutenant Morgan's name would be a noble thing to do," Oliver said approvingly. "The Brits consider him something of a war hero, do they not?"

Mr. Clarke's glasses were sliding down his nose. He took them off before continuing. "Indeed, they did, before all this business. He is said to have saved the lives of an entire unit in Africa. However, like Miss Wentworth, I prefer evidence over superstition. The truth of his demise may yet be unknown to us, but it is a fact that Lieutenant Morgan was transporting some fascinating curios that have gone missing since his death. Curios that must be found. Lives are at stake."

Emily frowned. "Surely, Mr. Clarke, the authorities will—"

"The authorities will do what they always do, Miss Wentworth. They will sweep this under the rug, chalk it up to an accident, and move on. By the time they have agreed to do anything more, the artifacts will be gone, and the truth with them. It is individuals with true initiative who will solve this case."

"Like you, I suppose?"

"Yes, like me. I have risked more for less."

"What if Lieutenant Morgan really was smuggling things

he shouldn't have been?" I asked. "Then you'd just be confirming the rumors if you found something. You can't clear the name of a guilty man."

Mr. Clarke shrugged. "We have been on this ship for less than a day, and already I have heard the most fantastic tales. Stories of people falling ill, equipment behaving strangely, and shadows where none should be. The crew are afraid, my friends. Perhaps Lieutenant Morgan was the unlucky victim of a tragic accident—but what if it was no accident at all? I believe we owe it to our fellow passengers to uncover the details of his untimely demise. Starting with the identities of his illicit contacts."

I didn't argue with him any further, but I had my doubts about whether Mr. Clarke's motives were entirely noble. There would be rather a lot of notoriety at stake for the man who broke a story like this one. Especially if Lieutenant Morgan's death had truly been the result of foul play.

"You young people are too prone to gossip. Idle minds are dens of sin, you know," chided Mrs. Henderson. "You should reconsider your plan, Mr. Clarke. It could be dangerous to meddle in these affairs."

Emily traded a glance with her brother. "Oh, come now, Mrs. Henderson. Do you not desire to learn the truth about what happened?"

"I do not," Mrs. Henderson replied. "Nor would you if you had any good sense. One should know one's place."

Mr. Clarke tipped his hat to the older woman. "You may be proven correct in the end, Mrs. Henderson. But I believe that a man must be bold—willing to go places others refuse to tread —when the moment calls for it."

Oliver elbowed me in the side. "What do you say, old man?

Fancy a bit of an adventure? It sounds like this fellow could use our help."

I shook my head. "What do we know about investigating smugglers? Or cursed artifacts?"

"What does anyone know about anything?"

"Try saying that when you need a doctor and see how it goes for you."

Mr. Clarke, it seemed, did not share my reservations. He offered Oliver a respectful nod. "I would be grateful for your assistance, Mr. Wentworth. Rest assured, I have covered more dangerous stories than this one before. You will not be placed in harm's way."

"Not to worry, Mr. Clarke," Oliver said, returning the gesture. "It would be unseemly for gentlemen like Mr. Kelly and myself to shy away from clearing Lieutenant Morgan's good name. Who are we to allow a soldier to die with his reputation so tarnished?"

Before I could muster up an objection to that, Emily spoke up.

"It would be rather like something out of a novel, would it not, recovering those missing artifacts?" she mused. Oliver's sister had taken to twirling a wavy strand of her hair around her finger. "I confess myself intrigued by the possibility of getting to the bottom of all this. You will have my help, Mr. Clarke, if you wish it."

"Thank you. With all of you assisting me, I stand a much better chance of uncovering the truth."

I groaned. My protest was ignored.

"Excellent! What should we do first?" Emily asked.

The corners of Mr. Clarke's mouth twitched. "While I appreciate your enthusiasm, you need only to inform me of any information you uncover while conducting your normal business. This ship provides us with, how do you say, a controlled environment for our investigation. The artifacts are still on board. Items of such value will not stay hidden for long."

My hopes for a quiet voyage evaporated like mist in the morning sun. The Wentworths were going to help Mr. Clarke investigate Lieutenant Morgan's death. There was no doubt about it. It was exactly the sort of scandalous intrigue they would be drawn to. This, of course, meant I would be investigating Lieutenant Morgan's death as well. That was how this sort of thing tended to go.

Irritated, I spun and hurled my last quoit at its target with more force than precision. To my surprise, it landed on the spindle and spun slowly to a stop as it wound its way down. My throw was excellent. I'd beaten Oliver.

Mr. Clarke inscribed a spiky, angular "3" on my side of the scoring slate.

"Well, I'll be damned." Captain Dinsmore passed a few coins to Mrs. Henderson, who tucked them away with her knitting needles. "I didn't think the lad had it in him."

"Watch your language, Captain," she replied. "Are you and Mr. Clarke not playing next? I fancy the newspaperman's chances, you know. You are not as young as you used to be."

"I should really be getting on with my investigation…" Mr. Clarke's voice trailed off.

"Nonsense!" roared Captain Dinsmore. "Your curse can wait. Step up and let's see what you're made of!"

Mr. Clarke grimaced before passing the scoring slate to Mrs. Henderson and joining the old sea captain near the quoits. Oliver crossed the deck to link up with his sister, but I lingered just long enough to overhear a snippet of the men's hushed conversation as they prepared to start their game. It was so quick I almost missed it.

"You would do well to be careful, son," cautioned the old sea captain, his bushy eyebrows squeezed so closely together they appeared to be joined. "Not everyone will take as kindly to your meddling as these children have."

Was that a threat?

I shared a significant look with Mr. Clarke, then hurried to catch up with the Wentworths, who were several paces away from me and already leaving the promenade through the aft staircase. If I didn't hurry, they would be halfway to D-deck before I reached them. I picked up the pace and crossed under the overhang just as the first quoit landed behind me with a thwack.

The companionway was crowded, but I weaved my way through the throng, following the sound of the Wentworths' laughter. I caught up to them just after the first bend. They acknowledged my arrival with twin grins, then carried on with their conversation, cracking jokes while we traversed the multitude of steps connecting the *Olympic's* decks together.

I elected not to join in. Instead, I took the opportunity to admire my surroundings. It always struck me how well kept this stairway was. Perhaps it was because the patterned linoleum tiles masked dirt so well, or perhaps it was because the landings were cleared of debris with such regularity one would be hard-pressed to find any accumulation in the first place. Either way, it was so unlike the disorganized chaos I'd grown up with on my parents' farm that I found it a bit unsettling.

As we descended further into the *Olympic*, I ran my hand along the smooth wooden railing, searching for further imperfections. There were none. Emily and Oliver were chatting about the case, but I'd lost track of their conversation, distracted as I was in my own musings. They were far more comfortable than I was on this ship. Of course, to be fair, they were from a much grander world than I. Neither of them had ever woken before sunrise to milk a cow or feed nesting hens.

We continued down the stairs until we heard the rising strings of music. The ship's band was set up just outside the library, playing a lively tune I didn't recognize. All around them, spread across the landing, passengers chatted with drinks in their hands. Some milled about near the base of the *Olympic's* stern mast, tapping their feet to the rhythm of the music, while others sat on cane furniture and gossiped the day away.

"I like this song," Oliver said as he maneuvered around a cluster of concertgoers. "Some of Godin's best work."

Emily hummed her agreement. "'Valse Septembre' will become a classic. I do hope someone will request 'Destiny' before they finish the show—I am partial to Baynes."

"The musicians are very talented, aren't they?" I asked, feeling a bit dim. I didn't know the names of many songs or composers.

"They are," Emily said. She moved easily through the crowd, humming along and swaying to the tune as she went. She held a smile for those we passed while she made her way to the other side. "If one closed their eyes, they could be forgiven for believing they were standing in a concert hall."

She was right. The band finished their song and launched into another number, a faster choice someone in the crowd had requested. We didn't linger to listen; instead, we walked the rest of the way through the hall, passed by the piano, and made our way into the second-class library.

The library was my favorite public space on the ship. Handsome sycamore panels proudly adorned its walls. Between them, flanked by silken curtains, large windows provided natural light for patrons to read and write by. There was an excess today. Sunlight from the promenade streamed through panes of sparkling glass, flowed across the room, and splashed onto the patterned Wilton carpet. I paused to soak it in.

Then, something eerie happened. My shadow lingered a half-step behind me.

What? I shook my head; all now seemed well. My shadow was still. *How bizarre. The light must have been playing tricks.*

We continued on, moving past my odd shadow and closer to our destination, a corner of the library where clusters of comfy chairs, dark wooden tables, and writing desks were available for us to claim. Emily headed straight for our favorite spot, a relatively private arrangement nestled under the port-side windows. We walked by two women speaking in hushed tones as their pens scratched against their papers. Near the ladies sat a pair of men hunched over a chessboard, their faces scrunched up in concentration. Another man dozed in a corner seat.

We reached our table and settled into our comfortable, tapestry-covered chairs.

"Well, this should be a wonderfully good time." Oliver rubbed his hands together and leaned forward in his seat. "I've always wanted to be involved in a conspiracy."

I took one last, hesitant glance toward the place I'd seen my shadow twitch. "Have you?"

"Who hasn't?" asked Oliver, grinning. "Listen, Jimmy, we need to get something out of the way. Your reluctance is becoming a nuisance. I understand wanting to be cautious, but I don't have time to waste! In no time at all, I'll be tucked away safely at Johns Hopkins, studying to be a doctor. My days of fun will be over. Helping Mr. Clarke could be my last chance for a grand adventure. You don't want to deny me that, do you?"

Oliver looked earnest. That wasn't reassuring. If anything, I felt even more unsettled by the reminder of his impending absence.

You see, after my parents died, and the weight of their debts forced me to surrender our family farm, the Wentworths invited me to live with them. They gave me a home when I needed one most. But with the three of us now finished with school, and with Oliver starting at Johns Hopkins, the time had come for me to move on. For things to change. The thought was terrifying. At eighteen, with no clear direction, I felt lost. *What would I do if I couldn't figure it out? If I failed? Where would I go?*

I squashed those feelings. It was better to focus on the present. And right now, Oliver was so excited that I didn't think I had it in me to deny him his wish to help Mr. Clarke. I owed him that much. And the journalist had assured us it would be safe...

"I don't want us to get involved with something we regret," I said, not quite ready to give in. "Nor do I want us to muddle things up for the authorities. Where does one even begin an undertaking such as this?"

"On the *Olympic*, of course," Oliver answered as if it were the most obvious thing in the world.

"Don't be droll. We'll need to investigate!" Emily leaned in closer, close enough that I got a strong whiff of her citrusy, orange-blossom perfume. "And we shall investigate carefully, just like it happens in Sir Arthur's detective stories."

Oliver clapped his hands. "Oh, this is going to be such fun."

I glanced between the Wentworths. Their twin sets of malachite eyes were sparkling with the same rabid enthusiasm. Given the debt of gratitude I owed their family, was I really in a position to refuse them this? *Did I even want to?*

"Fine," I said. "Have it your way. We can take a look around. But don't say I didn't warn you if this goes awry."

Oliver reached over to clap me on the shoulder. "Have no fear, Jimmy! One must be bold when the moment calls for it—or whatever it was Mr. Clarke said."

I warned you that everything you're about to read was Oliver Wentworth's fault.

2

IT'S CALLED THEORIZING

The *Olympic's* library served as our workshop that afternoon. All around us, passengers went about their business, many of them content to forget about the unfortunate death of Lieutenant Morgan. Such news simply didn't matter when there were parties to attend and cocktails to savor. If anyone talked about it, they did so with a smile on their lips and a playful, if not judgmental, wink and nudge. It was an accident, nothing more, destined to become an afterthought once we reached New York. An odd anecdote to an otherwise successful voyage.

It wasn't like that for the Wentworths and me. We were determined to help Mr. Clarke uncover the truth. Unfortunately, despite our enthusiasm, Oliver's confidence in our ability to act as detectives may have been misplaced. Our collective ignorance of Egypt, the Boer War, and detective work prevented us from making much progress. What it didn't do was stop the Wentworths from crafting increasingly absurd theories about the lieutenant, the rumored smuggling ring, and the allegedly cursed artifacts tying those threads together. Their speculations grew so outlandish that one could have written several novels using Oliver's suggestions alone. Say what you will about my friends, but they don't lack for wit.

After Oliver suggested that Lieutenant Morgan was still alive and parading around under an alias, wearing another man's clothes, I had to intervene. "Perhaps he leaped overboard to avoid hearing your theories," I said, taking care to ensure both he and his sister saw me roll my eyes.

The twins exchanged an amused look before dissolving into further laughter.

"Don't be such a bore, James," Emily teased, wiping away tears of mirth. "Where's the fun in that?"

"Well, I don't know—"

"None of us do. It's called theorizing! How does this sound —Lieutenant Morgan believed the artifacts were cursed and sacrificed himself to destroy them!"

"That sounds as likely as anything else," I said, strategically surrendering to the absurdity. "But why would he do such a thing?"

Emily's grin spread from cheek to cheek. "Well, I suppose it could be that he was a secret agent caught up in international espionage. In that case, the—"

But before she could finish, Oliver sprang to his feet. "No!" he exclaimed. Several nearby passengers startled at his outburst. He paid them no mind. Their worries were better saved for more tactful men. "You're missing the obvious answer—the lieutenant swam back to France!"

He took great relish in describing this feat, miming it with such enthusiasm you would think he was the one who had done it. His energy proved infectious; by the time he finished his tale, onlookers were laughing at his performance. I half expected them to give him a round of applause.

Emily looked impressed despite herself. "Not bad, Ollie, but if you think that's clever, wait until you hear this!"

And so it went. We spent quite some time working our way through the mystery. Some of our theories were realistic, many were outrageous, and none were based on a shred of actual evidence. Unfortunately, as entertaining as this was, it brought us no closer to the artifacts or the truth about Lieutenant Morgan. We were at a dead end. As the minutes passed, our laughter faded, replaced by an uneasy silence that was heightened by the steady ticking of the library's clock. There was something sobering about the magnitude of the task we'd taken on. No matter how many jokes we made, there was no avoiding that.

We eventually gave up our conversation as a lost cause and passed the time in our own ways. Oliver and I played several games of chess, discussing the case over his aggressive gambits and bizarre opening moves. While we battled it out, Emily borrowed a book on Egyptology from the clerk who managed the shelf. That was her way, I supposed, of searching for answers. She returned to her chair and settled in to read. Before long, the crinkle of her turning pages offered a measured accompaniment to the clatter of our battling pawns.

Upon finishing our third game, which ended in a rousing comeback for white, Oliver glanced at his pocket watch and stood up. "Well, I think it's about time I return to D-deck," he announced. "I booked a warm bath at 4:00, and I don't want to miss my turn."

Emily looked up from her book. "Did you really?"

Oliver winked before shrugging his jacket on. "A look this timeless doesn't come without effort, Em. Besides, if I head back now, I might be able to investigate a little on the way." He pivoted to face me. "Coming, Jimmy? You'd have our room to yourself to get cleaned up for dinner."

I glanced at Emily. She seemed content to continue with her reading. "I think I'll stay a bit longer," I said. "I'll escort Emily back to her stateroom when she's finished."

Oliver raised an eyebrow, but he didn't press. "Suit yourself." With a jaunty wave, he headed out, leaving me alone in the library with his sister. Emily returned to her book.

I wasn't sure what to do next. The library felt both smaller and quieter without Oliver in it. My mind wandered as I looked around the room, watching the passengers and crew carry on with their afternoon routines. It was all rather dull—until I shifted to look at Emily once more. I studied her, noting the fine lines of her face. There were several similarities between the Wentworth twins. They both had sharp features: high cheekbones, straight jawlines, and angular noses. But where Oliver was all energy, relentless in his enthusiasm, Emily was thoughtful, intense in her own way. There was an understated confidence in the manner she perched upon her chair.

She was captivating. Perhaps a little intimidating.

And I was staring. My mouth dried up, so I licked my lips, but that just made me feel more awkward. *Had she seen that?* I stood up and wandered to the nearby bookshelf, pretending to browse the collection.

"Do you need something, sir?" asked the wiry steward monitoring the library.

"I'm not sure. Just browsing, I suppose."

It was a silly thing to say. All the books on these shelves had the same bland, brown binding. There was no telling them apart. *What had gotten into me all of a sudden? Why was I so flustered?*

The steward looked me up and down, then glanced over at

Emily. A knowing smile graced his face. "Perhaps I could recommend something to pass the time while the young lady reads?"

"Yes," I said, grasping the lifeline. "Yes, please. That would be helpful. Something exciting, perhaps?"

"Would you like a newspaper? I brought a few along with me. There were new updates on the Senghenydd explosion and the HMS *Queen Elizabeth*."

I'd heard about the Senghenydd mining incident before leaving France. It was shaping up to be quite the disaster. "Is *Queen Elizabeth* the new British battleship?" I asked.

"Yes, sir. Ten 15-inch guns! The Kaiser won't know what hit him when she sets her sights on their fleet."

"I didn't realize Britain was planning on fighting with Germany."

The steward offered me another of his knowing smiles. "We wouldn't need a ship like that to handle the French. Now, do you want a paper, or shall I find you something else?"

"I was hoping for something a bit more entertaining," I confessed. "European news can be dreadfully bleak."

"Of course, sir. I have just the thing." He slid a book from the shelf behind him and held it out to me.

I took it. The cover was emblazoned with the logo of the White Star Line, but inside, the words *Theodore Roosevelt: An Autobiography* were spelled out in scrolling font.

"That just released earlier this year," the steward said. He handed me a borrowing ledger. "It was a popular request amongst American passengers."

"I'm sure I'll find it interesting." I signed my name and returned the paperwork.

"Very good. Enjoy your reading, sir."

Now that my business with the steward was done, I was

out of excuses to delay. I gathered up my courage and returned to our table. Once there, I tried to open Teddy Roosevelt's book, but my attention kept drifting back to Emily. Unaware of my dilemma, she shifted to pull her legs up onto her chair.

I continued to sneak glances at her. Again, I wondered why I was so anxious about this. Emily was, well, Emily. She wasn't a stranger. I'd known her for years. And yet, here I was, caught flat-footed with nothing to say.

It didn't help when I sensed someone looming behind me. I felt them lurking over my shoulder. *Had the steward forgotten to have me sign something?* I spun around, only to see... nothing. Like my shadow earlier, whatever had happened vanished as soon as I focused on it. Knowing that didn't help to quell my rising unease. I felt as if I was driving myself mad.

"Do you want to play chess?" I blurted out, unable to stand the silence any longer. "We don't have to, of course. But we can if you like?"

Emily looked up. "Are you offering me a challenge, James?"

"I am," I said, reclaiming my spot at the chessboard. I picked up the ivory pieces and arranged them in the starting position.

"Well then, consider your challenge accepted." Emily stood, stretched, and deposited her book on a nearby end table. She smoothed out her dress before taking her seat behind the black pieces. "I hope you can provide me with a good game, Mr. Kelly."

"I do, too." I shook my hands out and moved a pawn to e4.

She opened with d5. "I am less fond of taking risks than my brother, but I enjoy the thrill of a well-played gambit."

"Risk and I aren't on speaking terms."

We made a few more moves. Emily wrestled momentum away from me after the opening exchange.

"I have found that life is best when enthusiasm is balanced by caution," she said. "Incidentally, did you know that Florence Nightingale spent time exploring Egypt?"

"Was that in the book you've been reading?" I pondered the state of the board for a few moments before moving one of my bishops into a safer position.

"It was one of the few interesting passages. I suppose I should be grateful I managed to borrow it at all, considering the amount of interest everyone has in Egypt right now, but it makes for tragically poor reading. The man at the shelves told me Mr. Blackstone only just returned it a little while ago. And Mr. Clarke had it in his possession yesterday."

I frowned. "It seems strange that two people would check out the same book, only to return it a few hours later. Is it really that bad? Has it not taught you anything that might prove helpful?"

"That depends on what you mean by helpful," Emily said. She licked her lips before capturing a knight I'd left hanging. "The author goes on and on about priestesses and prophecies. Fortunately, someone already marked the pages that mention the Wings of Amun-Ra."

"Someone marked the pages? Who? What did they say?"

"Nothing sensical. The most promising line was about the artifacts stealing an unworthy priest's soul. If it were fiction, I suspect I would have enjoyed it. As history... I have my doubts. It is no wonder the others returned it so quickly."

"That does sound absurd," I agreed. But my curiosity had been piqued. *Had they returned the book because it was poorly written? Or had they returned it because they'd already learned all that they needed from its 'nonsensical' pages?*

We played in comfortable silence for a few more moves. Emily was a strong player. Every move she made either masked a future trap or launched a clever attack. My pawns bore the brunt of this, traveling over the board with the same level of security as soldiers in a minefield. I had a growing sense that their general might be outmatched.

"Let's talk about Lieutenant Morgan," Emily proposed. She moved her queen to put me in check. "What do you think about this curse business? Are our souls safe, or should I begin writing my will?"

"You're trying to distract me." I moved my last bishop to block.

She claimed my sacrificed piece with a satisfied, Oliver-like smile. "Perhaps, but I would still like to know your answer. What is your position on the cursed artifacts? Real or not real?"

"Well, the whole matter sounds rather far-fetched, but... it's difficult not to wonder. What do you think?"

Emily didn't look up from the board when she replied. "I do not believe in curses, and neither would you if you knew how many women were accused of witchcraft over the centuries." She bit her lip and made her move. "But I suppose what I believe doesn't change other people's thoughts. Smuggling is a serious matter. Those involved should face justice. That much is a universal truth."

"Agreed." I moved my remaining knight to threaten her queen. "I would like to clear Lieutenant Morgan of suspicion if we can. Oliver has latched onto the idea there is a nefarious plot surrounding this business. He's eager to prove it."

"Let's hope his eagerness doesn't get us into trouble. My brother is feeling pressure to enjoy himself before he dedicates his life to medical school. He faces more anxiety about that than he lets on."

"He's lucky, I think. It's good to have goals."

"For all his bluster, there is very little luck involved. Ollie has earned his opportunities. Tell me, while we are on the topic—what are your goals? What would James Kelly like to do with his life?"

"I—uh—don't know," I admitted. "I lost the farm settling my parents' estate, and I haven't been able to determine what I want to do next. It's thanks to your parents that I even have the blessing of a choice. It would have been the factory floor for me without them."

"One could never deny that you have been through a serious ordeal. You still have time to sort it out."

"What about you?" I asked, eager to shift the focus away from myself. "What are your plans?"

"Well, I—" Our hands brushed together on the board when we both reached for traded pawns. I was surprised to see a blush arise on her cheeks. "I would prefer not to say," she continued, not unkindly. "Perhaps another time."

Silence settled between us once more. The pieces shifted more slowly now as we weighed our next moves. After a few more quiet rounds, Emily spoke. "Do you know the origin of the term 'checkmate?'"

I perked up. "No, actually. I guess I've never thought about it before. Where does it come from?"

Emily moved her queen, setting up another attack and forcing me back on the defensive. "The word is derived from the Persian phrase 'shah mat.' It means 'the king is dead.'"

"Well, that's fittingly morbid, given the mystery we've gotten ourselves tangled in."

"Is it not?" Emily's hand hovered over the board. "Of course, we don't play to kill the king anymore. Now he's just... cornered." She slid her queen into a stronger position. "Trapped."

I moved my rook, but we both knew I was stalling. "I doubt kings have ever liked the idea of being killed."

"Who does?" Emily asked. She studied the board, moved her queen again, and pinned me. "That's checkmate, by the way."

I stared at the board. It was over. My king was surrounded. Yet, somehow, the loss didn't sting like it did when Oliver won. In some ways, losing to Emily didn't feel like losing at all. "Well played. Perhaps I'll put up more of a fight next time."

She flashed me a teasing smile. "I'll be waiting. Are you ready to go back downstairs?"

Before I could respond, the lights in the library flickered. Twice. I glanced around to seek the source of the disturbance, but the steward tending the bookshelves didn't seem concerned about the surge. I turned back to Emily, but she hadn't seemed to notice it, either. She was calmly gathering her things. *What had just happened?*

"Is something wrong?" Emily asked.

I shook my head. Each of the bulbs in the ceiling now burned bright and steady.

It must have been another trick of the light.

3
DINNER WITH MR. BLACKSTONE

That evening, as Oliver and I prepared for dinner in our stateroom on D-deck, we were no closer to discovering anything about the artifacts or the smugglers. Despite this, Oliver's enthusiasm for the search had only intensified in the time we'd been apart. He'd evidently done a good deal of thinking about it while taking his bath.

"I think I'll bring up Lieutenant Morgan's death at dinner," Oliver said as he styled his chestnut hair in front of the mirror. "Mr. Blackstone will be seated at our table with Mrs. Henderson, and you heard her talking on deck. She said her nephew is an expert in curses. Who better to ask about the artifacts than him? I'm sure a man like Mr. Blackstone has encountered a few smugglers in his life."

I was stretched out on the couch. It was a handsome piece, made from mahogany and covered in moquette fabric, complete with a matching pillow. "You want to ask Mrs. Henderson's nephew about the smuggling ring because he knows about curses?" I asked, straining to follow his logic. "I'm not sure that makes as much sense as you think it does."

Oliver tutted. "It's not just that, old man! Mr. Clarke wants me to investigate him. He told me that Mr. Blackstone was overheard bragging about some Egyptian jewelry he got hold of."

"When did you talk to Mr. Clarke?"

"On my way to the bath. He gave me the tip and asked if I could work on it."

"He suspects Mr. Blackstone?"

"Well, he didn't come out and say that. I suppose he got to thinking about the jewelry after Mrs. Henderson mentioned her nephew out on deck. Supposedly, there's a lively trade on board. An illegal one."

"I'm not sure that collecting old jewelry makes one a smuggler." I could already picture Oliver causing a scene at dinner. It wouldn't be the first time his enthusiasm had trumped his judgment. "You don't want to make a fool of yourself by jumping to conclusions and accusing Mr. Blackstone of breaking the law. Such behavior won't make you very popular."

Oliver snorted. A strand of his hair fell loose, but he folded it back in line with the rest before smoothing it down with oil. "I can be subtle. Fret not, Jimmy. It's not like I can stray too far over the line with Mother and Father there."

"Are you sure about that?"

"Well—no. But honestly, Emily is more likely to cause a stir than me. You saw what happened last night."

Dr. and Mrs. Franklin J. Wentworth had what many considered lax expectations for their children's conduct. Despite that, they still expected decorum to be kept. Emily fell in line with the few expectations placed upon her—unless something offended her sensibilities or beliefs. When that happened, she could be uncompromising in their defense. She had caused quite a stir the previous evening by arguing for women's rights at dinner. Mrs. Henderson, suffice it to say, was not a suffragist. The meal had gone somewhat sideways.

I smiled fondly at the memory. "I did. Your sister is as passionate as she is intelligent."

"Keep singing Emily's praises and old Mrs. Henderson will advise her nephew to steer clear of us entirely," warned Oliver, who was finished with his grooming. He stepped back to allow me a moment in front of the mirror.

I stood up, stretched, and made my way around my friend. I'm a little taller than Oliver, and broader in the shoulders. I needed to bend over to glimpse my hazel-eyed reflection. "That goes both ways," I said as I straightened my tie over the washbasin and turned a critical eye to my dark, tousled hair. "I doubt Emily would have a kind word to spare for her, either. Is Mrs. Henderson still upset about what happened at dinner?"

"She was up in arms over it this morning at breakfast. You should have heard her!" Oliver cleared his throat and affected a mousy voice before exclaiming, "'Why, the nerve of that girl! As if the world owes her everything!'"

"They managed to be civil on deck this afternoon," I said, chuckling at the passable impression of Mrs. Henderson. I picked up my comb, considered it, then set it back down. Fighting my hair was a losing battle. "Besides, Mrs. Henderson won't cause a fuss unless Emily does."

"Let's hope Josephine Beiderhase doesn't come up in conversation, then." Oliver glanced at his watch. "It's almost 6:30. Are you really going to leave with your hair in that state?"

I turned away from the mirror, emptied the washbasin into the cabinet, swept my hair back, and shrugged on my jacket. "Yes. Shall we?"

"After you."

Our stateroom, D59, was on the starboard side of D-deck,

near both the stairs and the dining saloon. Its location made it convenient for a quick trip to meals. I held the door open for Oliver. He passed me by and headed toward our dinner. I followed close behind him. The evening sun shone through an open porthole, bathing our walk in warm, amber light. Linoleum floor tiles shimmered with those sunset hues.

We passed through the double doors at the end of the hall just as a steward rang a gong to signal the start of the meal. The second-class dining saloon stretched the entire width of the ship, close to ninety feet in all. It could accommodate nearly 350 people for regular evening meals. Decorated in the "early English fashion"—Oliver's words, not mine—it was furnished with mahogany furniture, crimson leather, oak paneling, and an impressive sideboard.

"Perfect timing," I said. "Although your parents are probably already here."

"On time is late, if you ask my father. But what was I supposed to do? Rush my bath?"

"That would have been most unreasonable."

I did my best to keep pace with Oliver as he made his way through the crowd. Stewards rushed back and forth, carrying plates of haddock, curried chicken, and rice. The smell was divine.

"Come on, we can squeeze through these tables," Oliver said as he navigated a narrow gap between two passengers. "Do try to keep up."

"I'm right behind you."

The setting sun sparkled here, too, this time shining in from behind pivoted sidelights. Its brilliance scattered across silver plates and twinkling wine glasses. I held my hand over my brow to block the worst of it.

By the time we arrived at our table, our dinner companions

had already been seated. Dr. Wentworth commanded the corner chair. Fit and barrel-chested, with silver hair and an oiled beard, Oliver's father was an intimidating man. Beside him, Mrs. Wentworth appeared vanishingly frail. Her wispy hair and thin arms betrayed her compromised condition. Despite her poor health, however, Mrs. Wentworth's smile was the largest at our table, a reflection of the intelligence and wit of which she was still firmly in possession. She beamed at us.

Next to Mrs. Wentworth sat Emily, resplendent in a floor-length lavender chiffon dress. She was chatting with one of the few Black men on board, a photographer named Mr. Eli Carter. Mrs. Henderson, seated across from Mr. Carter, had angled herself away from their conversation to speak with her nephew, Mr. Reginald Blackstone—Oliver's prime suspect—who sat beside her. A former boxer, Mr. Blackstone was now a paunchy man, one whose thinning black hair was unable to be combed in a manner that could entirely mask his receding hairline. He was polishing one of his golden cufflinks with a white cloth. A cat's head glinted on its fine surface.

Generally, I sat next to Mr. Blackstone. That was my assigned seat. However, this evening, Oliver elbowed in and took it before I could. His father raised a steely eyebrow.

I intercepted him before he could say anything to his son. "Good afternoon, sir!"

Dr. Wentworth stared at Oliver for a moment longer. It was only with a good deal of reluctance that the Wentworth patriarch turned to face me. "Good evening, Mr. Kelly. Dare I ask why you and Oliver have decided to rearrange our dinner table? I rather thought your seats were assigned for a reason."

"Well, I—"

"Oh, Father, there's nothing to fear," Oliver said with a

grin wide enough to rival the Cheshire Cat's. "I just wanted to gaze lovingly into my mother's eyes. Is that a crime?"

Mrs. Wentworth scoffed, but she looked amused by her son's antics all the same. Her husband appeared decidedly less enthused.

A steward arrived with our first course. It featured bowls of consommé garnished with a sprinkle of fresh parsley. I reached for my outermost spoon, a silver one with a star on the handle, and took a test sip of the soup; consommé is generally a bit rich for my tastes, but this bowl had been prepared with great skill. I savored my first sip.

Oliver hadn't touched his consommé. Instead, he turned to speak with Mr. Blackstone. There was something distinctly mischievous about the smile on his face, something alarming about the predatory gleam flashing in his eyes. My heart sank. Unfortunately, just like the cat he so resembled, Oliver's sense had a way of vanishing when he needed it most. My friend was about to do something very unwise.

I gulped down my soup and cut in before he could say anything too tactless. "Mr. Blackstone, you must've come across some remarkable artifacts as a historian!"

Mr. Blackstone trained his beady eyes on me, unaware of how close he'd come to enduring Oliver's wit. "I have, yes," he said, squinting at me through his thick glasses. "But why the sudden interest in my work?"

"Well, we are the curious sort," Oliver replied. "So, what do you say? Do you have any unusual artifacts in your collection?"

"That's quite a broad term. What do you mean by 'unusual,' Mr. Wentworth?"

"Oh, you know. Exciting. Perhaps surrounded by tales of scandal?"

Oliver and Mr. Blackstone continued this line of questioning, but I caught Dr. Wentworth's scowl deepening with each passing moment. He wouldn't allow Oliver to continue in this vein for long. It was up to me to diffuse the tension.

"Sir, have you placed any wagers on our speed? Rumor has it we could cover 550 miles today."

That seemed to work. Dr. Wentworth's frown lines gave way to a small smile. "Indeed, Mr. Kelly. I have heard similar whispers. Have I told you yet about my meeting with the assistant doctor?"

"No, sir, I don't think you have."

"The poor man fell ill with the flu in Cherbourg. They let him disembark there, and rather than have the entire ship wait for them to find a replacement, I told Dr. Widmer that I would fill in if they needed my help. Afterward, the doctor let slip in conversation that Captain Bartlett believes we will have made it at least 530 miles by noon tomorrow. It boggles the mind that we would make even better time on the *Lusitania* or the *Mauretania*. The Germans may have made some advancements, but British engineering still rules these waters."

"The *Olympic* is an incredible ship," I agreed, grateful for the distraction from Oliver, who was now interrogating Mr. Blackstone about the antiquities trade. "And it was good of you to offer your services, sir. The doctor will be lucky to have you."

Dr. Wentworth waved my praise away. "It was nothing less than my duty. Ewan Widmer is an old friend."

Meanwhile, Emily was engaged in a lively conversation at the end of the table. "So, Mr. Carter, what brings you on this voyage?"

Mr. Carter smiled. "My grandfather—he is seated at the table next to ours, next to my sister Annabelle, just there—has been summoned to Kansas City to help settle his late brother's estate. We are his escort. But, more than that, I am hoping to see a bit of America. I have not been back home for many years. My mother used to tell me stories about the old family estate; I would like to see it with my own eyes. And, lest you think me idle, I have all of my photography equipment with me, and several appointments lined up."

"Do you often travel for your job?"

"Quite a bit, yes. As a matter of fact, I am going to do a photography series on a baseball team called the All Nations while my grandfather carries out his business. Have you heard of them?"

"I have! I admire the cause, Mr. Carter. By any chance, are you familiar with Maria W. Stewart?"

My attention was reclaimed by Oliver, who still persisted with his questioning. "Mr. Blackstone, surely some of your artifacts have come from your travel partners?" He glanced at the next table over, then lowered his voice. "Mr. Clarke tells me that the market on board is lively. Have you ever encountered anything rumored to be cursed?"

Mr. Blackstone forced out a chuckle. "Cursed, you say? My boy, you've been reading too many penny dreadfuls."

Before Oliver could respond, the main course arrived: plates of curried chicken and rice with sides of sautéed vegetables and boiled potatoes. Everything looked incredible; the food was so warm that the vegetables were still hissing.

"Ah, this dinner looks exquisite!" said Mrs. Wentworth. "Thank you," she added to her steward, who nodded politely.

I seized the moment to steer the conversation away from Oliver's probing. "Mrs. Wentworth, this curry is exceptional. Have you considered trying to make any of the dishes we've had on board once we're back home?"

She smiled. "I struggle more in the kitchen these days than

I would like, but perhaps I could attempt this one. It is divine. What do you think, Franklin?" she asked, turning to her husband.

Dr. Wentworth nodded. "It might be difficult to match this ship's chef, but I would never count you out if you say you are up for the challenge!"

Abandoning subtlety, Oliver dropped his elbow on the table and turned to face Mr. Blackstone once again. "Sir, I have heard Lieutenant Morgan might have smuggled some Egyptian artifacts on board. Do you know anything about that?"

I dropped my fork. Conversations died all around the table as everyone turned to face Oliver, with expressions ranging from shock, in Mr. Carter's case, to exasperation, in Dr. Wentworth's. Mr. Clarke, seated at the table behind ours, stopped his conversation with Captain Dinsmore to listen in.

Mr. Blackstone regarded Oliver through the thick lenses in his glasses. "I have heard whispers, yes, but I know nothing about curses or smuggled goods. Why do you persist in asking me?"

Oliver stared right back. "Oh, I'm just curious. Any insight you might have could be... enlightening. Say that I might be interested in making some purchases. Do you know anyone on board I should talk to?"

"Well..." The scholar fidgeted with his golden cufflinks. "No, no, of course not! Uh... that is to say..."

"Oliver!" I interjected. "Don't burden Mr. Blackstone with this over dinner. He doesn't look interested in such things right now."

He didn't. Lines of sweat had formed along his brow, sticking his thin hair to his forehead.

Oliver reluctantly turned away, but I knew he wasn't giving up. He was biding his time. Meanwhile, Emily resumed her conversation about American politics with Mr. Carter. Mrs. Henderson remained silent, her attention now divided between Emily's and Oliver's behavior. It was as if she couldn't decide which of the Wentworth twins was more offensive to her sensibilities.

As the evening progressed and dessert—a delightful plum pudding—was served, I hoped to keep the atmosphere light. If Oliver was going to get another chance to question Mr. Blackstone, we needed him to feel secure. "Dr. Wentworth, have you heard any more about the events they have planned for us this week? Anything exciting on the schedule?"

Dr. Wentworth, ever the gentleman, forced himself to look away from Oliver long enough to respond to me. "Why, yes, there is something. There has been a concert scheduled for Monday evening. It stands to be quite an event. Assistant Purser Haverford is organizing the affair, and I expect everyone traveling in second class will wish to attend. What do you say, Reginald? Interested?"

Mr. Blackstone grunted in the affirmative. "Yes, I dare say so. Aunt Edith—that's Mrs. Henderson to you all—wishes to attend. I shall be her escort."

"Splendid," Mrs. Wentworth said. "Perhaps we will see you there?"

"Perhaps."

An hour later, the evening sun had set. The dining saloon was now illuminated with electric lights. Their warm glow brought a more intimate atmosphere to our dwindling gathering, which was decreasing in number by the minute. A musician entered the room and began warming up at the piano for some after-dinner entertainment.

Sensing the moment was right, Oliver leaned over to speak with Mr. Blackstone again. "So, have you had a chance to think about it? Can you set me up with someone who wouldn't mind facilitating a little harmless smuggling?"

Oliver had finally pushed too far. Mr. Blackstone stood, drained his wineglass, and left without another word.

An uneasy silence settled over the table after that. The clinking of silverware against china resumed, but the tension was palpable. Dr. Wentworth eyed Oliver with mounting consternation. His wife looked exhausted; stress wasn't good for her condition. Emily and Mr. Carter traded glances, but neither of them moved to resume their previously lively conversation.

With the mood now irreparably damaged, Mrs. Henderson excused herself from the table. Mr. Carter departed next, saying something about his camera and a little nighttime photography. When Emily and her mother stood and bade us good night a few minutes later, it left only Dr. Wentworth, Oliver, and me at the table. For a few uncomfortable minutes, we sat in silence.

Finally, Dr. Wentworth set his glass down and leaned back in his chair. "Oliver," he said, his voice low. "A word."

Oliver glanced up. "Yes?"

"Your behavior tonight was inappropriate," Dr. Wentworth said, his nostrils flaring. "You—"

"Father, I was only trying to help Mr. Clarke! Surely—"

Dr. Wentworth was having none of it. "No. You are not a journalist, Oliver, and if you were, you would make for a poor one. Do you think you shall learn what you wish to learn by alienating people? You embarrassed Mr. Blackstone and disrupted the entire table. Your mother's condition cannot tolerate such foolishness, and I will not stand for it happening again—no matter who it is you think you are helping."

"Yes, sir," Oliver mumbled. He looked suitably abashed.

"Now, the night is still young," said Dr. Wentworth as he stood up and folded his napkin on the table. "Go for a stroll on the promenade. Head to the lounge, even, if you prefer, but do not cause any more trouble. Do you understand?"

"Yes, sir," Oliver repeated.

Dr. Wentworth looked at me. "Hold him to that, Mr. Kelly."

I gulped. Oliver could afford such a reprimand, but I could not. "Yes, sir," I promised. "I will."

4

MOONLIGHT MACHINATIONS

Oliver and I took his father's suggestion and ascended to the boat deck for an evening stroll. Rather than take the elevator, we climbed the aft stairs together. When we stepped out into the night air, we were greeted by the twinkling of an endless field of the brightest, whitest stars. They blanketed the sky, strewn across the heavens like a million grains of glinting sand. The moon, half-full, glowed more brightly than it ever could on land. There's something incredible about the night sky at sea.

A couple of years ago, the boat deck would have offered us an excellent ocean view. That changed after the *Titanic* disaster. Now, to meet safety standards, the deck was crowded with lifeboats, each thirty feet long and branded with the White Star Line logo. They were chained down and draped with canvas covers that rustled and flapped in the evening air. Towering davits, each many times taller than Oliver or me, loomed above them. Their presence should have been reassuring. In reality, however, they reminded me of curled fingers reaching up from the darkness. Like the hands of a giant.

I took a deep breath and inhaled the crisp night air. It sent a shiver from my neck to my toes. Exhaling, I stuffed my hands into the pockets of my trousers before we set off on our walk. Oliver laughed, but he, too, drew his jacket more tightly around himself. A rosy glow had already formed on his cheeks.

"We might have the place to ourselves," Oliver said as he led me up and around the towering fourth funnel. Unlike the forward three, which were belching black smoke, this one emitted a lazy, nearly invisible trail of exhaust. "The night is bitter."

"Which is why most will have taken their walks under the covered promenade."

But I knew Oliver would never compromise on that point. He loved the open air.

"Most are not having clandestine conversations about murder and smuggling."

"No, I don't suppose they are," I said as we completed a lap and settled together on a teak bench near the stern rail, looking out over the well deck. There were two boys down below us, steerage passengers perhaps a few years younger than Oliver and me, tossing a ball around. I watched them for a few moments. Judging by the sound of their laughter, they were having a good evening.

Oliver reached into his inside pocket and withdrew his cigarette case. He slid out a tightly rolled sleeve of tobacco, placed it between his lips, and ignited it with a flick of his Ronson lighter. He inhaled deeply before exhaling a cloud of smoke.

"Well," he said, "I think dinner went as well as one could expect."

I chuckled. It wasn't good manners for Oliver to smoke in public, but I wasn't going to correct his behavior. It was unlikely we would be disturbed here. Another reason he liked the boat deck.

"That's an optimistic take, even for you. Mr. Blackstone fled, did he not?"

"Yes, but you saw him, Jimmy. He went mad when I mentioned curses."

"You irritated him."

"Right. Because he's hiding something. He knows about the smugglers, I can tell."

I shifted to the edge of the bench; its bronze armrests were like ice on my forearms, chilling them through my dinner jacket. "Do you think so? I mean, what are the chances that the fellow who killed Lieutenant Morgan sits at our dinner table? It seems spectacularly unlikely."

"I never said that he killed him, just that he might know who did." Oliver held out his free hand, ticking off his fingers as he went. "First, we know that Reginald Blackstone is a collector of Egyptian antiquities. Second, we know that his beloved 'Aunt Edith' claims him to be an expert in curses. Third, we are looking for a possibly cursed, possibly smuggled Egyptian artifact. That's a difficult string of coincidences to overlook."

Suddenly, a third voice joined our conversation. "It is curious."

Emily was still in her dinner dress, but she'd donned a knee-length coat and swapped her formal shoes for a more comfortable pair of leather ankle boots. She waved her hand, and Oliver scooted down to the far end of the bench, making room for her between us.

"Emily!" I exclaimed. "I thought you'd gone to bed!"

Emily's snort was loud and unapologetic, a sound more suited to the stables than the dining saloon. "Not likely—not after the bumbling interrogation you two tried to pull on Mr. Blackstone at dinner. Oh, no, there was no chance of sleeping after that. I waited for Mother to fall asleep and then tracked you down as soon as possible."

I winced and offered her a rueful smile. "That's putting it rather mildly. Oliver claims it was a successful venture."

"Oliver is far too easily contented."

"Have you considered that your standards might be too high, Em?" Oliver rolled his cigarette between his fingers while he considered his sister. Proper etiquette demanded he put it out; naturally, he did no such thing.

"Hardly," Emily said, swatting her brother on the arm. "What were you thinking?"

"That Mr. Blackstone might spill something if I pressed him. And it worked! You saw how he reacted."

"I have no quarrel with your results. It is your methods I take issue with." Emily leaned over and straightened the collar of my jacket. Her fingers were much warmer than the cold air. "How will we ever get him to tell us anything else if he thinks you're out to get him? If he deigns to speak with you again, he will have his guard up."

Oliver raised an eyebrow. "Oh? I don't know about that. If we're persistent, that'll be enough. In fact, I thought we might try interrogating him again. Right now. What do you say, you two? Are you up for it?"

"What?" I said, somewhat distractedly. I could still feel the spot where Emily's hand had brushed against my neck. "Now?"

"Well, that is Reginald Blackstone, is it not?" Oliver asked, pointing his cigarette at the railing nearest to where Lieutenant Morgan had allegedly fallen. "Seems like as good a time as any for a second attempt."

Sure enough, Mr. Blackstone was creeping along a shadowed portion of the boat deck. He looked like he was searching for something amongst the looming davits and lifeboats. As he shuffled down the deck, peeking under every canvas flap and around every bracket, a cold draft brushed past. It was colder than the rest had been, cold enough to raise goosebumps on my skin. I couldn't explain it, but it felt like Mr. Blackstone was being hunted by someone—or something—much darker than us.

But that was insane, of course. There was no one here but us and the steerage kids playing on the well deck.

A nervous laugh escaped me as I watched Mr. Blackstone disappear into the shadows behind a lifeboat. I tried to shake off my unease by cracking a weak joke. "Well, I suppose that's lucky. We probably should talk to him."

"We need a plan," Emily insisted. "I will not endure a repeat of dinner. You cannot just—"

Oliver jumped to his feet. "He's up to something. We need to catch him before he flees again."

"And what if he decides to toss you into the sea?"

"Perhaps your sister has a point," I said. "Think about it, Ollie. If you're right about him, he might have kill—"

"There is, as they say, only one way to find out."

"Oliver, wait!" Emily hissed. Her brother froze mid-step. "We need to be tactful."

Oliver opened his mouth to argue, but Emily cut him off with a sharp look. "No! Your haphazard approach at dinner nearly ruined our chances. Father was most upset with you. Just... let me take the lead this time."

I nodded in agreement. The last thing I wanted was to allow Oliver to further upset Dr. Wentworth. "Your father asked us to stay out of trouble, did he not? Perhaps following Emily's plan would be wise."

It took Oliver a moment to decide on a course of action. When he acquiesced, it was with great reluctance. "Sure, Em. Why don't you show us how a real detective interrogates a suspect?" He paused, then added, "I recommend doing it carefully, so Jimmy doesn't get scared."

My cheeks warmed, but I don't think either of my friends noticed my embarrassment. They'd become consumed by their sibling rivalry. Emily made a rude, uncouth gesture. Her brother responded in kind, displaying the gesture with both of his hands.

Despite their silent disagreement and my misgivings, we stood and moved to approach Mr. Blackstone, who was still peeking around the lifeboats. His head snapped back and forth as if he expected danger to leap out at any moment. I suppose, in fairness to him, danger was about to leap out—if you considered Oliver, Emily, and me to be dangerous.

When we were within ten feet of him, Emily, who was leading the way, raised her voice and called out to the shady historian. "Mr. Blackstone! A word, if you please."

Mr. Blackstone froze. Slowly, he turned around, his face pale under the lights. "W—What is it? What do you want?"

"We need to talk," Emily said. "About your behavior at dinner."

"And about Lieutenant Morgan," added Oliver.

They were each as bad as the other, reckless and bold. There was no sign of fear in either of them. I adore the Wentworths, but I wasn't made up the same way. This confrontation was causing my stomach to flutter.

Mr. Blackstone looked as if he felt the same way I did. He took a step back, tripping over one of the thick chains holding the boats. "I already told you I know nothing about that!" he insisted. "Leave me be!"

Emily's voice held none of the apprehension I knew mine would have in her position. "We know you're hiding something, sir. We're not here to accuse you of murder, but we need the truth."

"I might be here to accuse you of murder," Oliver said. His grin appeared predatory in the darkness of the night. "So, weigh your words. If you aren't forthcoming, I'll find a master-at-arms and see how they feel about you snooping around here."

"Returning to the place where Lieutenant Morgan fell hardly casts you in a favorable light." Emily stepped up beside her brother. "If you truly are innocent, tell us, and we can drop this entire affair."

Mr. Blackstone licked his lips and glanced around, clearly hopeful that someone might come to his aid. Seeing that we were alone, he sighed, his round shoulders slumping in resignation. "Very well. We can talk. But not here." He gestured to a nook tucked away behind the fourth funnel. It was a small space, surrounded by lifeboats and shielded from the wind. "Follow me."

It was a tight squeeze. Despite the intensity of the situation, there was no way I could have missed Emily's proximity to me. Our arms were touching. If she noticed our closeness, however, she didn't comment on it. Her focus was on the crumbling facade of Mr. Blackstone.

"Well, Mr. Blackstone, you've chosen a cozy spot for this conversation," Oliver observed. "I daresay there isn't a more private place on this ship, aside from the lavatory. You don't want to reconvene there, do you?"

"No, no, this will do." Mr. Blackstone leaned in and

lowered his voice. "Now, you three listen here. I had nothing to do with Marvin's death. But, in the spirit of openness... I will confess that Marvin found something. Something that has everyone on edge. A pair of artifacts."

I glanced at Oliver and Emily, then spoke for the first time. "The Wings of Amun-Ra?" I asked. "We did some reading about them after Mr. Clarke mentioned them on deck."

"Not that it helped much," Emily muttered. "The only book about Egypt in the library was riddled with melodramatic warnings about our souls. It was hardly better than all these whispers about a curse."

Mr. Blackstone's face grew grave. "The rumors are true, I fear. Marvin had the artifacts, and now that he's died, the Wings of Amun-Ra have gone missing. I shudder to think what will become of us if they are not found soon." He fixed Emily with a knowing look. "I know you found that book's warnings excessive, Miss Wentworth, but the truth is that the Wings of Amun-Ra are a danger to all on board this ship. On that point, it was entirely correct."

"You checked out that same book, Mr. Blackstone," I said, suddenly remembering that Emily had seen his name on the ledger. "Why were you researching something you already knew about?"

He offered me a humorless smile. "I was curious how much of the legend had made its way into print. In the end, it included far less of the truth than I had feared."

"What did the book leave out?" Emily asked.

Mr. Blackstone may have been cornered by my friends and me, but you would never know it from the keen look on his face. He clearly had an interest in this topic. "Ah, well, that is a tale... and I suppose, given our current situation, it will do no harm to relay the basics. You see, my friends, from the time of the Ancient Egyptian pharaohs, there has been myths surrounding the powers of these two relics of Amun-Ra, god of sun and air. One version of the story holds that a sect of priestesses sought to harness the god's power for themselves, only to find that their creations had been cursed, spurned by the god they had so foolishly crossed."

Oliver looked thoughtful. Emily looked skeptical. I wasn't sure how I felt. "Do you really believe that?" I asked.

He shrugged. "It has always been the most plausible explanation to me. Treasure hunters are rarely men of science, so I cannot tell you these artifacts have ever met with the instruments of a laboratory. What I can say is they have vanished and reappeared throughout history, never long in one place. Each time they have surfaced, incredible stories have followed. Tales of empires formed and shattered."

As Mr. Blackstone spoke, a faint whisper drifted over us, carried like a snowflake on the wind. I couldn't make out what it said. But whatever it was, Mr. Blackstone seemed to recognize it. He stopped talking and backed into the wall behind us. His face was ashen.

"Sir?" I asked. "What was that?"

He wiped his hands on his jacket. "I—I don't know," he stammered.

I had the distinct sense he was lying. Before I could press him further on this topic, Emily cut in, determined to bring our conversation back on track. "How did Lieutenant Morgan get his hands on the Wings of Amun-Ra? They sound like they should be in a museum. Or in a vault somewhere."

"I don't know," Mr. Blackstone answered. He kept glancing down the deck, toward the engineers' promenade. "They are pieces of history, you know, so it could not have been easy—but regardless of how it happened, he did. Can you imagine it? He could have been the wealthiest man in Europe."

"What went wrong?"

"The daft fool underestimated how far his enemies would go to pursue the legend. Can you imagine what a modern nation might do with the powers of a god at their disposal? No battleship in the world could save them."

"His enemies?" Emily asked.

"I imagine they were plentiful. Marvin and his partner ran into a spot of difficulty, so they contacted some of my friends and me, looking for help to smuggle the Sundered Wings to America. I believe they thought the artifacts would be safer there, away from the politics of Europe."

Oliver crossed his arms. "I cannot help but notice that you've only just now noted your involvement in this little tale. Fascinating. Are you a regular smuggler of artifacts, Mr. Blackstone?"

"I had no involvement with Marvin's death. I swear it."

"That's not what I asked."

Mr. Blackstone pinched his lips together, then cursed under his breath.

"If you don't tell us the truth, the deal is off," Oliver said. "I'll take my concerns to Captain Bartlett. Or to a master-at-arms. Your choice."

Mr. Blackstone sighed, then spoke hurriedly, as if confessing more quickly would make the admission less painful. "Yes, you bedeviling boy. Yes. I admit it. I have smuggled goods a time or two in my life. But it isn't what you think! My friends aren't violent. To the contrary, our trades have always been harmless! No one I know was involved in this killing!"

Oliver's smirk radiated superiority. He basked in Mr. Blackstone's confession. "I knew it. Tell us about your friends. Who are your contacts?"

Mr. Blackstone fiddled with his cat's head cufflinks. "I—I know this may be too much to ask. You already have enough evidence to haul me in front of a master-at-arms. But allow me to keep this secret. I swear they are innocent in this matter."

"I don't think—"

"Can you tell us more about them?" asked Emily, interrupting Oliver. "Not your friends, but the Wings of Amun-Ra. What would someone searching for them need to look for? I'm wondering about size, weight, that sort of thing."

"You may as well tell us what you know about the curse, too," I said. "We need to know everything."

Mr. Blackstone straightened up and adjusted his glasses. I got the sense he was grateful for the temporary change in topic. "The Sundered Wings are sacred objects. Amun-Ra was said to take the shape of a falcon; the creators of these artifacts used that as inspiration, crafting a pair of golden wings befitting that divine form. And not just wings—legend holds the Wings of Amun-Ra were originally part of a magnificent statue, though they've long been torn away from that base."

"That's why you've been calling them that," Emily said, speaking in a tone that conveyed her satisfaction that at least one riddle had been solved. "They've literally been sundered."

"Sundered?" I asked.

Oliver answered first. "Broken, Jimmy. Snapped off. There's probably a wingless falcon buried somewhere in the sands of Egypt."

Mr. Blackstone grunted in agreement. "Indeed. Despite their origins, they are rumored to be breathtakingly beautiful. They were created by the greatest artisans of their time."

"But what about the curse?" asked Oliver. "Is it real?"

"Well..." Mr. Blackstone froze. From around the corner, the unmistakable sound of footsteps drew near. They were unsteady, rushed, and hurried, the sort of steps you might expect to hear at the end of a close race. Whoever it was would reach us any second.

"Get back!" Emily urged, yanking Oliver's sleeve into the shadows and leaning her torso into mine. "And hold still! We don't want to be seen out here!"

My imagination conjured all sorts of horrible possibilities, from Lieutenant Morgan's killer's return to the phantasmic appearance of an ancient Egyptian pharaoh. My heart, which had calmed down while Mr. Blackstone told his story, hammered away at my ribs. The steps grew closer. Any second now, we would see who they belonged to... for better or for worse.

5
A FORTUITOUS DISCOVERY

We didn't have to wait long to uncover the identity of the figure. Fortunately for us, it wasn't the reincarnated body of a pharaoh, the rotting mummy of a long-dead Egyptian priestess, or even a murderous smuggler shuffling along the deck. Someone much more mundane had joined us outside on this chilly autumn evening—Captain Dinsmore, the story-telling mariner.

The aged seafarer muttered to himself as he hurried from one end of the deck to the other, so engrossed in his own pursuits that he didn't notice us tucked away in our nook. His attention was elsewhere. While he was not doing it as thoroughly as Mr. Blackstone had done, Captain Dinsmore was clearly searching for something. He paused to examine the spot where Lieutenant Morgan vanished, took a swig from his half-empty bottle of liquor, mumbled something that sounded like, "Damned fool," and moved to another area to search. He repeated this pattern for several minutes, completing a circuit around the boat deck before disappearing into the companionway behind us.

Silence reigned on deck. The danger had passed, but we all hesitated to speak. None of us wanted to be the one who shattered our tense peace. It was only when I realized Emily's weight was pressing on me that I made to separate myself, fully aware of the impropriety of our position.

Oliver was the first to regain his ability to talk. "What was he doing out here?"

"The same as many others are doing, I suspect." Mr. Blackstone sighed and shook out his sleeves. "He's hunting for the Sundered Wings. Your friend Mr. Clarke is far from the only person interested in their recovery."

I made a quiet "hmm" sound. That explanation was certainly plausible, but it felt more to me like Mr. Blackstone was projecting his own motives onto Captain Dinsmore. Still, it was an intriguing notion. One that reminded me of what we were doing here. "You were talking about the curse," I reminded Mr. Blackstone. "I would like you to continue. What else do you know about the legend of the Sundered Wings?"

But Mr. Blackstone had rather lost his nerve. The enthusiasm with which he'd previously spoken was gone. "Well, nobody knows every detail, of course. The story goes that the group of priestesses imbued the Wings with the divine essence of the god himself. This power can grant incredible blessings or unleash devastating calamities."

"Blessings? Calamities?" Emily snorted. "How ridiculous."

"Doubt me all you like, but I know you felt Amun-Ra's power in the wind just a few moments ago. Or did you miss that?"

I shivered. I hadn't missed it, but I'd been hoping I'd imagined the odd voice.

Oliver looked uncomfortable. Emily's smile hardened. "It's

a cold night, Mr. Blackstone. Ships make noise. You'll need to try harder than that if you want to scare me."

"What do you want me to say, Miss Wentworth?"

"I want you to tell us the truth. Starting with the rest of the legend."

"Why should I?" Mr. Blackstone asked. "You won't believe me if I do."

Emily folded her arms. "You know very well why. Or have you forgotten what we caught you searching for? Do you think a master-at-arms would believe your friends are innocent?"

"At this point, I am considering whether it would be worth it to find out!" When it was clear none of us believed he would go through with this threat, Mr. Blackstone pinched his lips. "Very well. The fracturing of Amun-Ra's statue left the god's powers broken as well. Each of the artifacts can channel some of their original blessing, and each carries some of the original curse. According to legend, the Wing of Light can bring forth hope, healing, and the warmth of the sun."

"Like an ancient Egyptian doctor?" asked Oliver.

"No, no, boy." Mr. Blackstone waved him off. "I speak of real healing. Divine healing. Now, as for its twin, the Wing of Shadow..." He glanced over his shoulder before continuing. "Well, that one's different. Fear, plague, storm winds that can tear a ship apart. Separated, the Sundered Wings hold significant powers, but were they to be brought together, were Amun-Ra's powers to fall under the control of one man—well, the injuries one could inflict boggle the mind."

Emily wrinkled her nose. She opened her mouth to say something, but stopped herself before she got the words out.

"That doesn't sound much like a curse to me," I said, filling the space. "Who wouldn't want the power to heal someone or control the wind?"

Mr. Blackstone wagged his finger. "Remember this, boy—you catch the biggest fish with the finest bait. Everything in this world has a cost, and these artifacts' powers are no different. They curse their wielders. Steal their souls, even, if the legends are true. All for a taste of divinity."

"Why would anyone use them, then?" Oliver asked. "A soul seems a precious thing to wager."

Mr. Blackstone shrugged. "For some, the allure of godhood would be worth any price. Were that not true, we would have no need for tales of curses at all, would we?"

"Is there any evidence these artifacts carry such a curse?" Emily asked. She still looked confident that Mr. Blackstone was peddling snake oil. "Your story is fantastic, sir, but I have made it clear that I do not believe in such things as a general rule."

"You will believe what you wish to believe. Smarter men than I believe there is truth to the legend; certainly, Marvin believed the Sundered Wings were safer if he kept them separated and hidden. At least until he could deliver them to his contacts in America."

Oliver slid another cigarette out of his case, nearly dropped it, then began fumbling with his lighter. Only because I knew him so well did I notice how unnaturally still he was standing. "And you think he hid the artifacts on this ship?" he asked.

"Most definitely," Mr. Blackstone said. "Marvin Morgan was a capable man. He died to keep them away from his enemies. And before you ask, we were friends and shared contacts, but he did not confide in me the identity of his foe. Whoever killed him was after the power of the Sundered Wings... or the wealth they would bring on the open market. Either would be an appealing motive."

I considered him for a moment. "What's your angle, then? Are you after the Sundered Wings as well?"

Mr. Blackstone's voice dropped to a whisper. "Well—yes, I am. But I am trying to find them before our enemies do! I fear there are some dangerous people on this ship. Very dangerous people. I am not the first person to smuggle an artifact, lad, and I am far from the worst to ever do so."

"But—"

Emily placed her hand on my arm. "For now, we believe you are not likely to be a murderer," she told Mr. Blackstone. "But we will find your Sundered Wings. And when we do, we will turn them over to the authorities. Until then... stay clear of trouble."

"You won't be reporting me to Captain Bartlett, then?" he asked hopefully. "Or my friends to a master-at-arms?"

"Not tonight, Mr. Blackstone," Oliver said. He looked at me. "Jimmy? What do you say?"

I shook my head. "No. Not unless you force us to."

"I won't! You have my word!"

"For whatever that's worth," Emily groused. She was glaring at Mr. Blackstone. "The moment we have reason to believe your story is a lie, or that your friends are murderers, the deal is off. Do you understand?"

Mr. Blackstone nodded. Relief washed over his features as he backed away. "I do. You have nothing to fear! We are on the same side!" He took another step back and glanced over his shoulder.

Satisfied his escape route was clear, he bolted. The clambering sound of his feet colliding with the pitch-pine deck echoed in the frigid night air. We could still hear his hurried footsteps as he rushed inside. Their echoes bounced off the walls as he thundered down the stairs.

"You know, I'm not sure a word of his tale is worth believing," Emily mused, her gaze on the doorway through which

Mr. Blackstone had just vanished. "I would like to trust him. It would be my preference. But none suspected Dr. Jekyll of malfeasance before the truth emerged, did they?"

"I should hope that no Mr. Hyde lurks within Mr. Blackstone!" Oliver said.

"A Mr. Hyde lurks in all of us, brother mine. That's rather the point of the story."

"The two of you should be careful drawing comparisons to such tales," I said. "It's a wonder you don't see ghosts around every corner."

Emily shrugged. "They're entertaining. And I only intended to draw a comparison. You cannot deny that Mr. Blackstone is a strange fellow."

Oliver breathed out a cloud of smoke. "If he's strange, Em, the devil is misguided."

I think he meant it as a joke, but I couldn't find the energy to laugh. Something about Mr. Blackstone made me feel very ill at ease. And judging by the cigarette shaking in his hand, Oliver agreed with me.

An hour had passed since our conversation with Reginald Blackstone, but neither Emily nor Oliver had indicated that they were planning to return to our staterooms any time soon. They were too caught up in the mystery and too intent on finding another clue to consider calling it a night. Our earlier concerns about the cold had been forgotten, now that the twins' enthusiasm burned brightly enough to hold the chilly air at bay.

Or, perhaps, we'd simply grown cold enough that it was impossible to feel our faces. It was difficult to say.

Most of the other people on deck now were crewmen and staff. One of the ship's masters-at-arms, a dour-faced man named Mr. Harlowe, had passed by us several times, his greatcoat flapping around his ankles like a cape. His boots thumped as he stalked the boat deck. He had no way to know it, but he was retracing the same path that Mr. Blackstone and Captain Dinsmore had trodden earlier that same evening.

"It's late," he growled when he passed us by. Mr. Harlowe was an abnormally tall man, taller than any other I'd met. He needed to lean down to be heard when he spoke. "You should think about returning to your rooms."

A quick look at my father's old pocket watch told me we were approaching curfew, though it had not yet arrived. I exchanged a glance with Emily. Before either of us could reply, however, Oliver jumped in.

"Thank you for your concern, sir." He flashed the master-at-arms a winning smile. "We shall endeavor not to linger any longer than is wise."

Mr. Harlowe was not amused. "If it were wise to be here, I would be elsewhere. These are dangerous times. Hardier men than you have fallen prey to overconfidence."

"We won't be long," I assured him. "We'd like to take one more lap before we turn in for the night."

"So be it. If you are still here after lights out, you will hear from me again. And there will be consequences. Is that clear?"

"Yes, sir," we chorused.

Apparently satisfied, Mr. Harlowe resumed his solitary patrol without offering any parting words. As he walked away, I noticed his hand twitch. It was a subtle motion, one that pointed to a man dealing with stress, but it seemed out of place on someone so stern.

"We're fortunate he arrived when he did," Emily said the

second Mr. Harlowe was out of earshot. "If he'd interrupted us one second sooner..."

Oliver nodded. "Was it Shakespeare who wrote that 'truer words have never been spoken?' Because if it was, that old sod was correct."

"I don't believe anyone knows the origin of that phrase. But you're right, it wouldn't do for Mr. Harlowe to hear about what we're planning."

And we were back to this. Having exhausted the topic of Mr. Blackstone just before Mr. Harlowe arrived, our conversation turned to the possibility of searching Lieutenant Morgan's stateroom for evidence. I wasn't in favor of the plan, but the idea had caught hold of the Wentworths and taken up a prominent place in their imaginations. Oliver was especially eager, though I suspected his desire was at least in part connected to his need to regain control of the situation. He hadn't liked what he'd heard Mr. Blackstone say about the curse.

"We could figure out a way in," Oliver argued. "It's not like our rooms are locked up tight. We just need a plan."

"It will take some discretion, but it should be possible," agreed Emily.

"Discretion, dear sister, is my forte. Why, were I not named for our father, the word discretion would have made a splendid middle name for me."

"No, it wouldn't have. You're as discreet as a hurricane." Emily turned to me. "What do you say, James? Are you equal to the challenge?"

I wasn't, not really, but I took one glance at her hopeful features and found that I didn't want to disappoint her. "Let me sleep on it," I answered. "If it still seems like a good idea tomorrow, I'll devise a plan to get us a look around that stateroom."

"Thank you," she replied sweetly. "I trust you to think of a clever way to do just that."

I tried not to let my pleasure show. "Should we ask Mr. Clarke to help us?"

"No," Oliver said. "I don't want to bother him until we actually find something. Right now, all we have are theories and ideas." As soon as he finished speaking, something caught his eye, and he craned his neck to look over the darkened deck. "I say, is that your friend Mr. Carter, Em? What do you suppose he's doing out here?"

Sure enough, Eli Carter was on deck, camera in hand, capturing various angles of the ship under the moonlight. He was just brushing himself off from a shot that required him to lie flat on the ground when he encountered Mr. Harlowe, who was no more amused by Mr. Carter than he had been by us. It probably hadn't helped that Mr. Carter had taken a photograph of Mr. Harlowe as he approached.

Scowling, the master-at-arms bumped into the earnest man as he passed. "Move aside! And remove that infernal contraption from my sight!"

"It's good to know Mr. Harlowe wasn't just reserving his kindness for us," Oliver said, wincing sympathetically as Mr. Carter was knocked off balance. "That man is not one to cross. He's got a foul temper."

I was just glad that Mr. Harlowe's anger hadn't been directed at me. "Yes, he does. Mr. Carter seems a bit shaken up, does he not?"

"Let's go see if we can bolster his mood," suggested Emily. "He looks as if he could use a friendly chat."

Emily's suggestion was a welcome one; I'd also been about to suggest we speak with Mr. Carter, though for a different reason. I'd had an idea. If he was out taking photos this evening, had he taken some the previous evening as well? If so, might there be evidence in his camera, frozen in the black-and-white images he'd been collecting?

Emily took the lead once again. We followed her to where Mr. Carter was standing. His encounter with the master-at-arms seemed to have shaken him; Eli was still taking sidelong glances at Mr. Harlowe's retreating figure, his camera clutched in trembling hands. He held the device between himself and Mr. Harlowe as if he might use it to shield himself from the other man's sharp tongue.

"Mr. Carter," Emily greeted warmly. "How are you this evening?"

Mr. Carter licked his lips. "Fine, thank you. Out for a late-night stroll?"

"Something like that. Did you have a pleasant conversation with Mr. Harlowe?"

"That would be difficult to do. He is a most unpleasant man."

Emily laughed. "You speak the truth, Mr. Carter."

"Call me Eli, please. We are acquainted, are we not?"

"Of course. But one must recognize the formalities."

Eli inclined his head. "And so you have."

"Let's talk about something less drab. What brings you out on deck, Eli? What were you photographing?"

Eli pointed toward the horizon. "So many things, Miss Wentworth! The way the moonlight reflects off the waves is mesmerizing, and, of course, the *Olympic* is a marvel. I have been coming out to capture its beauty before heading to bed. Captain Dinsmore says that he has been in some of the first-class staterooms—I suppose he took a tour before we set sail—but, anyway, he told me how gorgeous the ship was and how much I might like to photograph it. And he was right!"

As he spoke, I peered at the camera around his neck. Its lens gleamed under the lights. "Say, Eli. Did you come out here last night to take any pictures?"

The further away Mr. Harlowe was from us, the more comfortable Eli seemed to be. His dark brown eyes brightened with enthusiasm. "Oh, yes," he gushed. "It was our first day at sea, so I took quite a few. The ship's architecture, the passengers, the crew... there are many things I would like to document."

"Do you think we could look at them sometime?" I asked, trying to sound as casual as possible.

"What a splendid idea!" Emily said. "James is right. We would love to see your photos."

Eli looked pleasantly surprised by this. "I would be delighted to share them with you, provided I can find a place to develop the films. This ship does not have a darkroom; it launched with one back in '11, but they removed it after the passengers abused the place for—"

"Mr. Carter," Oliver interjected. "This is all very interesting, but will you please tell us whether or not you can do it? Curfew is drawing nearer, and my dear sister is beside herself with curiosity."

Emily shot Oliver a reproachful look for his abruptness, but it was half-hearted. She, too, was eager to hear Eli's response.

Eli smiled. "Ordinarily, the answer would be 'no,' but you are in luck. I have some chemicals tucked away with my supplies, and I found a spot on board that I think I can use as a makeshift darkroom. How about tomorrow morning, between breakfast and lunch? I'll set up my equipment and bring a few samples to the library."

"That sounds perfect!" Emily said. "We are ever so excited."

Eli bade us a good night and set out to determine where Mr. Harlowe had gotten to. Satisfied that the master-at-arms was out of sight, and therefore too far away to interrupt him, the photographer checked over his camera before resuming his work.

We left him and walked back toward the stairs. The second we were out of earshot, Oliver asked the question that had likely been on his mind for the last several minutes. "Why do we care to see his photos? We can look at dingy images of a ship any old time."

I was about to answer, but Emily got to it before I could. "Use your head, Ollie. Do you not think it is possible that Eli captured something important in his photos? Something that happened on deck? At night?"

Oliver frowned. "Something to do with the case?"

"Yes!" I exclaimed. "Think about it. If Eli's been taking pictures all this time, he might've captured something related to Lieutenant Morgan's disappearance. He might not even realize he's done it!"

Emily was nodding along. "Exactly. This could be our first real clue! If there's anything in those photographs, we'll find it."

"Brilliant," Oliver said. "With all of us working together, we'll have this mystery unraveled in no time at all. Mr. Clarke will be surprised when he finds out we've solved his case for him!"

I couldn't help feeling that Oliver was a touch too optimistic in that appraisal, but I said nothing to correct him. Eli's photographs were a start, and after an evening that presented us with more questions than answers, a start was all we could have hoped for.

6
Nothing Worthwhile is Safe

Mr. Blackstone wasn't at breakfast the following morning. In fact, it was a lightly attended affair all around. Because of our late night out, Oliver slept in, deciding that his rest was more important than his appetite. He was insistent about it. I left him wrapped up in his blanket, his snoring having resumed before I could cross from his bedside to our stateroom door.

They weren't the only ones to miss the meal. Dr. Wentworth stopped by for coffee, but he left after ten minutes, explaining that Mrs. Wentworth was feeling poorly and preferred to dine in their stateroom. He didn't want to leave her there alone. Eli Carter stopped by long enough to grab a quick pastry, but then he, too, left the table, claiming that he needed some hours to develop his photographs before our scheduled meeting.

Mrs. Henderson, perhaps realizing that she did not want to spend any more time in Emily's presence than was strictly necessary, was the next to leave. She folded her napkin before rising to her feet and dramatically claiming that her lumbago was acting up. She went on to insist that she simply must call upon Dr. Widmer, the ship's most esteemed medical professional. "For my health, dears, you understand," she'd simpered. "It mustn't wait."

Mrs. Henderson's departure left Emily and me alone at the table, sitting at opposite ends.

"Are you going to join me down here, James?" Emily asked as she stirred her tea with a delicate spoon. "It seems strange to sit so far away when it's just us."

I smiled, picked up my cup, and moved to the seat beside hers. "Is this better?"

"Much. I think the quality of your company shall exceed that of Mrs. Henderson's."

"I can scarcely claim to deserve such praise."

Emily chuckled, set her cup down, and fixed me with a thoughtful expression. "Oliver is still asleep, and we have a few hours until we meet with Eli. Would you be keen to help me with something while we wait?"

"Is it about Mr. Blackstone?"

"No, nothing so serious. I want to send a wireless message to my friend Lilian in New York, you see, and I would like for it to be done today. But my father only gave me fifteen shillings to pay Mr. Haverford."

Mr. Haverford, the assistant purser, was famous for performing such favors for his patrons. He was always willing to ensure that our messages were sent out alongside those from the first-class passengers... if we were willing to pay him a small, unofficial fee to speed things along. Underhanded, perhaps, but I'd never heard much grumbling about it, either.

"Fifteen?" I repeated, doing some quick mental math. "After Mr. Haverford's five, that's barely enough to send her much more than a sentence."

"Precisely my problem!" Emily shook her head. "Who can be so concise as to fit everything they wish to say in one measly sentence?"

"Well, I'm happy to help you try."

"I hoped you would be. Shall we finish our tea and head to the library?"

"Certainly. Do we require a chaperone?"

"If you insist upon such a thing, I will write the letter without your help. I am my own woman, Mr. Kelly, and you would do well to remember that."

"Of course. I meant only to inquire."

"And inquire you have. My honor is intact."

We finished our breakfasts in companionable silence. The liveliness of the saloon provided an engaging backdrop for our blossoming two-hander. When it was apparent we were both ready to leave, I stood and pushed my chair in. Emily looked expectantly at me. It made my cheeks flush to do it, but I choked down my desire to flee and offered her my arm. "Shall we?"

She grinned and placed her hand on my outstretched wrist. "Let's."

I could have fainted.

From there, we made our way to the library. It wasn't a long walk to our destination, only one flight of stairs, and we engaged in playful banter all the while. It was fun to brainstorm possible messages. In fact, it was so fun that I forgot to be nervous.

"How about, 'Wish you were here—Emily,'" I offered as we reached the top step. "That's probably about as many letters as you've got to spend."

"It needs more personality. If I send such a message, Lilian will think I've grown terribly bland in my time away. She lives an interesting life. I need to keep pace."

"Alright," I said as we walked through the corridor to the library. "What if we included the phrase, 'Having adventure—Emily?'"

"That's better," she said. "It would be good if she thought I was on an adventure."

We entered the library together. Only a few other passengers were scattered around, reading or writing at the desks. Mr. Clarke was one of those present; he was reading a book he'd brought on board with him, one by Thomas Mann. Our usual spot was taken by a pair of men I didn't recognize, so we sat around an empty desk near the Swedish journalist. Emily and I gathered a set of writing implements and set to work.

"Well, if you want to sound exciting, why not tell your friend about our mystery?" I suggested. "How about, 'Cursed wings, big mess!'"

Emily grinned. "She would think I had lost my mind if I sent that. Although, 'Solving mystery' might not be an awful start…"

We made a few more serious attempts to resolve the message. After several revisions, we settled on something Emily could accept.

I picked up the paper and read our work aloud: "On ship. Solving mystery. Wish you were here. Having adventure. Your Friend—Emily."

"Oh, that might be the one. What do you think?"

I shrugged. "If your goal is to provide your friend with just enough information to pique her curiosity, I think you've succeeded."

"Excellent! Lilian will be pleased. She's always urging me to seek out new experiences."

"She sounds like a good friend."

"She is! Lilian's quite involved with the suffragist movement in New York. Before Mother's illness progressed, we had a dance class together—I love to dance, you know—and Lilian would regale me with tales of their rallies. She could recite Emmeline Pankhurst's best passages from memory. Have you heard of her?"

"Lilian? Just now, I suppose."

"No, silly. Emmeline Pankhurst!"

"Oh! No, I haven't," I admitted. "Does Mrs. Pankhurst live in New York?"

Emily chuckled. "No. She's from England—London, I think, or perhaps Manchester, I'm not sure which. I said Lilian recited her passages, not that they were acquainted. I imagine she'd faint with excitement if the opportunity ever arose for them to meet."

"May I ask what you think of Lilian's ambitions? Have you considered joining her at the rallies?"

A look of consternation flashed over Emily's face. "Yes, of course I've considered it. Were circumstances different... well, suffice it to say that I have yet to do so, but I find her inspiring, James. It means something when ladies band together to advocate for reform. She makes me ponder what might be possible if we dare to dream. Someday, I shall join her."

"Well, if anyone could make a difference in this world, Emily, it would be you."

A becoming blush colored her cheeks. "Perhaps," she said. Then, with a hint of her usual playful demeanor, she added, "But for now, we have our own little problem to manage, do we not? This message will not send itself."

"It won't," I agreed, suddenly aware of how long we'd been

alone together. "We should probably return to D-deck before anyone wonders where we've disappeared to."

"Very well. Shall we brave the journey to the purser's office together, Mr. Kelly?"

I offered her my arm. "After you, Miss Wentworth." Together, we set off to send her message, leaving the comfortable solitude of the library behind.

The assistant purser's office was two floors down from the library and one level past the dining saloon. We descended the stairs together, still walking arm-in-arm. When we reached the landing on D-deck, we ran into Oliver, who was making his way in for a late breakfast.

My best friend looked exhausted, but his face lit up at the sight of us. "Well, well, well," he drawled. "What are you two doing up so early? Searching for ancient Egyptian artifacts without me?"

"James assisted me in composing a letter to Lilian Graham." Emily tightened her grip on my arm. "We're on our way down to the purser's office to have it relayed to the Marconi men."

"Lilian Graham? The actress?" Oliver teased. "I didn't know you knew one another."

Emily rolled her eyes. "You know full well who I meant, Oliver Franklin. Lilian Graham from Manhattan."

"Ah, your mate from dancing lessons. Well, that's much less exciting." Oliver's grin widened when he spotted our linked arms. "This, on the other hand... I say, Jimmy! You're conducting yourself with remarkable propriety. How gentlemanly of you to escort my darling sister on her errand."

"Would you like to tag along?" I asked, ignoring his jab and trying to keep the conversation away from dangerous waters.

Oliver stroked his chin. "Do they have breakfast rolls in the purser's office?" he inquired, feigning serious consideration.

"I doubt it."

"Then no. You two have fun!" Oliver winked before sauntering toward the dining saloon.

"He's incorrigible." Emily smiled up at me. "Shall we continue on?"

"Certainly."

I guided her down the stairs to find a crowd waiting for us at the bottom. Led by Captain Dinsmore, a multitude of people were swarming the assistant purser's window, shouting questions and making requests. I spotted Mrs. Henderson, who, it seemed, had miraculously recovered from her lumbago. She was leaning on the railing and chatting with the steward assigned to our hallway, a young man with more freckles on his nose than hairs on his head. He looked harried.

The assistant purser was seated at a desk behind a window. He was older than Emily and me, though not by many years—perhaps four or five. He was dressed in an ironed uniform, its brass buttons a perfect match for his impeccably styled blond hair. The man exuded an air of relaxed confidence as he handled the passengers' requests.

"Next!" he called out. There were a few minor complaints about placement in line, but they were resolved by Captain Dinsmore shuffling to the window to be seen first.

"How are you this fine morning, Charlie?" the old sailor asked. "I have something here that will interest you, I think!"

Charlie—Charles Haverford—leaned forward with a smile. "Ah, my friend, but I find all my clients' needs interesting!" He looked around at the assembled crowd, then back to the captain. "What assistance do you require?"

Captain Dinsmore handed Haverford a sealed yellow envelope. "Open this before you send it on," he said. "Reggie and I think you'll find it entertaining. After you finish, forward it to the usual place."

"As you wish. Our typical rate?"

"That would be delightful! I appreciate you, Charlie, you know that. I wouldn't want to deal with anyone else!"

"Of course, sir, of course. Next up, please!"

Haverford drew attention like no one I'd ever met. People gravitated toward his window, eager to speak with him, and he was obliging to their requests. He was quick with a smile and delighted in conversation and inside jokes. His laughter filled the office with warmth. By the time it was Emily's turn in line, I'd grown weary of his charade—for I'd decided by then that it had to be a charade. I firmly believe nobody is as genial as Haverford was pretending to be.

"Ten shillings, Miss Wentworth, and you will be on your way." He smiled at her while she produced the money, his teeth as white as December snow. "I would give you a discount if I could, but those Marconi people are quite strict!"

"There's no need. I have the funds. Is it in your ability to make sure this message goes out today?"

She slid him fifteen shillings. It was a sign of how often he arranged such deals that he hardly batted an eye.

"Of course, ma'am, I meant you no offense," Haverford simpered. He took a long look at her before handing her a receipt for ten shillings. "Forgive me, but it is not every day I get to assist someone as charming as you, Miss Wentworth. If you ever need anything else, anything at all, you need only ask. Even... after hours."

Emily's expression remained calm, but her posture stiffened. "Thank you, Mr. Haverford, but we really must be going.

I have an appointment with someone and wouldn't want to keep him waiting."

Haverford's grin faltered. "Of course, I understand. The man you are meeting is lucky to have your company."

"Good day, Mr. Haverford." There was no mistaking that this was a dismissal.

As we left, I noticed the crowd pressing closer to Haverford's window, their faces turned toward him like flowers seeking sunlight. The observation settled uncomfortably in my stomach. I couldn't quite put my finger on it, but something about Charlie Haverford set me ill at ease. I was glad to be rid of him.

Emily exhaled in relief when we reached the top of the stairs. "That wasn't what I expected," she admitted. "I do not recall Mr. Haverford being so... odious."

"You handled him well."

"Flattery will get you nowhere, James. Now, let's hurry. We don't want to be late. Eli Carter will be waiting for us."

We made our way straight to the library to meet up with Eli. He was already there, pacing between the furniture, worry lines prominent on his scrunched brow. His expression was one of chagrin.

"I'm sorry, my friends," he said, closing the gap between us with startling speed. "The photographs are not yet ready. It's taking me longer than expected to work out how to manage the contrast. I have another set of negatives hanging now, and if they pan out, I have an idea for controlling the exposure. But I'm not finished yet. I need another couple of hours."

"No hurry, old man," Oliver replied. "I'm sure we can find something to do while we wait for you."

Despite Oliver's optimism, the hours dragged by in agonizing slowness. We tried to make the best of it by settling into conversation and pondering the whereabouts of Mr. Blackstone, who hadn't been seen since our meeting out on deck. Emily thought he might be avoiding us. When lunch came and went with no sign of him, though, his absence began to feel more than a little strange. Oliver thought he might have resumed his search for the Sundered Wings. We were all eager to press on with our own investigation, but Eli's photographs were our only lead. We had little choice but to be patient.

It was nearing 2:00 in the afternoon when we received word that we could come and view the images Eli had prepared for us.

Upon our arrival, Eli led Emily, Oliver, and me to a large table near the back of the library. He'd been busy in our absence. Waiting for us at the table were several black-and-white photographs spread out in neat rows. They captured various scenes from our voyage: passengers in animated conversation, still shots of the ship's interiors, and other candid moments that Eli had skillfully frozen in time. I chuckled when I recognized the photograph of Mr. Harlowe on deck.

Eli gestured to the table. "Here they are. I hope you'll find them to your liking."

Emily walked around the table, admiring the photographs. "Oh, but these are wonderful, Eli! You have done a splendid job with them."

Oliver tilted his head to the side as he examined a photograph of the ship's four tall funnels. "You have an excellent eye. I don't know how you managed this shot, but it's inspired."

I moved closer, drawn to a photograph of two crew

members. It showed Assistant Purser Haverford and Mr. Harlowe standing just outside the dining saloon, engaged in what looked like an argument. Their expressions were so vivid that I felt like I could hear their conversation. If I was reading the situation correctly, Mr. Harlowe looked especially nettled. Not that this would be out of character.

Eli smiled, clearly pleased with our reactions. "Thank you. I've always believed that a good photograph tells a story, and there are plenty of stories aboard this ship, that much I can promise you."

"Do you have any more of your nighttime photos with you?" asked Emily. "I would love to see how you captured the ship after dark."

Eli hesitated. "Most of those didn't turn out well. There just wasn't enough light. I tried to compensate for it, but I was limited without a true darkroom."

"Please, Eli," begged Emily. "I just know there's something worthwhile in them."

With a resigned sigh, Eli reached into his bag and pulled out another stack of photographs. "Don't expect too much," he said, spreading them out next to the others. "They really aren't very good."

Emily, Oliver, and I took seats around the table, leaned in, and examined the grainy images. As Eli had warned, most of them were difficult to decipher. I picked up a stack and flipped through them. They passed by in a blurry haze... until my thumb caught on the edge of a truly unbelievable photograph.

I gasped. Eli raised his eyebrows while a slow smile built on his face. "Find something interesting?" he asked.

Emily and Oliver didn't wait to see for themselves. They raced to my side, their twin expressions of eager enthusiasm reflected in both sides of my peripheral vision. I set the photograph down on the table so they could see it.

Like the other nighttime images, this photo was hazy. I needed to squint to make out the details. It looked like Eli had been standing close to the nook where we'd had our conversation with Mr. Blackstone when he'd taken it. A tall, uniformed man who had to be Lieutenant Morgan stood at the edge of the photo, nearly out of shot. His back was pressed against the rail with one arm raised over his chest. The other hung limply at his side.

"Is that Lieutenant Morgan?" Emily whispered.

Oliver's mouth was hanging open. "Has to be."

I tapped on the image. "Eli, when was this one taken?"

"Wednesday night." He froze. "You—you don't think... I saw nothing unusual when I captured it, but..."

I looked at the photo again, straining to make out any other details; Eli was standing a good distance from the attack, but I was sure that this image captured Lieutenant Morgan's last moments. It couldn't be anything else. In the background of the shot, facing the lieutenant, loomed another man, his frame barely discernible except for the faint glint of eyeglasses. The figure's arm was extended, holding something small and metallic—a revolver, perhaps. It was aimed right at Morgan.

Emily gasped. "Good Lord! You didn't just get a picture of the deck, Eli. You got a picture of Lieutenant Morgan's murder!" She paused, then glanced at Oliver. "I told you that curse story was nonsense."

I shivered. This was the proof we'd been searching for, but I didn't feel triumphant. I felt nervous.

"The curse might still be real," argued Oliver, though he sounded less than certain. "We don't know how these things operate, do we? You heard Mr. Blackstone—there's always a price to pay for power. What if Lieutenant Morgan died paying that price?"

Emily pinched the bridge of her nose. "That's absurd. We're looking at a man with a gun, not a ghost. There is no curse."

"You can't know that for certain! Mr. Clarke has heard things. Shadows in the cargo hold, disembodied voices in the engine room..."

"Are you serious?" Emily stood, turned her back on her brother, and leaned against the arm of my chair. "Control yourself, Ollie. You've seen no evidence of any such thing. Only rumors and suppositions."

"I am perfectly in control of myself, thank you. I merely question whether or not you have considered that the curse—"

"Setting the curse aside for a moment," I interrupted, trying my best to both ignore Emily's proximity and head off the argument, "I have a question. How did you avoid being seen by the assailant, Eli? You couldn't have been more than fifty feet away from the incident!"

Eli was clearly struggling with what he'd just heard. He swallowed hard, a visible lump forming in his throat. "I... I don't know," he mumbled. "But I know I want nothing further to do with this. You never cared to see my photos for their quality. You were looking for clues to aid in Mr. Clarke's treasure hunt! Well, it's fine for you to be tangled up in this mess, but I don't want to do anything to tempt the American authorities. Hand them over, please."

"You can't take them back!" Oliver's voice was louder than it should have been for the library. A few curious bystanders turned to watch him. "If you do, all the risks we've taken so far will have been for nothing! We need your photographs, Mr. Carter!"

Eli flinched. "But Mr. Harlowe—"

"Oh, forget about Mr. Harlowe," Oliver snapped. "Mr. Clarke can handle him. He's a professional!"

Eli gripped the back of his chair. "You don't understand, Mr. Wentworth. It isn't that I don't want to help you, it's that I cannot do so. I've listened to my grandfather's stories. I know what happens when people like me are caught in the wrong place at the wrong time. Helping you isn't worth crossing the Americans."

I didn't know what to say. Instead, I pulled the incriminating photograph closer, staring at the image as if it could offer me a solution. No luck.

Emily, as always, knew what to do. She stood up and crossed the room to stand by Eli's side. "You have my apologies, Eli," she said, resting her hand on his forearm. "You're right. This isn't fair to you. We should have been more forthcoming."

"You just don't understand," he repeated, turning away from Oliver. "You're taking such great risks..."

She guided Eli to the table next to ours. Once they were out of immediate earshot, they began to whisper. They were speaking too quietly for me to overhear.

I turned to deal with Oliver. He was fiddling with his Ronson lighter, thumbing the flint over and over, but never striking the flame. "Come on, Ollie. Let's take another look at this."

Oliver hesitated before relenting. He dragged his chair over beside mine and leaned in, staring at the hazy shapes in the photo without saying a word. His lighter clicked shut. Then he opened it again.

"Do you think this man could be Mr. Blackstone?" I asked. "Or one of the smugglers?"

"Could be." Oliver narrowed his eyes. "Mr. Blackstone wears glasses like these. It might very well be him."

Eli overheard us and gasped. "Mr. Blackstone wasn't at breakfast..." he whispered. "Nor was he at lunch! He could be out there looking for us, even now!"

I shook my head, trying to head off Eli's growing paranoia. "I don't think so. If he wanted to hurt us, he'd have done it last night. There wouldn't have been any witnesses out on deck. And we aren't exactly hiding in here."

Emily lent Eli one last look of understanding before she stood, crossed the distance between us, and reclaimed her seat at the table. "It is strange that he's avoiding everyone. If he were innocent, he'd want to maintain appearances, would he not? So why hide?"

"Perhaps he's lying low," Oliver suggested. "I know I'd hole up in my stateroom if people suspected me of murder. Perhaps he's having his dear Aunt Edith bring him food during the day, then sneaking around at night."

"Mrs. Henderson left breakfast early, but not with any extra food." Emily leaned forward and cupped her elbow with one hand, then tapped her lips with the other. "James and I saw her outside Haverford's office not an hour later. She'd have needed to hurry if she were going back to check on her nephew."

"Well, I don't know, then," Oliver grumbled. He stuffed his lighter back into his jacket pocket.

Emily sighed. "What we need is more information. This photograph is telling, but it cannot identify the man in the glasses and does not show the Wings of Amun-Ra. Where are they? Why hasn't anyone found them yet?"

The last thing I wanted to do was admit it, but I knew what we needed to do next. I sighed resignedly. "You were right last night," I said. "We need to get into Lieutenant Morgan's room. If the artifacts are still there, we might get to them before Mr. Blackstone does. And if not, we might at least be able to figure out what Lieutenant Morgan was doing with them."

"That's a capital suggestion!" Oliver punched me in the shoulder, seemingly reenergized by my proposal. "I knew you had it in you!"

I couldn't bring myself to match his enthusiasm. There were too many unknowns. Too many things that could go wrong.

Emily tucked a stray strand of hair behind her ear. "Let's say we find the artifacts in there. What then? What's our next move?"

"We could take them to Mr. Clarke," Oliver proposed. "He'd know what to do. As long as they're out of the killer's reach, they're safer than they are now. The idea of someone evil controlling the power of the curse gives me the shakes."

"Be sensible. We have proof now that nothing supernatural caused Lieutenant Morgan's murder," Emily said. Her tone left no room for argument.

Oliver looked far from reassured. He reached for his lighter again. "Mr. Blackstone disagrees. Who would know better than him?"

"Literally anyone else? He's a liar and a thief."

"What about Mr. Clarke? He believes in it. Is he a liar and a thief, too?"

"If we can get the Sundered Wings to safety, we can end this whole mess," I said, once again cutting off the feuding siblings. "Whoever killed Lieutenant Morgan did it to claim these artifacts. If we can find them, we can take away their motive to kill again. And clear Lieutenant Morgan's name at the same time."

"All due respect, but I will say again that I do not wish to be involved." Eli returned to our table and shoved the entire stack of photographs over to Emily with a grand sweep of his hand. "Take these, if you must, but you can forget we ever had this conversation. Don't mention me if you get caught with them, and don't mention me to your friend Mr. Clarke, either. This is dangerous, and I won't get myself caught up in it."

Oliver frowned before offering Eli a small smile. "Nothing worthwhile is safe, Mr. Carter. But you can trust we shall keep your involvement a secret."

"As far as I'm concerned, you were never here," I said. "But we're going to press on. I hope you understand."

Eli sighed. "You'll do what you must."

"Thank you for the photographs," Emily said graciously. "We appreciate them more than you know."

"Stay safe, Miss Wentworth," Eli replied. He took one last look at his work, which was still spread out on the table. "I pray that your foolish endeavor does not bring you to any harm."

7
HIDDEN AND HEARTFELT

"Are you sure you want to stay here, old man?" Oliver was leaning against the doorframe of our stateroom, thumbing the flint of his lighter. "My father would welcome your company. He and his mates will play cards with us until the lights turn out."

"Yes, thank you, but I'm sure." I was lying on our couch, having discarded my jacket and vest in favor of my suspenders and slacks. Though I wasn't quite settled in for the night, I was content to spend the rest of my waking hours flipping through the pages of Teddy Roosevelt's autobiography. "I think I'd prefer a quiet night in."

"Suit yourself," Oliver said. He grinned and pocketed his lighter. A second later, he was gone.

I let out a contented sigh. Alone at last. I hadn't had much time to myself over the last couple of days. I reveled in it now. Our room was quiet, save for the hum of the ship's engines and the occasional creak of the mahogany furniture. With nothing but the silence of my thoughts to occupy me, I leaned back and became rather absorbed in the 26th president's life story. Just as

Teddy Roosevelt's Rough Riders charged into battle on the page, a knock jolted me from my reverie.

"The door's unlocked!" I called out, expecting to see Oliver returning from the smoking room. "You weren't gone as long as you thought you'd—"

It wasn't Oliver. Instead, much to my astonishment, Emily strolled in. She had a small stack of Eli's photographs clutched in her hands. At some point, she'd let her hair down and traded her dinner clothes for a simple day dress and boots.

"Hello," I said, feeling a bit out of sorts. I didn't even have my jacket on!

"Hello, James. Where is my brother this evening?" she asked. She took in the state of our quarters with a raised eyebrow. "He isn't enjoying another bath, is he?"

"He's with your father in the smoking room." I tossed Teddy's book aside and reached for my vest.

Emily made a slight "hmm" sound. Her eyes settled on the title page of my book. "You got that when we were in the library yesterday."

"I did."

"I quite like Mr. Roosevelt," she said conversationally. "Jane Addams seconded his nomination last year at the Bull Moose Convention. Did you know that?"

"No," I admitted, fastening my vest and reaching for my dinner jacket. "I'm still at the part where he's gone to war with Spain."

"He's a respectable man. If only he had won the vote last year, we might have seen genuine progress by now. President Wilson is far too old-fashioned."

"I would have cast my vote for him if I were of age. Teddy Roosevelt, I mean."

"As would I, were the law different," grumbled Emily. "Alas..."

This entire conversation was surreal. I was alone with Emily Wentworth after dinner in my stateroom. "Uh—not that I'm not interested in this conversation, because I am, but why are you here?" I asked. "Shouldn't you still be with your mother?"

Emily shrugged half-heartedly. "You know how it is. Some nights, she is her old self, and others, she can hardly bear to stay awake, even when I read to her from our favorite novels. She fell asleep some time ago."

"But why have you left her? We agreed to wait until tomorrow to plan our break-in."

"Are you up for a walk?"

I didn't take much time to consider my response. "Where are we going?"

"The library, I think," Emily said. "It's not so late that the lights will be out, and I want to go somewhere more comfortable than your stateroom. I would also prefer to avoid the ire of the steward outside, which is surely stoked the longer I remain unsupervised with you. He was rather put out by the impropriety."

"Oh! Yes, of course. The library would be lovely."

She grinned. "Shall we go, then?"

Emily and I made our way back out into the hall, where, sure enough, a young, freckle-faced steward was waiting—the same one Mrs. Henderson had been harassing earlier in the day. He wore a look that landed somewhere between frustration and consternation.

"Miss Wentworth!"

"There's nothing to worry yourself over, Mr. Cunningham," Emily said. "My brother was not in, but Mr. Kelly will escort me to the library in his place. I shall be well cared for."

The steward nodded, placated. "Very good, Miss Wentworth," he said. "Please let me know if you need anything else."

"I will do just that." Emily took my offered arm, and we embarked on the short walk up to D-deck.

"So, Oliver has gone to play poker?" Emily asked.

"Yes. He was excited about it. Seemed to think he had a chance to win a few hands."

"My brother has too many tells. Those old men will take him for all he's worth."

"Given that he's only worth whatever money your father gives him, who truly stands to lose?"

"Well... perhaps they'll arrange it for him to win a hand or two."

"I would be surprised if they didn't," I said as we reached the double doors leading into the library. "After you."

Emily entered first. Only a few other passengers were present, and they were all absorbed in novels and other literary pursuits. None so much as looked up when we entered. A single clerk was scrubbing out the inside of a wine glass, humming a tune to himself. When he saw us enter, he nodded, a gesture we returned before claiming same table we'd written our letter on earlier that day.

"Well," I said. "What's all this about?"

"I was going through the photographs Eli left us," she explained, laying them out to show me. "He was telling the truth about these. The quality is poor. Most of them are worthless. But this one, I think, is interesting." She slid a photograph over to me and tapped it with her index finger. "Take a look and tell me what you see."

I leaned over to examine the image. It was grainy, just like the others had been. The presence of lifeboats to the left of the shot told me it had been taken on the boat deck, but beyond that, details were scarce. It was only when Emily pointed directly at the place she'd found interesting that I saw what she wanted me to notice.

There were people in this photo. At first, they were mere smudges, indistinct against the backdrop of the ship. But as Emily pointed out the details, two men emerged from the haze. Or their outlines did, at any rate. They were standing together at the waist-high gate between the second-class promenade and the engineers' promenade. Their postures suggested a tense conversation.

"What should I be looking for here?"

"Does nothing catch your eye?"

"Not yet. Can you give me a hint?"

Emily shook her head with a smile. "Well, I think this is—"

We were interrupted. Someone was coming up behind us, fast.

"Quickly, act natural," I urged, shoving the photograph back under the others in the stack.

Mr. Clarke emerged just as I slid it out of sight. He was dressed in his best black tuxedo. Grim faced, he was impatiently scanning the room, although for what, or whom, I could not say. Academic, thin, and bespeckled, the Swedish journalist would never be an imposing presence. Still, he was intimidating in his way, possessed as he was with an unknown purpose.

"Good evening, Mr. Kelly, Miss Wentworth," he said curtly. "I trust you are finding the library to your satisfaction?"

Emily and I exchanged a tense glance before nodding in unison.

"Yes, thank you, Mr. Clarke," I said. "Just... catching up on some reading."

"Are you?" He eyed the stack of photographs between us, his expression inscrutable.

I didn't know what else to say. I was very aware that neither Emily nor I were holding books, but there wasn't much I could do about that now. If Eli hadn't made us promise to keep his involvement a secret, we could have told Mr. Clarke what we were doing, but as it was…

"We are debating which books to check out next," Emily clarified.

"I see. And how is your investigation progressing?"

"Well, sir," I replied. "I think we've made a fair amount of progress. I know you've been meeting with Oliver individually, but perhaps we might all meet and speak about it soon."

Mr. Clarke seemed satisfied with that suggestion. "Very well. If I might impart upon you some advice?"

"Of course."

"The next time you wish to mislead a curious party, make your excuse more believable. Not everyone will understand your need for discretion as well as I." He looked between us again before spinning on his heels and heading to the forward exit. He turned back just before leaving the room. "Good luck with your work."

And then he was gone.

I sank back into my chair, exhaling as the tension of our encounter began to fade. "Thank goodness. I wonder what he was doing out at this hour?"

"Investigating, most likely," Emily said. "But we cannot tell him about Eli. We promised."

"I wouldn't have."

"Good. I don't like breaking promises. And say what you will, but if anything happens to Eli because of these pictures, it's our fault." Emily glanced around before she slid her hand back under the stack of photographs and pulled out the one we'd been examining. "But enough about that. What did you see when you looked at this image?"

"Well, I saw the two men," I said. It was difficult to find meaning in the smudges. "But there must be something more important than that here, or you wouldn't be showing this to me. What am I missing?"

Emily set the picture in front of me and indicated a few features with her nail. "Well, I believe that's Lieutenant Morgan on our side of the gate, right there. The image is grainy, so I cannot be certain, but this man appears to be wearing the same uniform Morgan was wearing in the other photo. Do you agree?"

"Yes, I think you're right!"

She smiled. "Good. Now, I want you to look at the man he is speaking with. Notice anything about him?"

"Well, whoever he is, he's standing on the engineers' promenade. He isn't on our side of the gate."

"Go on. What else do you see?"

It was genuinely difficult to make out any details, but if the man meeting with Lieutenant Morgan was a crewmember, he wasn't in uniform. If anything, he looked like he was wearing a similar tuxedo to the one Mr. Clarke had been wearing. It was different, fancier than the one the Swede owned, but of a similar make. Definitely an outfit meant for the dinner table.

"That man isn't an engineer!" I said, the thrill of discovery coursing through me like an electric shock. "Those are dinner clothes, not a uniform! He must have come from first class!"

"I believe the same," confirmed Emily. "Which means Lieutenant Morgan had an associate willing to cross class lines to meet with him. We cannot see the other man well enough to identify him, but I suspect he hopped the gate between the first-class promenade and the engineers' promenade. It would be easy enough to do."

"Why, though?" I asked. My chair creaked as I shifted to lean forward. "Why go to the trouble?"

Emily matched my posture. "I don't know. I came to look for you and Oliver before I figured that part out."

"I suppose it wouldn't be fair for me to continue expecting you to uncover everything." Realizing that I may have sounded rude, I hastily amended my statement. "Of course, this is a significant lead! One that we all overlooked this afternoon. Well done."

"Thank you, but I haven't done anything remarkable. It is all about paying attention to the details."

"You shouldn't undersell yourself, Miss Wentworth. You'd make a fine detective."

Emily chuckled, then snorted. "A detective, you say? I doubt that very much. I have always been more inclined toward writing. You, on the other hand, could be a fantastic detective."

"Me?" I shook my head. "I'm not suited for that."

"Nonsense. You're doing the work of a detective now, are you not?"

"With your help. And Oliver's, of course. I couldn't do it on my own."

"I think you have yet to try, and I also believe you are more capable than you believe yourself to be," Emily said. "But it was just a thought."

I mulled it over. There was a certain appeal to the idea, but... Emily was overestimating my abilities. That much I knew to be true.

"You flatter me," I finally said. "Now, I would like to do the same in return. I didn't know you aspired to be a writer! Why haven't you pursued it? You'd be wonderful!"

Emily's gaze drifted to the clock. Its minute hand was frozen in place to allow for the nightly adjustment of time. "Caring for my mother consumes my waking hours. When I'm not with her, there's always something to be done for Father or for the house. Parties to host, dinners to arrange, that sort of thing. Writing feels like a selfish dream when so many other things must take priority."

"I don't think your family would see it that way. They would encourage you."

"You only say that because you do not fully comprehend my situation."

"I'm willing to try."

She hesitated. "Well..." There was another pause, followed by a yearning sigh. "You must understand that my mother was formidable, once. Before you came to live in our home, before Oliver and I were sent to attend school with you, she was our tutor. Oh, James, you should have seen her! She was so bold. So fearless. Smarter than any man, and braver than them, too. She insisted I read everything in our library. That I learn everything she had to teach me. She married my father because his love was worth more to her than all the money in Europe. Do you know how rare that sort of woman is?"

I didn't know what to say. The library around us was as silent as a graveyard, and as somber as one, too. "She sounds incredible."

"She was—she is. But now that her sickness has progressed, she needs me to be strong for her. And it isn't just Mother; Father relies on me, too. Our house would fall apart without me there to care for it. Do you see now why I must remain content with my books? Happy to read about the fortunes of others, yet never to seek out my own?"

"I'd lived with the Wentworths for three years. Two of them had been overshadowed by Mrs. Wentworth's diagnosis. Only now, seeing the tired lines around Emily's eyes, did I fully grasp the weight of her burden. "It's not selfish to have dreams, Emily," I said, having recovered my voice. "Your parents would understand if you pursued yours."

"I wish it were so simple. Perhaps, one day, it will be. Perhaps I'll write novels or draft pamphlets for the suffragists. But that day isn't today. It can't be. I have far more pressing concerns."

She looked once more to the clock. Its hands had not stirred.

I didn't know what else I could say. I'd always thought of Emily as someone tenacious, someone who would never be denied what she sought. She never backed down in conversations with people like Mrs. Henderson. I didn't enjoy seeing her like this. *Was there something I could do for her? Did she want me to agree with her opinions? Or did she want me to challenge her assumptions?*

Emily must have noticed my dilemma, for she took pity on me and relieved me of my need to respond. "You need not say anything, James. Regardless of what you may be thinking, I know my responsibilities well, and I have made peace with them. I am not unhappy."

"But don't you ever wish for something different? Something more than tending to an endless list of duties?"

She snorted to cover up a small, bitter laugh. "Of course I do. This business with Lieutenant Morgan and the Sundered Wings has been a chance to embrace that. A chance to have an adventure of my own. It's awful, of course, but... I've enjoyed the challenge."

"So have I," I admitted. "I've never done anything like this before. We're planning to sneak into a dead man's cabin tomorrow, for goodness' sake!"

"I know. Isn't it invigorating?"

"It is. Frightening, too, of course, but... invigorating."

She smiled faintly. "It will all be over when we arrive in New York. The monotony of our daily lives will be waiting for us again. I dread that, in a way."

I nodded. That much I could understand. "I feel the same. I've been living on your parents' charity for too long. I know I need to strike out on my own, but truth be told, I'm not sure how to begin doing it. If Oliver hadn't convinced your parents to take me in, I don't know where I'd be. I owe them for that. I owe all of you."

Emily shook her head. "You shouldn't feel guilty, James. You may not realize it, but you've been a great help to my family. My parents adore you. You've been a comfort to my mother throughout her illness. In time, I believe you'll find your path. I know you lost your family, but you still have all of us. Don't forget that."

Her words stirred up something warm within me. It felt good to voice these worries to someone who understood. "Thank you. That—that means a great deal."

The corners of her mouth curled upward. "I have an idea."

"Oh?"

"A proposal, actually."

I sat up straighter. "I'm listening."

"I propose that we promise to hold each other accountable. I'll help you find your purpose. And you'll help me remember my dreams, even after we return to New York. We should not bear our burdens alone, not when we can share them with one another."

Emily was looking at me expectantly; she wanted an answer. It was an easy one to give. "It's a promise," I swore. "You can count on me."

"And you, me," she said, grinning. "I rather like the idea of having a confidant."

"Then you shall have one."

For a moment, the room stood still. Nothing made a sound but the renewed ticking of the clock over the mantle. Even the clerk behind the desk was quiet, having opened a book of his own on the countertop.

"Well! I think that's enough soul-searching for one evening," Emily said, stashing away the photographs and turning to face me. "I'm not ready to return to my stateroom just yet, but we have made all the progress we will make tonight. I do not wish to discuss the case any longer."

"Very well. What do you suggest?"

"Are you brave enough for another game of chess?"

"I think I can manage."

We sat together until after the clock struck midnight, talking, laughing, playing chess, and enjoying each other's company. I'll remember that night in the library for as long as I live. We officially became friends, then, I think. We'd always been aware of one another, but it was in that glorious couple of hours, bonded as we were by our promise and the mystery of the Sundered Wings, that we truly came to care for one another.

"Thank you for an interesting series of games, James," Emily said, wiping away a tear of laughter. "But I believe it is time for us to return to our staterooms. It would not be a good look for Oliver and my father to return and find us missing."

"Of course. We can reconvene in the morning to discuss your findings. I'm sure Oliver will want a look at that photograph."

As we rose from the table, I offered her my arm.

"Oh, how charming." She took it. "Shall we, then?"

We walked side by side through the quiet corridors while the gentle vibration of the engines thrummed underfoot. Emily's hair shone under the low evening lights. Her face seemed softer, more open than before. The sound of her boots on the wooden floor matched perfectly with mine.

She stole a glance at me. I grinned back.

I've admired Emily many times. I'm not ashamed to admit that. But this time, for the first time, I thought she might have been admiring me, too. I had to fight the urge to cheer like a fool. *Could such a thing be possible?*

Then reality hit, extinguishing my excitement as surely as a douter over a candle's flame. Emily and I were not suited for one another. Not in the eyes of society. I needed a job—a direction. Living off Emily's parents' charity wasn't an option if I wanted to stand beside her as an equal. And it wasn't just that. Dr. and Mrs. Wentworth trusted me to care for their daughter. I was almost certainly abusing that trust now, given that I was entertaining dreams of courting her.

When we reached the Wentworths' stateroom, I paused, tongue-tied once again. I was still wrestling with my words when Emily looked up at me. None of my indecision was reflected on her face.

"Goodnight, James."

"Goodnight, Emily."

She disappeared behind the door. I stood there for a moment, lost in thought, before making my way back to my room in silence.

8
MURDER IN THE LOUNGE

Knock. Knock. Knock.
"Hello?" called out an unfamiliar voice.
KNOCK! KNOCK! KNOCK!
"Hello? Mr. Wentworth? Are you there?"

I fumbled for my pocket watch and noted the hour—nearly 10:00 a.m. We'd overslept.

"Mr. Wentworth, I must insist that you answer this door!"

"That pounding is going to drive me mad," grumbled Oliver. I heard him pull his covers up. "Come back later!"

He sounded as tired as I was, which made sense, given the lateness of our night. I'd returned to our stateroom before him, but only by a few minutes. He'd been eager to chat upon his return. I caught him up on Emily's discovery in the photograph, and he caught me up on the latest rumors surrounding Mr. Blackstone. They were never in short supply. We stayed up well beyond curfew, trying to puzzle out the motives of the elusive man.

"MR. WENTWORTH! YOUR FATHER HAS NEED OF YOU, SIR!"

Oliver jumped out of his bunk and scrambled to pull a jacket over his nightshirt. The morning sun, obscured by clouds, cast a dim light into our stateroom. It wasn't much, but it was enough to see by. I rolled over to watch Oliver flounder. His hair, normally immaculate, resembled a bird's nest more than anything suitable for polite society.

"Looking sharp, Ollie."

Oliver responded with a rude gesture before yanking open the door and saying, with false cheer, "What can I do for you, good man?"

The same young steward Emily and I had spoken with the night before stood in the hallway. "Good morning, sir. Dr. Wentworth needs you to fetch his medical bag from his stateroom and take it to the first-class lounge. There's been an incident."

"Incident?" Oliver's smile vanished. "Is my father well?"

"Yes. You will learn more when you arrive, but please, make haste. He said you would know what he needed."

"Give us a moment to dress," Oliver said. He shut the door in the steward's face.

"Did you have to be so sharp with him?" I asked, sitting up and rubbing the stubble on my chin. "The poor boy looked terrified."

"I refuse to venture out half-dressed. Get up, Jimmy. You're coming, too."

"They didn't ask for me."

"I did. Come on, we don't want to leave my father waiting."

We dressed quickly—me in a navy blue suit, Oliver in a sand-colored jacket with a paisley tie. After a quick once-over to ensure we were presentable, we headed out.

The pale steward glanced sideways at me when we emerged

together. "Pardon, sir, but I was only asked to retrieve Mr. Wentworth. I wasn't expecting a second man."

"He's as good as a Wentworth," Oliver said as if that solved the entire problem.

Surprisingly, it did. The steward shrugged and accepted Oliver's explanation with little fuss. "Very well, sir. Shall we?"

We set off down the hallway as a group of three. It was silly, especially given the seriousness of the situation, but I had to work to keep a satisfied smile off my face. Being accepted as an unofficial member of the family was something I never took for granted. I drew strength from that sentiment on the short walk to the Wentworths' stateroom.

"My father's things are just inside here," Oliver said when we reached the door. He knocked. "Mother? Emily?"

The door swung open before Oliver could finish knocking. Emily stood on the other side with one hand on her hip, dressed immaculately in a high-collared blouse, honeydew waistcoat, and a skirt that brushed the top of her lace-up boots. Dr. Wentworth's brown leather satchel sat at her feet.

"Finally!" she exclaimed. "You took ages to arrive. Did Father call for us? Is there really a body in the first-class lounge?"

"Body?" I croaked. "A dead body?"

"Is there any other kind? Mother has already gone to speak with Assistant Purser Haverford. It's all so unusual; she wants reassurances about our safety. But she said Father would need his things and that I should stay behind and wait for you."

"Well, that's good thinking, then. Thanks." Oliver reached for Dr. Wentworth's leather bag, but Emily grabbed it before he could, looking reproachful.

"Can we please move this along?" our steward escort asked.

"The bag, please, Miss Wentworth. Hand it over to your brother."

"There's no need for that; I'll be joining you." When Oliver held his hand out again, Emily turned her nose up at him. "Thank you for your concern, Oliver, but I can handle this myself. Shall we go?"

The steward sighed. "Now, Miss Wentworth, this isn't the place for a lady to—"

"I wouldn't finish that thought if I were you," I said wryly. "Miss Wentworth has modern sensibilities. You aren't going to stop her if she's set on coming along, so it's best to accept it now and save yourself the trouble."

Emily beamed at me. "Too right," she said, looping her free arm around mine.

"Oh, very well," the steward conceded. "Is there anyone else you'd like to bring along? A distant cousin, perhaps?"

Oliver laughed. "What's your name, steward?"

The boy's face flushed a brilliant shade of red. He was younger than us, with sandy-blonde hair the same shade as Oliver's suit and a blizzard of freckles dusted across his pointed nose. "Pardon me, sir. It's Alexander Cunningham, sir. I beg apologies. I spoke out of turn."

"I like you, Alex; you've got spirit. Lead on!"

Alex first appeared confused by Oliver, but then, seeing my friend had no ill intentions, the steward relaxed. A bemused smile crossed his face. "Very well. I'll take you as far as the entrance to first class. An officer will be waiting there to escort you the rest of the way."

"Let's be off, then," Emily said. "It sounds like we haven't a moment to spare."

I'D BEEN at sea several times before, but I'd never been afforded the opportunity to visit first-class accommodations up close. I was curious, if a little apprehensive, to see what all the fuss was about. I didn't have long to wonder. Alex took us upstairs and out to the enclosed C-deck promenade; we'd barely stepped onto the pitch-pine deck when a group of children tore past, their laughter bouncing off the windows as they chased a ball across the floor. I watched them play until we reached the far end, where a narrow, unmarked door awaited.

A man was there, leaning against the bulkhead. A familiar man. William Harlowe, one of the *Olympic's* two masters-at-arms. Mr. Harlowe was about the same age as Eli Carter—just over thirty—though his wrinkled brow line and serious expression made him appear older than his years. He did not look especially pleased to see us.

Then again, that might have just been the way his face was. He never looked especially pleased about anything.

"Here's where I leave you, sirs, my lady." The young steward offered each of us a curt bow. "You'll be safe in the capable hands of Mr. Harlowe."

Mr. Harlowe grunted in reply. His piercing gaze roamed over us, stopping to rest on Emily, who flushed but stood firm under his scrutiny. "I expected one boy," he said. "Not the whole family."

"Sorry, sir." Oliver moved to place himself between his sister and Mr. Harlowe. "But where I go, they go."

"You don't make the rules, son."

"If I might interject, sir?" Emily spoke up. "We all just want to help my father. We're worried about him. You can trust us to be respectful."

Mr. Harlowe checked his pocket watch, a tarnished silver piece with scuffed, British military markings. "Very well. On your heads be it. Please do your best not to disturb the passengers; I dare say they've been through enough this morning." With that, he turned and opened the door. He was so tall he had to duck to fit under the frame.

Beyond it was a long hallway, not dissimilar to the one our staterooms were in, but more spacious by half. The floor tiles were earthy and offset by glimmering brass fixtures and walls of white. Electric lights burned brightly to guide our way forward.

"Not a bad set of accommodations," Oliver whispered to me. "One has to pay quite a bit to get these tickets."

"Not bad," I confirmed as we set off, trailing Mr. Harlowe.

We walked for an age. Eventually, the hallway opened into a magnificent room with beautifully pattered floors and an enormous, curved staircase. Intricate ironwork supported its sweeping oak balustrade, which was polished to such an exacting smoothness that I could see my reflection looking back at me on its surface. Several decks above, a glinting dome of iron and glass allowed natural light to pour in, bringing with it the cloudy mood of the sky overhead. The opulence of this room made my jaw drop.

For the first time, Mr. Harlowe displayed an emotion aside from contempt. He offered me a small, knowing smile. "The forward staircase is even grander. Now, come along. We're needed up on A-deck."

Mr. Harlowe began to climb. We ascended that grandiose staircase slowly, none of us speaking. I was drawn to the expert craftsmanship in its features: the rich handrails, the tiled floors, and the cherub statues that guarded either side of its flared entrance. Those statues were especially striking. Their childlike faces stared straight ahead, innocent bastions overlooking this palace of the sea.

The further we walked, though, the more like an impostor

I felt. My shoes felt out of place on these steps. My clothes felt shabby next to the fashion of the first-class passengers, high society men and women who passed by with an air of entitlement, their futures secured by their vast wealth. These people lived in the type of luxury once reserved for the kings and queens of Europe. And here I was, James Kelly, the orphaned son of two poor farmers. I stuck out like a sore thumb.

The atmosphere changed once again when we reached the top of the staircase.

A small crowd was gathered on either side of the hallway leading to the first-class lounge. They spoke in hushed tones, chattering amongst themselves as they craned their necks and stood on tipped toes to catch a glimpse of something just out of sight. Something hidden beyond a closed door. I couldn't see up ahead yet, but it was impossible to miss the tension in the air. We must be getting close.

"Make way, please, make way," Mr. Harlowe said as he carved us a path. Emily followed Mr. Harlowe with her head held high, Dr. Wentworth's bag swaying on her shoulder. Oliver was close behind her. I brought up the rear, my heart pounding with curiosity—and perhaps a little dread. I'd never seen a dead body before.

I held my breath as we pushed through a revolving door. Just on the other side, sprawled out near the lounge's entrance, was a man. He was still wearing his expensive dinner clothes, but his hair was mussed, his legs splayed out, his skin pallid in death. Open eyes stared vacantly at the ceiling. A small, glittering object lay near his outstretched right hand. I couldn't tell what it was.

Dr. Wentworth was kneeling beside the body. He was speaking with an unfamiliar, mustached man I assumed must be the *Olympic's* surgeon. I couldn't remember his name. "Ligature marks on the neck... and these others are signs of a struggle," Dr. Wentworth dictated. I watched him closely, noting every detail I could about the body: the bruises, the peculiar marks, and the odd object glinting in the dim light. It looked like a cufflink. In fact, I could have sworn I'd seen one just like it before, but I couldn't place where...

Emily handed her father his bag. He thanked her before waving her away, reaching in, and retrieving a stethoscope, which he positioned on the man's chest. I assumed he was confirming the absence of a heartbeat. Next, he pulled out a small magnifying glass, which he used to scrutinize the ligature marks before exchanging a few words with the other doctor. Finally, he used a pair of forceps to lift up the man's sleeve.

Oliver gasped and pulled up his collar. I couldn't blame him—it was all I could do not to be sick at the sight. Emily didn't notice it at first, but when she did, she backed away, hastening to stand behind her brother.

The stranger's left arm was so dry that it looked like something an archaeologist might dig up in the Valley of the Kings. Skin the color of parchment paper clung to the bone in leathery folds. Tendons lay exposed and brittle. The man's withered fingers curled inward as if clutched in a final, desperate grasp at something just out of reach.

The sight of such a grievous wound made my skin crawl. I had to fight the urge to turn and run.

"This is... unexpected," Dr. Wentworth muttered, half to himself, half to the *Olympic's* surgeon. "Something has withered this limb nearly to mummification, though I cannot hazard a guess what could have done it."

"Most peculiar," the other doctor said.

Dr. Wentworth shook his head. "I saw some remarkable

things in our war with Spain, my friend, but nothing so odd as this."

"I doubt whether many could say differently."

"Indeed. Oliver, hand me a syringe, would you?"

Surprised to be called upon, Oliver stepped up and fumbled with the bag before finding the instrument he'd been asked for. He handed it to his father. All the while, his eyes never left the man on the floor. He was transfixed.

Dr. Wentworth, on the other hand, was all business. "Thank you," he said before pulling the rubber cap off with his teeth. He inserted the point, drew a small blood sample from the man's good arm, and handed the syringe over to the *Olympic's* surgeon. "This fellow has not been dead long. I would say no more than a few hours."

"That lines up with the other information we have. He must have been brought here after the lights were turned out."

"I concur. I would like to investigate his effects next, if you have no objection."

"None."

Dr. Wentworth's movements were methodical. He lifted a flap on the dead man's jacket and pulled out a leather wallet; frowning, he opened it, leafed through some papers, and then folded it back up before handing it to Mr. Harlowe. He continued in this manner with the rest of the man's pockets. After a few more minutes of investigation, Dr. Wentworth sat back on his heels, his expression grave. He exchanged a tired look with the *Olympic's* surgeon.

"We have done what we can here." Dr. Wentworth picked the discarded cufflink up and turned it over. Its golden finish sparkled. "Without a proper autopsy, we cannot determine the exact cause of death or the source of this bizarre injury."

"Then the time has come to move the body to the ship's

hospital. We can perform a more thorough examination there. I have the equipment. Thank you for your help, Franklin; your expertise in these matters is widely regarded. I can see why."

"You are most welcome," replied Dr. Wentworth. He draped a cloth from his bag over the deceased man's face before passing the cufflink to the *Olympic's* surgeon. "We need to handle this with the utmost care. People will talk."

Oliver's attention remained locked on the body. "Who is he, Father? Have you identified him?"

"His name is—was—Theodore Eckert," answered Dr. Wentworth. "He was returning to the United States after a long stay in Egypt."

"Egypt?" I repeated.

"Yes, Mr. Kelly. Egypt. I hesitate to alarm anyone, but... this man's death was not natural. I do not understand how the injury inflicted on his arm could be the result of an infectious agent, but we need to be watchful for others who show signs of a foreign disease."

I suppressed a shiver. *How many times could Egypt come up before it was more than a coincidence? First Lieutenant Morgan, and now Theodore Eckert. Had the smugglers gotten to this man, too?*

The crowd parted to make way for a stately man dressed in a crisp uniform. I hadn't met him before, but he was unmistakable: Captain Edward Bartlett. The master of the *Olympic*, he was the ultimate authority while we were at sea. It was a sign of the seriousness of the situation that he'd joined us here.

Captain Bartlett strode confidently into the center of the lounge. Despite his position, the captain managed not to appear pretentious; a quiet charm was evident in his demeanor, even in a situation as serious as this one. Authority fit him like a glove. He scanned the room before settling on

Dr. Wentworth. His thin eyebrows lifted in recognition at the sight of the twins' father. "Dr. Wentworth, your reputation precedes you. Thank you for assisting Dr. Widmer. I am in your debt."

Dr. Wentworth waved Captain Bartlett's concerns away. "Nonsense. Your surgeon is more than capable, but I was happy to do my duty and lend a hand when called upon. I must admit, this is a troubling situation. Two deaths in a single passage..."

Captain Bartlett looked from the body to the cufflink. "What can you tell me?"

"Only suppositions at this point." Dr. Wentworth cleared his throat. "Mr. Eckert was found with ligature marks on his neck and bruising on his wrists, indicating a struggle. You can see for yourself that something strange has happened to his left arm. There are signs of forceful restraint on the right. Based on the evidence, I would hazard to guess that this man was interrogated before his death."

"Do we have any leads on who might have done this? Or why? Mr. Eckert seemed perfectly well at dinner last night."

"I should not speculate, but there was a cufflink found near the body. It appears custom made."

Dr. Widmer handed the ornament to Captain Bartlett, and the adults began a frenzied, whispered conversation. I strained to hear what they were saying to one another, but their voices were too low for me to follow along. There was nothing for it but to wait for them to finish.

Oliver wandered back to my side. We made eye contact before his attention drifted upward, fixating on a point above the lounge entrance. Whatever he saw there made his jaw drop. "Oh, no... Jimmy, Emily, look at the mascaron!"

"The what?" I asked.

He pointed over my shoulder. I followed his finger to the woodwork above the doorway.

The carving featured a woman's face resting in the center of an elaborate floral pattern. All around her, delicate flowers and vines wound through the wood, each petal rendered in painstaking detail. But while the flowers remained smooth, the woman's oaken skin had been damaged. Warped. Her eyes had been seared into empty hollows.

"I don't understand," I whispered. "What is this thing? Why is it there?"

Emily glanced at me before looking up to scrutinize the carving. "It's called a mascaron, James. They're decorative carvings ships have for... well, for luck, I suppose. They're supposed to ward off evil spirits."

"What happened to it?"

Oliver's eyes hadn't strayed from the decaying face. "It looks like something drained the life right out of her. You don't think... the curse..."

"Oh, be sensible," Emily said, but I could hear doubt creeping into her voice. "You cannot seriously think that a bit of old wood has anything to do with... well, with the Sundered Wings. Or the murder."

"You've been skeptical this entire time, Em, but even you must admit something odd is happening here. Mascarons are meant to fight evil. To watch over ships. Look at this one. Look at her eyes..."

"It is strange," Emily admitted. She didn't budge any further.

While the twins spoke, a seemingly unrelated memory stirred in my mind. One of Mr. Blackstone next to us at dinner, his hands moving as he spoke, the light catching on something shiny affixed to his wrist. I blinked as everything clicked into place. The intricate design, the golden finish, the cat's head—I'd seen it all before. I gasped, drawing looks from the twins.

"James?" Emily asked.

"What is it?" Oliver prompted.

I leaned in close. "Do you see that cufflink Captain Bartlett's holding? I think it's Mr. Blackstone's. He was wearing one just like it when we questioned him at dinner. I remember him messing with it."

Emily's hand flew to cover her mouth, and Oliver's face, if possible, became even paler. We all turned to look at Captain Bartlett, who was still examining the cufflink. He was oblivious to our whispered conversation.

"Do you think this means Mr. Blackstone is the murderer?" Oliver ran a hand through his hair. "But, then—what if he comes after us next? I don't want to end up like Eckert!"

"Calm down," I hissed, but it was too late. Captain Bartlett had noticed our exchange.

"You three, do you have something to add? What are you doing here? Who are you?"

I somehow gathered up the courage to speak first. "Uh, I'm Mr. James Kelly, sir. I'm a friend, or associate, I suppose, of Dr. Wentworth's... and I think I recognize that cufflink. It belongs to a man named Reginald Blackstone. He's... involved in some unsavory activities. He's a passenger, sir. In second class."

Dr. Wentworth and Captain Bartlett exchanged a look. "Thank you, Mr. Kelly. This is valuable information. I shall pass along your concerns to one of my officers. I think—yes, Master-at-Arms Harlowe will be leading this investigation. There's no man I trust more for the job."

Mr. Harlowe was standing off to the side of the room with his arms folded. His eyebrows rose at Captain Bartlett's request, but he straightened up, squared his shoulders, and accepted the duty with a curt nod. The captain's attention shifted back to Dr. Widmer. "Doctor? What would you recommend we do next?"

"Dr. Wentworth and I need to move Mr. Eckert's body to the hospital for a more thorough examination. An infectious room, I think—Room Two should be open. I shall have more information for you after completing an autopsy. Should we have someone contact New York?"

Captain Bartlett shook his head. "No. Keep the details to yourselves for now. I would rather avoid stirring up a panic."

"Understood. We'll proceed with the utmost care."

"Very good. Mr. Harlowe, would you have someone fetch me the carpenter? We need to do something about that mascaron."

Mr. Harlowe shrugged. "I can send a steward down to get him, sir."

"See it done."

As preparations were made to transport the body, Emily, Oliver, and I remained silent. *Was this the work of the smuggling ring? The curse wasn't real, was it? But what else could have done this? What damaged the mascaron, if not a curse?* I hadn't been sure whether there was anything to the story of the Wings of Amun-Ra before, but that was before a second dead body appeared. And that withered arm...

When things had progressed enough to allow for it, Captain Bartlett addressed the crowd of people waiting just outside of the lounge. "Thank you all for your cooperation. We have experts handling this situation. Please return to your rooms. We will keep you informed as we learn more."

It was difficult to miss the concern on the bewildered faces of the passengers. I had the sense that many of them were not accustomed to taking orders. Some weren't sure how to handle being asked to do so, which led to much grumbling. It was amusing to watch some of the most elite people in the world struggle to organize themselves. So much so that I nearly jumped out of my skin when a hand landed on my shoulder.

I whipped around to see Captain Bartlett standing beside me. "Can I help you, sir?" I asked.

"I fear that your presence here will draw more attention than you might think," he warned. "Keep your wits about you, lad. This ship is like a powder keg; one spark in the wrong place and we will all go up in smoke."

My heart was still thumping wildly. "Of course. I'll keep a low profile."

Captain Bartlett's grip on my shoulder tightened. "That may not be enough. You and your friends—Wentworth's boy and his sister—you need to keep your eyes open. I am not a superstitious man, Mr. Kelly, but I have seen enough to know when something is off."

"We'll do our best to keep a sharp lookout," I said, not sure I was saying the right thing. "You have my word."

He hesitated, glancing over at the mascaron still looming over the doorway. "See that you do. If you find anything amiss —anything at all—go straight to Mr. Harlowe. Is that clear?"

"Yes, sir."

"Good. Godspeed, Mr. Kelly."

9
DESTINY

After Captain Bartlett left the lounge, all that was left was for us to return to second class and plot our next move. Things had changed with the discovery of a second body; the smugglers who were after the Sundered Wings of Amun-Ra had once again proven their willingness to kill in pursuit of their prize. More than that, though, the twin horrors of the defaced mascaron and Theodore Eckert's withered arm had collaborated to spawn an atmosphere of creeping unease. I was fast approaching an absurd, yet inescapable conclusion: the curse was real. It had to be. What other explanation was there for such unsettling tidings?

I hated to voice such a thing aloud. Oliver would probably agree with me. Emily was more difficult to read.

It was decided that the three of us would not be returning to second class together. Oliver wished to accompany his father and Dr. Widmer to the *Olympic's* hospital for the autopsy and examination of the body. Despite the circumstances, my friend dreamed of becoming a doctor one day, and he was keen to follow along and observe the process. To my surprise, his father hardly protested before relenting. They even asked if I wanted to come along with them.

But I had no such desire. Neither did Emily. For a few moments, I feared we were going to be left behind. It didn't feel like anyone was paying us any attention. But there was nothing to worry about. When he realized we needed someone to take us back to our accommodations, Mr. Harlowe volunteered to do the job.

"I'll take the children," he'd said, which rankled at my sense of pride. "There's no sense in asking them to find their way back alone."

Don't be fooled by his charity. Mr. Harlowe acted miserably the entire way. His mood, always questionable, was downright foul. It was as if seeing Eckert's body had flipped a switch in him. He marched us to second class almost as if he were escorting criminals to prison, glowering at curious onlookers and snapping when people got too close. It was a long, awkward return trip that only ended when we reached the enclosed promenade from which we'd departed earlier that morning. No matter what Captain Bartlett said about trusting him, Mr. Harlowe was a difficult man. I couldn't have been more ready to leave the master-at-arms behind.

"Lunch should begin shortly," Mr. Harlowe said after we arrived. "It would be prudent to show yourselves. Best to head off whatever rumors you can." He turned and walked away, his heavy footsteps echoing down the corridor, before slamming the door behind him.

He was gone. Emily and I were alone. Seconds stretched out as we each waited for the other to speak.

"Should we heed his advice?" I asked. "I'm sure your mother will be wondering where we've gone."

It took most of my courage to suggest returning to the dining saloon. Truthfully, I wasn't sure if I was ready to see other people yet. They would want to know what we'd seen and what we'd done. The body. The mascaron. I didn't know if I had the strength to relive those things.

Emily shook her head and let out a shuddering sigh. "I find I have little appetite. Another man dead. It's dreadful."

I muttered my agreement before turning away to face a window. The sea outside was rolling, waves cresting and backing away with steady rhythm. There was a wind brewing. "Captain Bartlett told me to watch out for anything strange," I told her. "He's counting on us to find something."

Emily moved in close. Her shoulder brushed against mine. "Well, I think we need a break from all this. Even if it's just for a few minutes."

"What did you have in mind?"

"May we head up to the boat deck? I would like some air."

I hesitated for a moment, then offered her my arm. "Of course. I would be happy to accompany you."

As we ascended the decks, Emily's hand came to rest on mine. It made for a pleasant walk. At the top of the staircase, we paused for a moment, lingering on the threshold. The remnants of the morning sun had disappeared behind towering clouds, and a chilly, fast-moving breeze whistled around the funnels. It pulled the canvas lifeboat covers up and down with a steady, fluttering motion. There was a fresh smell in the air that hinted at incoming rain.

"It's not too windy for you, is it?" I asked.

"No. Let's go."

Our pace was slow. Neither of us was in a hurry. We had no destination in mind. But after a few minutes of pleasurable silence, I opened up about something that had been on my mind since I'd seen that marvelous staircase.

"I don't think I liked the first-class accommodations much," I confessed. "It was suffocating in there, surrounded by those high society types. I didn't have the faintest idea of how to behave."

If Emily was surprised by this random topic, she didn't show it. "It can be overwhelming, can it not? I, too, felt rather out of place."

"You did? But you were so composed!"

Emily shrugged. "Just because I look composed doesn't mean I am. I don't fancy mingling with that sort, I assure you. Most of them are far too interested in preserving their own privilege and far too disinclined to work on expanding such rights to others."

"I suppose that would wear on one as fair-minded as you."

"Very much so. Now, I have a question for you—Did Mr. Blackstone kill Theodore Eckert?"

I recognized the deflection, but I didn't fight it, nor did I protest our return to such macabre topics. "No, I don't think so," I said, watching an ominous line of clouds that was drawing near. "But he's involved. I'm sure of it."

"We're lucky you could identify his cufflink. Without that piece of evidence, I'm not sure they could have linked Lieutenant Morgan's death to Mr. Eckert's."

"I haven't done anything remarkable," I said, repeating Emily's earlier words back to her. "It's all about paying attention to the details."

"Your humility suits you, but in this instance, you should feel pride. It was an astute observation."

Her compliment warmed my cheeks. I shook my head. "Shall we continue our walk?"

We weren't interrupted again until the ship's band began playing somewhere below us. The sound of strings and keys drifted upward, lively and firm, dispelling the silence as confidently as it would have at a concert venue. I found myself swaying to the tune.

When the next song started up, Emily's frown gave way to a wistful smile. "Listen," she breathed. "That's my favorite song, 'Destiny.' I told you I was hoping to hear it."

I raised an eyebrow. "'Destiny?' Don't you think that's a bit of an ominous name?"

"No, I think it's lovely." She let go of my arm and fixed me with a defiant look. "Dance with me."

"What?" I choked. I glanced around to make sure we were still alone. "Is—is this the best time?"

"Name a better one, James."

I couldn't, and I knew it would only offend her to protest on grounds of etiquette. She took my hand, and we stepped into a small, open space on the deck. Our initial movements were awkward; we were too aware of our surroundings, too tense, and just too nervous to step into the waltz.

Slowly, though, we relaxed. All that existed on deck was the music and the two of us. The tension in our bodies melted away, replaced by a guilty sort of joy as we matched our movements to the rise and fall of the strings. It seemed insane to dance when everything around us was full of danger and darkness. I knew it was improper for me to do so when I had dreams of courting her. But just when my guilt was about to impel me to pull away, Emily laughed. It was a soft laugh, the kind of laugh that escapes despite one's best efforts to contain it. I couldn't help but join her.

"You're not too bad at this," she teased. I was startled to see that she had tears in her eyes.

"You're doing most of the work," I said, all thoughts of fleeing forgotten. "I would be out of step if you weren't leading."

As the song neared its end, we slowed our movements and came to a gentle stop. We stood like that, frozen in the moment, until the first raindrops started to fall. They pinged and plopped off the nearby machinery. Still, Emily made no effort to separate from me, even when droplets started clinging to our hair.

"Thank you," she whispered. "I needed that."

"You're welcome, but we should get out of the rain." I reluctantly pulled away from her.

"What happens next?"

I didn't know what she meant by that, so I went with the answer I felt was safest. "I think we should work on our plan to break into Lieutenant Morgan's stateroom. That's the logical next step of our investigation."

Emily looked thoughtful, glancing around at the few passengers who were still out on deck; they'd begun to scatter as the rain intensified. "I've been thinking about that. We've been trying to do everything ourselves, but perhaps that approach is overcomplicating things."

"What do you mean?"

"I mean we may not be thinking rationally. First it was Mr. Blackstone's story about the Sundered Wings, then it was Mr. Eckert's arm, and that awful mascaron. If we allow ourselves to fall under the spell of such tidings, or to believe in such fantastic things, the *Olympic* will fast become our own version of *The Castle of Otranto*."

I frowned, trying to remember if such a castle had ever been referenced in my studies. "I confess that I'm not familiar with that place. Should I be worried?"

"Oh! It's not a real castle," Emily said. The faintest blush spread across her cheeks. "Or it might be, I suppose, but I didn't mean to make a historical reference. Castle Otranto is from a gothic novel. One of my guilty pleasures, actually. Mother has an entire shelf of such stories in the library back home. She loves them. And she taught us to use them for inspiration when we find the mundane world lacking."

"I'm still not sure I understand."

"My apologies. I sometimes forget you didn't take part in our early tutelage." Emily glanced up at the imposing funnels, watching their blackened discharge mingle with the clouds. "*The Castle of Otranto* is an absurd story. Fanciful. I used it to remind myself that strange things are happening on board this ship, but their answers need not be equally so. We should be careful not to believe so heartily in the supernatural that we dismiss more ordinary explanations—or more ordinary solutions."

I was beginning to understand her point. At least, I thought I was. "Do you have a 'more ordinary' idea as to how we might get into Lieutenant Morgan's stateroom, then?"

"I believe I do," she said. Her lips curled into a satisfied smile. "There are people on this ship whose job it is to help us. What if we asked for their assistance? A steward could unlock the door. Now that we're working with Captain Bartlett, they might even be eager to help."

I blinked. "Would that work?"

Emily shrugged. "There's no way to know until we try, but... sometimes the simplest solution is also the best. That's one of Mother's lines, too, though I don't believe she thought of that one herself."

"Your mother is brilliant. Let's go find Oliver. The sooner

we get into that stateroom, the sooner we can get some answers."

Most travelers who book passage on the *Olympic* share living space with strangers. That's not something unique to the *Olympic* or to the White Star Line. It's just how things are at sea. I'm lucky that Oliver and I booked tickets to bunk together; we know each other and get along well. Had we not purchased two tickets for the same stateroom, we would have been given unfamiliar roommates for the voyage. That can be a mixed bag—sometimes you meet interesting people, and other times you meet people you'd rather not spend your time dealing with. Either way, you make connections.

If a passenger wished to secure their solitude, they would either need to part with enough money to ensure that outcome or hope that their passage was underbooked. Our passage was not underbooked, yet Lieutenant Morgan was one of those lucky few with his own room. One that he'd paid handsomely for. One that hadn't been opened since his disappearance. At least, that's what our steward friend Alex Cunningham told us when the twins and I tracked him down on D-deck. The evasive way Alex answered our questions made me eager to get inside and look around.

The trick was convincing Oliver's favorite steward to help us do it.

"Are you certain I should be aiding you in this matter?" he asked. "The last time I assisted you, we found a dead body."

Oliver made a calming gesture. "Don't worry, Alex. This is all legitimate. Captain Bartlett wants us to watch out for anything odd, and that's what we're doing. He's sanctioned the entire operation."

"He's right. We were asked to look for clues as to what's happening around here," I encouraged, even though I felt we were taking a very liberal view of Captain Bartlett's instructions.

Alex crossed his arms. "If Captain Bartlett gave you permission, I should not be the one to stop you. Still... this would be most unusual. That room has been on lockdown ever since the incident. Many have been desperate for a peek inside. Dinsmore has been hounding me all hours of the night!"

I suppose I could have guessed as much already, but it didn't escape my notice that Captain Dinsmore was still after the Sundered Wings. I wondered if the old sailor had managed to find anything.

"I'm certain that Captain Bartlett would appreciate you lending us your assistance, Mr. Cunningham," Emily said sweetly. "It is in the service of a most important cause. We are trying to exonerate a war hero. Finding the truth is important, is it not?"

Alex shook his head, but Emily's request had done the trick. "Oh, very well," he agreed. "If I don't help you, you'll just find another way in and make an even bigger mess. But we need to be quick about it! I do not want people hearing about this and queuing up for a peek of their own."

"We'll be finished before you know it!" Oliver slapped Alex on the shoulder. "Now, where are we going?"

Alex laughed, but it was a strangled sound, one that made him seem more stressed than relieved. "The lieutenant's room is one of the alternative bookings on E-deck. It's a bit of a walk."

"Distance is nothing but a minor obstacle. You can lead us there, can't you?"

"I can. Come along, please. And don't make yourselves conspicuous."

"Never fear. Inconspicuousness is my forte."

Alex snorted.

"We'll be on our best behavior," I promised before I stepped aside to allow the steward to take the lead. "We owe you one, Alex."

"Think nothing of it, sir."

We followed our escort through an enamel white corridor, away from the dining saloon, down the stairs, and back around to a stateroom with the identifier "E-33" marked above the entryway. It was a plain door, indistinguishable from the surrounding rooms except for a paper affixed to its front that read:

"Keep Out—Investigation Ongoing"

Alex hesitated. He was standing in front of us, his hands on the keys, but he wasn't making a move to open the door. "Are you sure about this? Captain Bartlett really ordered you to be here?"

"Of course," Oliver said. "This sign is talking about us, you know. We're the 'ongoing investigation.'"

"I had to ask."

Just as Alex inserted the key, pounding footsteps echoed around the corner. We froze, exchanging panicked glances—permission or not, we couldn't afford to be discovered snooping around here!

"Get this door open!" I urged.

"I'm trying!"

I clenched my fists as Alex fumbled with the key, its metal edges scraping against the lock with maddening slowness. My heart pounded loudly enough that I worried whoever was rounding the corner might hear it. Finally, the lock clicked, and we tumbled inside, pulling the door shut just in time.

I held my breath.

The footsteps stopped right outside. Emily's eyes were as wide as dinner plates. Oliver's jaw was clenched; a bead of sweat trickled down his temple.

Someone on the outside began turning the handle. It spun until it hit the lock. The stranger pulled on the door. It slammed against the jamb.

"Öffne diese tür!" a masculine voice called out in an unfamiliar language. The words sounded like they were demanding something. Probably for the door to be opened.

There was no chance I would be doing that.

We waited for several seconds. I could feel Emily taking shallow breaths beside me. Eventually, the intruder gave up. Their footsteps grew fainter as their owner drew further away.

"That was close," I whispered. "They tried to follow us in here!"

Alex nodded. "I did warn you that people have been desperate to gain access to this room."

"Yes, you did." Oliver wiped his forehead and began looking around. "We need to hurry. I don't fancy getting discovered by whoever—or whatever—that was."

"Whoever," Emily said. "They were definitely a person. I cannot place it, but I would even propose that their voice sounded familiar. Were they speaking German?"

Oliver laughed nervously. "I don't care if they were speaking Welsh, Em. They didn't strike me as the type we want to be crossing."

Emily was right. That voice had sounded familiar, somehow. But Oliver was also right to say that we shouldn't run afoul of its owner. As such, it made a great deal of sense to me not to spend any more time in this room than was necessary. We had a job to do.

I flipped on the lights.

Lieutenant Morgan's room was larger than ours, with beds for three and a mahogany desk shoved up against the wall. But where our stateroom felt warm and comfortable, the glossy white paneling here felt almost sterile. The air smelled of varnish and carbolic soap.

Emily knelt, swept her fingers across the glistening floor, and held her hand up to the light. "Mr. Cunningham, has someone been in here since Lieutenant Morgan's death? It seems very... clean."

"I rather doubt it. It's not like there was much opportunity for him to soil the place. We never even made his bed. We would have, of course. We planned to, even, although—"

Oliver snorted. "Relax. Are you planning to stay with us while we search?"

"Ah, um, no, I'm not." Alex cleared his throat. "In fact, now that our unwanted guest appears to have left us, I'd prefer to return to my work. You three may have permission to be here, but it would not be a good look for me to stay on E-deck for long. My peers would talk. I trust you can lock the room when you leave?"

"Of course," Oliver said. "We shall be nothing but respectful of the space."

"Steal nothing," Alex warned. He stopped with his hand on the doorknob. "And... be careful. Strange things are happening on this ship, sir. Strange things indeed." Then he left, closing the door behind him.

As soon as Alex had gone, Oliver threw Lieutenant Morgan's wardrobe open, abandoning all pretenses of caution. "Well, let's see what we can find! Remember, we're looking for anything that might explain these deaths or help us find the Wings of Amun-Ra."

I started by opening the drawers to Lieutenant Morgan's desk. The first one only held a comb and an unused shaving kit. In the second drawer, however, I found something. The bottom was uneven. I pressed down, and with a careful nudge, the board shifted.

It was a false bottom!

"Oliver, Emily, look at this!" I pulled out an unmarked manila envelope, slid it open, and revealed a large piece of parchment paper. "Could these be the Sundered Wings?"

The twins crowded around me to inspect a drawing of two exquisitely rendered falcon wings. Their jagged edges suggested they had been snapped from a larger whole, confirming at least a part of Mr. Blackstone's story. In fact, the artifacts looked much like I'd expected them to after hearing the smuggler's tale. He'd told us the truth about their appearance.

"Why would Lieutenant Morgan hide this here?" Emily wondered. "He already knew what the Sundered Wings looked like. He was the one transporting them, was he not?"

Oliver spun the parchment around to examine it from different angles. "It's hard to say. Perhaps he was trying to show them to someone? Or preparing to send this envelope on to another of his accomplices? It's not like he could carry the real things around. Jimmy, is there anything else in that compartment?"

"No," I said, double-checking as I answered him. I folded the drawing and tucked it into my breast pocket. "But let's keep looking. I think there may be more to find here."

"Whatever you say." Oliver moved back to the wardrobe and began rifling through Lieutenant Morgan's clothing. The cabinet was almost full, packed with both uniforms and civilian clothes. Oliver took his time going through everything. He methodically checked each pocket and seam. After a few minutes, he was rewarded for his efforts when he found a crumpled piece of paper. "Aha!" he exclaimed, unfolding it for us to see.

It was a steamer ticket granting passage from Alexandria to Marseille. Egypt to France. Many of the numbers were faded with wear, but I could still see the amount Lieutenant Morgan had paid for his ticket: twelve pounds.

Oliver grinned. "How's that for a clue? This proves that Lieutenant Morgan spent time in Egypt!"

"It's a shame it doesn't mention any cargo he might have had with him," I said. "Emily, what do you think? Can we use this to tie the smugglers to Lieutenant Morgan?"

Emily, who had been inspecting the washbasin, peered over my shoulder at the paper. "I cannot say for sure," she hedged. "Probably not. All this proves is that he liked to travel. Interesting, but circumstantial. It isn't illegal to travel to Egypt."

"Take it with you," I told Oliver. "We can try to figure it out later once we're out of here. Let me know if you find anything else."

"Sure thing, boss," he chirped, sliding the receipt into his pocket.

I shook my head before moving to the sofa, where I felt along the plush cushions. Nothing. I reached in between the sofa arm and the seat.

"Ouch!" I yelped. "I think I cut my finger on a spring!"

Emily quirked an eyebrow at me before reaching one of her

gloved hands into the sofa. "Let me help you with that," she said. "There's something to be said for a more delicate touch."

My finger stung, but not as much as my pride, which wilted when Emily deftly extracted an envelope from the couch. She wasted no time sliding it open. "This is odd," she said, holding the letter out for us to see. "It looks like some kind of code."

Oliver and I crowded around her to get a better look. The envelope wasn't addressed. The paper was plain White Star Line letterhead, the kind anyone could request from the purser's office. Written on it was a cryptic message composed of nonsense words:

PHHW PHDW HOHY HQFR PHDO RQHE
ULQJ WKHZ LQJR IGDU NQHV VFLV GDQJ
HURX V
—TE

My entire body tingled with the shock of our discovery. I couldn't believe what I was seeing. This was exactly the sort of clue we'd been hoping to find! If we could crack this code, perhaps we'd finally understand what really happened to Lieutenant Morgan. The truth was tantalizingly close.

Emily held the note up to the light. "For someone only on board a few hours, Lieutenant Morgan seems to have written and received quite a few messages. We've found two pieces of correspondence already, including the drawing, and these are just the ones he didn't send. He must have been a regular in Haverford's office."

"Better him than me." I reached out to take the note from her. As it slid from her hand to mine, a faint, unpleasant slickness clung to my fingertips. I rubbed them together, half-expecting to see some kind of inky residue there. Nothing.

"Did you feel that?"

Emily looked at me, then at my fingers. "Feel what?"

I glanced at the paper again. It looked perfectly ordinary.

"Nothing," I said, dismissing the sensation as a trick of my imagination. "We need to decipher this, if we can, though I confess to knowing precious little about codes. It seems as if it was bound for the purser's office."

"I would prefer to avoid speaking with Mr. Haverford today," Emily said. She tugged at her collar and grimaced. "He takes a particular sort of patience to handle."

Oliver laughed darkly. "We're in complete agreement there. That toerag has been even more insufferable than usual on this crossing, which is saying something after how he acted on our last passage. The way he struts around, all flash, you'd think the sun shines out of his—"

Emily cleared her throat. "Actually, I think the time has come for us to disclose some of what we've discovered to Mr. Clarke. We have a fair amount of evidence, but we'll need his help if we wish to unravel all of it."

"Is it safe for Eli Carter if we share his photographs?" I asked.

She hesitated. "We can explain ourselves without handing over everything he showed us. There's no need to break our promise."

Oliver reached for his lighter, then thought better of it, stopping instead to pat his pocket. "Fine," he said. "But let's keep this between ourselves and Mr. Clarke for now."

I wasn't sure about that suggestion. Captain Bartlett had specifically asked me to inform Mr. Harlowe of our findings, and Mr. Clarke was a journalist, not an officer. But one look from Emily changed my mind; she was nodding along with her brother. I trusted her judgment.

"Very well," I agreed. "Let's get out of here."

We left Lieutenant Morgan's stateroom quietly, but my mind was racing. *What was the significance of the drawing? What did the coded message mean? Who was 'TE?' And what did it all have to do with the Sundered Wings?*

10
A QUESTION OF TRUST

Now that we'd decided to contact Mr. Clarke, our next step was to find him. The *Olympic* was a massive ship, but the rain had forced everyone indoors, and the second-class public spaces weren't unreasonably large. It was just a matter of narrowing down which of them he'd sought refuge in.

We left Lieutenant Morgan's stateroom and worked our way toward the dining saloon, keeping an eye out for the Swedish journalist as we went. The afternoon was fast slipping away. Back on D-deck, dinner preparations were already underway; stewards hurried back and forth, carrying trays, silverware, and glasses in advance of the evening meal. The succulent aromas of roasted meat and baked bread wafted from the galley. They were divine... and they reminded me that Emily and I had skipped lunch. My stomach growled.

"Do you see Mr. Clarke?" Oliver asked as he scanned the hallway for the Swede's familiar salt-and-pepper hair.

"No, but then, it is difficult to see anyone in this crowd," answered Emily. "Perhaps Mr. Cunningham could be of assistance?"

Our hallway steward, Alex Cunningham, was darting between passengers with a stack of fresh linens in his arms. He met up with another steward, whispered something to them, and passed his laundered burden off. The exchange didn't take more than a few seconds. When Alex turned away, presumably to grab another stack, we flagged him down.

"Mr. Cunningham!" Emily called. "Do you have a moment?"

Alex stopped on a dime and sighed before crossing the distance separating us in a flash. He offered Emily a small bow before turning to Oliver and me. "Yes, sirs? Can I do something for you?"

"Hopefully so, old man," beamed Oliver. "Do you have time to do a little favor for us?"

Alex looked as though he very much did not have time. "What do you need?"

"We need to find Mr. Clarke. Have you seen him?"

"Not since this morning. I can check the public rooms for him if you would like me to do so."

"That would be splendid!"

Alex turned on his heels and made for the stairs.

"Wait!" I called after him, catching the steward just as he was about to head up to C-deck. "If you find Mr. Clarke, will you ask him if he'll meet with us? Tell him it's important. It has to do with the errand you helped us with earlier this afternoon."

His eyebrows rose. "Of course, sir."

We didn't need to wait long. Less than five minutes later, Alex reappeared, face flushed and parchment in hand.

Oliver darted forward to intercept him. "Mr. Clarke has

agreed to meet!" he exclaimed after he snatched the note away from Alex. "He wants to use the library and will be ready in twenty minutes."

"Excellent," Emily said. "Thank you, Mr. Cunningham. Your services, as always, are appreciated."

"You are always welcome, Miss Wentworth. Now, if you all will excuse me, I have duties to return to. I would like to see to them before you lasso me into another of your schemes." He offered each of us a respectful nod before scampering back to work.

After Alex disappeared into the dining saloon, I turned to the Wentworths. "Shall we gather our things and head to the library?"

"Let's."

We entered the room together, Oliver leading the way, to find that Mr. Clarke had already secured a table near the windows for us. There would be no using them for natural light today. The storm outside had only picked up in intensity through the afternoon. Rain lashed against the glass. It washed over the promenade, blotting out the sunlight with torrential sheets of water and howling gusts of wind.

Given the conditions, I wasn't surprised to see that Mr. Clarke had company in the library. Mrs. Henderson, who hadn't been seen in public for nearly a day, sat alone by a window on the opposite side, knitting. The light from her desk lamp highlighted the age lines on her face. Their deep grooves lent her the appearance of a brittle, somewhat weathered piece of bark.

Oliver tugged on my sleeve. "Is that Mrs. Henderson? Where's she been? She hasn't made it to a meal since Mr. Blackstone vanished."

"It is. We need to talk to her. If she can tell us where Mr. Blackstone is..."

"We shall stay back and observe her," Emily said. "If she makes a move to leave, we can step in. For now, we need to talk with Mr. Clarke. Mrs. Henderson can wait—for all we know, her nephew could show up here and save us the trouble of looking for him."

Oliver and I exchanged a quick look. After a silent conversation, we elected to follow Emily's lead.

We passed by Captain Dinsmore on our way to Mr. Clarke's table. Dinsmore was nestled in a plush armchair, engrossed in the same book about Egypt that Emily had checked out and returned on our second day at sea. His well-worn cap rested on the armrest beside him. There was a distinct smell of alcohol wafting off his person, strong enough to make my nose wrinkle. I was beginning to wonder if the old man planned to spend this entire voyage lost in the bottle. He'd been drunk more than he'd been sober.

Eli Carter's younger sister Annabelle, a spirited girl of about fifteen, sat near Captain Dinsmore. The beads in her braided hair caught the flash of each lightning strike. Curious and quick to laugh, she had formed fast friendships with several girls on board. Their table was alight with chatter and giggles. Too young to be aware of the impropriety, or perhaps too brazen to take heed of it, they weren't shy about their interest when Oliver passed them by. Each of them nodded appreciatively to one another as he drew closer to Mr. Clarke.

My lips twitched upward. It was comforting to know that some people were still enjoying this cursed voyage.

Oliver, however, ignored them. He had more important things on his mind. "Hello, Mr. Clarke," he greeted when we arrived at the journalist's table, sliding into the seat next to him.

"Wonderful to see you again. I hope you've recovered adequately from last night's poker game?"

"I left early precisely to ensure my continued good health," Mr. Clarke said, returning Oliver's welcome. I wasn't so sure about the veracity of that statement. Despite the warmth of the steam-heated room, he'd elected to don a woolen scarf to match his jacket and gloves. "James, Emily, please, come sit down with us. We have much to discuss."

We took the two seats opposite Oliver and Mr. Clarke.

Mr. Clarke placed a worn leather folder on the table before us. "I was pleased to hear you were ready to meet with me," he said. "Because I, too, have uncovered some disturbing information crucial to the investigation. It is time for us to compare our findings. What I am about to say must remain between us."

"We shall expect the same courtesy from you," Emily said. "We have yet to find the Wings of Amun-Ra, but we have made substantial progress in our search. Your discretion would be appreciated."

"Of course. You have my word as a journalist."

Oliver grinned. "Excellent. What have you found, Mr. Clarke?"

"I shall get right to it. I believe that at least one of the *Olympic's* crewmembers is involved in the smuggling ring. My sources suggest that someone well-placed enough to avoid detection met with Lieutenant Morgan just before his death."

"We found a photograph that might lend credence to that." Emily reached into her bag and presented Mr. Clarke with the blurry photograph she'd pulled from Eli's pile two evenings prior.

Mr. Clarke slid his glasses up to his forehead to get a better look. "Your mystery man is certainly on the promenade reserved for the engineers, but he looks like a passenger. You can see a dinner jacket. When did you say this was taken?"

"Wednesday night," I answered. "Sometime after dinner, not long before the murder."

"Remarkable. Do you have any other photographs like this I might take a look at?"

Emily and I locked eyes. She gave a very slight, almost imperceptible shake of her head. "None that show anything useful," I said.

She must have decided to hold back the photograph of the murder. I trusted her judgment. Some things were just too dangerous to share, even with Mr. Clarke.

"If we find any others, we'll share them with you," Oliver added, looking sideways at Emily's bag all the while. My friend was a terrible liar.

Mr. Clarke frowned. "I have been trying to retrace Lieutenant Morgan's last steps for two days, but this image does more good for the case than all of my mapping combined. I wonder if this man could be Theodore Eckert? The build is similar."

"We thought that as well," Oliver said. "Do you suppose he arranged to meet with Lieutenant Morgan before his death?"

"Such things cannot yet be known. Where did you three say this photograph came from?"

I answered before Oliver could. "We didn't. And we'd like to protect our source. You can understand that."

Mr. Clarke's eyes flicked to one of the other tables and back. "So be it. I am disappointed, but I understand the need for discretion in these matters."

"Thank you." Emily leaned forward and reclaimed the photo. "Now, how certain are you about the involvement of a crew member?"

THE CURSE OF THE SUNDERED WINGS 139

Mr. Clarke handled the change in topic well. "Quite certain. I spoke with some contacts I trust. They have noticed unusual behavior on this voyage. Secretive meetings late at night, strange orders, that sort of thing. Here, let me show you what I have."

While Mr. Clarke reached into his folder and rifled through the papers, my attention wandered. *Who on the crew could be working with the smugglers?* My first thought was of Mr. Harlowe, with his dour face and angry disposition. He was a man I wouldn't want to cross. And the master-at-arms would have ample opportunity to cover up his crimes. But then again, I wasn't so sure about that. Captain Bartlett trusted him, didn't he? He'd asked me to report anything odd to Mr. Harlowe. And the master-at-arms had had plenty of opportunities to hurt us in the last day. He'd taken none of them.

Who else did that leave as a suspect? I pondered. Probably hundreds of people. It wasn't like I knew everyone on the crew. I thought of Charlie Haverford's disagreeable countenance, but I dismissed that idea. I knew why I didn't like him. Resigned to the fact that this was a mystery I would not be able to solve, I turned back to face Mr. Clarke, who was still rooting around in his folder.

Then, before I could speak, the hair on the back of my neck stood up. Something was wrong. My skin was crawling. It felt like there were hundreds of insects swarming my neck, biting my arms, gnawing at me in the uncanny way the sixth sense sometimes does.

I whipped around.

There was no one there. Well, no one aside from Captain Dinsmore, who was still reading the Egyptology book. He didn't notice me staring. Mrs. Henderson looked up, but when our eyes met, she looked away, sewing needles moving all the while. Annabelle Carter sat just a few seats removed from the retired governess. She, too, avoided my gaze when she realized I was looking at her. A few hushed words were exchanged at her table. Afterward, her friends giggled and began stealing glances my way. I ruled them out as suspects.

There were no other potential culprits. No other obvious source of my unease.

Mr. Clarke cleared his throat. I turned back just as he pulled out a shaded sketch of the Sundered Wings. He unfurled it carefully, taking care to flatten the edges before setting a paperweight on one of the corners. I recognized the sketch instantly. It was an exact match for the one we'd discovered in Lieutenant Morgan's false drawer!

But how could that be?

I wondered, just for a moment, if Mr. Clarke had somehow stolen our copy. Oliver must have shared that thought, for he was already reaching into Emily's bag when I made eye contact with him. He gave me a slight, barely noticeable shake of his head. I took that to mean our copy was safe.

"This," Mr. Clarke explained, pointing to the artwork, "was found in Theodore Eckert's stateroom after his death. Mr. Eckert's copy wasn't the original, but it may interest you to learn that this copy was based on an etching, not a sketch. Whoever made it had firsthand access to the artifacts. Concrete proof that they exist."

"How did you come into possession of this?" Emily asked. She, too, was subtly trying to communicate with Oliver, who was now pointedly glancing between her bag and Mr. Clarke's drawing.

"From the fellow investigating Eckert's room. He understood how important my work is."

Mr. Harlowe had been assigned the case. *Was he working with Mr. Clarke?*

I didn't have time to pose the question. Oliver looked fit to burst. He was all but pointing at the two drawings.

"Oliver?" I prompted. "You may as well show him."

"Right. We have something you should see." Oliver pulled out the parchment drawing we'd found in Lieutenant Morgan's cabin. He smoothed it out on the table, then compared it to Mr. Clarke's copy. They were an exact match.

Mr. Clarke adjusted his glasses. "Good Lord. Where did you find this?"

"It was with some of Lieutenant Morgan's things," I said evasively, not wishing to reveal that we'd searched the late man's stateroom. "What do you make of him having a copy of the same artwork as Eckert? Do you think there's a connection between their deaths?"

For a moment, Mr. Clarke's confident facade cracked. He looked conflicted. Perhaps even pained. But whatever happened passed in a second. When he spoke, it was in the same brisk, nasally tone to which I'd become accustomed. There was no sign of emotion left on his face.

"It is a unique piece," he admitted. "The only way they could have the same copy is if one of them sent it to the other. Or, I suppose someone else may have sent it to both of them," he amended, stroking his chin. "When considered alongside your photograph, one is forced to conclude that the two men were, at a minimum, in communication with one another."

Emily bit her lip before interrupting Mr. Clarke. "Mr. Eckert was interrogated before his death. My father said as much. You don't think—you don't suppose the killer took—"

"We must assume the killer has not yet found the artifacts." Mr. Clarke wrapped his coat more tightly around himself.

"Eckert's death was an escalation, but it was also an act of desperation. His body would not have been left as it was if the killer had any choice in the matter. I believe the artifacts are still out there."

I felt a tickle on my neck. Confused, I glanced around the room, still wary of an unseen foe. "I don't see how Lieutenant Morgan's killer got to Mr. Eckert," I said as I scanned the library for anything out of place. There was a tightness in my gut I couldn't seem to shake. "Second-class passengers can't just walk over to the first-class lounge. And not because of physical barriers or locked doors, but because we stick out over there. We'd be recognized in a minute."

Emily was nodding as I spoke. "What if we aren't looking for one person, but several? A group that's turned on itself. I mean, think about it. There could be an entire network of people who buy and sell artifacts from each other. All of them would be suspects."

A dark look clouded over Oliver's handsome face. "If you're right, it would mean that Lieutenant Morgan had concrete ties to the smuggling ring. It would mean that—well, it would mean that he isn't innocent."

"I'm sorry, Ollie," I said quietly. "I know you were hoping to clear his name."

Mr. Clarke steamed ahead with his theorizing, either oblivious to or uncaring about Oliver's distress. "No, but this all makes sense! Theodore Eckert made a stopover in Germany on his way to Cherbourg. He had a run-in with the German authorities there." He pulled a statement from his folder and slid it over to us. "I have it from a trusted source that he was smuggling items of significant value and controversy out of Cairo. Eckert planned to bring those artifacts on board the *Olympic*."

It was Emily's turn to frown. "I don't understand. You think the German government caught wind of his find? And, what, that they tried to intercept the Wings of Amun-Ra en route?"

"I know how these things work. Lieutenant Morgan and Theodore Eckert must have been working together. They made the decision to split up once they secured the Wings of Amun-Ra. The Germans arrested Eckert when they should have been tracking his friend Morgan. An error on their part."

"It would have been a much simpler voyage for us if they'd stopped Lieutenant Morgan instead," Oliver agreed.

Mr. Clarke rubbed his brow before sighing in frustration and muttering a word I didn't recognize under his breath.

"It isn't all bad news, sir," I said. "We were able to uncover a connection between Lieutenant Morgan and Mr. Blackstone."

"Were you, now?"

Oliver nodded. "He confessed his smuggling to us. Jimmy even found his cufflink at the crime scene! Mr. Blackstone is our best link to the rest of the smugglers, I'm sure of it."

"His cufflink?" asked Mr. Clarke. A flash of something that looked like satisfaction crossed his face. "Well, that is compelling. Worthy of further investigation, at the very least. Well done."

"We need to find him," Oliver said. "We should go over to Mrs. Henderson right now and—"

"Wait!" Mr. Clarke interrupted. "Before you dash off, finish hearing me out. Reginald Blackstone is not our only suspect."

Oliver was already halfway out of his seat. He looked to me for permission; I shook my head. My friend folded his arms and collapsed back into his chair with a huff. His gaze never left

Mrs. Henderson, who was still working on her stitching over by the starboard windows.

Mr. Clarke plowed onward, uncowed by Oliver's stormy mood. "I believe you are correct about Mr. Blackstone's involvement. That man is as suspicious as they come. However..." Mr. Clarke paused. We locked eyes, and I felt that odd sensation again, like I was being watched from somewhere over my shoulder. I glanced around; once again, I saw nothing amiss. "There is another man aboard this ship as dangerous as Mr. Blackstone."

"Another man?" Emily repeated. "Dangerous, how?"

Mr. Clarke handed her our copy of the etching and replaced his own in the folder. "I have identified certain... irregularities in the cargo manifests that bear further examination," he said, reaching into his bag and pulling out a small, leather-bound book. "There are things in the cargo hold that ought not to be there. It is my assessment that someone organized it. Someone on the crew."

A shadow flickered at the edge of my vision. I turned my head, heart pounding, but I knew I wouldn't see anyone there. *What had gotten into me? Was I going insane?* I glanced back at Mr. Clarke as he continued to speak. "Officially, the manifests show only standard shipments, but I have found evidence of additional undocumented crates being loaded onto the ship in Queenstown and Cherbourg. We are carrying contraband. I do not know who is authorizing these shipments, but it must be someone with enough authority to—"

A sudden, sharp noise, louder than a gunshot, made us all jump. We turned toward the sound, but it was just Captain Dinsmore's book sliding to the floor. It seemed he'd fallen asleep reading. We turned back to Mr. Clarke, who looked unsettled.

"Good Lord, man," Oliver hissed. He reached for the manifest. "How did you get hold of this?"

"A man in the purser's office owed me a favor. He was willing to take a risk and get me a look at their records. But my research does not end there. I have a name for you. A potential suspect."

I exchanged a glance with Oliver, who raised an eyebrow. "You have a name?"

"Yes, I fear." Mr. Clarke looked over his shoulder. "I have already told you that a crewmember belongs to the smuggling ring. My information points to a man named William Harlowe. Mr. Harlowe has been active at odd hours, and some members of the crew have reported seeing him in areas where he should not be. He fits the profile."

Emily wrinkled her nose. "William Harlowe?" she asked. "The master-at-arms?"

"The very same. I believe he may be the one orchestrating the smuggling operation. He served in the Boer war at the same time as Lieutenant Morgan, and they were both involved with that nasty Black Week business in '99. They must have been familiar with one another."

So much for Mr. Harlowe and Mr. Clarke working together. Oliver's brow creased in concentration while he mulled that over.

"We saw Captain Bartlett tell Mr. Harlowe to investigate Mr. Eckert's murder when we were together in the lounge," I said, as much to Oliver as to Mr. Clarke. "Your contacts probably saw him investigating, like he was supposed to be doing, and made assumptions. It'd be easy for them to misinterpret what they were seeing if they didn't know Captain Bartlett had asked him to poke around."

Emily jumped in at the end of my explanation. "Mr.

Harlowe's disposition does not lend itself to fondness. It works against him in this. You may be confusing likeability with guilt."

It was Mr. Clarke's turn to look unconvinced. "Perhaps," he allowed. "But I have heard that Assistant Purser Haverford warned his associates to keep a close eye on Mr. Harlowe, and he would not have done so if the crew trusted him. No, even if you are correct, someone on this crew is working with the smugglers. William Harlowe is not to be trusted."

"Captain Bartlett trusts him," I said stubbornly.

Mr. Clarke was quick to reply. "The more pertinent question, perhaps, is whether Captain Bartlett has earned our trust."

"If he's involved with all of this, we haven't got a chance."

"A child's answer. Do not let your naivety lead you to ruin."

I crossed my arms. "I'm not naive."

"You have lost family, have you not, Mr. Kelly?" Mr. Clarke asked suddenly.

"I... yes, I have. My parents."

"Well, so have I," Mr. Clarke said. "And in my case, blind trust in the system only resulted in pain. One must be bold if one wants to be great. You are too timid for greatness, Mr. Kelly."

My heart sank. *Was he right? Had I been too careful? Was I wrong to trust Captain Bartlett?*

Emily jumped to my defense. "That isn't fair. I happen to agree with James. This is the transitive property at work—we trust Captain Bartlett, so we trust Mr. Harlowe. It's that simple."

"I don't know what to think, but if Jimmy and my sister

both trust him, I suppose I do, too," Oliver said. "Not every man will prove himself a villain."

"I forget that you are but children. Let us agree to disagree on that point." Mr. Clarke sighed and rubbed the back of his neck. "Regardless, I believe we are drawing nearer to the truth. That means we need to tread carefully. This conspiracy runs deep, and those involved will not hesitate to use violence to protect their interests. It has become imperative that we find out where Lieutenant Morgan stashed the Wings of Amun-Ra. What will your next steps be?"

Emily stretched her legs out and uncrossed her knees. "Mrs. Henderson is here. She may be able to connect us with her nephew. I'm sure she's scared, though; if she feels cornered, she won't tell us everything. I wouldn't be the best person to talk to her. We don't get along."

"I'll approach her," I offered, eager to do something that proved my worthiness. "I've had a few kind words with her before. She might be receptive to me."

"While you do that, Oliver and I can survey the ship, take a look for anything out of place. If we don't have any luck, we'll find Father. He's spent the day with Dr. Widmer. Perhaps they've discovered something about that strange injury to Mr. Eckert's arm."

Mr. Clarke looked on approvingly. "Very good. I, too, intend to continue pressing my contacts for more leads. If the opportunity presents itself, I will try to gain access to the cargo hold to look at those crates," he said, looking between us. "I think we have finished here... unless you have anything else to share with me?"

I'd almost forgotten. "We do have something else, as a matter of fact." I pulled the coded message from my pocket and handed it to him. "This was Lieutenant Morgan's. We think it's a code, but we haven't been able to make sense of it."

Mr. Clarke squinted at the letters on the page, mouthing some of them to himself as he read. "This is an intriguing clue," he admitted. "TE—could that be another reference to Theodore Eckert?"

"We think so," I said, while Emily said, "It's possible."

I smiled and indicated that she should speak first. She grinned back. "It's possible," she repeated. "We know they were in communication."

"I have a bit of a hobby in code-breaking," Mr. Clarke said. "Let me take a crack at this message, would you? I shall only need a moment."

Oliver had taken his lighter out at some point. He was fiddling with the handle. "Be our guest," my friend offered.

Mr. Clarke took out a small notebook and a pencil from his jacket pocket. He didn't take his gloves off before starting in on the code; his hands shook as he jotted down notes. "This message utilizes a complex cipher. It looks like a simple substitution, but..."

Mr. Clarke's pencil darted across the page as he tried various techniques to decode the message. It took long enough that I found my attention wavering.

That strange feeling of unease washed over me again, but I ignored it this time, balling my hands into fists and willing it to leave me be. Unfortunately, no matter how hard I tried, I couldn't shake the sensation that something was off about the library. Goosebumps sprouted up and down my arms. I shivered; Emily looked at me with concern, but I shook my head, dismissing her with a false smile.

Mr. Clarke sighed and set his pencil down. "I fear this is too complicated for me," he admitted. "It combines several sophisticated techniques. Whoever wrote it was quite the deft hand."

"We understand," Emily said, taking back the coded message and folding it into a neat square before handing it to Oliver. "Thank you for trying, Mr. Clarke."

"Think nothing of it. We are all on the same side, are we not?"

AFTER OUR FAILED attempt to decipher the message, it was clear our meeting had run its course. Mr. Clarke stood, collected his things and declared that he was going to return to his stateroom for a quick nap; it was evident that our conversation had taken a lot out of him. He looked rather ill.

Oliver and Emily left after that, intending to track down their father. My job was to speak with Mrs. Henderson. She was still sitting all alone at the small table near the window. She'd packed her knitting needles up and was now staring blankly at a book in front of her. This was my chance. I straightened my tie and made my way over to her, trying to appear casual.

"Mrs. Henderson," I whispered, pulling out the chair opposite her. "May I have a word?"

She looked up, startled. "Oh, Mr. Kelly. Is something wrong?"

"No, ma'am. It's just good to see you out. Everyone was growing worried something had happened to you."

She clutched her bag to her chest. "Me? Oh, no, dear. I... I am well. Quite well."

"I'm glad to hear that," I said. "But I couldn't help

noticing you disappeared right after your nephew got into a spot of trouble. Where has he vanished to?"

"Reggie is busy," scowled Mrs. Henderson with a dash of her old defiance. "He does not owe anyone an accounting of his day. Nor do I!"

I leaned closer. "Please, Mrs. Henderson. I need you to tell me what's going on. People have died, and more could be in danger."

"I have no idea of what you speak."

I took a deep breath. "Mrs. Henderson, I know you want to protect your nephew, but this isn't just about Mr. Blackstone anymore. If he's involved, willingly or not, we need to know. Lives hang in the balance."

She stiffened. "Reggie is a good boy. He has done nothing wrong."

"I do not suggest that he has," I said gently. "But if you decide against helping me to understand, more people could get hurt. Do you want that on your conscience?"

She clutched her bag even tighter, causing the pins inside to rattle. "You—you do not understand…"

"Help me to, then," I urged. "You care about your nephew, don't you? Show it by helping us keep him and others safe. Please."

She was silent for a long time. "He did not mean to get involved."

"Involved in what?"

"You already know the answer to that, I trust."

"The smuggling ring."

The elderly woman shook her head. "He assured me it was harmless. A few treasures here and there went missing, and a few men got richer. Nothing that has not been going on since long before any of us were born."

"He claimed it was harmless?"

"It was harmless!" she snapped, rising halfway out of her chair. But her posture collapsed as quickly as her outburst had come. She sank back into her seat. "Reggie is scared. He thinks death will come for him next. Last night, he was obsessing over you and the Wentworths. Trying to ascertain how much you knew."

My stomach twisted at the thought of our names being involved, but I tried not to let it show. "Well, you can tell him we're committed to uncovering who killed his friends. It would be helpful if we could speak with him again."

"I believe I can convince him to attend the church service tomorrow morning. You can talk with him after."

"Thank you, Mrs. Henderson. You've been very brave."

The uneasy feeling I'd noticed so many times this afternoon returned as I stood up to leave. Everything in the library looked to be in order—but, somehow, I knew it wasn't. My heart was racing. I steadied myself and crossed the room, searching everywhere for the source of my discomfort. Just as I reached the door, the air grew thick, as if something unseen, something enormous, had entered the room. I summoned my courage and spun around.

A shadowy figure slipped behind the bookshelves.

Someone had been watching me.

11
CLOSE YOUR EYES

I wasn't thinking straight. How could I have been? Hearing that Mr. Blackstone was inquiring about us—about Emily—was too much for me to ignore. And now I had confirmation my stalker was a real, flesh-and-blood person. My hands were trembling as I stared at the place the shadowy figure had disappeared from. How dare someone skulk around and put her in danger? What gave them the right?

But then, who was I to stop them?

Fear gnawed at my insides, crawled up into my chest, and gripped my heart in its icy hands. I wilted under its grasp. It was like my lungs couldn't expand, like my stomach was being compressed. I was seconds from losing control when something else sparked within me—something fierce, something I couldn't yet name. It built in intensity until it burned even brighter than my doubts. The heat seared away my fear, leaving only a charred remnant behind.

The remnant felt a lot like resolve.

I couldn't run from this. Not anymore.

I charged through the library, brushing past Captain Dinsmore, who grunted in confusion. There was no time to worry about him.

The library was wide, but it wasn't especially deep. It didn't take me long to cross through it and out onto the landing. I emerged right by the elevator. Two children were climbing over each other and wrestling on a wicker couch beside it; next to them, their mothers sat with their heads together, deep in conversation. I snapped my head right and left. There was no sign of my mystery stalker.

"Excuse me?" I asked. "Have either of you seen anyone come through here?"

The women looked up at me, startled to be addressed. One of them, a dark-haired woman with a fabulous, two-tiered hat, responded, rather breathlessly, "Why, no, dear. I cannot say I have."

"He went downstairs!" said her friend in an equally hushed voice. "Angry-looking fellow, he was. I dare to say he was most upset."

I didn't stop to thank them. There was no time. The elevator door opened, and the boy working the controls shouted something about slowing down. I ignored him and took the stairs two at a time, my pulse pounding as I jumped the last three steps. I landed with a clatter at the bottom.

The doors on my right and left, each leading to the dining saloon, were closed. There was nobody in sight.

"Damn it," I hissed. *Which way had my stalker gone?*

I gambled that I wouldn't have chanced running through the dining saloon if it were me who was fleeing from someone. I continued to dash down the stairs to E-deck. A stitch formed in my side as I hurtled forward, digging deeper with every step. My shoes weren't meant for running. They cut into my ankles. I kept going.

Two men were walking together on the landing between flights. I tried, unsuccessfully, to slip past them; instead, I rammed one of them in the shoulder. Pain seared through my chest. I clenched my teeth when my shoulder lifted, nearly ripping itself from its socket. The man spun around. I almost fell over, but I caught myself on the railing.

"Pardon me!" I called out. I started running again.

"Well, I should say so! How uncouth!"

I continued on. The next deck passed in a blur. I'd run quite a distance through the *Olympic* at this point, and it was getting harder to catch my breath. I put my hands on my knees as I looked from right to left for any hint of my quarry. There was no sign of them.

"Whatever is your hurry, man?"

Coughing, I turned to face the speaker. I stood just outside the window to the chief second-class steward's office, and though I'd never talked to the severe-faced man standing inside, I assumed he must be the office holder. He looked none too pleased with me.

"I'm looking," I said, panting, "for a man. He would have just come by here a minute ago."

"Of course you are." The chief steward raised an eyebrow. "He just came thundering down this hallway in about the same state as you. It's nonsense! I won't tolerate horseplay on this deck; I will tell you that much! You, sir, are far too old to—"

I was gone, chasing after the culprit. There wasn't time to lose entertaining inane conversation. I hurtled down the next hallway, closed doors flashing by in a haze of enamel until I heard them. Voices. I stopped on a dime, just around the corner from Haverford's office. Leaning against the wall, I tried to slow my breathing; it was difficult to hear over the rushing blood in my head.

"I will not have it, sir!" shouted a man whose nasally tone I would recognize anywhere. Reginald Blackstone. *Was he the man I was chasing? If so, why had he been spying on me?*

Unable to resist eavesdropping, I crept around the corner and darted into a small side passage. From there, I could just see inside the cracked office door. Mr. Blackstone, his face red and sweaty, was arguing with Haverford, whose delicate blond hair was mussed and out of place. He was also red in the face, though in his case, I suspected it was more from anger than exertion. I'd never seen him look so furious.

"You don't get to come here and give me orders!" Haverford snarled. "After everything you've gotten yourself involved in, now you develop a conscience? Now!?"

"I'm trying to help you!" shouted Mr. Blackstone. "You know there's something off about this storm! Marvin was trying to save lives, Charlie! If he knows about the Sphinx Society—"

"Don't mention Marvin Morgan to me," Haverford snarled. He moved out of my line of sight, said something else, and then slammed the door to his office shut. The pamphlets in the display outside shook. One slid from its holder and drifted down to the floor.

I could still hear shouting within the office, but it was time to go. Emily and Oliver needed to know what I'd found. Not only was Mr. Blackstone alive and well, but he was friends with Haverford!

I took a steadying breath, emerged from my hiding place, and made a break for the stairs. At the same time I was escaping, Mr. Clarke was shuffling up from somewhere down on F-deck. We nearly collided on the landing. I had to grab onto the railing to avoid stumbling and falling.

Our co-investigator looked even worse than he had an hour

ago in the library. There were deep stress lines on his face. A thin sheen of sweat coated his blotchy skin and dampened his shirt. "Pardon me," he said thickly, his accent blending the words. "I was just coming up from the toilets; I—I believe I am suffering from a bit of seasickness."

I took a reflexive step back. "I'm sorry to hear that, sir. Perhaps you should go lie down?"

Mr. Clarke nodded with a grateful smile. "Thank you," he said. "I may just do that."

We walked together. With each step, I became more convinced that something was seriously wrong with the journalist. Something more than seasickness. His steps were heavy, as if each of his feet weighed a ton. The joints in his knees protested with each rise and fall. It didn't help that he was so pale he seemed to absorb the brilliance of each light we passed. The veins in his forehead were prominent on his brow.

"Are you sure you don't need the hospital, sir?" I asked him when we parted on D-deck, just outside the dining saloon. "I can walk you the rest of the way there."

"No, no, I merely need to rest," he said. "I've had a long week of travel. Give my apologies to the others at dinner, would you, Mr. Kelly? I doubt I shall be up to attending."

"Of course, sir."

I watched Mr. Clarke shuffle away and said a quick prayer that he wouldn't collapse before reaching his room. It looked as if that was a real possibility. His progress was painstakingly slow. Thankfully, he made it, and I breathed a small sigh of relief when his door closed behind him. At least he hadn't died in front of me.

With Mr. Clarke safely in his stateroom, I was free to take a moment to walk back to my own. I needed to catch my breath and think about what I'd seen. *Mr. Blackstone had been spying on me, but why? Was it because I'd been speaking to his aunt? Or, as she said, was it because James, Emily, and I were getting too close to the smuggling ring? Why would he go to the assistant purser for help? Could Haverford be the inside man Mr. Clarke had warned us about?*

I opened the door to our room to find it empty. Oliver and Emily must have already gone to dinner. I stepped to the washbasin, splashed some cool water on my face, and tried my best to look presentable. Despite the fatigue I was feeling and the threats I was facing, I felt lighter than I had all day. I'd tracked down the person stalking me. I'd learned something new about our case. Emily would never believe me when I told her what I'd done.

I CAUGHT up with the Wentworths only a few minutes later. They were already sitting at our familiar table in the back of the dining saloon, their plates laden with food. A server was adding wine to Mrs. Wentworth's glass. Despite the best efforts of the crew, however, there was an ominous atmosphere in the room. The overhead lights struggled to hold back the darkness of the storm. The sky outside had turned black. It was such an eerie sight that I double-checked my pocket watch to make sure I hadn't somehow confused the time—I hadn't. The clouds had simply overtaken the sun.

Oliver was sitting across from his father. They were deep in conversation. Mrs. Wentworth was leaning over to speak with Mrs. Henderson; she looked healthier this evening, her alabaster complexion the only visible sign of her illness. Emily and Eli were similarly engaged, smiling as they regaled each other with stories about their siblings. Annabelle sounded like she was as mischievous as Oliver. When Eli finished explaining something about a tiger, Emily erupted into a peal of laughter, much to Mrs. Henderson's chagrin.

The sound of Emily's laughter brought a smile to my face. It was a smile I needed after pursuing Mr. Blackstone through the *Olympic*. My hands were still shaking as I came down from the rush.

The seat next to mine, Mr. Blackstone's, was empty. No surprise. I hadn't expected to see him here; after all, he was probably still arguing with Haverford. Taking care not to bump into anyone, I settled into my chair and spun it around to face Oliver and Dr. Wentworth.

"Good evening, sir," I said, addressing Dr. Wentworth. "I'm glad to see you back from helping Dr. Widmer."

Dr. Wentworth shook his head. A piece of fish dangled on his fork. "I am glad to have returned. Mr. Eckert's death was an unexpected tragedy."

Oliver leaned over. "Father was just telling me about his findings. Fascinating business."

"Neither Dr. Widmer nor I know what to make of it. It is as if Mr. Eckert was mummified." Dr. Wentworth took another bite, chewing slowly to give himself time to think. He opened his mouth to continue, then stopped and let out a sigh instead. "But enough of that. It was a rather morbid day, and I believe it would be my preference not to relive it at dinner."

"Of course, sir," Oliver said. "I just get excited by your work. I cannot wait to begin my own medical training."

It was as if Oliver had flipped a switch in his father's brain. Dr. Wentworth swelled with pride. "And I cannot wait for the day you join me in the practice of medicine," he said. "Johns Hopkins will be better for you having attended. I say that with certainty."

Eli Carter overheard us. "I say, Oliver, that's quite the ambition you have! A doctor, eh? And at Johns Hopkins, no less!"

"Oh, yes, I suppose so." Oliver had the decency to blush. "I have worked hard, but I have also benefited from my parents' support and connections. I recognize that."

Emily joined the conversation. "That may be so, but you have earned what you are receiving now. Your grades have always been exceptional."

"What about you, Emily?" Eli asked. "What do you plan to do with your life?"

"Well..." Emily started. She bit her lip. "Well," she started again, in a falsely bright voice, "I would like to continue helping my mother. She requires support, of course, and with Father working, our home requires a good deal of maintenance..."

"Emily is a brilliant writer," I blurted out. Everyone turned to look at me. Even Mrs. Henderson, who had been gazing at her own reflection in the back of her soup spoon, was now staring at me. My hands, which had only just stopped shaking, began to tremor again. I set down my fork.

Emily closed her eyes and took a deep breath. When she opened them, her expression was inscrutable. Despite the flush of heat rising on my face and neck, I held firm. If she wanted to be a writer, she would have my support, especially in front of her family. We'd made a promise. I wasn't going to let her back down from her dreams.

The silence stretched on. I felt as if I was waiting for a verdict.

Finally, Emily exhaled. A bemused, almost exasperated smile replaced her frown. "James is being kind," she said. "I do like to write, but my focus now is on my family. Perhaps, someday, things will be different."

"Perhaps they will be," mused Dr. Wentworth as he looked speculatively between Emily and me. "We all know you are a talented woman. I dare say you could accomplish almost anything you set your heart to."

"Thank you, Father," Emily said.

"Any daughter of ours should be possessed of lofty goals," Mrs. Wentworth agreed. The twins' mother straightened in her chair. For just a moment, a spark of her old fire burned, and I could see traces of the formidable woman Emily held so much admiration for within it. "Goals beyond living to dote on her old mother, that is. I am pleased to learn of this ambition."

Eli Carter clapped his hands. "Well said! And what about you, James? What are your plans?"

I hadn't minded being in the spotlight when Emily's dreams were the topic of discussion, but I minded it very much now that it was my life under the microscope. Everyone turned to stare at me once again. I let out a strangled laugh.

"Come on, Jimmy," Oliver encouraged. "We all have to make a choice of career eventually, do we not?"

The pressure was palpable. Absurdly, the first answer that came to my mind, unbidden, was the one that Emily had supplied me with the day before when she'd said I could be a fantastic detective. Somehow, the idea had taken hold, and I was beginning to find it an attractive one. I didn't know the first thing about detectives. I didn't know how someone became one, or how much they were paid. But if I tried my utmost to succeed...

But no. I couldn't say it. It was foolish. Childish, even. I'd be laughed at for suggesting such a thing.

"I don't know!" I answered, too embarrassed by my ridiculous thought to say it aloud. Emily looked disappointed, which was the worst part of it. She'd been expecting me to give a proper answer.

"Well, I suppose you still have time to decide," Mrs. Wentworth said bracingly. "Franklin and I will not rush you out of our home."

"Thank you," I mumbled. *How could my only goal be so stupid? Who in their right mind wanted to be a detective?*

Frustrated and embarrassed, I stabbed at the last portion of my dinner more aggressively than I intended. It wasn't my pudding's fault I had clammed up, but its gelatinous surface was a brilliant target for my antsy hands. I went to work dismantling my dessert with my cutlery. I tried not to picture Eli Carter's well-meaning face in it, but the temptation was difficult to resist. He couldn't have known the firestorm his words would ignite within me. I knew that. But after the day I'd had, such scrutiny was the last straw. When I imagined the glimmer of Mr. Blackstone's ostentatious golden cufflinks in my pudding, I stabbed even harder.

"Please excuse me, but I think I would like to return to my stateroom." Emily abruptly stood. "James, I see that you have finished with your meal. Would you be so kind as to escort me back there?"

"I—yes, of course, I'd be happy to," I said, freezing midstab. "Are you ready to go now?"

"Yes, I am."

"Then I would also like to be excused."

It was a kindness that nobody protested this. Rather than comment, Dr. Wentworth leaned in to speak with Oliver about classes at Johns Hopkins. Mrs. Wentworth and Eli began a conversation about photography. Mrs. Henderson looked bored with the entire affair, and perhaps she was, but she made no move to interrupt except to offer a quiet "good night" to me as I passed.

Emily and I swept by the stewards managing dessert and passed through the double doors to the D-deck landing. Once we were clear of the crowd, Emily let go of my arm, looked me up and down, and sighed.

"You could have handled that with slightly more tact, but I understand why it upset you. It is as we discussed in the library."

"I didn't mean to lose my composure," I muttered. "And I do not mean to be petulant, you understand. It's just... this is a sore spot for me. That I don't know what I want to do with my life. The only thing I could think to say was 'detective,' but they'd laugh at that. It isn't a real dream."

Emily moved closer, grabbed my hand, and squeezed it. It was a personal gesture that was inappropriate to undertake in public, but I didn't shy away from her touch. "I told you before, I think you would be a fantastic detective. I meant it."

I looked at her, doubting her words but wanting to believe. "I'm not like you and Oliver, Emily. I'm... well, I'm timid," I finished bitterly.

Emily shook her head. "That's Mr. Clarke talking, not you. You stood up for me at dinner, did you not?"

I didn't answer.

"Close your eyes for me."

"What?"

"Close your eyes," Emily repeated. "Do you not trust me?"

I did trust her. I closed my eyes, even though I felt ridiculous and exposed, standing as we were on a heavily trafficked landing that anyone could enter at any time.

"Good," Emily said. "Now, think about what you have seen and done on this voyage."

"Everything?"

"The important things."

I did as she asked. With her gloved hand in mine and her citrus perfume swirling around me, I reflected. I remembered dancing on deck, our late night in the library, my frantic run through the ship, and my fumbled conversation at dinner. I expected to be terrified by the power of my own recollections. Somehow, though, I wasn't. Far from feeling scared or intimidated, I felt empowered by my actions, especially those I'd taken today. Proud, even. I smiled when I opened my eyes.

"Thank you," I said. "For believing in me."

She released my hand and grinned back. "You simply required a reminder that our promise goes two ways. Now that we've settled your crisis of confidence, you can tell me all about why you think I would be a good writer on the way back to my stateroom."

"I'd be happy to, but would you like to hear about how I chased Mr. Blackstone all the way from the library down to E-deck first?"

Emily stopped, looked at me, and snorted. "Yes," she said, laughing. "Let's start with that. 'Too timid,' honestly..."

12
SERMON IN THE SALOON

I awoke on Sunday morning to thunder rattling the water basin. A flash of lightning ignited the sky outside of our porthole. The bolt arced across the rolling clouds, its jagged edges heralding the imminent return of thunder's pounding drum. It was a dreary morning. The kind that makes you want nothing more than to pass the day away with a book and a drink, absconding from all responsibility.

    I stayed under the covers in my bunk for several minutes, relishing the warmth of my blanket and the steady pitter-patter of the rain. My pocket watch warned me I didn't have much time to delay, but moving was difficult; inertia, after all, is a powerful force. Thunder rumbled again, but I clutched my blanket to my chest. It was cozy. Warm. For a moment, I closed my eyes and considered drifting back to sleep.

    But no. I couldn't. I sat up, yawned, and reluctantly slipped out from under my blanket. Bracing myself, I tested my weight on the first rung before climbing down from the top bunk. Each lurch of the *Olympic* threatened my balance. Though I only needed to descend a handful of feet, I was mindful to keep my footing. Oliver would never let me hear the end of it if I fell out of bed.

I reached the ground safely. The floor was cool, so I opened my trunk and fished out a pair of socks, pulling them on one at a time before unleashing yet another yawn. The staccato beat of raindrops on glass was my sole companion. Oliver was there, I suppose, but he was sprawled out in the lower bunk, mouth agape, snoring softly. If I'd had Eli Carter's camera, I would have preserved the moment to laugh about later. It was not a dignified sight.

As I dressed, I considered how lucky I was to be traveling on a modern ship like the *Olympic*. It wasn't so long ago that a storm like this would have meant death for those caught in its grasp, but the ocean liners of today fare far better in such conditions than the ships of yesteryear. Only three years ago, in 1910, newspapers reported that the Cunarder *Lusitania* encountered a monstrous wave over one hundred feet high. It drenched her, broke windows, and swallowed most of the beautiful ship in its jaws, but she emerged from the encounter with nary a scratch, a true marvel of modern engineering. And the *Olympic* was an even more impressive vessel than that! Between her state-of-the-art design and her Marconi wireless set, there wasn't a ship afloat that could match her for safety.

The rain continued on. Call me mad, but I like storms, even at sea. There's something centering about a breezy autumn gale.

Oliver stirred just as I was fastening the last button on my jacket.

"We stayed up far too late, Jimmy," he muttered, rubbing his eyes. Another flash of lightning lit up the room. He groaned and covered his face with his pillow. "I'm going to skip breakfast. Give the others my best, would you?"

"It's Sunday, Ollie," I reminded him as I glanced at my pocket watch. "You've already missed breakfast. In twenty minutes, they'll be looking for us in the dining room for the church service."

Oliver threw his blankets off in a panic, all tiredness forgotten, just as another rolling wave of thunder vibrated through the ship. "You ought to have said something sooner!" he moaned. "Mother will be furious if we run late!"

As it happened, we didn't run late. In fact, we arrived right on time, and we arrived with the good fortune to obtain seats alongside Dr. Wentworth, Mrs. Wentworth, and Emily, who looked stunning in a tailored, ankle-length dress of cerulean blue. As was her style, she wore lace-up boots that peeked out from beneath the hem. She smiled at me as I took my seat beside her father, two chairs down from her, with the venerable Mrs. Wentworth sitting between them.

"Good morning, sir," I said, greeting Dr. Wentworth, who was peering at Oliver's crooked tie. "I trust your morning is more agreeable than yesterday's?"

"Quite. I must thank you for ensuring my son's punctuality. He has always been fond of a lie-in on the Sabbath."

"Yes, thank you, James, dear," said Mrs. Wentworth. She adjusted her collar and rested her hand on her husband's arm. "It is a comfort to know you two are looking out for each other. Heaven knows my son needs all the support he can get."

Oliver made a noncommittal noise that might have signaled his agreement. He wasn't always pleasant first thing in the morning. My friend was saved from further conversation by the arrival of the organist, a familiar man dressed in the crisp uniform of the *Olympic's* crew—Assistant Purser Haverford. It seemed that he would be playing the music this morning. My last memory of Haverford was of him shouting in his office, though there was no trace of that anger in him now. He was glowing under all the attention being foisted upon him.

"Good morning," he said, his voice rich and melodious. It struck me then that he was probably an excellent singer. "My name is Assistant Purser Charles Haverford, and I will guide you in hymns this morning."

"He looks a lot happier now than he looked while speaking with Mr. Blackstone yesterday," I whispered to Oliver. He turned back, scrutinizing Haverford with renewed suspicion. The crowd, dressed in their Sunday best and blissfully unaware of our conversation, greeted the assistant purser. Those still milling about said their goodbyes before taking their seats. Side conversations dwindled to whispers.

"Thank you." Haverford smiled at us and spread his arms wide. I couldn't help but notice the golden pocket watch shining on his vest. It matched the gaudy signet ring he wore on his left hand. Large, impressive cufflinks glinted on his wrists.

"He's done quite well for himself, hasn't he?" Oliver whispered. "Fellow has more gold on him than the Pope."

"Now is not the time," Dr. Wentworth hissed out of the side of his mouth.

Oliver shrugged before settling back into his seat. "Doesn't make it less true."

Haverford cleared his throat and smiled his gregarious, toothy smile. "Now, while I will be providing you with music throughout the service, Master-at-Arms Harlowe will lead the ceremonies. Please give him a warm welcome."

It was immediately apparent to me that Haverford didn't like Mr. Harlowe much. His charming smile didn't fade as the tall, flat-footed man stepped up to the pulpit, but there was a definite wrinkle in his too-straight nose, a disdainful expression that hadn't been there before. Haverford was Mr. Harlowe's opposite in many ways; he was charming, debonair, effusive, and popular, whereas Mr. Harlowe was rude, callous, reserved, and a bit of a loner. But regardless of how favorably he compared, it was undeniable that Haverford nursed a grudge. *What had happened between them?*

Mr. Harlowe either didn't notice Haverford's reaction or he didn't care about the assistant purser's opinion. It was hard to tell which. The master-at-arms was stone-faced and impassive, his aura so commanding that even Haverford leaned away when he passed him by on his way to the pulpit.

"Good morning," Mr. Harlowe began. "As we gather here on this blessed Sunday, let us take a moment to center our hearts and minds on the Divine. We are grateful for the safe passage granted to us thus far and seek continued protection and guidance as we journey onward."

The congregation nodded in agreement with his solemn words. Mrs. Wentworth bowed her head in prayer.

"It figures they'd send the fellow with the morbs down to us," Oliver muttered, keeping one eye on his father's stern features. "I'll bet they got Captain Bartlett to do the service in first class. He's at least got some charm." I suppressed a smile, but Oliver caught it. "See? You know I'm right. Mr. Harlowe is far from an inspired choice."

After Haverford opened our service with the hymn "Lead Us, Heavenly Father, Lead Us," Mr. Harlowe made a show of pulling a well-worn Bible from the bag he carried with him. His voice was steady as he read from the Book of Ephesians. "Anyone who has been stealing must steal no longer," he read. "But must work, doing something useful with their own hands, that they may have something to share with those in need."

As he read, the passengers listened. Some nodded along in agreement. I couldn't help but wonder at Mr. Harlowe's choice of scripture—*if Mr. Clarke was right about him, wasn't he condemning himself? Could this verse instead be a sign of his innocence?* Either way, I had no doubt he was referencing the smuggling ring in front of our entire congregation. That was a bold move.

Emily seemed to think that was what Mr. Harlowe was doing as well. She couldn't say anything to me, separated from my side by her parents, but she did her best to get my attention. Once she had it, she stared at the space between Haverford and Mr. Harlowe before turning back to me. I nodded to show my understanding.

Oliver poked me in the arm. "Looks like Haverford hated that bit of scripture, doesn't it?"

"I think he might just hate Mr. Harlowe," I whispered, looking away from Emily to return my attention to the service. Even from a distance, it was evident that I was correct. Haverford's jaw was clenched tight.

"The purser's office wouldn't be a terrible place to cover up a smuggling ring, would it?" Oliver asked. "Perhaps we should be taking a closer look at Haverford. You saw him with Mr. Blackstone, so we know there's a connection, and they must have been yelling at each other for a reason. We should ask him what the Sphinx Society is."

"You first. And Haverford's been upset since before Mr. Harlowe started reading... I think we're missing something."

"Right, that's what I'm saying! Haverford is very well-liked. What do you think they'd do to us if we accused him of aiding the smugglers?"

"Nothing compared to what I shall do to you if you do not show respect for this service," Dr. Wentworth hissed. He spoke so quietly that I almost missed his reprimand, but he was firm enough that I clamped my mouth shut at once. My cheeks burned with embarrassment.

Oblivious to our side conversation, Mr. Harlowe began his sermon. "Today, we are reminded of the virtues of honesty and integrity. In Ephesians, we are called to put away falsehood and to speak truthfully. The scripture further admonishes those who have stolen to do so no longer. A lesson many could learn, I believe."

He paused. "In our daily lives and interactions, let us remember the value of truthfulness. When we speak honestly, we honor our neighbors and ourselves, both here on this ship and in our lives beyond this voyage."

We all bowed our heads in contemplation. I was mulling over Mr. Harlowe's words when Oliver jabbed me in the arm once again.

"Where's Mr. Blackstone?" he asked. "You said he'd be here, didn't you?"

I tried to look around as subtly as I could. Mrs. Henderson was present, but her nephew was nowhere to be seen. Instead, the old woman stood with Captain Dinsmore. Dinsmore was dressed in a black three-piece suit. At least he'd left his brandy behind for the service.

"No," I whispered back. "It appears Mrs. Henderson failed to persuade him to attend."

"Are you going to talk to her again?"

"After the service, perhaps, though we might have more luck waiting and calling on her in her stateroom."

"Mr. Blackstone could be hiding out in there. It's not a bad idea."

Haverford began playing a new hymn, "Dear Lord and Father of Mankind."

Oliver made a show of mouthing the words like he was singing along, but he continued our conversation. "Mr. Blackstone isn't the only one who's missed church. Where's Mr. Clarke?"

"He looked ill yesterday. He might not have been up to making a public appearance."

"This storm has a great number of people feeling seasick. I saw old Mr. Carter, Eli's grandfather, when I was in the hospital yesterday. He wasn't well at all. I think Dr. Widmer wanted to keep him overnight."

"I hope he recovers, for Eli and Annabelle's sake."

"As do I."

Back at the pulpit, Mr. Harlowe looked like he was ready to end the service. "May the Lord bless you and keep you," he said, raising his hands in a gesture of blessing. "In your darkest moments, may His blessings bring you peace. Go forth in the grace and love of our Lord. Amen."

The congregation dispersed. Mr. Harlowe left the saloon as quickly as he'd arrived, only stopping to exchange words with a few grateful passengers. In contrast, Haverford looked like a man who wasn't in a hurry to vacate. Nothing could stop him from rubbing shoulders with anyone willing to chat. He settled in, laughing with some nearby passengers while he performed more music.

"I don't think Mr. Harlowe is our killer, but I think he knows something," Emily said. She'd detached herself from her parents, who were moving forward to join the crowd surrounding Haverford. "Why else would he choose those passages for the service?"

Oliver was bouncing on his toes. "Do you think he suspects someone in second class?"

"Well, if he was after Haverford's confession, it didn't

work," I said as we fought to work our way through the crowd. Most people were shuffling toward Haverford, but we were trying to get to the back of the dining saloon. "That man is shameless."

"He's a brilliant performer, though," Emily admitted. "Everyone wants to be close to him."

She was right. From where we stood, Haverford's styled blonde hair was practically glowing. His presence drew others near to him in the same way a blazing torch might draw in a moth. It would have been impressive if I hadn't seen him treat Emily like she was some sort of prize to be won.

"I don't like him. He's slippery."

"You and Mr. Harlowe will be fast friends, then, Jimmy," Oliver said. "But the two of you are not in the majority. Assistant Purser Haverford is popular. Even with that conversation you overheard yesterday placing Mr. Blackstone in his office, there's no way we could accuse him of anything without more evidence."

Emily tugged Oliver's sleeve and led him to the door. "I think we need to find out what Mr. Harlowe knows," she said. "If he doesn't like Assistant Purser Haverford, he must have a reason. We may be able to help each other. He should at least be told that James spotted Mr. Blackstone."

I inclined my head in agreement. "We should see if he's still nearby. Captain Bartlett put him in charge of the investigation into Mr. Eckert's death. If we could get him to talk, perhaps we could convince him to help us in return. Quid pro quo, you know?"

"Whatever you two want to do." Oliver didn't sound as convinced as Emily and I were, but then, he'd been leery of trusting Mr. Harlowe ever since Mr. Clarke had first warned us about him.

We filed into the corridor at the foot of the aft staircase. Away from the relative comfort of the dining saloon, it became apparent that the storm outside had once again increased in ferocity. The once gentle swaying of the ship had transformed into a more pronounced up-and-down rhythm. Rain lashed against the portholes, each droplet sounding like the sharp, insistent notes of a frenzied song. It felt like we were under fire from a damp Gatling gun.

I glanced at Oliver and Emily, ready to comment on the storm. Before I could speak, a figure barreled toward us, collided with Oliver, and sent him sprawling to the floor. He landed with a resounding thud.

"Oliver!" Emily rushed to his side. "Are you hurt?"

While Emily saw to her brother, I turned, fists raised, to deal with our new arrival.

It was Eli Carter. Our friend was hunched over and gasping.

"Oliver! Emily!" he exclaimed. "Oh, thank God, I found you!"

"What's wrong, Eli?" I asked. When he didn't answer, I grabbed him by the shoulder and gave him a shake. "Eli!"

"It's Annabelle," he cried. "She's gone missing! Something terrible has happened. I just know it!"

Oliver clutched his elbow. "Missing?" he asked as Emily helped him sit upright. "Since when? And do you always greet people by plowing them over?"

Eli flinched. "I—I'm sorry!" he stammered, raking a hand through his curly, disheveled hair. "I don't know when she disappeared. She was with me at breakfast, but when I returned to get ready for church, she was gone! Her things are still in our stateroom, but she's nowhere to be found!"

Emily raised a gloved hand to her mouth. I ignored the

trembling in my own hands as I bent down, grabbed Oliver's arm, and hauled him to his feet. Once I was sure he was steady, I turned back to Eli.

"Where have you searched so far?" I asked.

"Everywhere I could think of! The library, the promenade deck, Grandfather's hospital room, even the smoking room... please, help me. Come back to our stateroom. Perhaps you'll see something I've missed."

"Lead the way."

The Carters were housed in adjoining rooms on E-deck. It wasn't a long walk down there, but with the ship rolling harder now, the journey took more time than it should have. Our footsteps were unsteady on the shifting floor. All the while, I felt my sense of unease growing. I didn't know the Carters well, but Annabelle didn't strike me as the type to disappear without explanation. She was a capable girl. There was something very wrong if she'd vanished without a trace.

When we reached the Carters' room, Eli flung the door open and led us inside. His sister's belongings were scattered all over the place. Dresses were draped across chairs and half-falling from the bed. Books and clothing lay scattered across the floor.

I looked around, trying to think logically despite my rising fear something terrible had happened. "Did Annabelle say anything to you this morning, Eli? Anything that might indicate where she was going or who she might be meeting?"

He shook his head. "Nothing out of the ordinary. She was excited about the day! She even spoke of joining us all for lunch."

"Have you seen this?" Emily asked. She picked a piece of White Star Line letterhead up from the desk. It was folded, with one word printed on the front in meticulous handwriting: *Carter*.

"N—no. That wasn't here before! I swear it!"

"It has your name on the front," Emily observed. "Perhaps Annabelle sent you a message?"

"I cannot open it. I... what if..." he choked on his words. "Please, Emily... will you read it?"

Emily nodded. Swallowing nervously, she unfolded the letter. Her face paled as she read it aloud.

"Cease your involvement in affairs that do not concern you. Do not go looking for the girl."

Eli looked faint. "They've taken her because of me," he whispered. "Because of my photographs. They found out! They know I helped you. Oh, God, what have I done?"

Oliver placed a reassuring hand on Eli's arm. "It's not your fault, Eli."

He didn't say it, but I knew what the next part of his sentence should be—the fault was ours.

My stomach twisted up. It was even worse than that. I was the one who suggested that we use Eli's photographs. He'd gotten involved because of me.

Emily took a shaky breath. "We need help. This is too much. We don't know what we're doing."

"Mr. Harlowe," I said. "We need to find Mr. Harlowe. He's the master-at-arms. If he's on our side, he'll help us. He's been investigating these men. He'll know where to start."

"I—well—are you sure?" Eli argued. "You saw how he treated me. Can we trust him?"

"We'll have to. Unless you have a better idea?" I asked.

"No. If—if you insist he's trustworthy, I believe you. But what if we're too late?"

"We won't be," I said firmly, trying to infuse my voice with the confidence Eli lacked. "But we can't afford to waste any time. Given what happened to Lieutenant Morgan and Theodore Eckert, we know how serious this is."

None of us felt the need to share the harrowing thought that Annabelle Carter would soon be the third body found on the *Olympic* in as many days.

"We shall need to divide our efforts," Emily said. "Eli, you accompany Oliver. Retrace your sister's steps. Look for anything we might use to find her. James, you and I will seek out Mr. Harlowe. We shall inform him of the situation and hope he can help us find Annabelle."

Oliver clapped Eli on the back. "Of course. If there's anything there, we'll find it."

"Annabelle..." Eli paused to look at each of us in turn. His words were thick with emotion. "You must understand. My sister is the most precious person in the world to me. I cannot bear the thought of losing her."

"You won't," I promised. "Let's go."

13
THE ENGINE ROOM

Emily and I hurried through the maze of white corridors that separated Annabelle Carter's cabin from the last place we'd seen Mr. Harlowe. Details blurred as we hurried past an endless array of rooms and closed doors. I couldn't stop imagining Annabelle, alone and terrified somewhere aboard this behemoth of a ship, trapped in some forgotten corner, or worse...

No. I couldn't start thinking like that. There was still time to save her.

The *Olympic* lurched hard to starboard, a slow, groaning tilt that made me fear the whole ship might roll over. I grabbed wildly for the railing. Somewhere behind one of the cabin doors, I heard a chair scrape across the floor, a muffled curse, and the heavy thud of something toppling over.

Emily lost her footing. I caught her before I could consider the propriety of my hand closing over hers. The *Olympic* continued to roll. A wave of panic washed over me when I realized Emily might still slip away.

I wrapped my free arm around her waist.

We stayed like that for an age. Then, slowly, the ship righted herself. The deck leveled out beneath our feet. I glanced down at Emily. She was holding on as tightly as I was, one hand locked around mine, the other clenched around my jacket. The glove separating her skin from mine felt impossibly thin. Her fingers were warm.

"Thank you, James," she said breathlessly. The blood had all but drained from her face. "That fall could have been most unfortunate."

"Think nothing of it."

Despite the chaos surrounding us, both Emily and I grew still. A few moments passed. Then, as if steeling herself for the challenge ahead, she closed her eyes, exhaled, separated from me, and continued on without another word. I pushed myself to follow her. Emily's auburn hair clung to her forehead, but there was no give in her, no hesitation.

I wish I could say the same for myself. My legs, no longer conditioned by daily farm work, burned with every step. Each breath came harder than the last. The corridors twisted and turned with no end in sight. Each stretch was identical to the last. I wanted to stop, but we had to find Mr. Harlowe. Annabelle needed him.

I pushed on.

Every porthole and window we passed was drenched in rain. The storm was as relentless as Emily; it howled and battered loose fixtures, producing a chorus of sharp, metallic clatters. The sea was more turbulent than I'd ever felt it before.

We slowed down when we reached the assistant purser's office on E-deck. The service windows were pulled shut, their glass fronts sparkling each time lightning flashed. A note was affixed to their front.

*I have gone to church and will return at 12:00.
Assistant Purser C.S. Haverford.*

"He's late," Emily muttered. It was now well past noon. "He must still be in the saloon."

I stopped to catch my breath. "Along with most of second class."

"Unfortunately, that's of no help to us." Emily turned and marched up the stairs. "Come on, then! We haven't a moment to spare. Annabelle is counting on us!"

I followed her. The *Olympic* was a steady ship, over 880 feet long and as even keeled as they come. But the waves we were breaking over now weren't to be trifled with. It was difficult for me to keep my balance. When we reached the landing on D-deck, there was no sign of Mr. Harlowe, but music and the rumble of unconcerned laughter echoed from the saloon. Many of our fellow travelers seemed to be riding out the storm there, enjoying the company of Assistant Purser Haverford.

"We're never going to find Mr. Harlowe like this," I said. "What if he's already left second class to return to the officers' quarters?"

"Alex," Emily said.

"What? Yes, he would be helpful, too, but—"

"No, look!" She grabbed my arm and spun me around. "It's Mr. Cunningham!"

Serendipitously, Oliver's favorite steward, Alex Cunningham, was at that moment scrubbing up a spilled mess on the stairs leading up to C-deck. He straightened up, wiped his brow with the back of his hand, and stared at us. The dampness clung to his uniform like a second skin, giving him the appearance of some sodden, woebegone creature of the swamp.

He shoved his mop into its bucket, its contents sloshing to the brim. Satisfied, he took it out and slapped it on the floor.

"Alex!" I called out.

"What do you need, Mr. Kelly?" he asked. He sounded exhausted. "Somebody spilled half a bottle of brandy here and left it without alerting anyone. I've been picking up glass for twenty minutes!"

"We need a master-at-arms." I didn't waste time with pleasantries. "It's urgent. Do you know where we can find Mr. Harlowe?"

Alex wiped his hands off on his cleaning rag. "Why do you need Mr. Harlowe?"

"I'm sorry, Mr. Cunningham, but we haven't time for explanations," Emily said. "Do you know where one might find him? Please, it's important."

Alex fought a brief war with himself. It played out on his face as his expression ranged from pinched to frustrated to resigned. "He's in the engineers' mess, talking to the second engineer. They've been having some trouble down there, if you must know, and he headed that way right after the service. It's the talk of the ship."

"Please take us to him," I said, bracing myself as the ship lurched. It wasn't an alarming motion, but it was enough of one that I heard a glass shatter in the saloon. A roar of laughter followed. "Just get us there."

"It would mean much to us, Mr. Cunningham," Emily insisted. "Can you take us to the engineers' mess?"

Alex looked Emily up and down. "They won't be happy to see you there, Miss Wentworth. It isn't any place for a proper lady to be."

"Fortunately for you, I can decide for myself where it is best for a proper lady to be. Mr. Kelly will ensure no harm comes to me, won't you?" Emily looked up at me with a mischievous smirk, eerily similar to one I'd seen her brother wear many times. I smiled back and offered her my arm. She took it.

"You heard her. She wants to come along."

Alex sighed dramatically. "You're the most baffling passengers I've ever had the pleasure of caring for—no disrespect intended, of course." He dropped his mop into its bucket. "Very well, then. Follow me." He led us back downstairs to E-deck, where he swiped a key from the Chief Steward's desk.

From there, he opened a door near the forward staircase and ushered us into a long hallway that teemed with sailors, stewards, and engineers in white uniforms. Some were splattered with grease or damp from their labors. "It's not far from here," Alex said, "but try to keep pace. I do not want to lose either of you. The American authorities would be liable to quarantine the whole ship."

I'd never seen a place like this before. The corridor teemed with activity. It was massive, a glorious mess of exposed pipework and ventilation ducts. Crew members and steerage passengers alike bustled about, using this passage to cross through the chest of the *Olympic* unimpeded. It was one of the most diverse crowds I'd ever seen. Shouted conversations in a multitude of languages surrounded us like we were in ingredients in Zangwill's melting pot.

In a less stressful time, I think I would have enjoyed it.

"Where are we going?" I shouted. It was difficult to hear over the clanging metal, loud voices, and rhythmic pounding of the engines below.

"To the engineers' mess hall, sir. Master-at-Arms Harlowe should still be there!" Alex called back.

As we hurried along, several bewildered people stopped to

gawk at us. The steerage passengers were especially fascinating; many were Eastern European, with languages and customs different from those I was familiar with. Our sudden arrival seemed to excite them. The majority looked away after being caught staring—the division of our classes meant they shouldn't speak unless spoken to—but the crew were less demure. The engineers and cooks looked upon us with raised brows and open mouths; one burly man dropped his sack of potatoes and approached us for conversation, but Alex waved him off. He backed down, and we continued on.

The constant hum of machinery grew louder as we descended deeper into the bowels of the *Olympic*. The floor was stained with oil.

I wondered if we'd ever find Mr. Harlowe. Or if Alex Cunningham actually knew where he was going.

Finally, after several more near encounters with the people who worked in this strange place, we arrived at a door marked "Engineers' Mess." Alex knocked twice and pushed it open without waiting for a response.

There were several people eating their lunch in this small room. Upon our entry, the sounds of scraping cutlery and animated voices ceased. The engineers turned to face us. I paid them little mind, so relieved was I to see that we'd tracked down the object of our search: Mr. Harlowe. He was leaning against a wooden cabinet with his long arms folded like a pretzel, speaking to a man who was probably the second engineer. The master-at-arms did not look happy to see us.

"What's the meaning of this?" he demanded. "Steward, why have you brought these two down here? It's highly inappropriate for these passengers, especially a young woman!"

I stepped forward, still breathing hard from our mad dash

through the *Olympic*. There was a stitch in my side. "Mr. Harlowe, sir, please. We have little time. Annabelle Carter's life is in danger, and we need your help to find her."

Mr. Harlowe narrowed his eyes. "Start from the beginning, Mr. Kelly. And make it quick."

I exchanged a glance with Emily. "Well, sir, we were leaving the dining saloon after church when Eli Carter came running up to us. He told us that his sister, Annabelle, had gone missing. He was frantic—he said she disappeared after breakfast and left no clues about where she went."

Emily nodded along. "We searched everywhere he could think of, but there was no sign of her. Then we found this." She handed Mr. Harlowe the note she'd discovered on Eli's desk. "It's a warning. Whoever's behind these murders is trying to intimidate us. And Eli."

Mr. Harlowe scanned the note. "I don't need to tell you how serious this is. What I want to know is how the lot of you have gotten involved with this business. Care to explain?"

"Well, someone needs to find out the truth about these events, don't they?" I asked. "Sir," I added as an afterthought.

"Yes," Mr. Harlowe said slowly. "Yes, they do. Which is why Captain Bartlett asked me to do that very thing."

"Pardon, sir, but we were looking into these artifacts before you were ever assigned to the case," Emily said. "We are working with Mr. Clarke—he's a journalist, and that's his job. We've been helping him with his investigation."

Mr. Harlowe looked as if he wanted to say something, but he sighed and handed the paper back to Emily. "I trust that's proven favorable for you? No major complications have arisen as a result of that choice?"

"We don't need your insults, sir," I said, feeling distinctly nettled. "We need your help. Annabelle's disappearance is connected to Lieutenant Morgan and Theodore Eckert' deaths and the smuggling they were caught up in. We think we've uncovered some information you might be able to use."

Emily jumped in right after I finished. "We've pieced together evidence suggesting Mr. Reginald Blackstone is in on it," she said. "We told you about him when Mr. Eckert was found, remember? Please, Mr. Harlowe, we can explain everything later, but we must act now!"

Mr. Harlowe looked from me to Emily, weighing our words. The engineer he'd been speaking to, a burly man with a grease-stained coat, glanced up from his meal. "Cursing in German," he muttered, loud enough to catch Mr. Harlowe's attention. "Heard it coming from somewhere in the engine room earlier. I thought it was strange. Sounded like an argument."

"That's why we called you down here in the first place, Mr. Harlowe," another man said. "Peculiar business, all of this. You told us to watch out for anything strange, and we did. A girl goes missing, and then we hear strange shouting. Perhaps this German fellow is involved in your case?"

Mr. Harlowe's expression hardened. "Very well, Mr. Kelly. I will help you search for Annabelle Carter. We will start by tracking this lead in the engine room. You will follow me, speak when spoken to, and listen to any orders I might issue. Is that clear?"

"We understand," I said. "Lead the way."

Mr. Harlowe grabbed his hat from a hook by the door and made to leave the room. Upon passing by Emily, he stopped to look down at her. She stared right back. I was worried he might protest her presence, but after studying her face for a few seconds, Mr. Harlowe nodded curtly. "Try not to be a distraction," he muttered. With that, he strode out. We followed him.

The engine room was only a short walk from the mess hall. Mr. Harlowe pulled the door open when we reached the entrance and ushered us onto a metal catwalk, closing it when we were all through. The air was hot. It reeked of oil and metal. Below us, the ship's massive reciprocating engines filled the cavernous space with the clanking of pistons and the hiss of steam. The scale of this room was overwhelming. It felt like we had entered an entirely new world.

Emily glanced at me. "Do you think the German intruder that Mr. Harlowe is chasing could be the same man who followed us to Lieutenant Morgan's stateroom?"

"If it is, then he's probably the one who went after Annabelle," I said as we descended a narrow set of metal stairs. "I wonder who he would have been arguing with down here?"

"It's difficult to say. I don't know how anyone even managed to overhear it. Everything is so loud!"

"I don't either. Hang on; I think we're near to the end."

We were. The colossal machinery of the engines towered overhead. I'd hardly had time to register that they were taller than most houses when we were approached by a man in a smudged uniform. He removed his cap upon seeing Emily, clearly confused by her presence in our strange party.

"What's all this about, sir?" asked the engineer.

"I'm not sure yet," Mr. Harlowe replied curtly. "I've heard you may have an intruder down here."

I only caught snippets of the rest of Mr. Harlowe's and the engineer's conversation. The engines were just too loud to hear anything clearly.

Eventually, the engineer nodded. Mr. Harlowe turned back

to face us. "We're going back up a level to investigate the engineers' quarters," he said. "That's where they heard the commotion earlier this afternoon."

We started climbing the stairs again. If the hallway above us was the *Olympic's* chest, I decided, this place was more akin to its heart. The engines' constant vibration made it feel like the entire room was alive. Every shudder of the machinery felt like the inner workings of a massive, steam-powered body. As we passed the workshop and neared our next stop, a shadowy figure darted across our path. It disappeared into the darkness with the sound of a slamming door.

"There!" I shouted, pointing.

Mr. Harlowe drew his revolver. "Stay close and follow me."

We gave chase down a series of catwalks. The shadowy figure was elusive, always just out of reach, but we were getting closer by the second. Finally, we turned a corner and found ourselves in a dingy corridor that contained the engineers' sleeping quarters and lavatories. One of the doors was ajar. Mr. Harlowe stepped forward and kicked it the rest of the way open.

Slumped against the wall, clinging to life, was Mr. Blackstone. He looked like he'd been drawn from the depths of some musty crypt. His wrinkled shirt clung to his newly skeletal frame like funeral wrappings. Whatever had been done to Mr. Eckert—supernatural or not—had also been done to Mr. Blackstone. I was sure of that.

I closed my eyes and chanted a prayer before stepping into the room. This was something I knew I needed to see for myself, no matter how scary it was. Unfortunately, the closer I got to him, the worse things got. The historian was a shell of his former self. His skin, stretched tight over protruding bones, bore the desiccated look of something long dead. His glasses, perched askew on his nose, had one lens cracked. Behind them, his eyes were sunken deep into their hollow sockets. His breathing was labored. Each inhale was strained.

Mr. Harlowe knelt beside what remained of Mr. Blackstone and checked for a pulse. "He's alive, but this isn't the figure we were chasing. This man can barely move."

My heart pounded as I noticed a crumpled piece of paper clutched in Blackstone's withered hand. I pried it loose from his brittle grip. *Would we finally get answers? What was causing these injuries?* I unraveled the note. A single, cryptic phrase stared back at me:

Potato Sack.

Emily read over my shoulder. "'Potato sack?' What on Earth does that mean?"

Mr. Harlowe rose to his feet. "I haven't the faintest idea," he muttered. "But I know who does." Without warning, he kicked Mr. Blackstone in the side. "Wake up, you lout!"

Mr. Blackstone startled awake, grasped my arm, and pulled me in close. "The wings are real," he rasped. "Marvin, he—he found them... tried to hide them... but he got to him. Teddy—he lost it. The storm is... proof. Ask—ask—C—"

"Ask who?" Mr. Harlowe barked. "What are you saying, sir? To what does this message refer?"

But Mr. Blackstone couldn't finish. His grip tightened, eyes wide with terror, before he let out a final, shuddering breath and went still. His hand fell from my wrist and landed with a thump.

I exchanged a grim look with Emily, who looked horrified. Whatever smuggling Mr. Blackstone may have done, he didn't deserve this fate. No one did.

"Good heavens!" exclaimed a new arrival. Another of the ship's engineers, an especially thin man, was stumbling backward, a hand clasped over his mouth. "That fellow has died in my room! Whatever was the matter with him?"

Behind him, another man hurried down the corridor with his cap pulled low over his face. The eyeglasses on his nose glinted in the low light.

"Send for Dr. Widmer," Mr. Harlowe growled to the startled engineer. "What a fine mess this is. 'Potato sack,' indeed. I fear we have been reduced to pursuing the craven whims of a lunatic."

The engineer scurried off, clearly afraid of both Mr. Blackstone's haunting corpse and Mr. Harlowe's boiling wrath. Once he was gone, Mr. Harlowe knelt over the body. He paused for a moment, as if considering his next move, before leaning over, holstering his revolver, and closing Mr. Blackstone's eyes. After that, he pulled Mr. Blackstone's jacket open and began to search his pockets. The silence was broken only by the rustle of fabric and the thrum of the reciprocating engines.

"Sir?" I interrupted tentatively. "Do you have any other ideas where we might find Annabelle?"

"No. We will need to regroup and organize a search. If luck is with us, we will find your friend before our mystery assassin does."

BAM!

The door behind me flew open and slammed into the wall. A young crewman stumbled into the room, his face as white as a sheet, his hands fumbling with motion. He doubled over.

"Mr. Harlowe, sir!" he wheezed. His attention darted between us and Mr. Blackstone's withered remains. "There's been another disturbance! In the cargo hold, sir."

Mr. Harlowe did one last cursory search of Mr. Blackstone, then stood, pocketing one of the dead man's distinctive cufflinks. "What manner of disturbance?"

The crewman's throat bobbed. He glanced over his shoulder "Well, they're saying it's unnatural, sir, if you understand my meaning. They told me there was a rush of wind that knocked them over—inside the ship, mind you, not on deck—and that shadows were moving about on their own. Cold spots, too. Like walking through a ghost. That's what they said, anyway."

Emily and I exchanged glances. I could see skepticism already taking shape on her face, but truth be told, the hair on my neck was beginning to stand on end. I'd seen too many strange things on this ship to dismiss the story outright.

Mr. Harlowe, however, looked as if he agreed with Emily. His lip was curled in distaste. "Balderdash," he said. "Nevertheless, this... report... must be investigated. Posthaste."

"Do you think this could have something to do with Annabelle's disappearance?" Emily asked.

"I don't know what to think," growled Mr. Harlowe. He looked us up and down. "But I know that the two of you are thoroughly entangled in this affair. If Miss Carter is involved with whatever is happening in the cargo hold, you might prove useful. I would welcome your assistance."

Emily lifted her chin. "We are at your disposal, Mr. Harlowe," she said.

"Yes, sir," I agreed. "We're with you."

"Hmph," Mr. Harlowe grunted. "Very well. Stay close and remain vigilant. With any luck, we shall uncover the truth of this mess today." He rounded on the young crewman, patting his revolver before saying, "I don't truck with curses or specters, lad, but I am duty-bound to investigate any disturbance on this ship. I will investigate the cargo hold."

"Of course, sir. May God protect you."

"May He protect whomever I find skulking about in there," Mr. Harlowe said. "Before this day is done, they'll need your prayers more than me. Of that, I can assure you."

14
IN THE SHADOWS

After taking care to lock Mr. Blackstone's body away behind us and instructing the crew not to disturb it, Mr. Harlowe led us back through the engine room. Our ascent up the sweltering stairs was a silent affair. One that left me plenty of time to think. I couldn't shake the image of Mr. Blackstone's frightened face from my mind. Couldn't stop replaying his ominous last words. *The Wings are real... The storm is proof.* It was such an absurd claim that I struggled to believe it. But it had to be so, for nothing natural could have caused those wounds.

Alex was waiting outside. "Miss Wentworth! Are you well? What's happened?"

I glanced at Emily. She wore a stony expression. "Trouble," I said, sparing her the need to answer. "We found another body. Mr. Blackstone."

Alex gaped at me. His patience gone, Mr. Harlowe pushed past the young man with a muttered, "Excuse me, lad," and headed back in the direction we'd come from, nearer to second class. His determined stride left no room for hesitation.

We followed him.

Mr. Harlowe led us down the long corridor we'd entered with Alex only an hour before. Passengers and crew craned their necks to catch a glimpse of us as we trudged through their domain. Conversations and remarks followed us as we went, but they were held in a smorgasbord of linguistic flavors, seasoned with countless different regional dialects. It was too chaotic for me to even attempt to understand them.

Then we passed by a wrinkled man cloaked in tobacco smoke. There was a sweet hint of apple wood in the furling cloud surrounding him, a faint dash of roses in the air. I would recognize that blend anywhere; my father's was uncannily similar, cured with wood from our orchard. This stranger must have used a similar process. In fact, were it not for the lingering odor of oil and grease from the engine room, I could have closed my eyes and imagined myself back on the farm, spending time with my father under the shade trees.

It felt like he was with me again, if only for a moment. The memory of his loss sent a sharp twinge through my chest.

But I couldn't afford the luxury of such reflections. Not now. My father, like Mr. Blackstone, wasn't coming back. There was no sense in dwelling on him.

We kept walking.

Just after the smoking man was a group of women huddled near a doorway. Some of them had the fair skin and light hair of the Baltic regions, while others had the darker complexions of the Mediterranean. I supposed some of them might have been Italian. Their ages ranged from young girls in their teens to grandmothers with lines of wisdom on their faces. Despite their financial circumstances, they carried themselves with grace. There was a certain sort of old-world strength in their posture.

Seeing this, Emily tugged on my jacket, and I leaned over so she could whisper in my ear. "These women... they're nothing like what one hears in the press."

"What do you mean?"

"Have you not heard the things reporters say about Italians?"

"Well—"

She interrupted me before I could finish. "Of course you have. It's just, the way some people talk, you'd think they were all unwashed and wretched. But look at them. They're so... dignified."

"Does that surprise you?"

"Yes—no—it's just, seeing it for myself, it gives me hope, you know?"

"Hope?"

"For them," she clarified. "For their future in America. That they can grow to be part of our society."

I offered her a hesitant nod. "Emily," I said carefully, "I grew up around people like this." I gestured toward the group of women. "My father was a farmer. His father came from Ireland. Most of our neighbors were immigrants. I already knew those things were lies. They've been part of my life for as long as I can remember."

Emily let out a small gasp. "Oh, James, I... I didn't mean to imply... I support Jane Addams, you know, and Florence Kelley—"

"I know," I assured her. "It's nothing."

She fiddled with the cuff of her cerulean sleeve. "No, I was insensitive. You have my apologies."

"There's nothing to apologize for."

Emily didn't say anything else. The silence between us stretched as we moved deeper into the corridor.

It couldn't have been more than five minutes later when we encountered another group of people. Men, this time, huddled together in a small circle. They wore heavy woolen trousers and loose-fitting shirts. A few sported caps pulled low over their brows. Others had bare heads. Many sported mustaches impressive enough Oliver would have been jealous.

As we approached their group, one of them, an elderly man with a long beard, stepped forward. He shook his fist and said something snappy to Mr. Harlowe in his native tongue.

Shockingly, Mr. Harlowe responded in kind. "*Odsuń się!*" he snarled. "*To sprawa oficjalna!*"

The man's eyes widened in surprise. He stepped back, muttering, "*Przepraszam, proszę pana,*" before his group dispersed, casting furtive glances over their shoulders as they went.

"What language was that, Mr. Harlowe?" asked Emily.

"Polish," he grunted, not breaking stride.

I whistled. "Where does a man learn that sort of thing?"

"In my line of work, you pick up a bit of everything, Mr. Kelly. Now, less gawking and more walking, if you please."

We entered the third-class public area. It, too, was crowded with immigrants. We made our way through them, tailing Mr. Harlowe as he led us further into the ship. No others dared to challenge the master-at-arms. The men stepped aside, pressing themselves against the walls to let us pass. It seemed word about Mr. Harlowe had spread quickly.

Emily leaned in closer. "James, do you think any of these people might have seen something? They could be good witnesses."

Before I could respond, Mr. Harlowe answered her. "If they had, Miss Wentworth, they wouldn't tell us. Leave the investigating to me."

Emily made a pinched face at me when he wasn't looking. All I could do was offer her a sympathetic shrug. Like the steerage men, I had no desire to go toe-to-toe with an angry Mr. Harlowe. I had more sense than that.

Our path took us through the firemen's mess next. The atmosphere in the den of the stokers was thick with sweat and coal dust. It stung my nostrils. Men sat at long tables, their faces and hands smudged with grime. They regarded our group with open distrust, some scowling as we hurried past. I would not have wanted to be here without Mr. Harlowe. In that sense, his presence was a virtue.

One surly fireman spat on the floor near our feet. "What's the fancy folk doin' down 'ere?" he growled.

Mr. Harlowe's hand moved to his hip, where his revolver was holstered. "Official business," he said coolly. "You'd best find your manners, son, before I haul you in front of Captain Bartlett and let him find them for you."

The fireman's face paled beneath the coal dust. "Sorry, sir. Lost me head."

"I thought so," Mr. Harlowe muttered. He turned back to us. "Come along, now. It won't do us good to dawdle here."

We continued until we reached the firemen's stairs. They were arranged in a tight spiral of steel planks wound around a central pole, the steps themselves barely wide enough for one person to pass at a time. The metal was worn smooth from countless boot strikes. It creaked under our weight.

"Watch your step," Mr. Harlowe warned.

We descended in single file, the stairwell growing darker and more claustrophobic with each trip around the spindle. Every moment brought us closer to our goal, but it also seemed to squeeze the walls in more tightly around us. It felt like we were being swallowed whole by the ship. Even the sound of our footsteps had no room to escape this place.

After spiraling downward for an eternity, we reached the bottom.

Cargo Hold #3 was a vast cavern of steel, filled to the brim with stacks of crates that loomed out of the darkness like the towers of an ancient city. Empty walkways displaced the windswept streets of my imagination. Distant bangs and dings on the hull did the same for any sound of animal life. Where the sky should have been was nothing but a roof of darkened metal. Canvas tarps rippled as a draft blew through, the suction generated by some far-off fan doing its best to channel the spirit of the wind.

On second thought, this was no ruined metropolis. It felt more like the castle dungeon from one of Emily's gothic stories.

There was another reason this place felt like a dungeon. For the first time on the *Olympic*, I was struck by how dark it was. Something was wrong with the electric lights. They were flickering, struggling to stay lit, burning a sickly orange instead of a strong yellow.

Luckily, Mr. Harlowe had brought along a battery-powered flashlight. He ignited its beam. "Stay alert," he cautioned. "Whatever caused that disturbance could still be here."

As if in response, a chill swept through the hold and crawled up my arms like the skittering legs of a thousand spiders. I gasped. The sensation raised goosebumps on my skin.

Emily's hand found mine. "James," she whispered, "did you feel that?"

I could only squeeze her hand in response. How else could I describe what I'd just felt?

"Stay sharp," Mr. Harlowe said. "Remember, we must keep a keen eye out for anything out of place."

"Do you think Annabelle could be here?" Emily asked.

"Perhaps." Mr. Harlowe cleared his throat. "Hello? Is anyone there?"

A crewman emerged from behind a stack of crates, holding up a hand to block out the beam of light that had been aimed his way. "Mr. Harlowe, sir. I've been expecting you."

Mr. Harlowe lowered his flashlight. "Is that right?"

The crewman nodded. "Yes, sir. I'm the one who sent Jones to find you. Strange things are happening down here. I thought you might come to investigate."

"What kind of strange things? Your man spoke of unnatural occurrences. Oddities."

"Noises, sir. Shadows moving when they shouldn't. And..."

"Yes?" Mr. Harlowe prompted. "And what? Spit it out, man."

"Well, it might not be my place to say so, but a Swedish man was down here for around an hour with another official-looking fellow. That was this morning. After they departed, I heard a voice. German, I think. Angry-like. But there was no one else here, sir. I swear it. I was by me lonesome."

Emily and I exchanged glances. *Yet another mention of our mysterious German man.* And it sounded like Mr. Clarke had succeeded in his quest to access the cargo hold.

Mr. Harlowe's face remained impassive, but I noticed his grip tighten on his flashlight. "Did you see or hear anything that might relate to a missing girl? Annabelle Carter, about sixteen years old?"

The crewman shook his head. "No, sir. No sign of any girl. Just the Swede and his friend... and that voice."

"Show us where you heard it."

The crewman shivered, but he nodded. "Right this way, sir."

As he led us deeper into the hold, I couldn't shake the feeling that we were being watched. Emily's hand found mine once again. I gave it a reassuring squeeze, though I was feeling far from reassured myself. I was on edge. More than once, I spun around, certain I'd seen movement out of the corner of my eye, only to find shadows. It was unnerving. They moved independently of our flashlight beam, flowing across the floor and walls, acting as sentinels of this maze of cargo and steel.

We kept walking.

Time didn't seem to exist here. Things simply were. With each plunge the *Olympic* took, the towering stacks of items around us shuddered, dancing to the beat of the storm. The beam of Mr. Harlowe's flashlight swept across the crates, its light revealing nothing but clutter and grime. It did nothing to combat the oppressive feel of this place.

Something in the darkness was watching us. Waiting.

I was startled when the crewman spoke again. "This is the place, sirs. This is where I heard the voice."

"Thank you," Mr. Harlowe said. He turned his light to the crewman. "Do you have anything else to add? Any other detail you might have omitted?"

"No, sir. None."

Mr. Harlowe nodded. "In that case, you have fulfilled your duty here. I would like for you to head upstairs and ensure Captain Bartlett learns of the rumors you shared with me. Tell him I am on the trail of a missing girl, Annabelle Carter, and that I am pursuing all leads. Can you do that?"

"You want me to go to Captain Bartlett himself?"

"Yes. Try not to make me repeat myself."

The crewman muttered words of acknowledgment before vanishing into the darkness. Soon, we were quite alone, standing in the middle of a section full of passengers' belongings. Suitcases and boxes surrounded us on all sides. It was difficult to spy what was up ahead of Mr. Harlowe, but to his right, a trunk had been thrown open, its contents bared for the world to see.

"What do you suppose happened here?" Emily asked.

"I do not yet know. These—these are Marvin's things," Mr. Harlowe said with a slight stutter. "I'd recognize his trunk anywhere."

As he bent to examine the luggage, something caught my eye. A scrap of fabric protruded from beneath a nearby crate. I let go of Emily, crouched down, and pulled it free. It looked like part of an old British uniform.

"Mr. Harlowe?" I asked, holding up my find. "Was this Lieutenant Morgan's as well?"

Mr. Harlowe frowned as he took the crumpled fragment from me. He slid his flashlight under his elbow, held the garment up, and tapped a faded insignia on the sleeve. "Yes. This patch is from our—his old unit."

"Sir? Why isn't this with the rest of his things?" Emily asked. Her brow was furrowed; she must have picked up on Mr. Harlowe's slip of the tongue, too. "Shouldn't it have been in his trunk?"

"You need to be more observant, Miss Wentworth." Mr. Harlowe folded the tattered shirt up and reclaimed his light, sweeping its beam across the floor in a wide arc.

I gasped.

It looked as if Lieutenant Morgan's entire life had been thrown out onto the cold metal. Certainly, the majority of his earthy possessions had been. A silver pocket watch caught our flashlight's beam, its face cracked and hands frozen at 2:20. Boots caked with mud lay alongside socks rolled up in balls. There were other effects too, both personal and utilitarian, all tossed about the same way. It was a mess.

Scattered photographs crunched under our feet as we moved closer. I bent down to pick one up, brushing off the dust. It showed a younger Lieutenant Morgan, beaming, his arm around a pretty woman hardly older than me.

"His wife, Clara." Mr. Harlowe peered over my shoulder. "She passed in 1905."

I took another look at the two people in the photograph. They seemed happy. "I didn't know he was married."

"For a few years, yes."

As we stood there, surrounded by the scattered remnants of Lieutenant Morgan's life, the shadows pressed in closer. The sense of violation was palpable—not just of Lieutenant Morgan's privacy, although that was pervasive, but a violation of something deeper, something more primal. Despite every shred of logic I had screaming that it could not be so, I felt as if I was being watched, observed by something that sent a chill down my spine. It was the same way I'd felt throughout our conversation with Mr. Clarke in the library.

All was not well in this place.

"Do you think whoever did this is responsible for Annabelle's disappearance?" Emily asked.

"It is likely," Mr. Harlowe replied. "Disregarding whatever else happened here, someone was looking for the artifacts Lieutenant Morgan was smuggling. And no specter did anything of the sort, of that I can assure you. Our quarry is a man."

A gust of cold air swept through the hold, extinguishing Mr. Harlowe's flashlight. In the pitch darkness, I heard Emily gasp and felt her press against me. For a moment, the only sound was our strained breathing.

Then came a whisper. One so faint I thought I might have imagined it. *"Get out..."*

"Annabelle?" Emily whispered.

Mr. Harlowe's flashlight flickered back to life, revealing his tense face. "Did you hear that?" he demanded.

We nodded, but as we looked around, there was no sign of Annabelle or anyone else. The shadows were more agitated than ever, reaching out with inky fingers that always retreated just before touching us. A rending sound—the heavy *whoosh, whoosh* of enormous wings—echoed from the air above. From somewhere beyond the crates arose a clattering of hooves, stomping and marching through the hold. Just when things seemed at their strangest, the lights overhead snapped back on, flooding the cargo hold with steady light. The wingbeat ceased. The clattering vanished.

"W—What was that?" I stammered.

Emily had my hand gripped tighter than a vise.

Mr. Harlowe took a deep breath. "Nothing. A trick of the storm."

"Do storms have wings?" Emily asked incredulously.

"The brain seeks out patterns, Miss Wentworth, even where there are none to find."

Emily gaped at him. "You cannot seriously believe that."

"I do not have a choice!" he snapped. "What would you have me do? Arrest a ghost? Cease this talk and help me search. We will have more luck with the lights on."

By mutual, unspoken agreement, we didn't push Mr. Harlowe to continue to discuss what we'd just witnessed. There would be time for that later. The master-at-arms directed us to fan out and examine every nook and cranny between the towering stacks of crates and trunks. We called Annabelle's name, our voices echoing in the cavernous space, but we received no response.

Emily focused on smaller hiding spots, peering behind boxes and into barrels. I helped Mr. Harlowe move some of the lighter crates, hoping to uncover a clue that could help us in our search. He was trying not to show it, but I could tell that he was unnerved. His hands were shaking, more so with each new shred of Lieutenant Morgan's life that our search uncovered. I realized then that Mr. Clarke had been right about one thing—Mr. Harlowe had known Marvin Morgan. Known him well, even. He was too affected by this search for that not to be so.

We combed through row after row of cargo, our hopes diminishing with each void we uncovered. The hold stretched on endlessly, a labyrinth of goods bound for distant shores. There was an infinite amount of material here. But no trace of Annabelle or the person who had searched Lieutenant Morgan's things.

After what felt like hours of fruitless searching, Mr. Harlowe admitted defeat. "We need to regroup with the others," he said, removing his hat and wiping grease and dirt from his brow. "We're missing something."

I stuffed my hands into my pockets. I was a bit surprised to remember that they weren't empty; the crumpled paper I'd taken from Mr. Blackstone was still there. Wearily, I drew it out, reading the words upon it once more: *Potato Sack*.

Perhaps it was because my father had been on my mind earlier. Perhaps it was just that potatoes made me think of the farm. Whatever the reason, my thoughts again drifted to my childhood. I remembered how hard my father had worked for our family. I remembered how strong and calloused his hands were. And I remembered the dirty vegetables he'd taken so much pride in harvesting. *There was something to this note. There had to be.*

"Sir," I ventured. "Are you sure there aren't any potato sacks here?"

The look Mr. Harlowe gave me could have killed me on the spot. "We will not be wasting time on a madman's ravings," he hissed. "It is time to return to the upper decks and locate Captain Bartlett."

I was sure there was a clue in Mr. Blackstone's cryptic last words, but I didn't know how to convince Mr. Harlowe of that. He spun on his heels and charged away before I could formulate a good response. I glanced at Emily; she shrugged sympathetically. We took off after Mr. Harlowe. Despite the bright overhead lights, a palpable sense of unease festered in each shadowy corner we passed. By the time we reached the central corridor off of the engine room, we were all on edge. It was the worst for Mr. Harlowe. With each step we took, his previously unflappable demeanor slipped further into malaise.

"I cannot help but feel as if we are the last crewmen on the *Demeter*," Emily whispered. "I still hesitate to believe in such strange tidings, but..." she trailed off, her pretty face scrunched up with an uneasy sort of thoughtful malcontent.

That was a rare literary reference I did recognize, though I had no idea how to properly respond to it, nor any words to quell Emily's fear. The entire crew of the ill-fated *Demeter* had been slaughtered to sustain an unholy monster. *Were we, too, ferrying a cargo akin to the Count's coffin? Were the Sundered Wings truly so dangerous?*

I shivered. It was unsettling to think that the events of our voyage called for Emily to reference *Dracula*.

We'd undeniably stirred up something in the cargo hold.

Something that wasn't going to let us go easily. The phantom creatures might have stayed behind, but the sense of being followed lingered, even in the brightly lit corridor. It didn't help that engineers and crewmen were crawling out of what seemed like every open door. Their raised voices and shouted questions were like fuel on a raging fire.

When people called out to Mr. Harlowe, he ignored them. The master-at-arms had developed tunnel vision. He was determined to find Captain Bartlett.

I saw several familiar faces on our march. Alex, the steward, joined our number; Emily began catching him up on what we'd found. When we passed by an especially strong, bearded man, I had a burst of realization. Potatoes! *I knew what potato sack meant!* Hadn't I seen this same man carrying a sack of potatoes only a few hours ago?

"Mr. Harlowe!" I cried. "Wait!"

To my surprise, he stopped. He turned his head just enough to glance at me. "Yes?"

"I have an idea!" I broke ranks and jogged back to the burly crewman, who was eyeing me warily. "Excuse me, sir?" I asked. "Did I see you with a sack of potatoes earlier?"

Mr. Harlowe groaned. I ignored him.

"Aye," the man grunted. "They called for 'em up in the galley."

"But where did they come from? Where did you find them?"

"The potatoes?" The man raised a hairy forearm and jerked his thumb back over his shoulder. "Storage room. That's where they keep all of 'em. Sacks and sacks, you know 'ow it is."

This information was all Mr. Harlowe needed to change his mind about my hunch. He sprang into action and shoved his way around the muscular sailor, who watched bewilderedly as the master-at-arms fought through the assembled crowd. I reached the storage room door just behind Mr. Harlowe. It was closed, tucked behind an already-open collapsible gate.

"This is it," I said, my hand already on the knob. "Are you with me, sir?"

Mr. Harlowe drew his revolver. "Yes. Let me go in first."

When I opened the door, Mr. Harlowe rushed through the gap, his weapon at the ready. I went in just after him. Emily was behind me.

This storage room was the most bizarre place I'd yet seen on the *Olympic*. Rows of potato sacks reached the ceiling. There were hundreds of them, enough to form a veritable maze of burlap. As my eyes adjusted to the lighting, I realized this must be some kind of pantry, for there was no other explanation that could justify this trove of tubers.

"We should spread out," I suggested. "If this room is the place Mr. Blackstone was trying to tell us about, we need to check everywhere."

"Be careful, avoid taking risks, and call for me if you see any sign of something amiss," advised Mr. Harlowe.

After exchanging one last look, we fanned out, each of us taking a different path into the spuds. It was slow going. The room wasn't especially large, but I made sure to keep an eye on Emily; I didn't want to lose sight of her in this place.

I heard a faint rustling.

"Hello?"

No response. Emily looked over at me, and I pointed to the place where I'd heard the sound. Together, we moved toward the noise, creeping along the maze, until... there she was. Annabelle, slumped against the wall, her wrists tied together with rope and a filthy potato sack crumpled over her head. The tips of her braided hair poked out from under its fraying edge.

"Annabelle!" I exclaimed. I ripped the sack away and pulled a gag from her mouth. "Annabelle, are you hurt?"

She shook her head. Tremors traveled up and down her arms, which were chilly to the touch. I helped her to her feet, shrugged my jacket off, and wrapped it around her shoulders. Emily began working on the ropes binding her hands.

"Thank you," Annabelle croaked. Tears sparkled in her eyes. "I thought... I thought I was going to die."

Mr. Harlowe held his revolver at the ready. "Who did this, girl? Was it Blackstone?"

She hiccupped. "No. Mr. Blackstone tried to save me!"

"He tried to save you?" Emily asked incredulously.

Annabelle nodded. "That's—that's not all. He told me Marvin Morgan failed, and everyone on this ship is in danger!"

15
FACING JUDGMENT

Annabelle's pronouncement stunned us all into silence. Perhaps most concerningly, it appeared to leave Mr. Harlowe uncertain about how to proceed. The master-at-arms always looked downcast, but he looked even more so now, with his shoulders slumped and his head bowed in thought. It was as if the latest mention of Lieutenant Morgan had sapped the rest of the fight out of him.

Seconds ticked by, yet he made no move to take charge.

"Um. Mr. Harlowe?" I asked. "Are—are you quite well?"

He turned and looked at me with haunted eyes. I'd never seen a man who stood well over six feet tall look small, but Mr. Harlowe was managing it. Despite the tenacity he'd shown up to this point, he now looked more vulnerable than imposing, even with his revolver drawn.

Emily and I exchanged a glance. She shook her head. For her part, Annabelle was now sobbing, quivering in my suit jacket in the center of the room. Emily took her from me, whispered soothing words, and wrapped her in a hug. I tried to back away, to give them space, but I bumped into a sack of potatoes and sent several of them tumbling to the floor. The dull thuds startled Mr. Harlowe more than my words had done. He twitched, and for a moment, I worried he might accidentally discharge his weapon.

"Sir, we need your help," I said, trying again to get through to Mr. Harlowe. "We're all a bit shaken, but Annabelle needs you. We don't know what to do next."

My words didn't seem to make much of an impact. To make matters worse, the crowd of engineers, crewmembers, and steerage passengers outside the door swelled as more curious people joined it. Their voices built into a low, rumbling chorus, not at all dissimilar to the thunder booming outside. Soon, the noise was overwhelming, a horrid combination of chatter, gasps, and exclamations that pressed in from all sides. It was more suffocating than the song of summer cicadas.

The crowd pressed around the door, each trying to be the next to glimpse Annabelle, Mr. Harlowe, Emily, Alex, or me. The pressure of so many bodies threatened to crush us. We were seconds from being swarmed when two workers from the galley peeked in a back entrance, unaware that a crime had been committed in their strange potato room.

"I say," one of them exclaimed. "What are you all doing in here?"

"That's the master-at-arms!" replied the other. "We've gotta show him some respect, don't we? We can't just go asking that sort of question!"

"Well, he doesn't seem all that with it now, does he? Looks as if he's seen a—"

"Mr. Harlowe," a stern voice interrupted, sending the cooks scurrying away. "What the devil is going on here?"

I'd never been so happy to see Captain Bartlett. He was soaking wet, drenched from his hat to his boots, as if he'd swam down to E-deck from the bridge. Usually an affable man, there was no trace of humor on his weary facade, no hint of a smile on his weather-beaten face.

Mr. Harlowe stared at him. For a moment, the master-at-arms struggled to answer. His breathing grew shallow. It was like he was far away, no longer present in the room.

"Mr. Harlowe," Captain Bartlett repeated, more softly this time. "Are you alright, son? You're on the *Olympic*. You're safe. Breathe. There's a good lad."

Mr. Harlowe blinked, closed his eyes, and took a deep breath as he fought to regain control. "Sorry, sir. It won't happen again. But there's—you need to know that there's been another killing. The victim was one of the suspects I was pursuing from the smuggling ring, Reginald Blackstone. His body is locked up in the engineers' quarters."

"Good Lord. I met your man on the way down, but he made no mention of that. What happened to him?"

"The same as what happened to Theodore Eckert, I would wager. I didn't stay to document things. We had a lead on a suspect. As that lead could have led to the whereabouts of Miss Annabelle Carter, I elected to pursue it. We found her bound and gagged in this room."

"I'll send Dr. Widmer down to confirm the time of death," promised Captain Bartlett. He turned to look at Emily and me, then over to Annabelle. "What scoundrel is responsible for this, Miss Carter?"

"I... I don't know, sir. I didn't see his face."

"Do you need to see the doctor?"

Annabelle shook her head. "No. I want to stay with Emily and James."

Captain Bartlett paused. "Very well," he said, after taking a moment to gather his thoughts. "In that case, I would like all of you to accompany me to the bridge. It may be unorthodox, but we can debrief in the officers' smoking room. We will not be interrupted there."

"Even me, sir?" Alex asked.

"Yes, lad. Even you. Mr. Harlowe, would you be so kind as to lead the way?"

Mr. Harlowe holstered his revolver and motioned for us to follow. The crowd of engineers and crew parted as we moved, their curious whispers following us as we worked our way down the long hallway. Captain Bartlett wrapped a protective arm around Annabelle to guide her firmly away from the onlookers. He stopped only once to murmur instructions to a tall, bearded man I thought might be the chief engineer.

"Take the long way, Mr. Harlowe," Captain Bartlett said after he dispatched the bearded man down to the engine room. "I would prefer not to risk the promenade again."

"Of course, sir."

Walking together, we turned heads and invited comments from those we passed. The steerage passengers did double takes. Some of them raised their eyebrows. Others nudged their companions and whispered behind calloused hands. It wasn't every day that Captain Bartlett walked this corridor. A few crew members offered respectful nods to him, their eyebrows rising when they glanced at the rest of us. We were a mismatched bunch.

Emily grabbed my hand, her gloved fingers curling around mine with surprising firmness. I felt a rush of warmth. The fabric of my shirt became uncomfortable around my neck. It was one thing for us to comfort each other privately on deck, or in the cargo hold, but this step was too bold, no matter how much I wanted our relationship to progress. We could not be seen in public holding hands. Contact like this was not acceptable. People would talk.

Before I could protest, she leaned in close and whispered, "Be quiet, James. Let them judge. I need this right now, and I'll worry about what people think later."

"I wasn't going to say anything," I lied.

As we continued our walk, I noticed a shift in the glances from the passersby. What had before been mild curiosity now felt more like scrutiny. It might have been my imagination, but the ladies began whispering just a bit more furiously when they eyed Emily's hand in mine. The gentlemen frowned, shaking their heads in disapproval. Once respectful nods from crew members transformed into looks of surprise and judgment.

If that wasn't bad enough, our pace was agonizingly slow. The storm's fury still battered the ship from outside, requiring us to stop and brace ourselves every time the mighty liner pitched and rolled in response to the unrelenting swells of the Atlantic. It felt like hours passed, though it was likely only minutes before we reached the familiar landing on D-deck.

At last, after everything, we were back in second class.

"Emily! James! Over here!" It was Oliver, accompanied by Eli Carter. Eli's hair was frazzled; it looked as if he'd been running his hands through it ever since we'd left. At the sight of Annabelle, he let out a cry of relief. Tears of joy streamed down his face.

Oliver's attention, however, was on Emily's hand in mine. A troubled look replaced his initial happiness at our reunion. Emily's grip faltered for a moment, and I let go, the sudden absence of her hand leaving mine cold.

"Eli!" cried Annabelle. She broke free from Captain Bartlett's hold.

"Annabelle! Thank God you're alright!" Eli rushed forward

to meet her, wrapping his arms around his sister in a tight embrace. "I thought I'd lost you. I was so worried!"

Captain Bartlett cleared his throat. "We need to keep moving," he said firmly. "Mr. Carter, Mr. Wentworth, you may come with us. It is time to discuss what has been happening on my ship."

Eli, who kept one arm wrapped around Annabelle, nodded. Oliver took longer to respond. He stood rooted to the spot, looking back and forth between Emily and me. An uncharacteristic frown marred his handsome features. Emily squared her shoulders and walked right by her brother, but I held Oliver's gaze. We looked at each other for several long seconds. Finally, after an eternity, he snapped off a sharp nod to signal his agreement with Captain Bartlett's suggestion.

And so it was that we were once again setting off, heading for the bridge. This time, though, Emily and I stayed apart. She stuck close to Annabelle and Eli, whereas I fell back to walk with Alex Cunningham, who was bringing up the rear. Getting to the bridge required passing through the same nondescript door into first class we'd taken the day before. Dressed in their evening finery, passengers turned to stare as our disheveled group passed by, but a single stern look from Mr. Harlowe kept them at bay.

We went further forward on this trip than we did the last time we'd entered first class. I thought I'd seen luxury the first time, but that was before I ascended the *Olympic's* most magnificent feature: the forward Grand Staircase. Dignified oak paneling covered the walls, and as I ran my hand along the railing, I felt the skill behind its intricate scrollwork. It was adorned with delicate bronze flowers and twisting iron foliage.

A great flash of lightning lit up the dome above us. It illuminated the stairway's centerpiece. This magnificent carving, which depicted two female figures holding up a clock, showed an hour I thought was impossibly late. We'd missed dinner! Dr. and Mrs. Wentworth would be worried sick by now. The sight was so disconcerting that I almost missed it when Captain Bartlett unlocked a side passage that led to the bridge.

Beyond the door was a much more utilitarian space. Gone were the finished walls and immaculate floors of first class; they were replaced by white paint and practical features more reminiscent of what we'd seen down near the engine room, though this hallway was much narrower. The ceilings were bare, with rivets and steel plating exposed for all to see, and the floors were of the same red and white linoleum pattern that adorned much of second class. Once we were through, Mr. Harlowe stepped aside, allowing Captain Bartlett to lead the way. The captain passed a few more doors, turned to his left, and knocked before opening one of them.

"Make yourselves comfortable," he said.

Easier said than done. I was taken aback by the lingering odor of cigar smoke, so much so that I needed to stifle a sneeze. It came out like a strangled cough. I heard Oliver snort, but when I turned to face him, he looked away.

Sighing, I took stock of our surroundings. The officers' smoking room reminded me a bit of one Oliver and I had visited back in Paris. It was all dark paneling, vintage paintings, and oaken furniture. One of those styles that never seems to fall out of favor. The table in the center of the room bore many circular, cup-shaped stains, enough that I knew this must have been a popular meeting place for the crew.

Surrounding that table were a few leather chairs. Their green upholstery creaked as we chose our seats and settled in. Oliver elected to take the one beside mine, though he was still steadfastly avoiding eye contact. An outside observer might have thought us strangers.

That bothered me more than I wished to admit.

Against another wall was a couch, well-worn and dark, though fitted with brass studs that glinted in the lamplight. Emily sat there. She perched close to one end, legs curled up beneath her, and offered comfort to Annabelle, who sat beside her, still wrapped up in my suit jacket. Eli sat ramrod straight at the far end of the couch. It looked to me as if he was doing all he could to maintain his composure.

Near the couch stood an elegant roll-top writing desk. Its surface was cluttered with navigational instruments, maps, and a solitary brass lamp with a green glass shade. Alex stood near it. He seemed like he was doing his best to stay apart from the rest of the group.

Now that we were seated, Captain Bartlett moved aside to welcome two stewards, who entered the room with trays balanced in their hands. They exchanged a brief, confused glance, clearly unprepared to see so many unfamiliar faces. I couldn't blame them.

Regardless of their shock, they got to work offering us refreshments and hors d'oeuvres. The moment their duties were completed, Mr. Harlowe ushered them out and closed the door behind them.

"Well, then." Captain Bartlett cleared his throat. "I believe it is time to address the matter at hand. What is happening on my ship?"

"It is best to begin at the start, I think." Mr. Harlowe stepped away from the door, strategically positioning himself so he could see everyone and watch both entrances. "Captain, you know that I have been investigating a smuggling ring ever since I was transferred to the *Olympic*. The so-called Sphinx Society."

"I heard Mr. Blackstone mention that!" I exclaimed. "He was arguing with Mr. Haverford when he brought it up. He was a part of it, wasn't he?"

"I..." Mr. Harlowe glanced at Captain Bartlett.

"You may as well tell them, William. They are involved now, whether or not we want them to be."

"Very well. I suppose it is time they learn the truth."

16
MR. HARLOWE'S TALE

"What I am about to say cannot leave this room. Is that clear?"

I nodded my assent. So did the others. Nobody spoke, though I could sense their anticipation building. Emily leaned in closer to Mr. Harlowe. Oliver tried to look nonchalant by playing with his lighter, but he, too, sat up a little straighter.

"I am currently assigned to work with the White Star Line as part of a special arrangement with the Metropolitan Police," Mr. Harlowe said. "I am investigating the individuals behind a recent surge in smuggled artifacts. An unbelievable number of stolen pieces have made their way to New York from Southampton and Cherbourg in the last twelve months. All orchestrated by a group of men who identify themselves with a self-aggrandizing moniker: 'The Sphinx Society.'"

Oliver whistled, his feigned disinterest already forgotten. "How did you get assigned to something like that? Does the rest of the crew know?"

"Until now, the only one who knew was Captain Bartlett," Mr. Harlowe said. "As for how I found my way to the Met, I was recruited directly after my time in the Boer War concluded."

I asked the question that had been eating at me since our time in the cargo hold. "Mr. Harlowe, did you know Lieutenant Morgan?"

The tall man sighed, picked up his glass, and drained his water. "Yes, I did. Marvin and I served together in South Africa," he answered in a faraway voice. "I knew him well. I even introduced him to his wife, Clara. But our time in the Boer War was... difficult. I prefer not to talk about Black Week. It left me... well, you've seen how it affects me." He paused. "I saw a lot of depraved things in that place. But Marvin was one of the good ones—a decent man. He saved my life, and I his. Such was the way of it, then."

"He sounds like he was a good friend," I said.

Mr. Harlowe shrugged. "There was no other man I would have preferred to have on my side. I imagine I did not feel much differently about him than you do about Mr. Wentworth."

Oliver doggedly avoided my attempt to catch his eye.

I probably deserved it.

"You believe Lieutenant Morgan was involved, though?" Emily asked. "In the smuggling ring, I mean. A part of us hoped we could prove him innocent and clear his name."

"The evidence is incontrovertible," lamented Mr. Harlowe. "Marvin accrued substantial debts caring for Clara, then got wrapped up with Theodore Eckert while trying to resolve them. Eckert set him up with the others in the Sphinx Society. I do not wish to speak ill of the dead, but Eckert was a most unpleasant man to cross. The world is a better place with him out of it."

"Who else is a member?' Oliver asked.

"The only names I can supply you with confidence are Eckert, Morgan, and Blackstone," Mr. Harlowe answered. He glanced at Captain Bartlett. "Any other suspects I have are just that—suspects."

Oliver frowned. "That won't do. What about the others, what about—"

"I would rather not say more names at this time."

I moved to speak, but Captain Bartlett cleared his throat to stop me. "Mr. Harlowe's integrity in this matter is not to be questioned. He has been invaluable to this investigation, and his unique insights are the reason we have been able to piece together as much as we have. Suffice it to say, with these recent deaths, it is clear the stakes have been raised. Do you have anything else to add, Mr. Harlowe?"

"I do. I have come to believe that a German agent has been dispatched to recover the artifacts Marvin brought on board. While there remains a possibility that these recent events stem from an internal betrayal within the ring, my growing suspicion is that the Sphinx Society is facing an external assault."

"We encountered a man we think is German while we were investigating." I was hesitant to admit where we'd been snooping when he'd cornered us. "He showed up when we were getting close to a clue about the artifacts. We never saw his face."

Mr. Harlowe nodded thoughtfully. "Intriguing, but not immediately actionable. Do you have any idea what it was he was looking for?"

At that, Oliver perked up. "I do. Blackstone—Mr. Blackstone, I mean—he told us a story that might help you understand why Lieutenant Morgan did what he did and what the German man is after. He said Lieutenant Morgan found these ancient Egyptian artifacts called the 'Wings of Amun-Ra.' He was smuggling them to the U.S., but he died before he could get them there. Supposedly, they're cursed—incredibly powerful, of course. But cursed."

Emily sighed. "I found Mr. Blackstone's tale to be patently absurd. I wish I still did. But we have seen things—things that are difficult to explain. Unnatural things. The cargo hold was... strange."

"It advantages our adversary if we chase such leads," Captain Bartlett said. "It is Mr. Harlowe's belief—and mine—that the killer is deliberately arranging evidence to make it appear as if these killings have a supernatural cause. I have been at sea for a long time, my friends; sailors are a superstitious lot."

"We didn't imagine what we saw in the cargo hold, sir," I said.

"I do not mean to insinuate that you did. But you may not have seen what you thought you saw. You were under an extreme amount of stress, were you not?"

"How do you explain the bodies of Theodore Eckert and Mr. Blackstone?" I asked, ignoring his last prompt.

Oliver gasped. "Mr. Blackstone is dead?" He turned to Emily, who nodded in confirmation.

Captain Bartlett was frowning now. "Ah, yes. Dr. Widmer is rather at a loss with the Eckert case. He has elected to keep the body in an infectious disease room, but he does not believe the threat is communicable at this time. I am hopeful a natural explanation will be uncovered in due course."

"Mr. Harlowe?" Emily asked. "What do you think?"

Mr. Harlowe sighed. "I do not know what to think. I believe it best if we set aside such things for now and focus on what we can prove." He turned to face Oliver. "Son, you mentioned that Reginald Blackstone discussed the Sundered Wings with you. Anything you know might help me in my search. Can you describe them?"

"Oh. Well, yes, I can try. Mr. Blackstone told us that one of the artifacts, I forget which one, brings hope and sunshine. The other one brings storms and destruction. He seemed to think they were a tempting enough prize for dangerous people to go after them."

Mr. Blackstone's last words resurfaced in my mind. "He said something strange just before he died," I added as Oliver looked away. "Mr. Blackstone said, 'He found them... this storm is proof.' I think he was talking about the Sundered Wings."

Annabelle, who had been resting against Emily until now, scooted away and rubbed her eyes. "Mr. Blackstone talked about that with me, too," she whispered. "He thought that the storm we're sailing through was spun up by the power of Amun-Ra."

"Balderdash," Mr. Harlowe muttered. He scoffed defensively when he realized we'd all heard him. "What? I respect that you believe what you have been told, young lady, but..."

Captain Bartlett raised his hand, and Mr. Harlowe fell silent. "I think what Mr. Harlowe means to say is that the time has come for you to tell us about what happened to you, Miss Carter. I apologize for allowing you to wait for so long. I know you have been through an ordeal."

"I'll be fine, sir." Annabelle took a deep breath and began to tell her tale. "It's embarrassing, but I was surprised and grabbed from behind. I didn't see who it was. They whispered something, I think in German, before they held a cloth up to my face. I passed out. When I woke up, my hands were tied up and I had a bag over my head. I didn't know where I was. I didn't even know if anyone knew I was missing." She shivered, rubbing her wrists where the ropes had chafed her skin.

"German?" Mr. Harlowe interrupted, perking up at this piece of information. "This kidnapper must be the same man the crew heard shouting in the engine room and the cargo hold. The one I've been searching for. It is concerning that our enemy could get so close to vital machinery."

Captain Bartlett looked troubled. "Indeed. We must double our shifts."

Mr. Harlowe uncrossed his arms and began to pace. "Tracking down the rest of the Sphinx Society has become even more imperative. We cannot let the assailant get to them before we do. If you would permit me to interrogate—"

"We have had this discussion already, Mr. Harlowe, and you do not have the evidence to make that accusation," warned Captain Bartlett. "Not when he has the weight of a lord behind him. Don't think I didn't hear about your little stunt at this morning's church service."

Mr. Harlowe frowned, but he didn't retort. He raised his arms in surrender before turning back to Annabelle. "Please continue, Miss Carter. My apologies for the interruption."

I couldn't help but wonder what name Mr. Harlowe had been about to say. *Was it Haverford? Or did he have another link to the Sphinx Society he was keeping to himself?*

Annabelle sniffed. "Well, I wasn't there very long when Mr. Blackstone found me. It wasn't me he was looking for, though; he believed some treasure was hidden there. When he saw me, he wanted to help me, but..." Her voice faltered, and she glanced at her brother for support. He gave her an encouraging nod, and she continued, "But he didn't have any time. Someone came in after him. He told me to stay quiet and that he would lead the attacker away. That help would come. He saved my life by doing that."

"Did he say anything else? Anything about who might be behind this?"

"He wanted me to tell someone that one of the Sundered Wings had been found and that we were all in danger. That Lieutenant Morgan had tried to hide them, but he messed it up. I didn't understand what he meant before, but now..."

"Why you?" interrupted Mr. Harlowe.

"Sorry?"

Mr. Harlowe cleared his throat. "My apologies for interrupting once again, but why did our German friend come after you? Forgive me, but Mr. Clarke would have been a far better target based on my understanding of this unsanctioned investigation. Or even one of the Wentworths."

"That's my fault, sir," mumbled Eli. "She wasn't involved in this mess. I was. I obtained some information I should not have. Dangerous information. I shared it with the Wentworths. The German must have learned of that, somehow."

Immediately, Oliver, Emily, and I protested, our voices coalescing into a maelstrom of denial.

"One at a time, please," Captain Bartlett insisted.

"Eli is a photographer," I said, doing my best to take control of the conversation. "He captured some incriminating evidence. Nothing identifiable, but enough to help lead us in the right direction. The killer must have found out about it."

"Our foe was trying to get us to give up the chase," Oliver added. "He must have thought threatening Eli would do the job."

Eli had become very still. I jumped in again, knowing I could say more to assuage his guilt. "Eli was just trying to share his pictures with us. We dragged him into this mess."

Emily nodded. "The fault lies with us. He isn't to blame."

"The fault lies with our mysterious enemy," Mr. Harlowe corrected. "But thank you. That clarifies things for me. Mr. Carter, I would be grateful if I could look at those photographs."

"I have them, sir," Emily said. "In fact, I have several things that might aid you in your search. I'll get them to you first thing in the morning."

"That would be appreciated, Miss Wentworth."

"Is there anything else?" Captain Bartlett asked. When none of us answered, he launched into his plan. "Thank you. Mr. Harlowe, I do not need to tell you that your next steps are crucial. Continue your investigation with the utmost discretion. If you are right, your suspect may make a move during tomorrow night's second-class concert. I have my reservations, but you have my permission to take them into custody if they do."

"Understood, sir. Thank you."

Next, he turned to the rest of us. "Listen carefully, all of you. It is too late to keep you out of this investigation, but your safety is my priority. Until we have this situation under control, no one travels alone. Stay together, and if you see or hear anything suspicious, report it to me or Master-at-Arms Harlowe immediately. Is that clear?"

A chorus of agreements filled the room.

Captain Bartlett gave a final nod. "Good. You are not officers on this ship, and you would do well to remember that." The captain turned to Alex, who had been silent throughout the meeting. "Young man, I need you to escort Miss Carter and the others back to their quarters. Make sure they get there safely."

Alex straightened up and nodded. "Yes, Captain."

The meeting was adjourned. The Wentworths and I followed Alex out of the room, but Mr. Harlowe elected to stay behind to talk with Captain Bartlett. His hand still rested on his revolver.

As soon as we were out of earshot and descending that magnificent staircase in first class again, Oliver began to wonder aloud. "What could be so important about the concert?" he mused. "Why would Harlowe's suspect choose that moment to make a move?"

I was so happy he was talking to me again that I speculated with him. "It's a public event with a lot of people—almost the entirety of second class. It'll provide cover for whatever they're planning."

"James is right. In addition, if this storm keeps up, the crew's attention will be divided between the concert and the weather," Emily said. "It's the perfect distraction."

Eli, still holding his sister close, frowned. "You need to be careful. I almost lost Annabelle today. It could be any one of you next."

None of us knew what to say to that.

It didn't take long to reach the familiar corridor outside the second-class dining saloon. From there, it was only a matter of moments before we reached Emily's stateroom.

Alex paused outside the door. "This is where we part ways, Miss Wentworth."

"Thank you, Mr. Cunningham." Emily squeezed Annabelle's hand before stepping around her and nodding to Alex. The steward knocked. There was some shuffling, and Mrs. Wentworth opened the door, her thin face lined with worry.

"Emily!" Mrs. Wentworth exclaimed. She pulled her daughter into as tight an embrace as her condition allowed. "I have been so worried! Last I heard, you were looking for Annabelle, but, dear, so much time has passed! Oh, and Oliver, you're safe as well! Thank goodness. Your father said not to worry, but..."

Oliver flushed, but I thought it was with pleasure rather than embarrassment. He was grinning at his mother.

Emily returned the hug. "We found her, Mother. Everything's fine now, thanks to James and Captain Bartlett."

"Of course, dear. Please, come in and get comfortable. I shall send for a warm towel. Are you sure you are quite well?"

"Yes, mother. I'm sure." Emily flashed us one last smile before disappearing into the stateroom. Her mother's concerned questioning followed her inside.

Oliver and I were next to reach our stateroom. Alex paused with one hand on the doorknob. Lightning shone through the porthole, highlighting his freckles. "Stay together and lock your door," he instructed. "If you need anything, send for me or Mr. Harlowe. Don't take any unnecessary risks."

"We'll be careful, Mr. Cunningham," I promised. Almost as an afterthought, but not ungratefully, I added a quick parting line. "Thank you for your help today. We couldn't have saved Annabelle without you."

"Of course, sirs. I'll see you in the morning." Alex let us file into the room before he closed the door behind us.

Now free from the presence of the others, Oliver slumped onto his bed, running a hand through his hair. Keen to give him some space, I walked over to our porthole, pressed my hand against the cool glass, and took a moment to watch the turbulent sea. As I stared out into the vast expanse of the ocean, rolling thunder echoing overhead, I found myself believing Mr. Blackstone's claim that this storm wasn't natural.

There was a weird sort of power in it. A pressure I couldn't explain.

I turned away from it to see that Oliver had recovered himself. He was sitting straight up and looking more serious than I'd ever seen him. When he spoke, it was with intensity.

"We need to talk about Emily."

17
DEADLINE

"We need to talk about Emily," Oliver repeated.

"I suppose we do." I sank onto the couch opposite Oliver, who was perched on the edge of his bed. "You want to know why we were holding hands, I imagine?"

Oliver grimaced. "Among other things. You knew this was coming, Jimmy."

"I suppose I should have known it was."

My friend glanced around our cramped stateroom. Then, he abruptly stood and crossed over to the washbasin. His lighter, never far from his hands these days, glinted in his reflection. He took a drink, started to speak, and then stopped. He ran a hand through his chestnut hair. "I can't—I need—" He took a deep breath. "Fancy a trip to the smoking room?"

"What?"

"The smoking room, Jimmy. The room where people go to smoke."

"I know what the smoking room is. Is that safe? With a murderer on the loose?"

Oliver chuckled. "Perhaps not, but I'm going to need a stronger drink than water for this conversation. It doesn't suit me to be the voice of reason."

I looked up at him and saw a hint of something somber in his expression. Hurt, perhaps, or was it something worse? Betrayal? He wasn't giving it away, but I knew what I'd seen. My chest tightened. I wanted to explain myself, but no words came. Everything I thought to say felt hollow.

On second thought, perhaps his suggestion to move to the smoking room wasn't so crazy after all.

"Sure, Ollie. We can go. All Mr. Harlowe said was not to venture out alone. We aren't alone."

He offered me a hand to stand up. "Don't fret. I'll keep you safe."

I took it. "I'm more worried about the poor man who tries to attack us with you on the job."

"Too right."

We left our stateroom, closing the door behind us. The hallway was empty. Often, there would be a steward close by. Not this evening.

"Which way do you want to go?" Oliver asked. He glanced hesitantly at the nearby aft staircase.

"Let's take the forward stairs. I don't fancy trying our chances out on deck."

"Fine by me. I've heard they're turning people back, anyway. Captain Bartlett is worried we'll get swept overboard."

"He's probably right. Here, after you."

I held the nearest door open, and we stepped through it into the quiet dining saloon. The glasses and cutlery already set out for breakfast shone eerily in the semi-darkness. It was silent, save for our footsteps. The atmosphere was so still that I could have sworn I caught a faint hint of last night's dinner lingering in the air.

I wondered for a moment if I might see more strange shadows here, but none came. Everything was exactly as it should have been. There was an exit at the back of the saloon that led to the same companionway I'd used to chase Mr. Blackstone. We took it, making our way up to the smoking room via the winding stairs, neither of us speaking much along the way. It was like that until we passed by a pair of stewardesses. They were the first sign of life we'd seen on our late-night walk.

"I told him I wouldn't venture down there alone," one of them was saying. "No cutlery is worth risking our lives!"

The other nodded vigorously. "I told Alexander Cunningham the same thing. This ship isn't safe!"

"Did you know they found another man dead?"

"Dreadful business. And that nasty Harlowe fellow was there—you know, our new master-at-arms? The Swede staying on D-deck is convinced he's the one." She lowered her voice. "The killer."

Her friend hummed in agreement. "Well, I've heard that journalist has gone and gotten himself injured. Won't let the doctor tend to him, either..."

Their voices faded away as they headed down to a lower deck. If Oliver had a comment to make about what we'd just overheard, he held it close to the vest. I didn't volunteer my thoughts, either.

We arrived at the smoking room just as the clock struck 11:00. It was a comfortable place, decorated in a variation of what Oliver had once assured me was the Louis XVI style, although I couldn't really tell one fashion from another. They were all fancy to me. The furniture was oaken, covered in dark green leather, and spread out to accommodate conversation. It was the sort of room where deals were made and plots were hatched.

At one table, tucked away in the back right corner of the room, Mr. Clarke nursed a drink while he took down notes with a fountain pen. Our partner looked dreadful. There were dark, prominent circles under his eyes, and his hair was lank. Greasy. It was as if a storm cloud had migrated inside, positioned itself over his head, and dumped its contents on the poor man.

He was chatting with Captain Dinsmore, who was quite obviously drunk. Dinsmore was hanging over the side of his chair, his loud voice cutting through the otherwise polite atmosphere. "I've told you before, Fred," he was saying, "I've heard they work around-the-clock up in the wireless shack. But Charlie told me a way, he said..." Dinsmore's speech trailed off as he lost his train of thought. "Well, everyone needs a break sometimes," he continued after a moment. "That's what he said, anyway."

"Is Mr. Clarke's first name Fred?" Oliver asked me bemusedly. For a moment, the tension between us ebbed away as we shared a smile over Mr. Clarke's misfortunes. Dinsmore had leaned over so far he was nearly lying on top of him.

"He'd prefer Frederick, probably," I said, following Oliver to another of the corner tables. "Strange that he's here. I thought he was too ill to leave his room."

"Well, rumors abound. We just heard he was injured, too, but does he look injured to you?" Oliver asked. He drew out his lighter, struck it, and then took a long drag from one of his cigarettes. "Oh, look, Jimmy! My father is here."

And so he was. Dr. Wentworth sat in the center booth with some friends. He looked up and offered a wave of greeting, but otherwise, he stayed well clear of us, which suited me just fine. I love the man like he's my own blood, but the conversation Oliver and I were about to have was not one I wished him to overhear.

A steward stopped by. Oliver ordered a double Scotch with a splash of water while I opted for a glass of Old Tom. The steward returned minutes later, balancing a silver tray. He set our drinks down on the table. First the whiskey, then the gin.

"To whom should I send the bill for these drinks, sir?" asked the steward.

"Dr. Franklin Wentworth," Oliver said without missing a beat. He waved once more to his father, who offered one of his own in acknowledgment.

"Very well," the steward said. "Should you require anything further, please don't hesitate to ring."

"Does your father know he's paying for our drinks?" I asked as soon as the steward was out of earshot.

"I rather doubt it," Oliver said, brushing ash from the tip of his cigarette. "But he won't mind."

"If you say so."

With nothing more to distract us, the purpose of our visit here returned to my mind: Emily.

I could see that Oliver shared my thoughts. He took a long sip of his whiskey and leaned back in his chair. "We may as well get to it, then."

"I suppose so."

"Listen, I respect you, Jimmy. You're like a brother to me. That's what makes this so devilishly difficult."

"I meant nothing by it, it just—"

"Don't brush this off. I've known you for a long time, and I know you're interested in my sister. But holding Emily's hand in public... it can't happen again. This isn't just about you."

I met Oliver's gaze, my drink untouched. "I understand. Things got away from me. From us. We were swept up in the moment. It's just... Emily's not one to be denied, you know? When she wants something, she takes it. That's no excuse, and I am responsible for my actions, but... it is the truth. She wanted to hold my hand, and I allowed her to."

"I understand." Oliver took another sip of his drink. "Emily's like me. She gets caught up in things. I'm not surprised to see her take liberties with you. You, on the other hand—well, it caught me by surprise to see you with her. You're generally more mindful than either of us."

He was right. Without wealth or a clear future, a man of my standing had no business holding hands with a woman like Emily. Etiquette was a fortress built to maintain the social order, to keep people like me in our place, and to protect families like the Wentworths from scandal. I'd known that all along.

"I'm sorry," I said. "It isn't my station to admire her. I stepped over the line."

Oliver shook his head. The ghost of a smile was discernible on his face. "You dolt. You think that's what this is about?"

"Is it not?"

"Definitely not." Oliver finished his drink and called for another. "You must understand, Jimmy, the rules we live by are there for a reason. If this scandal isn't nipped in the bud, it'll ruin her reputation. And yours. The things people will assume..."

"I've already told you that I understand," I said sullenly. "I'll leave her alone. It's only right."

"Stop doing that—I will not have you talking down on yourself when I'm trying to give you a stern talking to. It's not right." When I didn't respond, he gestured to me, his cigarette dropping ash on the table. "I don't want you to leave her alone, you fool; I want you to do the opposite! Court her properly!"

"Court her?" I repeated, disbelieving. "You—you're not angry with me?" I'd braced myself for a reprimand, even a demand to stay away from Emily. Yet here was Oliver, telling me to pursue his sister as if it were the most natural thing in the world.

"I can be angry and still want you to be successful, Jimmy."

"But—I mean, how can I? I'm just—"

"First of all—and this is very important—take Emily off whatever pedestal you've placed her on. My sister is lovely, but she's far from perfect. God has never crafted a more stubborn creature. Hell, I don't think we'd even be having this conversation if she hadn't decided to pursue you; I know you didn't start whatever this is. It isn't your style to break with convention."

"That isn't fair."

"Neither is you saying you can't court my sister. I assume you're worried about your living situation? Or your finances? Perhaps how the two of you will be judged?"

"I don't come from a family like yours," I asserted, needing him to understand. "Life doesn't work like this for me."

"Why not? You're already a Wentworth, as far as I'm concerned. We may as well make it official. Go to my father and ask him to court Emily. Do everything properly, the way it should be done. Send her gifts, write her letters, do whatever you must."

"This is insane."

"It's what I must do to see Miss Rowan. You don't hear me complaining about it, do you?"

"No, of course not, but I'm—"

"Damn it, Jimmy! Courting Emily is what you want, isn't it?"

Of course it was. I wanted that more than anything. *But what if I was misreading the situation? What if Emily didn't feel the way I did?*

"Emily would kill me if I asked your father to court her before I asked her how she felt about me," I said. "I wouldn't want to put her in a bad position with your parents—what if she refused me, or worse, didn't, out of some twisted sense of obligation?"

"So break protocol and ask her privately first," Oliver suggested. "I don't care how you do it, but I don't want either of your reputations ruined because the two of you caused a needless scandal."

"Can I really go through with this?"

Oliver shrugged. "It's your life. I'm trying to persuade you to fight for what you want, but I can't force you to do so."

"I'm not what your family would have chosen for Emily," I said. "I don't have many career prospects. I don't have a job lined up, a college selected, or a source of income. I have nothing to offer her but my loyalty and love."

Oliver chortled. "Do you think some pompous gentleman will respect her the way you do? Emily needs someone who will honor her independence, not try to stifle it. That's you. If you work hard, I'm confident my parents won't fight the match. They're less concerned with status than you might think. After all, it's practically tradition for us. My mother was wealthier than my father, too."

"I didn't know that."

"Well, now you do. Use them as an example. Find a career, make something of yourself, and nobody who matters will question whether you belong with Emily."

"I've thought about trying to become a detective."

"You'd be brilliant at it."

"Seriously?"

"I'd say. You're doing a fine job with Mr. Clarke's case."

"But could this become a career? It isn't as sure as becoming a doctor."

Oliver waved me off. "Jimmy, my becoming a doctor is far from certain. I'm terrified I'll fail—that I won't be good enough for all the stiff-lipped old money at Johns Hopkins... or for my father. God knows what it would do to my poor mother if she saw me stumble. But I have to try, don't I?"

"Because it's your dream."

He inclined his head. "And it's worth the risk."

I sat back, considering Oliver's words. Could I do this? Part of me wanted to laugh, to tell Oliver he was insane. But the other part... the part that couldn't forget the feel of Emily's hand in mine, the part that had chased Mr. Blackstone through the *Olympic*... that part wanted to fight for her. Because while the thought of taking the next step was daunting, losing Emily was even more terrifying. *Could I strive for the career I wanted? For the woman I was growing to care deeply for?*

I had to. I had to seize this moment. If Emily was willing to challenge the status quo to be with me, then I had to be brave enough to stand by her side. And I had to earn it.

"You're right. I have to ask her. I can't lose this chance."

Oliver tipped his glass to me in a small salute. "Then your path forward is clear. I don't care what happens between now and Wednesday as long as you get this done. I expect you to have approached my parents before we arrive in New York. If you haven't, I'll have to say something to them. For both of your sakes."

"You have my word, Oliver. I'll do what's right."

18

THE MAN AT THE CENTER OF THE UNIVERSE

Monday morning dawned dark and dreary. Far from abating, the storm engulfing the *Olympic* had intensified overnight. Its vibrations resonated through the ship's hull even more intensely than the rumble of the engines. The situation was serious enough that Captain Bartlett had announced his decision to ban passengers from going out onto the boat deck late the previous night. Better sensible than sorry, as the saying goes.

I grunted and rolled over. A quick glance at my pocket watch told me it was 8:17 a.m., hours past sunrise, yet the horizon beyond our porthole was a dismal abyss, blacker and more foreboding than the ship's own steel-plated sides. There would be no sun today.

"Oliver," I whispered, peeking over the side of my bunk. "Are you awake? They've rung the breakfast gong."

Oliver turned away. "No."

We hadn't returned to our stateroom until just after midnight, and I knew by the absence of his snores that my friend hadn't fallen asleep before me. For all I knew, he hadn't slept at all.

Deciding to give him a few more moments of rest, I dressed in silence and slipped out of our stateroom. The hallways were buzzing. Our fellow passengers, most of whom were still strangers to me, engaged in animated conversations as they made their way to and from the dining saloon for breakfast. Feeling the pangs of hunger myself, I joined the flow, mindful of Mr. Harlowe's warning to avoid traveling alone.

When I arrived at breakfast, I found Dr. Wentworth at our table, engrossed in a book, his coffee untouched. Next to him, Mrs. Wentworth conversed with Mrs. Henderson, who seemed to be barely holding it together. Her red, teary eyes and black attire spoke of a woman in mourning, which, I supposed, she was. Mr. Blackstone had been her nephew.

Emily and Eli Carter were at the end of the table. Emily slowly sipped her coffee, her usual enthusiasm replaced by tired silence. Eli was moving the oats around on his plate with his fork. He, too, wasn't saying much of anything, though he was casting frequent looks at Annabelle, who was seated next to their elderly grandfather. Evidently, the old man had checked himself out of the ship's hospital.

"Good morning, sir," I greeted Dr. Wentworth. Up close, the fatigue in his eyes and the tension in his jaw were more pronounced. It seemed that he, too, had been plagued by a restless night.

The doctor turned over a corner of his page to mark his spot before he closed his book. "Good morning, Mr. Kelly," he said wearily. "Late night?"

I nodded as I laid out my cutlery and built a plate of Yarmouth bloaters and fresh fruit. "Yes, sir. After yesterday's excitement, it was hard to get to sleep."

"You and Oliver stayed later than even I," he said, smiling. "You must have had a lot to talk about."

"We did." Not wanting to wade any deeper into that conversation, I changed the subject. "This storm is something else, is it not?"

"It is. I spoke with the chief engineer yesterday; he shared that Captain Bartlett ordered our speed reduced, in the interest of safety. After hearing that, I placed a wager on the day's run with Dr. Widmer. He could not believe that a ship as grand as this one could be slowed by a storm."

"How much distance did we cover?"

"Nearly 600 miles," Dr. Wentworth admitted. He cleared his throat. "I shall not be taking hints from the chief engineer again, that much I can assure you. Slower, indeed! We shall set a record if we keep this pace up."

That struck me as odd. *Shouldn't the ship cover less distance if it was moving slower?* I considered probing further, but I was reminded of something else I wished to ask Dr. Wentworth about. "Speaking of the engineers, sir, have you heard what happened in the engine room yesterday?"

"Ah, yes. Terrible business. After all the madness was over, I was called to assist Dr. Widmer in determining Mr. Blackstone's cause of death."

I took a bite of my fish. "What did you find? Anything interesting?"

At the table behind ours, Mr. Clarke was leafing through some papers, his glasses resting on the edge of his nose. Out of the corner of my eye, I saw him turn his head. He was listening to our conversation. Down the table from the Swedish journalist was Captain Dinsmore, who was munching on a breakfast roll, watching the waves splash up against the portholes at the end of his table.

Dr. Wentworth glanced at Mrs. Henderson. "Between you and me, the wounds on Mr. Blackstone were similar to those we found on Theodore Eckert. I would wager the same attacker handled both murders, though I still haven't the faintest idea what could cause such injuries."

"Is this an appropriate conversation for the table, dear?" Mrs. Wentworth interjected, holding one of Mrs. Henderson's trembling hands while she clutched a handkerchief in the other. "Mrs. Henderson has been through enough. Could we talk about more pleasant things?"

"Of course, darling," Dr. Wentworth said. "My apologies, Mrs. Henderson. Are there any happier topics we might take up?"

"Annabelle is very keen to attend the concert this evening," Eli said, glancing again his sister's way. "They say that Assistant Purser Haverford will be playing music with the band again. I'm told he was a delight to listen to at church."

"Oh, he is good," gushed Mrs. Wentworth. "When that man is in the room, I cannot look away. I just feel happy around him; all the women are saying it, and some of the men, too."

Eli set his fork down. "I know what you mean. Why, I even think he glows a little in photographs! It is the most curious thing. I suspect my eyes are playing tricks on me, but..."

"Mr. Carter, you are being silly," chided Mrs. Henderson, wiping her eyes. "I suppose a little levity will do us all a bit of good. I am still planning to attend. It is what Reggie would want."

"I agree." Mrs. Wentworth turned to face her daughter. "What do you say, dear? Are you excited about the show?"

Emily was still staring into her coffee cup, absent-mindedly stirring the liquid within with a silver spoon. Her blazing hair, usually so full of life, hung limply around her heart-shaped face.

"Emily!" Mrs. Wentworth repeated. "Did you hear me?"

"Yes, Mother," she replied curtly. "I am excited to have you all watch Haverford like he embodies the sun, and we are all just his... little... planets..." Emily's lips parted in a silent gasp. She paused, her brows furrowed in concentration, before fixing her malachite gaze on me.

"Can I help you?" I asked, bemused.

"Possibly?" Emily opened and closed her mouth, shaking her head. It was as if she were struggling to find the right words. "I just... it is... well, it is rather insane. But... it makes sense..."

"What is it?" Mrs. Wentworth asked. She elbowed Dr. Wentworth, who had reopened his book. "Dear, what do you suppose is the matter with Emily?"

"Pardon?"

Behind me, Mr. Clarke gathered up his papers, nearly dropping them in a rush to leave the saloon. In his haste to reach the doors, the Swede bumped into Eli, who was engrossed in his breakfast. The collision caused Eli's spoon to fly out of his hand. Oats spilled onto the table.

"*Achtu*—Ah, sorry," Mr. Clarke muttered, glancing at Eli as he steadied himself. "Seasick." The journalist rushed out of the room, muttering to himself as he went.

"Well, I say!" Mrs. Henderson said. The breach of decorum appeared enough to snap the conservative woman out of her grief. "That was rather rude!"

"Poor Mr. Clarke has been ill all weekend," Mrs. Wentworth said, frowning reproachfully at her companion. "Not to mention the Herculean effort he has undertaken to get to the bottom of all of this unpleasantness. He should be afforded some grace."

"Indeed. I'm sure he must be feeling more pressure to solve the case than ever." Eli leaned back so a steward could clean up the mess left behind by Mr. Clarke's abrupt exit. "Would you not agree, Emily? You and your friends know him better than anyone."

Rather than reply, it was now Emily who sprang to her feet. "James," she said. "I need you to take me to see my brother. We have something to discuss."

"Now?" I said, my plate still half full. "What's the matter?"

"Yes, now," she urged, stepping around and pulling me out of my seat. She turned to her parents with a placid smile. "Everything is fine, so do not worry. I need only to speak with James and Oliver for a moment."

If there was one person in the world I never wanted to doubt, it was Emily Wentworth. I followed her without asking any more questions.

"Wake up, you great lout!" Emily commanded, not waiting a moment after I opened the door to accost her brother.

Oliver tumbled out of bed, scrambled to his feet, and brandished his nearby hair comb as a makeshift weapon. "Don't come any closer!" he warned. When he saw it was only us, a sheepish grin spread across his face. "Oh! Uh—having a good morning?" he asked casually, acting as if we hadn't just seen his reaction.

I held the door open as Emily marched into our stateroom. "I've just had an idea, Oliver. I might be losing my faculties, but I need you two to hear me out. We may be about to have a breakthrough."

Oliver looked between us with confusion. "Very well," he said, sinking back onto his bed, comb still clutched in hand. "What's this all about?"

Emily began to pace. "I have been thinking about the curse," she said. "About all the evidence we've collected... and about the bodies..." she sighed. "I still do not want to believe such a thing could be real, but... after what James and I saw in the cargo hold... what if it is?"

"I've begun to believe that it must be," I confessed, relieved to admit it out loud. "Those sounds were most unsettling."

Emily frowned as she flopped onto the small couch opposite Oliver. She tugged at the ends of her hair while she considered how to continue. "It's not just what we experienced in the hold. I cannot stop thinking about Mr. Blackstone's body. You saw it, James. He looked like a mummy."

"Did he look similar to Theodore Eckert?" Oliver asked.

"Worse," Emily said. "It was grisly. Yet, despite his injuries, Mr. Blackstone fought to ensure that his last words were useful. He warned James that the storm outside was an omen."

As if it were waiting for a cue card, a mighty flash of lightning ripped through the sky outside. It harshly emphasized the frown lines on Oliver's handsome face.

"He said that," I confirmed, thunder rumbling behind my words. "I didn't think you believed him."

"I didn't," Emily sighed. "I don't? I am reluctant to believe it, even now. But something peculiar is afoot. A smuggling ring as sophisticated as the Sphinx Society must have been in operation for months, perhaps even years. Why are these deaths occurring only now?"

Oliver rubbed his face. "Well, because Lieutenant Morgan brought those damned Sundered Wings aboard. We know that. Mr. Harlowe thinks the Germans are after them."

Emily clasped her hands together. "Hear me out, please." She took a breath before diving in. "Lieutenant Morgan has smuggled goods before. Theodore Eckert got him involved in the trade. It has, to this point, been a bloodless pursuit. Are we in agreement on this premise?"

"Yes," I said.

"Unfortunately," Oliver agreed. "Where are you going with this?"

Emily shushed him and leaned forward, her words tumbling out faster with each new idea. "One would already know that if one had the patience to listen. As I was saying, Lieutenant Morgan is an experienced smuggler, but this trip is different because of the Sundered Wings. They drew too much attention to him. He realized he was being targeted, so he hid the artifacts—somewhat unsuccessfully—before he was killed."

"But where are the Sundered Wings now?" Oliver asked.

"I'm growing more confident that Lieutenant Morgan gave one of them to Theodore Eckert," I said. "That explains why he was killed and why his body looked so strange. And, if we're embracing the idea of a curse, it explains the mascaron as well."

Emily nodded. "If we are willing to consider all of our evidence, Eli's picture is further proof. He captured an image of Eckert and Lieutenant Morgan together on the night of the first killing. They might have made the exchange then."

"The storm started on Saturday night," Oliver interrupted, his comb still clutched tightly in his hand. "If you're right, and our killer stole one of the artifacts from Eckert, they could have started cursing us with it that afternoon!"

"Is it odd that I'm still not willing to fully embrace that?" Emily said, twirling a strand of her hair. "It just seems so fantastic..."

I chuckled. "Perhaps a little. Doesn't your theory rely on the Sundered Wings being real?"

Before she could reply, Oliver snapped his fingers. "Mr. Blackstone! James identified his cufflink next to Eckert's body, remember! He must have killed Eckert for the artifact! He's our killer!"

"Not unless he later killed himself," Emily said. "No, I'm inclined to think that Mr. Blackstone was being hunted like Mr. Eckert was. His cufflink could have been planted to throw the authorities off."

"Well, I suppose that makes sense..."

Emily smiled. "It does. Anyway, with Mr. Eckert dead, we must assume that the killer had one of the artifacts in their possession. The other one has been trickier for them to locate. That's what I am basing this theory on. I've had an idea where it is."

"Go on, tell us, then," Oliver urged.

Emily turned to me. "James, how did everyone at breakfast describe Haverford?"

Surprised to be called upon, I stumbled over my words. "Well," I began, "I think they... like him? Mrs. Henderson called him the center of attention, and you said he was like the sun."

"Like the sun," Emily echoed. "Sound familiar? Let me ask you this—where would be the safest place to hide something of great value on board this ship?"

Oliver pumped his fist. "You think Haverford is in the Sphinx Society! Do you suppose the artifact has been stashed away in that scoundrel's office this whole time? While he carries on as normal?"

"Yes, I do. And I wouldn't say he's been acting normally. That's my whole point. Think about it! Is it not strange that people have gravitated so intensely around him? Nobody made a fuss about him the first night, did they? And yet, ever since Lieutenant Morgan disappeared, it's as if people can't help but be drawn to him. The women at breakfast were practically swooning."

I walked a few steps over to lean against the cabinet. "You're saying the Sundered Wings' powers might be abstract? That they don't just cause storms and sunshine, but change people's feelings and emotions? That they can make someone the center of attention without anyone else realizing it?"

"Why not?" Emily asked. "I still despise putting stock in this curse business, but I cannot deny what I've seen. Someone going after the Sundered Wings is our killer. I believe Haverford has at least one of them in his possession. By all logic, he must be our killer. Or the killer's next target."

I considered her words. "What do we do? Our case against Haverford is weak. All we really have is your theory and a single overheard conversation. We need evidence."

"What we need is to get into his office," Emily said. "If we can prove Haverford has one of the artifacts, we can take it from him, get it to Captain Bartlett, and let the crew protect it."

"But how?" asked Oliver. "The purser's office is always busy. Plus, Haverford works there. Do you think he'll let us poke around?"

Emily smoothed out the folds of her dress. "Well..." she started. "He did ask me to seek him out if I ever needed help. Perhaps I should take him up on his offer."

"I don't like it," I said. "What if he can tell you're lying? What if he tries to hurt you?"

Oliver frowned. "James is right, Em. This feels risky. It won't be like it is in your books."

"I'll be diligent," Emily promised. "And, should I fail, a time is approaching when Haverford won't be in his office to stop us. When we could all explore together, unimpeded by witnesses."

I snapped my fingers. "The concert! You're suggesting that we check the purser's office during the concert tonight?"

"If I am unsuccessful this afternoon, yes. But we shall need a plan. We cannot break in without a strategy."

"We need to tell Mr. Clarke and Mr. Harlowe about this," I said. "Mr. Clarke has been ill, but he's still our partner. And Mr. Harlowe might not believe us about the curse, but we can at least tell him we suspect Haverford. I think he was about to accuse him when we were talking to Captain Bartlett."

At the mention of the master-at-arms, a small, forced smile replaced the frown on Oliver's face. "Mr. Harlowe dislikes Haverford enough to preach to him about stealing in front of the entirety of second class. I think it's safe to assume he shares our point of view."

"I hope so," Emily said grimly. "Because if there is a curse, I cannot be the only one who has worked this out. It's only a matter of time before Mr. Harlowe's German shows up at Haverford's door looking for the artifacts."

I exchanged a concerned glance with Oliver. I could tell he was thinking the same thing I was—if it came down to Charlie Haverford to protect the Sundered Wings, they were as good as gone.

19
EMILY'S GAMBIT

After we finished our conversation in our stateroom, Oliver set out to find Mr. Clarke. He pounded on the journalist's door for several minutes before a steward interrupted him to explain that Mr. Clarke was too ill to see us. Meanwhile, Emily and I tried and failed to locate Mr. Harlowe. The master-at-arms was nowhere to be found. After coming up empty in our search for both men, we were forced to accept that no outside help was coming. We would be entering Haverford's office on our own.

Defeated but not deterred, we returned to our stateroom and began to work out the details. A little over an hour later, after a rushed round of negotiations, we were ready to carry out Emily's audacious plan. We wasted no time putting it into action.

Each of us had a duty to perform. Oliver secured a spot on the landing between D-deck and E-deck, where he would be strategically placed to monitor the dining saloon doors above and the purser's office below. He leaned against the railing, looking casual, with a full glass of water in his right hand—my idea. If anyone tried to get around him, Oliver would engage them in conversation. If he couldn't stall them, he'd "accidentally" drop the glass, creating a mess to slow them down.

I took up a position on the landing below Oliver. From my perch on the stairwell between E-deck and F-deck, I had a clear view into the purser's office through the open window. Emily had insisted on this vantage point, arguing it was the best place for one of us to monitor Haverford while she was in the room with him. She was nervous about spending too long in his presence without backup. More than that, I could intercept anyone coming up from the staterooms below.

Our plan wasn't perfect. Passengers could still come to the purser's office from forward on E-deck, and someone might slip by Oliver or me on the stairs. It wasn't like we had the authority to arrest them or take them captive. Still, it was the best we could do with the time we had. At least we could watch over Emily and give her some cover if she needed it.

As soon as the line at the purser's office broke, Emily hurried down from her spot near Oliver. She approached the service window where Haverford awaited her. Up close, I saw what Emily meant about the assistant purser. There was something unnatural about him. His whole body glowed as if an unseen electrical cord connected him to the ship's generators.

The longer I watched him, the more intensely a strange, foreign warmth spread through me. It was similar to the way that memories of my mother felt. Warm. Fond. Even loving. My throat grew thick with a sudden, illogical fondness for the assistant purser.

But wait—that wasn't right. *Was I going mad? Haverford wasn't my family. I didn't even like him!*

I broke into a cold sweat. There was something eerie happening here, something unnatural. I shook my head and turned my attention to Emily. Whatever Haverford was doing to us, she'd felt it, too. I hoped he hadn't noticed the flash of disgust on her face; for just a moment, she looked like she'd bitten into a sour lemon.

When I looked back to Haverford, I examined him again, more warily this time. His blond hair still shone under the lights, but not as much as his eyes, which were so greedily focused on Emily he looked like he might devour her right then and there. He bore a striking resemblance to a toad preparing to snatch a fly.

"Miss Wentworth," Haverford said, licking his lips. "What a pleasant surprise. Do you have another message for me to pass along?"

Emily smiled back, stepped closer, and surrendered herself to his orbit. "Not today. I was just passing by and thought I might take you up on your offer to say hello."

"All the better that this is a social call, then." Haverford looked Emily up and down, smiling with appreciation for what he found. "I'm afraid you've caught me at an interesting moment. The wireless has been giving us trouble."

"Oh?" Emily asked with wide eyes, employing the sort of practiced innocence that had often kept her nose clean from Oliver's playground schemes. "Nothing serious, I hope?"

Haverford affected a conspiratorial whisper. "Equipment failure," he confirmed. "Between you and me, my dear, it appears the *Olympic* has lost her wireless entirely. The Marconi men will have their work cut out for them when we arrive back in New York."

"Are you certain it was an equipment failure?" Emily asked. There was a note of real concern behind that question. She was hinting at sabotage.

Haverford missed it completely. I did not. It seemed impossible for such a modern ship to be cut off from the rest of the world, but without access to a wireless set, the *Olympic* was now unable to signal for rescue in the event of a tragedy. This played right into the hands of the killer—and of our mysterious German foe. I felt more certain than ever that our opponent would make their next move soon.

At that moment, thunder boomed, shaking the glass in Haverford's office window. I had to strain to hear his reply to Emily.

"As certain as I am fortunate you stopped by, Miss Wentworth. But enough of such dreary business! I confess that I am far more interested in getting to know you than in any issues with a fussy wireless set."

Emily smiled. "Well, sir, I feel the same. I have heard a great deal about you since we last met."

Above me, I heard Oliver engage someone in conversation. A part of me hoped he would abandon the plan and allow this person to pass him by. Between hearing about the wireless and experiencing Haverford's strange aura, I was quite ready to escape this place. The stairwell, for all its beauty, rose up around me like a cell, claustrophobic and confining. The walls were pressing in.

Haverford leaned forward, and I felt that pull again, the strange, foreign warmth in my chest. His smile radiated heat. A soothing laugh bubbled up from his throat. "All good things, I hope?"

Now it was Emily's turn to chuckle, though hers came out as more of a giggle, light and flirty. "You seem to be quite popular these days," she said. "Why, I imagine you have all sorts of interesting stories to tell from your time in that office."

I gripped the railing tighter. Emily was acting. I knew that. Yet, I'd barely resisted whatever pull Haverford was exerting, and I despised him. *Just how insidious of an influence on our behavior could he affect? How much of our will could he claim for his own?* Suddenly, our plan seemed very foolish. We'd underestimated Haverford. There were too many unknowns. Too many ways this could go wrong.

"Would you like to come inside?" Haverford asked silkily. "I would be happy to show you around."

It was precisely the invitation we'd hoped to hear, but now I desperately hoped Emily would turn it down. Instead, ever bold, she said, "Oh, yes, please. That sounds fascinating."

Emily squared her shoulders and stepped into the room. Haverford closed the door behind her with a sly grin. I wanted to shout and pull her away, but I knew I had to trust her. Emily could take care of herself.

That didn't mean there was nothing I could do. Haverford's door may have been closed, but his window was open. I could still hear their conversation. I crept closer, listening hard.

"You are quite the piano player." Emily sounded breathless. "And, of course, a man with a lot of responsibility. It must be challenging keeping track of all the valuables on board."

Personally, I thought she might be laying it on a little thickly. Evidently, so did Haverford, for his next response was much more guarded. "It can be, yes. But I manage."

Emily whispered something. I missed it. Unable to stand being out of earshot, I crept even closer to the window. Emily was leaning in, facing Haverford, her eyes wide with feigned admiration. "That's incredible," she was saying. "I cannot imagine the pressure you must be under, especially with all the recent... excitement."

I reached the window. Standing off to the side, I leaned over and peered in. A wave of nausea swept through me when Emily laughed and touched Haverford's arm. His answering smile was so arrogant that he deserved to be placed beside the word in Webster's dictionary.

I didn't know what to do next. *Should I interfere? Was Emily doing what she wanted, or was Haverford guiding her moves?*

There was nothing for it. I forced myself to turn around and focus on the hallway—I still had a job to do. It was lucky that I did. I'd missed Oliver dropping his water. My friend was coming down the stairs, trying and failing to wrangle the much larger Captain Dinsmore. The old man seemed hellbent on reaching Haverford's office.

"Come now. Can your business not wait?" Oliver asked, extending an arm to intercept Captain Dinsmore. "Surely, you can spare a moment to speak with me. The assistant purser is a busy man, after all, and—"

"Nonsense, my boy! Charlie will be happy to see me!" Dinsmore boomed as he pushed his way around Oliver. "We go back a long way! I've known his father longer than you've been alive!"

Dinsmore, Oliver, and I converged on the landing at the same time Haverford burst into laughter from somewhere inside the office.

"Of course, darling, there are valuable items in here," he said, his voice dripping with toxic sweetness. "But I cannot show you the interesting ones until I am off duty. Perhaps we could discuss this later? In private?"

"I shall think about it, Mr. Haverford," Emily said coyly. "I appreciate your time; I know you are a busy man. But I should be going."

"I am never too busy for you." Haverford pulled the shade down, blocking my view. "It seems such a shame to let you leave now. In fact, I insist you stay. My quarters are just around the corner here. Would you—"

Oliver's and Captain Dinsmore's argument reached the window, where Dinsmore shouted, "Charlie! Are you there?"

Haverford cursed. "Dinsmore, you fool, come back later!"

"No! I have something to say!"

"It can wait!"

"Oh, but you don't know what I'm gonna say, boy! You'll want to hear this!"

I dashed the rest of the way to the door and flung it open. Emily was standing with her back to me, but I reached in, grabbed her by the hand, and yanked her into the hallway. Haverford came after her, but he was too slow to catch us. I don't think he saw any part of me but my back.

"Oliver, hurry! This way!" We raced down the corridor. Just before we turned the corner, I looked back and saw Haverford being distracted by his belligerent, probably inebriated associate.

"Come now, Charlie!" slurred Dinsmore. "You'll never guess what I've found!"

I didn't care to listen to Haverford's reply. All I cared about was escaping. Sweat dripped from my brow as adrenaline surged through my veins. Emily clutched my hand as if her life depended on it. We didn't stop until we were two decks above the purser's office, just outside of our stateroom. I fumbled with the doorknob before thrusting it open. We slipped inside. Oliver slammed the door shut behind us.

"Forget Haverford!" Emily exclaimed as she slumped over on our couch. "He's loathsome. We're breaking into that office during the concert. Consequences be damned."

My heart was still pounding. "I prefer that to leaving you alone with him again. Something about him isn't right."

"There's something strange going on," Oliver agreed. "I don't know if it's the Wings of Amun-Ra or some other trick, but he had me feeling an odd way. For a moment there, it felt as if I liked him." He shuddered. "Can you imagine? Makes my skin crawl just thinking about it."

"I felt it, too," I said. "It was... powerful."

Oliver shook his head. "I know this will sound unbelievable, coming from me, but... might it be smarter to leave him alone? There has to be another way to learn what we need to learn."

"Absolutely not," Emily said. "This matters, Oliver. We're up against a man who thinks he can use his connections and these artifacts to manipulate and control others. We must show him he won't get away with it!"

"We need to find Mr. Harlowe," I said, massaging my temples. "If we're right about Haverford, he needs to know what we're planning. I'm not going in again without backup."

"I'll go see if Alex can find him for us," Oliver said. "I'll go now. Jimmy, take care of Emily. Make sure she gets back to her stateroom safely."

"You can count on me."

Oliver and I nodded to each other before he swept out of the room.

With her brother gone, Emily and I were now quite alone. I turned to face her. Though her expression was composed, I could see the stress lines on her face and the tension in her shoulders. She was holding herself together. Barely.

"How are you feeling?" I asked.

Emily smiled weakly. "Fine. It's just a bit... overwhelming. All of this."

I took a risk and sat beside her on the couch. The cushion

dipped beneath me. "I don't know if it means anything, but I think you were brilliant today."

Her lips parted slightly in surprise. "It means a great deal," she admitted. She sighed and leaned back against the couch pillow. "You've done a brilliant job holding up your end of our promise, you know."

"Think nothing of it. If not for you, Haverford might have gotten away with everything. Now we have a chance to stop him."

Our hands brushed together. I took hers in mine. She shifted her weight from the pillow to my side and rested her head on my shoulder.

"I've always wondered why the governess in *The Turn of the Screw* felt compelled to write down her story," Emily said. "The events at Bly were so horrible, their description so unbelievable, that it feels as if they should never have been shared at all. But now that my life has become just as strange as hers... I sympathize with the character. One can learn a great deal from macabre tales. If we survive this, James, I would like to write down our story. Even if the truth might make me seem mad."

I should have known Emily would have a book ready to reference. She always did.

"If you wish to write about our journey, I'll be the first to read your work," I said. "One can only hope your novel will end with the villains in irons."

"Would you, really?"

I blinked, caught off guard by her quiet question. "Of course. We're friends, are we not?"

Emily snuggled closer to me.

I reached over to brush her hair away from her face.

I could hardly breathe when Emily tilted her chin up to face me. She was close enough now that I could count the faint dusting of freckles on her nose. I drew nearer. She matched my movement with her own. We were mere inches apart...

A mighty burst of thunder split the sky. Emily let out a startled yelp as a sudden lurch of the *Olympic* sent us both tumbling forward. I caught her by the shoulders. Her hands clutched the front of my shirt. For a breathless moment, we stayed frozen in place.

Then we separated. Emily smoothed her skirt as a blush colored her cheeks. I cleared my throat.

"You've made a regular habit out of catching me, James," she managed.

"You're lucky you keep falling where I happen to be."

She smiled, then repeated my word back to me, slowly, as if testing its fit on her lips. "'Lucky?' I suppose that's a fair way to describe it."

I didn't know what to do. My heart was beating a million miles an hour. My hands felt shaky. "Well, I promised Oliver I would walk you back to your stateroom," I said. "I—I wouldn't want to upset him."

Emily looked away, but not quite quickly enough to mask the look of disappointment that crossed her face. "Yes, of course. We wouldn't want to worry anyone."

As we left the room, I couldn't help but wonder what might have happened if we'd been interrupted even a second later. *How would I have reacted if we'd managed to cross those last few inches of distance? Would I have been exhilarated? Terrified?* Either way, one thing was certain—my feelings for Emily Wentworth were becoming impossible to ignore. I needed to speak with her about my desire to court her, and soon. We couldn't keep finding ourselves in situations like this.

But that conversation wouldn't happen now. It couldn't.

My bravery was gone, and no matter how hard I tried, I couldn't summon it back.

It didn't take us long to arrive at her stateroom door.

"Well... here we are," I said. I'd never felt so awkward. "I suppose I'll see you at the concert."

Emily's hand lingered on the doorknob. "I cannot tell you how much I despise Haverford right now."

"What? Why? Has he done something else?"

"No. It's just—well, were things different, were we not obligated to investigate him—I would have been very much looking forward to sharing another dance with you tonight."

"And I, you," I whispered, watching as she disappeared into her stateroom, dumbstruck by what had just taken place.

I LINGERED in the corridor for a moment after Emily disappeared into her stateroom. An echo of her citrus perfume clung to my jacket, making it difficult to think about anything but her. But there was no time to dwell on what had passed between us. Not as long as Haverford was out there, free to use the Sundered Wings to harm others.

Keen to clear my head, I pulled myself away from her door and went to find Oliver. I needed to keep busy.

When we finally met up just outside of the smoking room, my friend shared with me that nobody seemed to know where the master-at-arms was. Not even Alex Cunningham, who had the uncanny ability to find anyone, had seen the elusive Mr. Harlowe. Our only remaining hope was that he was planning to attend the second-class concert. If we didn't see him there, we would have to break into the purser's office without his help. Not an appealing proposition.

Resigning ourselves to the fact we'd done all we could, we returned to our stateroom. The remaining hours of the afternoon flew by in a whirlwind of last-minute preparations. Oliver took another bath. I made sure my face was smooth and my teeth were brushed clean.

Soon, we were putting the finishing touches on our outfits.

"Ready, old sport?" Oliver asked as he finished adjusting his collar in the mirror. His reflection winked at me before he spun around, flashing me his most confident grin.

My friend was a sight to behold. He looked every bit like a dashing gentleman in his tailored black tuxedo. His hair was slicked back, highlighting his angular jawline and sharp cheeks. Tonight, he looked less like the mischievous companion I was accustomed to and more like a man plucked straight out of Emily's Jane Austen novels. He made it look effortless.

"Ready as I'll ever be," I replied, crushing my envious thoughts. I straightened my tie for what felt like the hundredth time. I'd taken extra care to ensure my outfit was perfect, but I knew my more elegant friend had overshadowed me. He always did.

As we walked down the corridor toward the dining saloon, I scanned the faces of the passengers we passed.

"Where do you think she is?" I asked.

Oliver rolled his eyes at me. "Worry not, Romeo. My sister probably went on ahead with my parents."

"Don't say that so loudly! What if she hears you?"

"Then my life probably becomes a great deal simpler."

"What if your parents hear you?"

"Same answer, with extra steps." Oliver grinned, but he sobered when he saw my panicked face. "Come now, Jimmy. Be reasonable. We both know they are already inside. My parents will have arrived an hour ago, so as not to be late, and Emily will have wanted as much time as possible to survey the room. You know how she is."

I bit my lip. "There's a lot riding on tonight."

"So, don't make it more difficult than it needs to be. This is the easy part."

We pushed the doors open and entered the dining saloon. The party was in full swing, roaring with laughter and conversation. Table lamps, special lighting they didn't set out for regular meals, sat atop every surface, casting their intimate glow on the finely dressed passengers. The ambiance was immaculate. Stewards moved among the guests, balancing trays of sparkling drinks and hors d'oeuvres.

I spared little time on the mingling socialites. There was only one person I wanted to see. I scanned the room, not lingering for long on any one face or feature.

And then, there she was. A beacon that made the rest of the concert seem dull by comparison.

Emily wore a striking emerald gown. Bold, modern, and a little daring, its fabric flowed over her like water, hugging her curves as it spilled from her shoulders to the floor. Her hair was swept into an intricate bun. A few loose curls fell to frame her beaming face when she threw her head back in laughter.

She looked up. Our eyes met. And her smile transformed into something radiant.

I reached up to adjust my tie. "Emily, you look incredible!"

"Thank you, James. You clean up quite nicely yourself."

Emily stood with her parents, who were both elegantly attired and immaculate in their presentation. Dr. Wentworth was wearing a classic black suit; Mrs. Wentworth dazzled in a sophisticated golden gown that hid the thinness of her frame under its forgiving lines.

"Greetings, Mr. Kelly," Dr. Wentworth said. "I hope this evening finds you well?"

"It does, sir," I said, trying not to stare at Emily while I answered. She'd worn a pair of flat shoes. Most of the other women were in heels. Then again, most of the other women weren't planning to be involved in a heist.

"You both look so handsome!" complimented Mrs. Wentworth, beaming at her son and me. "Oh, my boys. I am ever so glad we have this night together. It promises to be one to remember."

"Yes, it does," Emily said, moving to stand with us. "I hope this evening will prove to be a rewarding experience for all of us."

Annabelle Carter appeared next to Oliver. Despite her recent ordeal, she carried herself well, making no effort to hide the bruises on her wrists. Her dress was stylish and light. Eli looked equally handsome in a charcoal-gray suit.

"Good evening," Eli said. "Mrs. Wentworth, you look stunning. As do you, Emily."

Both women smiled and nodded their appreciation for his compliments.

"Are you all ready for the big event?" Annabelle asked. "I must say, celebrating when the journey has been this difficult seems ever so strange."

Oliver answered with a charming smile. "Of course I'm ready. And, not for nothing, I would posit that the difficulty of our journey makes the timing of this party even more appropriate. Do you not agree?"

Annabelle blinked a few times, then looked away. "I appreciate your optimism. Grandfather is waving to us, so for now, I bid you a good evening. We'll see you soon!" She and Eli headed for their table.

The Wentworths and I began circulating the room, making the required social calls. We kept a sharp lookout for Mr. Harlowe. I spotted him as a flash of lightning streaked across the sky, illuminating the darkened sea and shining on all the silver dinnerware and cutlery. The master-at-arms was standing sentry near the back of the dining saloon. His posture was as rigid as a gargoyle's. The only reason I'd noticed him at all was the host of golden buttons affixed to the front of his navy-blue jacket.

"There's our man." I nodded toward Mr. Harlowe. "Let's go say hello."

Emily, Oliver, and I separated from their parents and made our way over to the master-at-arms. Mr. Harlowe's expression remained impassive. If I didn't know better, I would say he'd never met us before. The man was an excellent actor.

"Good evening, Mr. Harlowe," Emily said when we reached him. "We need to talk."

"Urgently," I added.

"I had a feeling you three would seek me out tonight." Mr. Harlowe glanced at the other officers and crew members around us. "Wait until after dinner, then meet me on the landing outside. We can talk there."

"Of course, sir," Oliver said. "Enjoy your meal."

We joined Dr. and Mrs. Wentworth at our corner table after our conversation with Mr. Harlowe. I sat beside Oliver in my usual seat. The rich scent of baked haddock and roasted potatoes made my mouth water, but the knots of anticipation twisting in my stomach almost immediately worked to kill my appetite. I picked at my food, moving it around with my knife. It was difficult to take a bite.

Across the table, Mrs. Wentworth laughed at something Eli Carter had said, her golden gown shimmering in the light.

Emily was sitting next to her mother. She glanced my way and offered me an encouraging smile.

By the end of the meal, I'd somehow choked down most of my food, but my potatoes sat untouched. Their golden-brown skins were inviting, but every glance at them reminded me of Annabelle's capture and that strange potato room. I couldn't bring myself to eat them. Mrs. Henderson, sitting beside Eli, ate even less than I did. Her fork moved mechanically as she picked at her dinner.

As the last course, a generous helping of Waldorf pudding arrived. It was a rich dessert, a bit heavier than I generally prefer, constructed from a creamy base of vanilla pudding, flavored with nutmeg, accented with diced apples, and finished with sultana grapes. Despite the seriousness of our situation, I smiled when Oliver made sure a double serving found its way to his plate. At least my friend wasn't allowing his nerves to impede his love for all things sweet.

The lights dimmed. An anticipatory hush fell over the dining saloon when the band entered and took their places near the piano. Thunder rumbled while they set up their instruments. The band leader, a youthful man with dark hair, raised his hands. With an elegant swipe, he began to guide the others.

The sweeping notes of a waltz filled the air.

"'Saints and Sinners,'" Emily said, commenting on the band's chosen song. "Seems appropriate, don't you think?"

"Very," I replied, wishing I had thought of something more charming to say.

As the band played on, Haverford made his entrance. The assistant purser was dressed in his formal uniform. In the low light, his golden cufflinks, buttons, and epaulets only reinforced his unearthly glow. They sparkled each time he passed by a table. His movements were graceful. His smile was warm. He drew the admiration of everyone in the room, posturing as he exerted his gravity on the crowd. The man truly was a sun among planets.

"Good evening, ladies and gentlemen," Haverford began. "We hope you are enjoying your meal and the delightful music. We have a special treat for you tonight, a performance that promises to make this voyage one to remember. No storm shall dampen our spirits!"

The crowd let out a sigh of appreciation, but Oliver saved me before I could be sucked in by Haverford again. "What a cad," my friend said in a mock whisper.

Emily snorted, much to the chagrin of Mrs. Henderson. Dr. Wentworth shushed his wayward son.

Haverford continued to speak. "I must commend our musicians for their dedication. Despite the adverse conditions, they will be playing a selection of pieces to entertain you all. Please give them your best."

As the band launched into another lively number, Haverford moved through the room, engaging with the passengers and cultivating an almost magical atmosphere. When he neared our table, Mr. Harlowe ducked out into the corridor.

"It's time," I said. "Mr. Harlowe is moving. We need to go."

"Please excuse me!" Emily said. She smiled at her parents before darting from the table. Oliver and I were a little slower, but we followed behind her, whispering our excuses. We needn't have bothered; everyone around us was so taken by Haverford that they didn't notice us leaving.

After we closed the double doors of the dining saloon behind us, the music and chatter faded away, replaced by the distant rumble of thunder. Mr. Harlowe was waiting for us, checking his pocket watch and tapping his foot. He stowed his timepiece away in his jacket when we arrived.

"Well?" he said, crossing his arms. "What do you have for me?"

20
THE WING OF LIGHT

Emily's voice was steady as she laid out our theory and our need to search the purser's office. Mr. Harlowe's frown deepened with every revelation.

"Very well," he said. "I have my own reasons to suspect Haverford, and I would rather not miss this chance to turn the screw on him, but we need to be discreet. He has friends in high places. Our evidence must be incontrovertible."

I'd suspected as much from the moment Captain Bartlett had prevented Mr. Harlowe from accusing someone the previous afternoon. "We're with you, sir. You can trust us."

"Then, let us make haste."

We left the landing outside of the dining saloon and descended the aft staircase. The overhead lighting cast lengthy, bizarre shadows on the steps; they were phantasmic creatures of shade and darkness, only broken apart when lightning flashed and sent them scurrying. For just a moment, I was grateful for the storm. Its light dispelled the worst of what my imagination had conjured.

The eternally grim-faced Mr. Harlowe led the way. Oliver

walked beside him. Emily and I were behind them; it had been an almost subconscious motion for me to extend her my arm, but I was glad I had done so. We descended the stairs together.

When we reached our destination, I was pleased to see that the hallway was empty. Everyone, it seemed, was up in the dining saloon. The purser's office was dark. The windows were closed, and the shades were pulled down. Mr. Harlowe leaned over the railing, peeked around the corner, and then nodded.

"We appear to be alone," he said. "We should move quickly."

"Did you see Haverford left a note on the door?" Oliver asked, tapping the parchment pinned to it. "How thoughtful."

> *"Closed for the night. Please join us in the dining saloon for an evening of fellowship."*
> *Assistant Purser C.S. Haverford*

"I doubt Captain Bartlett permitted him to close this office," Mr. Harlowe groused. "It's just like Haverford to break the rules first and ask forgiveness later."

"Yes, we know he's a dolt. But how will we get into his office if he isn't here?" asked Oliver, looking at me as if I might have the answer. "Can you pick a lock, Jimmy?"

"Why would I know how to pick a lock?"

"I didn't mean to imply anything, old man. But if one of us would know..."

"It would be you!"

"Boys!" Emily quieted us with a word. "This isn't helpful. I see no reason to resort to burglary when we have the support of the master-at-arms for our endeavor."

"Ah, yes. That does make sense," Oliver admitted.

Grunting his assent, Mr. Harlowe produced a set of keys. He tried two: the first one didn't work, but the second, a small bronze key, turned the mechanism. The door swung open.

Mr. Harlowe turned a round light switch next to the entryway before stepping aside for us to file in after him. Thunder rumbled outside, the sound converging with the faint strains of music emanating from the saloon. "Spread out and search," he instructed. "We have little time here before someone notices our presence. If we're caught, there'll be hell to pay."

There wasn't much room in Haverford's tiny office for us, but we did our best to follow Mr. Harlowe's instructions. The windows were pulled closed, but various things were laid out on the desk just inside: books, papers, and writing utensils, many emblazoned with White Star Line iconography. I rifled through the papers, searching for anything that stood out. Anything that might lead us to the Sundered Wings.

Behind me, Emily was rustling around in Haverford's personal desk, pulling out all sorts of things and setting them on its wooden surface. She made a "hmm" sound each time she found something new before setting it aside to join her other discoveries. She'd collected a coffee cup, a feathered quill pen, three postcards, and even what looked like a model train engine.

Mr. Harlowe knelt by the safe, muttering under his breath as he tried one combination after another, his hand flashing over the dial. He didn't seem to be having much luck. Oliver pulled back the curtain separating Haverford's personal quarters from the rest of the office. He was rooting around in the assistant purser's wardrobe, but I couldn't see much else of what he was up to from where I was.

I noticed something odd when I returned to my search. A

photograph had been hidden among the cluttered papers and ledgers on the purser's desk. It was black and white, clearly taken with a professional camera, and depicted a sculpture of Anubis, the Egyptian god of the dead. The statue's jackal head was depicted with a stern expression.

At the bottom of the photograph, a hurried note was scribbled in dark ink:

Take a look at this.
— Dinsmore

Dinsmore! So, he and Haverford were in cahoots. Was he another member of the Sphinx Society? Dinsmore's handwriting was uneven; it looked to me as if it had been inscribed by a shaking hand. A yellowed stain was covering up what might have been a post script. Curious, I turned the photograph over and found more writing on the back. This time, it was in German, the precise letters contrasting with the scrawled note on the front. The text was brief:

Mitternacht. Bootsdeck. Komm alleine.

I thought I recognized the spiky handwriting, but I couldn't place where I'd seen it before. "Emily, Oliver, come here and look at this," I said. "What do you suppose this means?"

Emily glanced at the note, her nose wrinkling. "It's German," she said. "But I can't read it. I think *'nacht'* means night?"

Mr. Harlowe stood up and snatched the photo from my hand. "Midnight," he translated. "Boat deck. Come alone."

"That's when Lieutenant Morgan was killed," Oliver pointed out. "I guess Captain Dinsmore isn't the harmless old drunk I thought he was."

Emily frowned. "Captain Dinsmore? Is everyone on this ship involved with Lieutenant Morgan's smuggling ring? Such a thing seems impossible."

"I would be wary in his presence, but I do not believe Dinsmore is our murderer," Mr. Harlowe said slowly. "No, whoever wrote the German message on the back of this photo is our man. Dinsmore must have come across it in his search for the artifacts. Why he elected to share it with Haverford is anyone's guess."

"Well, what about Haverford?" demanded Oliver. "Could he have written on this after Captain Dinsmore found it? Does he speak German? Is he working for them?"

Mr. Harlowe shook his head. "Not to my knowledge. He may be duplicitous, but he is an Englishman. I suspect Haverford was only shown this message after Dinsmore found it for him."

"You already knew Haverford was innocent?" Emily asked. "Why are we spending time investigating him, then? Why are we here?"

Mr. Harlowe sighed. "I do not believe Haverford is innocent of smuggling. I believe he is innocent of murder. That is an important distinction. The German agent I am tracking has committed several murders in pursuit of the artifacts that the smugglers have tried to hide."

"What's the German's angle?" Oliver asked. "Are they after wealth? Power?"

"Such a man could have many motives, but given our other evidence, sabotage is most likely."

"Sabotage? You think this German fellow wants to make the White Star Line look bad?"

"I do, but it's more than that," Mr. Harlowe explained. "There's a lot of national pride tied up in the *Olympic*—and the *Lusitania* and *Mauritania*, of course—especially following the *Titanic* disaster. The British want to show the world that our engineering and maritime capabilities are second to none. The Germans, on the other hand, want to undermine that reputation."

Oliver frowned. "Let's say you're correct. What's Captain Dinsmore's role in all of this? What's Haverford's?"

"I suspect Haverford, at least, has ties to the Sphinx Society. I just don't have enough evidence to be sure. That's why we need to find out if he has one of the Sundered Wings. It would be an undeniable link between he and Marvin."

"One you could use to open a proper investigation," I said.

Emily followed my thought with one of her own. "Haverford might prove to be enough of a lead to allow you to unmask the German, too."

"Precisely so, Miss Wentworth."

We resumed our search. Having exhausted the wardrobe, Oliver kneeled down to open the sliding drawers under the cabinet. It wasn't even a minute later when he found something. "Look at this," he said, pulling a folded paper out from the inside of a comfortable pair of slippers. "Whatever does it mean? The letters are all jumbled up."

"It's a Caesar shift." Mr. Harlowe took the paper from him and smoothed it on the desk. "Marvin and I used one when we were in the service. Every letter in the alphabet is shifted forward three spaces. For example, 'A' becomes 'D,' 'B' becomes 'E,' and so on. They are effective, if fairly simple to crack."

He pointed to the top of the page, where precise handwriting outlined the pattern:

$$A \rightarrow D$$
$$B \rightarrow E$$
$$C \rightarrow F$$

I peered over Oliver's shoulder. "So, if we were to decode a message written in this cipher, 'HELLO' would become 'KHOOR?'"

"Yes," Mr. Harlowe confirmed. "Anyone with a basic understanding of spycraft would be familiar with the pattern, though I'd imagine the boys in the wireless office were mighty confused about sending communication out in this fashion."

Oliver gasped. "We found a message written with this cipher in Lieutenant Morgan's room! He must have taught the other smugglers to use your code!"

"Should I ask what you were doing in Marvin's stateroom?" Mr. Harlowe asked. Oliver opened his mouth to answer, but Mr. Harlowe cut him off. "On second thought—never mind it. What's done is done. It goes without saying that I'll need to see that note."

Oliver grinned. "Of course, sir. It's in my other jacket. Or at least I think it is. I can look for it after—"

"Look at this!" Emily interrupted. She pulled a wooden box out from under Haverford's bed. "I... I think I found something!"

The box was elegant, carved from rich, dark mahogany, with hieroglyphics inscribed along its edges. A relief showing a falcon was etched on the lid, the details so fine that it was hard to believe a human hand could have crafted them.

Emily's fingers lingered on the latch. She looked up at me. "Should I open it?"

I nodded.

She cracked the lid.

Resting within the box, upon a lining of deep red velvet, lay what could only be one of the fabled Wings of Amun-Ra. It had a surface of pure gold, adorned with ancient hieroglyphics I couldn't begin to understand. Each line was highlighted in ageless blue paint the same color as a cloudless sky. The craftsmanship was exquisite. Carved feathers formed the backbone of the artifact, each so intricately detailed they seemed ready to flutter in the breeze or float through the air. A real wing wouldn't have looked much different; in fact, if you'd told me that this wing had been torn from a falcon and dipped in molten gold, I would have believed you. Every delicate cut glimmered as the ship rocked in the storm.

But that wasn't all. The same gravity I associated with Haverford poured from the Wing of Light; it washed over us like an overfilled chalice, one filled to the brim with promise and eager for a new drinker to share in its blessings. The artifact felt like it had a heartbeat—like it was alive.

I felt a sudden, almost irresistible urge to reach out and touch it.

And I wasn't alone.

Desire flashed across Emily's face. Her lips parted. Her neck flooded with color. Even her hands, still wrapped around the box, trembled with anticipation. She cast a furtive glance at me, then turned to face me fully, her eye contact now quite firm. I knew then that it wasn't just awe she was feeling—it was longing. Desperate longing. It was written all over her face. I was confused, just for a moment, before I recalled Mr. Blackstone's words, spoken so long ago that it felt like they'd been dredged from my ancient past. "*I speak of real healing,*" he'd said. "*Divine healing.*"

Divine healing. I knew of at least one person who was in desperate need of such a power. We all did. *Was Emily thinking about using the Wing of Light on her mother? Was it right for me to ask her not to try it?*

"Incredible," Oliver whispered.

"Can you feel that?" I asked the others, posing a different question from the one that had been lingering on the tip of my tongue. "That... pulsing?"

"Yes," Mr. Harlowe whispered. "I cannot believe Haverford thought an artifact like this would be safe under his bed!"

I shook my head. "You forget how arrogant Haverford is, Mr. Harlowe. He probably fooled himself into thinking it was safest in here."

"He is a bit of a plonker, isn't he?" Oliver said, regaining some of his composure.

Chortling, I brushed the back of my hand on the Wing of Light. Burning heat seared through my skin. I lost myself in that moment, so startling was the warmth emanating from the artifact. Touching it was like experiencing a thousand embraces simultaneously, each whispering promises of strength and love. The sensation was so profound, so deeply moving, that it was almost beyond words.

I forced myself to pull away. "This is too much," I whispered, turning over my trembling hand. "Too powerful. We can't trust this. It'll eat us alive if we allow it to."

Emily hiccupped. There were tears streaming down her cheeks. She'd touched the Wing of Light, too. Felt its caress upon her skin. There was a remnant of its warmth still burning in her eyes.

"I need to take the artifact to Captain Bartlett," Mr.

Harlowe said. "Right now. It is far too dangerous to be left out in the open. With the Wing of Light in hand, there's no way I will be refused an interrogation of Haverford. The Sphinx Society will be brought down tonight."

He held out his hand to take the box from Emily.

She didn't give it to him.

Several seconds passed.

I started to get nervous.

Finally, Emily let out a shuddering breath, closed the lid, and handed the box to Mr. Harlowe.

He tucked it under his arm. The master-at-arms had no idea of the sacrifice Emily had just made on his behalf. "Very good. Now, you three must return to your stateroom with the cipher. Use it to decode your message. When you have the contents ready, send a steward to me, and I'll send someone down to bring you up to the bridge. Speak to no one else about what has happened here."

Oliver was the first to leave the room. Mr. Harlowe followed him, the Wing of Light tucked safely under his arm, his manner one of grim determination. Before Emily could leave, I reached out and grabbed her hand. She turned to look me. We locked eyes.

As before, I thought I saw a hint of something burning in her malachite stare. Something much older than either of us. It had started to fade, but its smoldering presence was unmistakable. I wondered if she saw the same thing when she looked at me.

"I know what it cost you to give that up," I said.

Emily blinked more tears away. "It was a fool's dream," she admitted, lacing her fingers with mine. "The Wing of Light would have taken more from us than it could have ever given her. I remember Mr. Blackstone's warning."

"So do I. That doesn't mean I don't understand."

"Perhaps it is best that Mr. Harlowe took it from me. Were we to be faced with such power again, I have little trust in my own restraint."

"If such a thing happens, you won't face it alone. We look out for each other, remember?"

A small, resigned smile replaced her determined frown. She released my hand and wiped the last of her tears away. "We do. That promise is proving to be one of the best ones I have ever made."

Her eyes looked normal once more. The unnatural glow was gone.

"I plan to continue keeping it for as long as you'll allow me the pleasure," I said. When her cheeks flushed a brilliant red, I looked over her shoulder and out into the empty hall, aware that my face might betray similar emotions. Now was not the time. "Do you need a moment, or are you ready to go?"

"When all of this is over, I suspect I shall need many moments. But I am ready."

We left Haverford's office together. Our companions were out of sight, but we caught up to them just after we turned the first corner on the staircase. They were standing with their backs to us. Opposite Oliver and Mr. Harlowe, with a frightful look upon his sallow face, was Mr. Clarke. We'd evidently interrupted some sort of confrontation.

The journalist looked startled to see us, though not as surprised as I was by his appearance. His illness had advanced in the hours since we'd last spoken. Seasickness now appeared to be the least of his concerns. Mr. Clarke's cheeks were hollowed out and empty; the dried edges of his lips were drawn and cracked. Far from flattering his thin frame, his dinner clothes hung on his gaunt figure. His once sharp eyes now held a glassy, fevered look.

"What are you doing here?" he snapped, though the question felt like an accusation. He glanced at the elegant wooden box in Mr. Harlowe's arms. "Are you not enjoying the concert?"

Mr. Harlowe stepped forward. "Mr. Clarke, as I have told you once already, this is an official investigation. Please return to your cabin and stay there until I give you further notice."

Mr. Clarke hesitated. His bloodshot eyes drifted from Mr. Harlowe's stern expression to the box. For a moment, it looked like he might argue. He certainly wasn't happy with Mr. Harlowe's order. In the end, though, he turned away and continued down the stairs, his unsteady footsteps scraping along the floor.

I felt a little guilty for cutting the journalist out of our investigation, but there wasn't any time to argue with Mr. Harlowe on his behalf. We resumed our hurried trek up the stairs. The storm outside roared desperately, like an animal backed into a corner. It seemed absurd that anyone could still be enjoying the concert through the tumult, but the rising sound of strings echoing from the saloon was confirmation that they were. A multitude of laughing voices could still be heard behind the double doors.

We reached the point where we would need to part ways.

"You have the cipher?" Mr. Harlowe asked.

"Yes," I confirmed, patting my jacket pocket.

"Then you know what must be done," he said. "Find the message you lifted from Marvin's room, decode it, and send for me right away once you have the riddle solved."

I nodded just as a deafening crack of thunder split the sky above. "You can count on us, sir. We won't let you down."

21
KNIFE'S EDGE

Oliver threw open the door of our stateroom, dashed to the wardrobe, and immediately started rummaging through his jacket pockets. I let Emily pass me by, then closed the door behind us. It felt safer to have privacy.

"I have it!" Oliver exclaimed. The note we found in Lieutenant Morgan's room was clenched in his hand. He moved to our water basin and shoved the bowl into the cabinet. With that out of the way, my friend flattened the note on the wooden surface. Long, wavering shadows played on the walls as the three of us huddled together around the familiar mess of jumbled letters.

PHHW PHDW HOHY HQFR PHDO RQHE
ULQJ WKHZ LQJR IGDU NQHV VFLV GDQJ
HURX V
—TE

"And here's our cipher," I said, drawing out the crumpled paper. "Let's see what Mr. Harlowe's theory is worth."

I flipped it over so that the lines of letters were facing upward. Oliver held the encoded message up beside it. "Do you think this will work?" he asked.

"There's only one way to find out. Budge over." Oliver obliged and moved out of my way.

I began to decode the first line. The room fell silent, save for the occasional boom of thunder and our steady breathing; before long, it was evident that Mr. Harlowe was correct about his old friend. Lieutenant Morgan was indeed using a Caesar shift. When my work was complete, I set my pencil down and held up the finished message.

"Is that it?" Oliver asked eagerly. "What does it say?"

"See for yourself."

MEET ME AT ELEVEN
COME ALONE
BRING THE WING OF DARKNESS
C IS DANGEROUS.
—TE

Emily's fiery hair brushed against my shoulder while she read. Being near to her wasn't quite as distracting as touching the Wing of Amun-Ra had been—but it was close. "Someone does have the Wing of Darkness, then," she said when she finished. "If this was from Mr. Eckert, and if Lieutenant Morgan followed through with his request, he lost it days ago."

I exhaled slowly. We were too late. Too slow in decoding the message. "We can't know that for sure," I said, though I was confident she was right. "If it was him, whoever killed him probably stole it."

"'Cis dangerous?'" Oliver asked, his brow furrowed. "What does that mean?"

"I think it's supposed to say, 'C is dangerous,'" corrected Emily. "Who is 'C,' though? Dinsmore was a captain. We know he has some involvement in all of this. Or Mr. Blackstone—his first name was Carrington, wasn't it?"

Both were good guesses, but I couldn't shake the feeling we were missing something. Something big. It was on the tip of my tongue. "I think we're forgetting about someone," I said. "And it can't have been Mr. Blackstone. He died, remember?"

Oliver scratched his jaw. "He could have killed Lieutenant Morgan first, though. And then gotten himself killed later."

"Mr. Harlowe doesn't think so. It would be helpful if we could talk to Mr. Clarke..." I trailed off. Alarms were blaring in my head. *Mr. Clarke. C.*

"James?" Emily asked. "Are you well?"

"Mr. Clarke," I whispered. "What if this note is a warning about Mr. Clarke?"

"Really? I mean, I suppose he might have been investigating them," Oliver said fairly. "That's his job, right? To poke around and uncover wrongdoing? They'd have wanted to share that with each other."

Emily bit her lip. "Mr. Harlowe said the Caesar shift should have been simple to decrypt. Is it possible Mr. Clarke lied to us about being able to read the message?"

"He wouldn't do that," Oliver insisted. "We saw him try to work it out! Besides, using Jimmy's logic, someone like Alex Cunningham might as well be our killer. Should we run around accosting everyone who shares the consonant?"

I wasn't convinced. But, unable to reach a consensus on the

identity of "C," we decided to wait until after reconnecting with Mr. Harlowe to speculate any further. Following the master-at-arms's instructions, we left our stateroom to buzz for a steward. As luck would have it, we didn't need to wait long. Alex Cunningham, arms laden with a stack of laundered linens for the dining saloon, nearly collided with us in the corridor.

"Mr. Cunningham!" I exclaimed, reaching out to steady his teetering pile of laundry. "Just the person we needed to see."

He sighed. "Good evening, sirs. What can I do for you? You... um... haven't stumbled on another murder, have you?"

"No, of course not. Might we trouble you to convey a message to Mr. Harlowe?" Emily asked kindly. "It is critically important that it reaches him. With all haste."

Alex glanced at his burden and then at us, his shoulders drooping. "Of course it is," he muttered under his breath. He sighed once more. "Let me drop these off. I'll be right back."

"Time is of the essence," interjected Oliver, his tone apologetic. "We'll help you with your linens, old man. Just pass them to us and be on your way."

Alex looked like he might protest, but the determined expressions on our faces must have convinced him not to do so. "Very well," he conceded, shifting the stack of warm towels into Oliver's arms. "Though this is highly irregular. What is the message?"

"Take this to him. Tell him we've just decoded it, and it's urgent he learns its contents," I said, handing over the marked-up letter. "If you say that, he'll know what to do."

Nodding, Alex adjusted his cap and started down the corridor. "I'll find him straight away," he promised over his shoulder. "You can count on me, sirs!"

As he disappeared around the corner, Oliver juggled the stack of linens and shot a wry grin at me. "I haven't the faintest idea what to do with these," he admitted. "Would it be dreadful if I were to hide them somewhere? How many towels does a ship like this need?"

"Oliver!" Emily chastised. "You're going to get Alex in—"

Unsteady footsteps echoed from somewhere down the corridor. They were slow, shuffling footfalls; their owner must have been half-dragging themselves to move. As they drew closer, I recognized Captain Dinsmore's broad frame and unsteady gait. He was upon us before we had a chance to consider fleeing.

"Good evening, Captain Dinsmore," I said cautiously. "Are you not having a good time at the concert?"

"Ah, yeah, good evenin,'" Captain Dinsmore slurred. He peered at us. "Me and Charlie, see, we took a little break. The band is playin' now. But that's... why aren' you in there?"

"Is everything alright, Captain?" Emily asked, neatly dodging his inquiry. "You seem... ill at ease."

He waved a hand dismissively, causing him to lose his balance. "Oh, I'm jus' fine. I jus'... need a bit o' air. And another drink... or two."

Oliver set Alex's linens down. "Captain, as long as you're here, we must ask you about something. It's important."

Dinsmore squinted at us, then nodded. "Wha' is it?"

"We found a message. It mentioned someone dangerous, someone whose name starts with 'C.' Do you know anything about that?"

Dinsmore's face twisted into a half-smile. "C? Jus' look out the window, lad, and the sea will be all you see!" He laughed, loud and from his belly, a rich, incongruous sound entirely inappropriate for the moment. "No, lads, I don' know who your dangerous 'C' is. I don' know why you'd be askin' me, anyways. I don' know nothin.'"

"Don't lie to us," Emily pressed. "We know you're involved with whatever is happening around here. We saw your Anubis picture. We know about Assistant Purser Haverford."

Dinsmore's smile faded. Almost as if he couldn't stop himself, the old sea captain clutched his wrist. I looked down. There, shining on the end of his sleeve, was a gleaming golden cufflink. The twin to the ones I'd seen Mr. Blackstone wearing at dinner on Thursday night. The cat's head was exactly the same.

"Where did you get that?" I demanded. "Did you steal those from Mr. Blackstone?"

"No, no, they're mine," insisted Dinsmore. He took a step back, swaying dangerously. "Now, you listen. I've... occasionally smuggled a thing or two. Harmless stuff. But when people started dyin'—good men, friends—I wen' low. I didn' want to end up like Marvin or Carrington. Blimey, even Ted was a good bloke if you could handle calling him 'colonel.' He's the one that gave us these." He looked down, twisting his cufflink. "I didn' sign up for murder, lads. I jus' wanted a few extra coins in my pocket."

"And Assistant Purser Haverford?" I urged, feeling a little nauseous. "What's he got to do with this?"

"Well, he's the boss, o' course, now that Ted's gone," Dinsmore muttered, twisting to look over his shoulder. He suddenly seemed to have realized there was a risk we might be overheard. "He's dead scared, though. Someone has been hunting for the Sundered Wings, see? And it's only me and him lef' now, so he's nervous. Wants me to find them, for all the good tha's done. And tha' reporter won' leave us alone, houndin' us all hours o' the day..."

Hurried footsteps sounded from behind Dinsmore. We stopped and turned to face their owner. It was as if the universe itself had planned for him to be brought up in conversation, had known that he would be needed here, and was only saving his arrival for dramatic timing. Assistant Purser Haverford, the subject of our inquiries, shot to the stop of the stairs and turned the corner at a run. He was frantic, wide-eyed, his wavy blonde hair askew. He looked far from the composed figure I'd seen at the concert earlier that evening.

"There you are, Dinsmore!" barked Haverford. "I've been looking everywhere for you, you drunken fool! Do you have any idea what you've done?"

Dinsmore flinched, retreating a step. "Charlie, I—"

"Save it!" Haverford snapped. "I warned you yesterday, didn't I? 'Watch my office,' I said, and what did you do!? Went off to DRINK! And now, the Wing of Light is GONE!"

Haverford's gaze shifted, landing on Emily and me. "Wait..." His voice dropped to a menacing whisper before rising once more. "You two... you've touched the Wing, haven't you? You have! I can see its light on you!"

I took a step back. "I—I don't know what you're talking about."

"Oh, yes, you do, you little thieves. I have already told you; I can see it. The Wing of Light leaves a trace. An aura. It clings to everyone who touches it. I am on to your game now, Miss Wentworth. You have played your part well, but your race is run."

Emily reached out and grabbed my hand. "We were just trying to help," she said. "That Wing belongs with Captain Bartlett, not with you! You're nothing but a criminal."

"Help?" Haverford sneered. "You have no notion of what you have done, you impudent girl. That artifact holds power beyond your comprehension. Where is it?"

"We don't have it," Emily confessed. "And you'll never see it again if we—"

Without warning, Haverford lunged at Emily, a flash of steel in his hand.

Time slowed down. The only things I could see were the gleam of a blade and Emily's wide, terrified eyes.

Instinct took over. I threw myself in front of her, everything else forgotten. The frosty edge of the knife sliced into my upper arm. Pain exploded, white-hot and blinding, but I swung back at Haverford, my hand knocking against his wrist. The knife clattered to the floor. I shoved the assistant purser away. He slammed into the enamel-white wall, then collapsed to the ground in a heap.

"James!" Emily screamed.

The pain was intense. I could feel my heartbeat pulsing, pumping blood onto the ruined sleeve of what had been my best suit.

"I know you have the Wing of Light!" Haverford raged, spittle flying from his lips. "Give it back!" He lunged at me again, but someone grabbed him from behind and pulled him back.

"Stand down, Haverford!" Mr. Harlowe barked, his grip like iron. The master-at-arms had arrived just in time.

"You fool!" Haverford shouted, swinging a fist at Mr. Harlowe. "You don't understand! I need that artifact! It's mine!"

Mr. Harlowe dodged and countered with a swift jab to Haverford's gut. Haverford staggered, gasping for breath, but quickly recovered, launching himself at Mr. Harlowe with renewed anger. They grappled, the pair of them appearing only as a blur of fists and grunts in the narrow corridor. I slid down the wall as I watched them fight. My energy, it seemed, was spent.

Emily dropped to her knees beside me and grabbed one of the linens from the floor. "Hold still, James," she urged, her hands trembling as she pressed the cloth against my wound to staunch the bleeding. It was quickly soaked crimson.

Dinsmore, swaying unsteadily, tried to move toward Mr. Harlowe and Haverford, but Oliver stepped in between them and grabbed the old man by the shoulders. "Stay out of it, Dinsmore," Oliver warned, but Dinsmore struggled, trying to break free.

As Dinsmore twisted in Oliver's grasp, Alex Cunningham rushed in to join the fray. He helped Oliver wrestle the drunken captain to the ground. "Hold still, damn it!" Alex grunted. Together, they pinned Dinsmore's arms behind his back.

Stateroom doors began to open. A few curious passengers who had skipped the concert, either by habit or by seasickness, peered out at the commotion. I could only imagine what was going through their minds.

Mr. Harlowe and Haverford continued to exchange blows. Finally, with a well-placed punch to Haverford's jaw, Mr. Harlowe sent the assistant purser sprawling to the floor.

"Enough!" Mr. Harlowe shouted, his chest heaving. "You're not helping anyone with this madness!"

Haverford lay on the ground, groaning. "The Sundered Wings... if he has both of them, Harlowe, you won't be able to stop him. Nobody will."

Mr. Harlowe scoffed. Emily and I moved closer to Haverford while Oliver and Alex kept Dinsmore subdued.

"We need to know everything, Haverford," I said firmly, my

voice steady despite the throbbing in my arm. "Who is 'C?' Who's hunting you?"

Mr. Harlowe hauled Haverford to his feet, his grip firm on the man's collar. "Start talking. Now."

Haverford's eyes darted around the corridor, clearly looking for assistance from the passengers, who were watching in stunned silence.

Mr. Harlowe glared at them. "There's nothing to see here! Everyone, back to your rooms!" he ordered. Abashed, the passengers closed their doors one at a time until nobody was left to watch.

Out of options, Haverford sagged in Mr. Harlowe's grip, defeated. "Very well," he said, surrendering. "But I'm not saying a word until Captain Bartlett has been summoned. I will not allow myself to be manhandled by you brutes."

"On your way, then," snarled Mr. Harlowe, shoving Haverford forward. "He's waiting for us, with your artifact in hand."

Haverford smiled. It was a cold smile, utterly bereft of its usual warmth. "You should have said so sooner."

Mr. Harlowe led us up the stairs. Haverford was in front of him, his arms pulled behind his back, being led in a frog march by the taller man. Behind them, Oliver and Alex supported Captain Dinsmore, who had passed out in the excitement. The old man's arms were draped over their shoulders. Emily and I brought up the rear; she kept the linen pressed against my arm, which still throbbed.

When we reached the C-deck landing, Mr. Harlowe led us out onto the enclosed promenade, heading toward the same plain door we'd grown accustomed to taking into first class.

Out here, it was clear that conditions had deteriorated even further. Sea spray splashed on the windows. Beyond them, between flashes of lightning, I could see the dark, churning sea. Waves crested to such peaks a mountain would feel envy.

"Keep moving," Mr. Harlowe commanded. "You know the way."

Our steps echoed in the enclosed space. Two forgotten dolls, their porcelain faces gleaming, stared unblinkingly at us from one of the benches as we passed. I thought of their owners; what were they doing now?

We were almost at the end of the hallway when the vast expanse of the ocean outside dropped away. The ship rolled over several degrees, enough to make Emily and I grab for the inside railing. Oliver shouted, waking Dinsmore, who offered a drunken, "Wha's happenin?'"

A flash of lightning outside illuminated something horrifying: a towering wave, perhaps over one hundred feet tall, barreling down on the *Olympic*. There was no time for the ship to dodge it.

"Get down!" Oliver cried.

It was too late.

Emily clung to me as the windows shattered.

Icy water surged in and swept us down the length of the promenade. Everything was a blur of ocean and broken glass. Salt stung my eyes, blinding me as I fought to regain control. The wind was knocked out of me as I slammed into the aft end of the promenade hard enough to see stars. Emily's hand slipped out of mine. She crashed into me before being pulled away. We stretched out to each other; our fingers brushed before the current pulled us apart.

Haverford decided this was the moment to make his escape. The assistant purser thrashed against Mr. Harlowe's grip, twisting and jerking his body to gain leverage. Mr. Harlowe tightened his hold, but the slickness of the seawater gave Haverford an advantage. The assistant purser drove his shoulder into the master-at-arms's chest. Mr. Harlowe stumbled. Haverford broke free, slamming Mr. Harlowe's head into the wall before fleeing into the ship.

"No!" I shouted. "Get back here, you coward!"

Haverford disappeared around the corner. Summoning every ounce of my remaining strength, I forced myself to my feet, the icy water swirling around my knees. "Emily!" I shouted. "Emily, are you safe?"

She was. She had to be. I couldn't lose her. Not before I'd had a chance to confess.

"I'm here!" Emily's voice was weak. She surfaced and crawled toward me, drenched and shivering; I grabbed her hand and pulled her to her feet. Her hair was plastered to her shoulders. Her brilliant emerald dress was soaked through. A jagged cut, red and angry, welled up on her collarbone. She pulled a piece of glass from it. "We need to get to Mr. Harlowe," she said, tossing the glass aside. "I haven't seen him come back up."

"He's there!" I said. "Oliver has him!"

The master-at-arms was slumped over, unconscious, leaning against the interior wall. His forehead had split open. Oliver and Alex were already by his side, trying to lift him up at the same time they kept a frantic, newly reawakened Dinsmore under control. "Jimmy, help me!" Oliver yelled. "I can't lift them both!"

Emily and I stumbled over to her brother. We traded glances before each of us took hold of one of Mr. Harlowe's arms and pulled his limp body from the water. Satisfied that the two of us could keep the master-at-arms from drowning,

Oliver switched to helping Alex subdue Dinsmore, who was thrashing and speaking nonsense.

We dragged the unconscious Mr. Harlowe back inside, away from the shattered windows and the relentless storm. The ship lurched again. "Where should we take him?" I asked, panting.

"Library," Oliver grunted. He was beside us, pulling the inebriated Dinsmore by his feet. He'd passed out again. Alex was carrying Dinsmore's other side.

It was a good suggestion. The four of us dragged Mr. Harlowe and Dinsmore into the library, hoping that the dimly lit room might offer us momentary respite from the chaos outside. It was thankfully devoid of people. We shoved some furniture out of the way and lowered Mr. Harlowe onto a couch. He didn't stir.

"Stay with us," Emily urged, pressing a torn scrap of the floral curtains to his wound. "This is bad. He needs a doctor, Oliver."

But even as she spoke, the lights flickered and went out, plunging us into darkness. "Damn it!" Oliver cursed. "The electricity is out!"

"That isn't a surprise. We're fortunate we didn't founder," I wheezed.

Emily hesitated before tentatively asking, "We aren't sinking... are we?"

"No. At least, I don't believe so. I still feel vibration from the engines," Alex said. "We aren't dead in the water. It may just be C-deck that's lost power; either way, the engineers will fix everything, don't you worry."

Not worrying was easier said than done. The only light now came from the occasional flash of lightning outside. It was eerie, watching the storm from the darkened library. It didn't help that the air carried the metallic scent of blood. Mr. Harlowe and I were almost certainly ruining the carpet.

"We need to keep moving." I wrapped my hand around the cut on my arm, which was stinging mercilessly. The salty sea water wasn't doing me any favors. "Haverford can't have gotten far. We can still catch him."

"But what about Captain Dinsmore? Mr. Harlowe—" Emily began.

"I'll take care of things here," rasped the master-at-arms.

I jumped, startled to hear his voice.

"Mr. Harlowe!" Oliver exclaimed.

"Go after Haverford," the injured man begged. "We need him. Only he can lead us to the German."

He held out his revolver for Oliver to take. After a moment of indecision, my friend reached out and grasped its custom hilt. Another flash of lightning illuminated the exchange.

Emily stood up, wiped her hands clean, and nodded. "Very well. We bid you farewell, sir."

"There's no time for the niceties, Miss Wentworth. The safety of everyone on this ship depends on you."

22

TOGETHER AT LAST

Mr. Harlowe double-checked that Oliver understood how to load and fire his revolver, then collapsed back onto the ruined couch. He looked utterly spent. I wished we could do more for him, but there was nothing for it. It was time for us to go.

Emily led the way back out onto the promenade. I followed right behind her. Oliver brought up the rear.

We had nearly reached the door when I reached out and braced myself against the dampened frame. I sighed before holding up my other hand to bring Oliver to a stop. Emily turned around; I inclined my head back toward the master-at-arms. Leaving a wounded Mr. Harlowe behind felt wrong. *What if something else happened? What if Dinsmore awoke and he couldn't handle him?*

"Mr. Harlowe, are you sure—"

"Son, you need to go. Marvin didn't sacrifice his life for us to allow Haverford's escape. I'll be safe here."

Oliver and I shared a skeptical look. "All due respect, sir, but will you? You can't even stand."

Alex patted Mr. Harlowe on the shoulder, took the master-at-arms's keys, and handed them to me. "We can manage things here, Mr. Kelly. Please find Assistant Purser Haverford before anyone else gets hurt. You're the only ones who can."

"Thank you, Mr. Cunningham," Emily said. "As always, your services are invaluable. Oliver, James, are you ready?"

We were. The three of us raced back onto the C-deck promenade, where a few inches of water still covered the floor. The windows were shattered. Wind and rain whipped around in their absence, drenching the walls with brine and peppering our exposed skin with salty sea spray. It felt like we'd stepped into the heart of the storm. Incredibly, one of the porcelain dolls had survived the wave; it now floated aimlessly in the water, vacant eyes staring at the ceiling. The poor thing's painted lips were frozen in an eerie half-smile.

"This way!" I called out as I turned to the right. "Haverford was heading toward first class!"

The ship groaned and creaked around us, but it seemed she'd righted herself for the time being. That was a relief—I wasn't sure how many more waves like that the *Olympic* could take. Wasting no time, I swung open the same door Mr. Harlowe had used on Saturday. Passengers, disoriented in the darkness, filled the hallway. Their faces were cloaked in shadow under the low emergency lighting.

"Hey, you lot!" Oliver shouted. "Have you seen the assistant purser?"

A short man with silver hair and soaked pajamas nodded. "Aye, yes. He ran by just now, drenched from head to toe! But... who are you?"

"Well, sir, I'm—"

"No time for that, Jimmy! Speed is of the essence!" Oliver insisted. He overtook me as he dashed down the narrow corridor. When he turned back, I was still in the same place. "Don't just stand there! Try to keep pace!"

Emily and I took off after him.

"I say!" another man shouted when we shoved by him, all thoughts of decorum forgotten.

As we neared the end of the corridor, Oliver sprinted even further ahead, outpacing both Emily and me by a fair margin; in our defense, I was wounded, and she was attempting to run in a sodden dress. "The stairs are right up here!" he shouted over his shoulder. "Haverford will have been heading to the bridge—he wants the Wing of Light back!"

Suddenly, the ship lurched as another wave struck. A pair of ceiling panels broke free, swung downward, collided with a deafening clang, and came to rest vertically in the darkened hallway. Sparks flew as electrical wires shorted out. The nearest emergency lights failed.

"Oliver!" Emily cried. Her brother, my best friend, was out of sight, separated from us by the barrier of debris.

"We're cut off!" I yelled. Emily and I stepped back. The air was pungent, filled with the smell of ozone from the electrical short. "Oliver, are you there?"

"Jimmy?" It was Oliver's voice, coming from the other side of the obstruction.

"Oliver!" I shouted. "We're not hurt, but we're stuck here! We can't reach you!"

I heard rustling on the other side of the fallen tiles. The bulkheads groaned.

"There isn't time to get through!" Oliver yelled. "I'm going to try to find Haverford!"

"Be careful! We'll find another way around!"

Emily tugged at my sleeve. "We need to hurry."

I nodded, glancing around for an alternate route. The

debris and water made everything more difficult. "I think we need to backtrack," I said. "If these hallways are arranged like those in second class, there will be another corridor running parallel to this one. We just need to find a way over to it."

"I'll be right behind you."

We pushed through the crowded hallway. Confusion reigned as passengers tried to navigate the darkened, waterlogged corridor. We made it about halfway back to the promenade before Dr. Widmer bowled me over.

"What's happened?" he asked. "Are we sinking?"

"No," I assured him. "At least, I don't think we are. The *Olympic* is tough."

Dr. Widmer's posture sagged in relief. "Well, thank the Lord for that. Do you have any casualty numbers?"

"No, but sir, you're needed in the second-class library," Emily said. "Master-at-Arms Harlowe is in a bad way."

"Has he sent you here?"

"No. We're on our way to see Captain Bartlett." I winced when a passing man bumped into my arm. "We have information he needs."

The doctor nodded. He glanced at my wound, which was bleeding through the linens wrapped around it. "If you need to see Captain Bartlett, the fastest way will be to go back the way I came from. The hallway on the other side of C-deck is clear. I will see to Mr. Harlowe."

With a rushed "thanks," we set off down the narrow, deserted passageway that Dr. Widmer had just come flying out of. We passed several doors as we ran, staterooms belonging to the chief steward, restaurant manager, and assistant doctor. All of them were closed. When we reached the far end, the exit refused to open. It was locked. Cursing, I reached for Mr. Harlowe's keys and started trying them.

Emily leaned against the wall and took a moment to catch her breath. Her elegant dress was soaked with seawater, her hair tangled with grime and sweat. The silver necklace around her neck shone under the emergency lights. It took all of my willpower to look away from her and focus on the task at hand. A part of me worried she'd be gone when I turned back.

If that wave had swept her away... If I hadn't blocked Haverford's knife...

My hands were trembling, though whether that was from adrenaline or exhaustion, I couldn't say. "Emily..." I started, fumbling with the loop of keys. They were labeled with metal tags, but I didn't have enough light to read the words. "I know this is bad timing, the worst possible timing, but I have to say this now, or I might never get the chance."

She looked up at me. "What are you talking about?"

"If we survive this, I want to court you," I said, the words spilling out before I could lose my nerve. Emily's mouth fell open. "I know I don't have the wealth or status your other suitors might have, but I can earn those things. I can't promise you much, but—"

She touched my arm and smiled. "James, you jumped in front of a knife for me. What's more valuable than that?"

"Gold?" I joked as I tried yet another key.

Emily chuckled. "One should not downplay their accomplishments when proposing courtship. Are you prepared for what this will entail? I am no traditional woman, Mr. Kelly, but people will expect certain traditions to be followed."

"I know that I'll have to ask your parents, of course," I said, trying another key. It, too, failed to open the door. "I'm planning to do that. I just didn't think you'd take kindly to hearing about my feelings from them before you heard about them from me. You've told me many times that you're your own woman. I wanted you to have the chance to turn me down in private."

"You're right. I am my own woman." Emily stepped closer, her gaze steady. I was awash in a citrus haze.

"Does that mean you're interested?" I asked, my mouth suddenly dry.

She leaned in and answered my question with an urgent kiss. All around us, the hallway trembled with distant crashes, shouting voices, and the groan of the ship twisting in the storm. But for a moment, none of it mattered. Her lips were warm against mine. Every shared glance, every brief touch, every unspoken word between us since that first day on deck had led us here.

It was a desperate kiss, the kind you share when you're afraid the world is about to end.

All too soon, it was over. We pulled apart, breathless and staring at each other in wonder.

"I've been waiting for that all night," Emily whispered, grinning devilishly. "Ever since that moment in your stateroom. People may judge me for it, but I needed you to know I feel the same way you do."

"I know—I mean, I do. That is, we feel the same way," I stammered, then added more firmly, "I won't tell anyone what we just did. Your reputation is safe with me."

Emily's smile was warmer than the Wing of Light. "I trust you, James, or I wouldn't have done it. Now, let's get this door open, shall we? Oliver is waiting for us."

"I'm trying," I said, my hands still trembling as I fumbled with the heavy keys. "There are a lot of keys here." I tried another one, the second to last on the keyring. This time, it turned the lock with a satisfying click. We stepped through the door and back out into a central corridor.

"Let's go!" I grabbed Emily's hand and took off down the hallway. "Oliver should still be close! If we hurry, we can catch up with him!"

We burst onto one of the middle landings of the magnificent Grand Staircase. Outside, the storm still raged, its fury illuminating the iron dome up high above us. The red and white pole of a barber shop shone in the intermittent light.

"James, I hear someone running up ahead!"

Emily had barely had time to finish her sentence when Haverford came flying out of the room straight ahead with a look of sheer panic on his face, Oliver hot on his heels. They rounded the corner and dashed up the staircase. Haverford took them two at a time, so desperate was he to escape.

"About time you two made it!" Oliver called out over his shoulder. "Come on, we can't let him get away!" His voice was drowned out by the rain, which was hammering the glass dome above with the force of a dreadnought's broadside.

Emily and I glanced at each other, then charged after them. We reached the next landing right as the electric lights came back on. They flickered once before burning strong.

The return of the lights startled Haverford enough that he missed the last step. He went flying into a nearby palm, smashing the pot and sending soil everywhere. It was a sign of how much conditions had deteriorated that this was hardly the only plant that had tipped over on the B-deck landing. Cane furniture, normally arranged in a manner to encourage conversation, was strewn about haphazardly, and the tiled floor was slick with water.

Haverford picked himself up off the floor. He stopped long enough to glare at us before turning away from the stairs and resuming his mad dash forward, desperation fueling him more effectively than any logic ever could. We continued our pursuit;

my legs burned with the effort, each footfall aggravating the jagged wound in my arm. It throbbed along with the beats of my racing heart.

Room numbers flew by—B-97... B-81... B-63...

We nearly caught him on the forward staircase, our hands just inches from his coat, but he scrambled up to the next landing on A-deck, pivoted, and continued up toward the boat deck. We were losing ground. Just when it seemed he might escape, he tripped again. Arms flailing, Haverford sprawled out, coming to a crashing halt under the dome. Our chase was over.

"Stop, Haverford!" Oliver cried. "There's nowhere else for you to go!"

But Haverford wasn't done yet. With surprising agility, he leaped to his feet, rammed his shoulder into a wooden door, and dashed into the gymnasium. We followed him. The electric camels and horse stood tall in the dark; these state-of-the-art products, some of Wiesbaden's finest engineering, were the only things separating us from our quarry.

Emily and Oliver flanked me as we advanced. Haverford was trapped. He looked around, wildly searching for an escape he must have known didn't exist. The windows rattled with the wind. Rain hammered against the glass.

"There's nowhere left to run," Emily said. "Give it up."

Haverford backed against the wall, his chest heaving. "You don't understand," he wheezed. "I kept the Wing of Light safe!"

We surrounded him, panting as we, too, fought to catch our breaths.

"Tell us what you know, Haverford," Emily pressed. "Cooperate, and we can help you."

"If I talk, I need guarantees, protection. Otherwise, I'm a dead man."

Before we could respond, Oliver lunged, grabbed Haverford by the collar, and slammed him against the wall with enough force to make the wood paneling shudder.

"Start talking," Oliver demanded. "Who is 'C?'"

"I won't t-t-tell you." Haverford's breath escaped in short, terrified gasps. "Not—not unless you promise me protection!"

"We'll do what we can to keep you alive." I tightened the linen wrapped around the wound on my arm, wincing as a fresh wave of pain shot through me. "I can't promise more than that. Now, do you want us to help you, or do you want to try your chances out there with the murderer?"

"No! I—I'll talk." Haverford looked between us frantically. "I was keeping it safe from him!"

"From whom?"

"I don't know! I don't have the name you want. But I have something... something I was going to show to Captain Bartlett! I was just heading over to meet him!"

"You were doing no such thing," Emily sniped. "You wanted that artifact for yourself. You were coming here to steal it, not to talk with the captain."

"I do! I mean, I was. But not for the reason you think! I can show you if you'll let me down!"

Oliver looked questioningly at me, and I nodded. He released Haverford but drew Harlowe's revolver, training it on the deceitful man. The White Star logo gleamed on its metal handle.

His attention focused on the gun, the assistant purser reached into his pocket and pulled out a crumpled note. The paper was damp, the ink smudged. He handed it to Emily. She read it before giving it to me.

I know you have the artifact. Bring the Wing of Light to the library in second class at 3:00 tonight, or you'll be the next to die. Come alone.

"Ominous," Oliver commented idly. "How do we know this isn't a forgery?"

"It isn't. I—I recognize this," I said. "That handwriting, I've seen it before..."

But where? My mind raced, trying to place it. The answer was just out of reach, locked away in my head, but I knew it was there. It tugged at the edge of my memory. It had been something trivial. Something unimportant. I closed my eyes, trying furiously to remember...

And then it hit me.

Quoits.

A slate scoreboard.

And a spiky number '3.'

My eyes flew open. "Yes!" I exclaimed. "I have seen it! And so have you!"

"Have I?" Emily asked. She looked at the smudged note again. "Are you quite certain?"

"Yes. It's the '3' that I remember," I said, pointing to the spiky numeral. "See how distinctive it is? Mr. Clarke wrote this, I'm sure of it. He used the same number style on the scoring board for our game of quoits!"

Emily let out a small gasp. "Mr. Clarke? Do you think he really is 'C?' But what about his seasickness? He was too sick to even meet us earlier—"

"His writing is similar to the message on that Anubis picture, too." I was growing surer by the second.

Oliver scoffed. "Come off it, Jimmy. Do you seriously think Mr. Clarke is the German? He's on our side!"

"No, he isn't. That was all an act."

I received backup from a most unexpected place—Haverford. "Clarke's been sniffing around Dinsmore and me for days. He must have guessed we knew about the other artifact. That bastard fooled us all... even the bloodhound Harlowe failed to suspect him."

"Mr. Harlowe was so busy following you he missed Mr. Clarke," I said, feeling the pieces continue to fall into place. "Think about it. Mr. Clarke has an accent, right? How different does Swedish sound from German? Could he be faking it?"

"Quite different," Emily said, wringing her hair out as she spoke. "But he could probably pass one off as the other if he worked at it."

Oliver shook his head. "This is madness. He's a journalist! His job is to investigate crimes, not commit them. How could he be..."

"I know it's difficult to believe, Ollie," I said, stretching and flexing my fingers. My wounded arm was growing stiff. "But Mr. Clarke told us himself that Eckert ran into the authorities in Germany before this voyage. They must have been the ones who sent him to the *Olympic* to steal the Sundered Wings. Mr. Clarke knew about the connection between Morgan and Eckert, so he started with them and worked his way through the smuggling ring from there."

Emily was nodding along now. "Oh, James. It makes so much sense! Mr. Clarke knew that Lieutenant Morgan was connected to the smugglers, so he scheduled the midnight meeting to discover more. It went badly, and Mr. Clarke murdered him, but only after he found out the lieutenant had already hidden the artifacts!"

"So, all this time... he's been using us?" Oliver slammed his fist into the nearby punching bag; it rattled on its chain, spun around, and narrowly missed Haverford, who was warily eyeing the revolver in Oliver's other hand. "We've been feeding him everything he needed!"

"Marvin gave me the Wing of Light for safekeeping on Wednesday night," Haverford added helpfully as he climbed to his feet and dragged himself over to lean on the mechanical horse. "I wasn't supposed to touch it, but... curiosity, you know. After he died, I figured I was as good a person as any to inherit his goods."

"Noble of you to wait for his body to cool," Emily deadpanned. Haverford shrugged.

I cleared my throat and spoke again. "He trusted you with one of the Sundered Wings, Haverford, and gave the other to his partner, Eckert. Eckert was 'TH.' But Mr. Clarke knew about their connection. He snuck into first class and murdered him for it."

"The other artifact must be what's causing those strange, mummified wounds," Oliver suggested. My friend was still breathing heavily, but he seemed to be coming down from his angry outburst. "It must have been used to kill Eckert. And Mr. Blackstone."

Emily let out a resigned sigh. "Unfortunately, we must also presume that Mr. Clarke is the person who used it on them."

It was a sobering thought.

"Oh! And the storm!" Oliver continued, snapping his fingers. "The storm started the night Eckert was killed! Mr. Clarke has probably been using the artifact ever since he found it! Just like Mr. Blackstone said!"

"We saw Mr. Clarke the night Eckert was murdered, James," Emily said, awestruck. "He passed by us in the library, remember? He was dressed up in his tuxedo. That outfit wasn't meant for us in second class—he wore it to blend in with the people in first class!"

"Unbelievable," I muttered.

Oliver sat down on one of the benches. "What about Mr. Blackstone's cufflink? How did that end up next to Eckert's body?"

"Those cufflinks aren't unique," I said, remembering Dinsmore's slurred confession. "We saw some on Dinsmore's jacket, too. Remember? He said Eckert gave them to him."

"We all have them," admitted Haverford. He'd been so quiet I'd almost forgotten he was present. "They were a gift from Theodore, back when we first established the Sphinx Society. A gesture of goodwill. He was probably wearing them the night he died."

"So, it's true, then?" I asked. "You're part of the Sphinx Society?"

"Yes. Or I was. Not many of us left, are there? Theodore, Dinsmore, Reginald, and I were the founding members—collectors of fine artifacts, unbound by the rules and laws of nations."

Oliver frowned. "What about Lieutenant Morgan? Wasn't he a part of your team?"

Haverford snorted. "Marvin worked with Theodore, but he never wanted to dirty his hands with the rest of us. Joining the Sphinx Society was a step too far for our so-called war hero."

"He wasn't a part of your smuggling ring?" Oliver asked.

"Marvin was no saint," Haverford drawled. "But no. He wasn't one of us. Not officially, anyway."

I shook my head. "How did you manage to stop Mr. Harlowe and the authorities from uncovering your plans? They were hard after you."

"There's honor among thieves, boy. We took an oath."

"That's it? You just agreed not to tell anyone?"

Haverford rolled his eyes, and for a moment, a spark of his old fire returned. "That's how secrets tend to work. We couldn't have dodged the authorities if we made a habit of screaming our business from the mountaintop, could we? And I thought you were intelligent…"

I glared at Haverford. "Be that as it may," I ground out, fighting to unstick my teeth, "I guess that explains the cufflink. Mr. Clarke knew we suspected Mr. Blackstone—after all, he was the one who told us we should investigate him in the first place! So, when we told Mr. Clarke we found the cufflink alongside Eckert's body, he let us believe the killer left it behind. He's known about you all along."

Haverford lapsed into a coughing fit. When his hand came away from his mouth, glistening red blood shone on it.

"Are you well?" Emily asked.

"I have been growing weaker all evening," Haverford confessed in a whisper. "But never fear. I shall be whole again after I reclaim the Wing of Light. Everything will be fine once I have it back."

I didn't know how to respond to that, but Oliver, for the first time, looked pityingly upon the assistant purser. "Let's say I believe that Mr. Clarke is our man," my friend said. "How did he pull this off? Where did he go after killing Eckert?"

"Well, at that point, Mr. Clarke had one of the Sundered Wings." I folded my arms and began to pace. "But he still didn't know where Lieutenant Morgan stashed the other one.

He met with us and lied about being able to decipher that coded note—but he knew we were getting close. So, to silence us, he went after Annabelle. Unfortunately for him, Mr. Blackstone figured him out. They had a fight, and Mr. Blackstone ended up dead. Cursed."

A flash of lightning illuminated the gymnasium. Shadows streaked from the stationary equipment.

Haverford cleared his throat. "I never considered using the Wing of Light to carry out such violence. Every time I touched it, I felt like the sun blessed me with its power. It's intoxicating to feel so loved and to be so loved. I constantly saw new possibilities, new avenues for use. The Sundered Wings are limited only by imagination. Clarke's is clearly darker than mine."

"Yes, well, you aren't a German saboteur, so causing damage wouldn't have been at the top of your priority list," Oliver said bitterly. "You're just a greedy fool who got in over his head."

"Perhaps." Haverford dropped to his knees and coughed again, recoiling at the sight of more blood on his hand. "Although, it might have something to do with which of the Sundered Wings I had. Mine is beautiful. Helpful. Warm. The other one, the Wing of Shadow... I suspect it exerts a rather more sinister pull on its owner."

"You're plenty sinister on your own," Emily snapped.

To his credit, Haverford had the sense to look chagrined. "All I wanted was to be someone who matters. Someone special. But I haven't felt right since I lost it. Something is wrong with me. I need the Wing of Light back. I'm cold without it."

"Are you sure about all of this?" I asked, ignoring his lamentations. "Sure that everything you've told us is true?"

Haverford looked up at me; he was growing paler by the second. His face twisted in anguish when he spoke. "I am sure. I—I did not mean for things to go this far. I just..." he trailed off.

Another lightning strike illuminated the gymnasium. It highlighted every cut and bruise on our faces. The resounding crash of thunder that followed rattled the *Olympic* to such a degree I could feel it reverberating in my chest.

"There you have it, then." Emily looked down on Haverford with intense dislike. "We have unraveled the mystery. Mr. Clarke is using the Sundered Wings to sink the ship."

"You're wrong," Haverford wheezed. Despite his deteriorating condition, he seemed delighted to know something we didn't; a chuckle escaped his ruby lips. "The entire crew is baffled by these weather patterns, but I understand them."

"What do you mean?" I asked.

"Only that it benefits Clarke to get to New York as quickly as possible."

Haverford pointed to a carved oak installation on the wall opposite the door. On it, an intricate cutaway showed an Olympic Class ocean liner and a map with the travel routes of the White Star Line. "By my reckoning, we covered over 600 miles yesterday. This voyage will crush Cunard's record crossing time; I'd be surprised if we weren't passing Ellis Island by noon tomorrow, Blue Riband in hand."

I remembered my breakfast conversation with Dr. Wentworth. He'd been told that the *Olympic* had been ordered to slow down. *Could Haverford be right? Was this why she hadn't done so?*

"Fine," Oliver snapped, his features tightening again. "Mr. Clarke isn't trying to sink the ship, which throws Mr.

Harlowe's theory out the window. Instead, he's trying to use the biggest storm of the century to rush to New York and slip away with the Sundered Wings. How did we miss this?"

"More importantly, how confident are you in this theory?" I asked Haverford.

"Does it matter, Mr. Kelly? We'll be in port tomorrow; Clarke is out of time to find the other artifact. That's why he made his move tonight."

"But we messed his plan up," Oliver said.

Emily finished his sentence for him. "Because we broke into your office. He wasn't counting on that."

"None of us were counting on your interference, girl! If Dinsmore hadn't cracked, I'd still have my warmth. We would be safe."

"I rather doubt that." I watched as Haverford sank lower to the floor, overcome by a heaving cough. "But what's done is done. We need to get to the bridge and find Captain Bartlett. Someone has to secure the Wing of Light before Mr. Clarke steals it out from under their noses."

Oliver nodded, his face set with determination. "It's up to us now."

"What should we do with him?" I asked, gesturing to Haverford. "We promised to protect him."

Emily answered first. "We'll have to leave him here and trust he will remain safe until we return. All that matters now is reaching Captain Bartlett before Mr. Clarke does."

I took one last look at the assistant purser. He no longer seemed to be aware of his surroundings. "You're right. Let's go."

We left the gymnasium, our footsteps echoing in the empty landing as we headed toward the officers' quarters. Everything we passed was in disarray. Handsome furniture was strewn about, its blue upholstery ripped and damaged by the wave. A heater on the wall gently hissed as it released a steady trickle of steam. It felt as if an unnatural hush had fallen over the ship, the usual white noise swallowed by a suffocating silence. The *Olympic* was holding her breath. Waiting.

"Do you think Mr. Clarke might have already gone to the bridge looking for the Wing of Light?" Oliver asked. "He must know that Mr. Harlowe had it when we encountered him outside Haverford's office."

I began to jog. "Yes. He's been one step ahead of us all week. This is our last chance to stop him."

Oliver cursed. "I hope they had the sense to put a guard on the damned thing."

A loud crash echoed from somewhere up ahead, followed by muffled shouts. We froze, exchanging alarmed glances.

"I—I think that came from the officer's quarters," whispered Emily.

The unmistakable crack of gunshots rang out. *POP! POP! POP!* The sound reverberated through the corridor and onto the landing where we stood.

"That must be him!" I said.

Olive cursed again. "What do we do now?"

Emily pointed to the narrow passage connecting the Grand Staircase to the bridge. "This way! We can intercept him if he tries to escape back into the ship!"

Oliver and I didn't need to voice our agreement aloud. She was right. We broke into a run.

Just before we reached the door to the officers' quarters, it slammed open with a deafening crash. We were too late. Mr. Clarke emerged, wild-eyed, with a smoking revolver clutched in his left hand. His right hand was raised. Clutched in it were two golden artifacts. Artifacts that pulsed with a strange, ethereal light.

Our worst fears had been realized—despite our best efforts to prevent it, the Sundered Wings of Amun-Ra had been reunited once more.

23
THE CURSE OF THE SUNDERED WINGS

I froze. The room, grand as it was, shrank under the oppressive weight of Mr. Clarke's presence. He was neither tall nor broad, but he towered over the staircase, casting a shadow many times his size. A shadow with two massive, rippling wings.

"Mr. Clarke?" I gasped. "Good Lord, what's happened to you?"

There was no answer. The Wings of Amun Ra had twisted him beyond recognition. His skin had taken on a corpse-like pallor. His veins stood out like the dark, twisted roots of an ebony tree. He wasn't yet as dehydrated or brittle as Mr. Blackstone, but it was close. I'd seen a mummy before, in the British Museum—he looked like one returned to life.

Emily is one of the bravest people I know, but even she was recoiling from the awful energy surrounding the man we had thought to be our fellow investigator. Our friend. "What's wrong with him?" she whispered. "Why does he look like that?"

"I think it's the Sundered Wings. He's cursed."

Mr. Clarke loomed over the room. It was as if he was in a trance, somehow aware of his surroundings but unaware of our presence. When he did finally notice us, a gruesome smile crossed his withered face. "Well, if it isn't the Wentworths—my favorite *junge detektive*. I have no time for you, children. Step aside and let me pass."

"We know what you are," I snapped. "We know what you've done. It's over."

"It's time for you to hand over the Wings of Amun-Ra, Mr. Clarke," Emily said.

Oliver's grip tightened around Mr. Harlowe's revolver, but he didn't raise it. He was staring, transfixed, at Mr. Clarke. "You were supposed to be on our side! You were helping us find out what happened to Lieutenant Morgan! I trusted you!"

Mr. Clarke cackled as hissing magic snaked around him like a boa constrictor. "You should not have."

"But—how? Why? You killed him! Admit it!"

"I did." The aura pulsed, its dark tendrils coalescing around his torso. It moved with a sinister grace, slithering up his arms, around his neck, over the satchel he wore across his shoulder, and into his chest. The air around him felt cold; it stank of decay.

Oliver continued to stare at the monster wearing Mr. Clarke's clothes. "I hope it was worth it," he seethed. "You have everything you wanted now, don't you?"

"I do."

"The curse will come for you. It's come for everyone else. You can't escape it forever."

"I don't think Oliver can see it," Emily said. "That horrible magic, I don't think he can see it!"

She was right, though I couldn't fathom how that could be. *Was it because he'd never touched the Wing of Light?*

Mr. Clarke glared at Oliver; the spy's veneer of calm was chipping away with each pressing question. "As wonderful as it is to see you, my witless assistant, I've already told you I don't have time for a reunion." He winced as the magic of the Sundered Wings crossed over his heart. "I have killed enough in pursuit of this prize. I would rather not kill you as well. So, if you would be so kind as to get out of my way…"

"How do you think you're going to escape, exactly?" I asked, taking a cautious step forward. "We're in the middle of the Atlantic Ocean. There's nowhere for you to go. You're trapped!"

"Can a lion be trapped with an antelope? No, my friends, no help is coming for you. I have destroyed the wireless set. It is you who are trapped with me—until I make my escape."

Emily responded with a humorless laugh. "We're all trapped on board the same cage, Mr. Clarke. You may have power, but the lion is no freer to roam the zoo than any other creature."

"Silence! You know nothing of which you speak!"

"You're deranged," Oliver declared. "Absolutely demented."

The shadows coiled more tightly around Mr. Clarke's chest. His eyes bulged; it was like something snapped in him. The last strands of his sanity seemed to fray and break apart. "Deranged!?" he screamed. "I have gained the blessing of Amun-Ra! United the Sundered Wings! With them, Germany will rise to unparalleled glory!"

"That's what this is about?" I demanded. "Politics?"

"Talk to me about the value of political power when it's your father butchered at the hands of the French!" Mr. Clarke shouted. "When it's your mother forced into servitude to make ends meet! When it's your brother drafted into the army, dead at nineteen, killed in a needless African squabble! YOU—KNOW—NOTHING!"

"I—"

"No! I've had enough of you, Mr. Kelly. For the last time—move aside!" His gaze, once sharp, now burned with fanatical fire. "I am taking these artifacts back to Germany. My people will rise above all others!"

"You're wrong." Emily's voice was firm. "Nobody will rise to anything if they need to use the Sundered Wings to do it. They're twisted. Can't you see what they're doing to you?"

Mr. Clarke ignored her. He stowed the artifacts in his satchel before marching toward the door that led outside, but each of his labored steps was further proof that Emily was right about the cost of Amun-Ra's power. His joints were stiff and reluctant to bend. He looked like a human puppet. One whose strings were controlled by an unseen, supernatural master.

"Stop. You're not going anywhere, Mr. Clarke." Oliver raised Mr. Harlowe's revolver with shaking hands. "This ends now."

Mr. Clarke took a step forward, aiming his own pistol at Oliver. "Drop it, *dummer junge*," he hissed. "A man should never present a firearm unless he is prepared to discharge it."

"I am prepared," Oliver snapped. His knuckles whitened as he gripped the revolver tighter.

"You are not." Mr. Clarke turned his weapon to Emily and me, his presence overpowering, the aura around him tangible. "You know nothing of war. Of death. Shall I show you what resolve looks like?"

I stepped forward to shield Emily. But Emily, no damsel in distress, pulled me back beside her. "We face him together," she said. "I will not hide behind you when I can stand beside you."

She grabbed my hand, and we embraced our destiny as partners.

Mr. Clarke's smile twisted into a manic grin as he shifted his aim between us. "It matters not whether I shoot one of you or all of you! Mr. Wentworth, don't even try it—I will get a shot off before you so much as twitch," he warned Oliver. "Lower your weapon... or they die."

Reluctantly, Oliver lowered his gun.

"*Gut*," Mr. Clarke hissed. "Now, drop it and back away."

Oliver did so. "I'm sorry," he mumbled, looking devastated. "I just... I couldn't. I couldn't do it. He would have killed you if I'd tried."

"I understand," I said. "Truly, I do."

There was a commotion behind the cursed journalist. Shouts erupted from the corridor leading back to the bridge.

"Move," Mr. Clarke commanded. He gestured toward the door with his pistol. "I've changed my mind. We're all going out on deck together."

"And if we refuse to be your hostages?" I asked. "What will you do then?"

"I'll shoot you. Or I'll introduce you to the charming effects of these artifacts. Your choice."

"I don't see where we have much of one."

"Start walking, Mr. Kelly. Or I'll begin with your beautiful friend."

We began to make our way to the door. After Emily and I passed by Mr. Clarke, I took the opportunity to glance down at her. Her grip on my hand tightened. "We'll get through this," she whispered. "If you get a chance to get the Sundered Wings away from him, take it. I'll back you up."

"Be safe," I whispered back, knowing it was an impossible request.

We let Mr. Clarke lead us from the first-class entrance to the boat deck. The stormy expanse of the ocean stretched out before us, a vast, heaving field of nothingness that pitched and rolled at the direction of the Sundered Wings. The sky was an angry swirl of black and gray clouds. Rain lashed at us with stinging ferocity. The deck beneath our feet was slick and treacherous. It would be all too easy to be swept away by the gale. I held onto Emily as tightly as possible; if we fell from here, there would be no coming back.

"Can you feel it?" Mr. Clarke asked. The aura's tendrils pulsed, each beat synchronized with his erratic heartbeat. "The power I possess? I have brought on the storm! And now it will cover my escape!"

"You started as a spy, Mr. Clarke," I shouted. "That much, I can understand. But this? This is madness! Why are you doing this?"

Mr. Clarke's face twisted in a grimace. "Madness? Do you think I wanted this? I saw an opportunity, *junge*, to better my country. To make Germany great. I sacrificed only what duty required! Any man of courage would have done the same!"

Mr. Clarke stepped nearer to one of the towering lifeboat davits. For the first time, it was clear that he was unsure what to do next. A massive, quarter-wheel gear was affixed to what looked like a crank, but I didn't see how one could operate it alone—and evidently, neither did he. He yanked at the ropes and levers with growing frustration, each pull and twist only tangling the lines further. The mechanisms clicked and banged under his desperate attempts.

"You can't seriously think you'll be able to take those artifacts back to Germany!" I stepped forward, releasing Emily's hand. "You'll never be able to get that boat free! Even if you do, what's your plan? To sail to America?"

"*Halt die Klappe!*" Mr. Clarke snarled. His glare was murderous, but there was no denying the truth. The German was many things—a spy, a murderer, and even brave—but a sailor, he was not. He didn't know how to operate the equipment holding the lifeboats.

I heard shouting from inside the ship; help was close.

"You can't kill all of us!" Oliver shouted. "Just give up and hand over the artifacts!"

"Don't tell me what I can't do!" Mr. Clarke screamed. The once confident man now appeared pitiful, consumed by the curse inflicted on him by the Sundered Wings. Nevertheless, he plunged his right hand into his satchel and raised one of the artifacts high, begging for aid—the storm roared with approval, intensifying its gale and hammering us with all it had.

"Grab onto something!" I shouted. I looped my arms around a nearby railing and strained to pull Emily close enough she could do the same. Beside us, Oliver wrapped his hands around the railing, his hair plastered to his face in the rain.

"I have secured the power of Amun-Ra!" cried Mr. Clarke as he returned what must have been the Wing of Darkness to his satchel. "I have won!"

"It's killing you!" Emily said. "Why can't you see that? Are you not afraid?"

Mr. Clarke cackled. "Fear? Oh, yes, girl. I know it well. But *mein Deutschland* will dominate their rivals with these artifacts! My people shall never again need to feel such a weak emotion!"

I let go of the railing and started making my way around to where Mr. Clarke stood. His attention was focused on the Wentworths; he didn't even seem to notice that I'd moved.

"You're insane!" Oliver shouted. "Mad! Our countries aren't even at war!"

"They will be!" Mr. Clarke was straining to be heard over the storm. "It's only a matter of time! Germany will need every edge it can get—and I shall provide it!"

Oliver saw me sneaking up on Mr. Clarke. He seized the opportunity to keep our adversary's focus on himself. "Do you really believe Germany can take on the world? America won't stand idly by if you start a war!"

"*America*?!" Mr. Clarke laughed again. "Your people are feeble and impotent, Mr. Wentworth! They won't intervene until it's too late!"

I edged closer, careful to stay out of Mr. Clarke's line of sight.

"Is that what you think?" Oliver pressed. "That the world will just let Germany run wild? Forget about America; Britain and France won't stand for it, either. And when they fight back, the entire world will be dragged into your chaos! Millions will die!"

"The old empires are already dying," Mr. Clarke spat. "Germany is rising, and these artifacts will make us unstoppable! I will bring glory to my nation. You will be dust beneath our boots!"

I was just a few feet away. Mr. Clarke's back was turned.

"A worldwide war, Mr. Clarke? Is that the legacy you want to leave?"

"You cannot understand!" Mr. Clarke roared, brandishing his bag at Oliver. "How could you? This is my destiny, my power! These artifacts will forge a new world order for Germany!"

Mr. Clarke whirled around and aimed his pistol at me. "You fool! You dare to defy me? I can—"

I didn't let him finish. It was now or never. With a surge of adrenaline, I lunged and tackled him to the deck. My wounds burned in the salty water. His pistol went off, but the shot was lost in the chaos. I knocked it away. Mr. Clarke was much smaller than me, but I was injured, fighting with one good arm, and he was desperate. We were evenly matched.

Emily held true to her word and came to my defense. She closed the distance between us and kicked Mr. Clarke, hard, again and again, hammering away at him for all she was worth. He growled and shouted. It was for nothing. She was relentless. We were relentless. Unable to throw us off on his own, Mr. Clarke screamed to the heavens, calling for the wind to aid him. It whipped up, somehow fiercer than before, with a bitter edge that spoke of powers beyond any mortal understanding. Under that pressure, Emily lost her footing and spun toward the sea—I froze, terrified, sure that all was lost—but, with the grace of a dancer, she turned her fall into a slide. She grabbed onto one of the bent railings and clung to it for all she was worth.

"James!" she shouted, fighting against the rain to be heard, "Don't give up! Get the Sundered Wings away from him!"

Mr. Clarke and I fought ferociously, each of us pounding away at the other with everything we had, until, finally, his strength faded. He'd pushed himself too far. I didn't recognize it for what it was at the time, but that was when I saw the first spark of fear in his eyes. His control over the situation was fast slipping away. With one last blow, I knocked his bag away from him. The Sundered Wings tumbled out and skittered across the slick surface of the deck.

"Oliver, grab them!" Emily shouted, but it was too late. Another massive wave crashed over the side and swept the artifacts to the edge. With an almighty clang, they caught on the side railing, suspended hundreds of feet above the heaving Atlantic. One more wave would sweep them away for good.

Mr. Clarke froze when he noticed that the Sundered Wings were teetering on the brink.

He let out a guttural scream, thrust his arms out, and managed to throw me off. I landed hard on my back. He scrambled toward the artifacts, but I dove after him, grabbed his ankle, and pulled him away.

I heard someone screaming my name. It had to be Emily.

Mr. Clarke tried again to snatch the Sundered Wings, but I lunged alongside him, sliding on the rain-soaked pine. I made it there first. As my hands closed around the artifacts, electricity surged through me. For one glorious, absurd moment, indescribable power flowed through my veins. It made my entire body vibrate with energy.

The storm's fury responded to my touch. If I wanted them to, the winds would bend to my will. I was sure of it. The ship beneath my feet was insignificant, a mere toy in the face of the power I now wielded.

A voice, ancient and commanding, filled my mind. *"You could have it all. Use my power to end this fight. Kill Clarke. Embrace your destiny. Put your trust in me."*

This was far beyond the sensations I'd felt when I touched the Wing of Light. The artifacts must have enhanced one another. Empowered each other, somehow. I was tempted to embrace the voice. Sorely tempted. But I resisted. I thought of Emily. And Oliver. And Dr. and Mrs. Wentworth. The people who needed me. I steadied myself, and for a moment, I thought I'd regained control.

"Perhaps the outcome of this battle is not enough for you... but I can give you the power to be with her," thundered the ancient voice. A vision flashed before me—one of Emily, smiling, radiant in a white dress. *"Wealth, glory, all would be yours. She could not refuse you if you had my*

power. You would command the respect you have long craved. I can elevate you to your rightful place!"

But no. Emily was her own woman, wasn't she? The choice should be hers.

The ancient voice growled. **"What is choice to a god?"**

My brain was itching, urging me to accept the Sundered Wings. I knew it was wrong, but the pressure was so intense, so visceral—I screamed, trying to resist. It was overwhelming. The voice was burrowing into my thoughts, working its way down to the depths of my soul...

But it was wrong. I didn't need to be a god. Being James Kelly was good enough.

"You've never been good enough."

My heart was splitting open. One by one, my insecurities were dredged up from the darkest pits of my being. I saw them all. I was alone. And I always would be.

But that wasn't true!

With the last of my free will, I pushed back one more time, fighting to remember my friends. I thought of Oliver's smiling face as he insisted I was a Wentworth, of Mrs. Wentworth's motherly smile as she called me one of her boys, and of Dr. Wentworth opening their home to me in my time of need. I thought of Emily's coy smile, and her lips on mine...

"Get out of my head!" I cried as I shook free. With a surge of defiant will, I thrust the Sundered Wings overboard, watching as they disappeared into the blackness of the night, swallowed by the raging sea. Their power ebbed away, leaving me hollow and trembling.

I'd done it. I'd won. My soul was my own.

"No!" Mr. Clarke's scream was one of pure anguish. He scrambled toward the edge of the boat deck, his eyes wide with disbelief.

The storm, no longer under Mr. Clarke's control, began to lose ferocity. For the first time since Saturday afternoon, the wind settled enough that I didn't have to shout to be heard. The rain softened. It was as though an ancient rage had been quelled.

I waved at Oliver. "We need to..." My voice cracked. "We need to capture him." I was shaking madly; sparks of electricity still ran up and down my arms from where I'd touched the artifacts.

"Right." Oliver stepped forward, holding Mr. Clarke's discarded revolver. "Step away from the railing, Mr. Clarke. I won't hesitate this time."

But Mr. Clarke didn't hear him. The man was broken. If he cared about what Oliver was saying, he didn't show it. The aura around him had dulled, but it was still palpable; the curling tendrils, so like snakes, bit and gnawed at him, taking from him all that they could. He didn't seem to care about that, either. His gaze was somewhere behind us, deep in the Atlantic Ocean. There was hunger in his expression. A burning desire that couldn't be satiated by anything but the artifacts he'd lost.

I knew what was about to happen.

"Wait!" I shouted.

It was too late. Mr. Clarke dove over the edge, unable to stand being parted from the Wings of Amun-Ra. He was gone before anyone could stop him.

Shocked, I made to stand up, but the shaking in my arms only intensified. My vision blurred. A searing pain shot through my temples. My legs buckled. I had just enough time to look at Emily before blackness crept in on the edge of my vision. She was the last thing I saw before I passed out.

24

RETURN OF THE SUN

Consciousness crept back to me in brief flashes. First, I remembered being carried. I thought Emily might have been with me then—I certainly remember smelling citrus—but I lost consciousness before I could find out. The second time, I felt people poking and prodding at the knife wound on my arm. It hurt, though not to the degree that it had earlier in the evening. I smelled alcohol; I tried to open my eyes, but I couldn't do it. I passed out again.

The third time I returned to consciousness, I kept my eyes closed. My body felt heavy. Thankfully, this time, I was dry; I savored the warmth of the comfortable sheets I'd been wrapped in. It was difficult to know for sure, but I didn't think it could have been more than a few hours since I first passed out on the boat deck. My wounds still stung and ached.

Then I heard whispering. I even recognized the owners of the voices: Dr. Wentworth and Dr. Widmer.

"He is fortunate to be alive," Dr. Wentworth said. "Those Sundered Wings were insidious artifacts. I was worried we would find him in the same state we found Reginald and Theodore."

Dr. Widmer grunted in agreement. "Thank God we didn't. He's stable, which is more than can be said for that Clarke fellow. He never resurfaced, did he?"

"No. Poor Charles isn't faring well either, is he?"

"Mr. Haverford is beyond my help. I fear he's well and truly lost his mind."

"To be so young and so afflicted. Alas, what can be done? My children told me what he used the artifacts for... I believe he made his choice."

They were silent for a moment.

"I'm going to the other room to check on Mr. Harlowe," Dr. Widmer said. "Will you be quite well here?"

"Yes. I am comfortable seeing to Mr. Kelly."

"Lock the room up when you're ready to leave, won't you?"

"I will."

I heard a door open and close. Dr. Widmer was gone. Deciding I had waited long enough to reveal myself, I opened my eyes. "Dr. Wentworth?" I asked, surprised by the weakness in my voice.

"Ah, Mr. Kelly. Excellent. I was hopeful you would wake soon." Dr. Wentworth was sitting with his hands folded together at my side. "How are you feeling?"

I tried to sit up. As I adjusted on the bed, a sharp sting in my arm made me wince. The sterile smell of antiseptic burned my nose. "A bit sore, sir, but... alive. What happened? Where am I?"

"You are in the hospital," Dr. Wentworth said. He dabbed at a cut on my forehead. "You endured quite the ordeal last night. It was close, but we got you here just in time."

The night's events came rushing back. "What happened after I blacked out? Is everyone safe? Are Emily and Oliver well?"

"They are. By the time that help arrived, Mr. Clarke was gone," Dr. Wentworth said. "My children were frantic, claiming you had touched the Sundered Wings and needed immediate medical attention. You were brought here."

"They were so powerful. I felt them, you know? It was like... well, it was like nothing I've ever felt before. The power, the temptation... I understand how they lured in Mr. Clarke and Assistant Purser Haverford."

Dr. Wentworth placed a comforting hand on my shoulder. "You did well, Mr. Kelly. I cannot fully comprehend the nature of those objects, but your resistance to them shows great fortitude."

"I tossed them overboard," I confessed, basking in the relief brought on by saying those words aloud.

"You did. I am proud of you—your parents would be, too."

I let out a sigh. "Thank you, sir. And thank you for taking care of me."

"We both know my children would never forgive me if I did any less."

"They were incredible," I said. "I don't know what I would have done without Emily. She was brilliant."

"I do not doubt it." Dr. Wentworth offered me a small, knowing smile. "I ordered both of my children back to their rooms for the night, but I assure you they will be here in the morning. They insist you saved their lives, you know. They were reluctant to leave your side."

"We saved each other."

"Be that as it may," Dr. Wentworth said, "I am in your debt. Should you ever need anything, do not hesitate to ask."

I don't think Dr. Wentworth intended for me to respond immediately, but there was something else I needed to ask him, and this seemed as good a time as any. I'd promised Oliver I would have this conversation, after all. If I couldn't do it now, after everything I'd endured, I would never be ready.

"Actually, sir? There is something."

Dr. Wentworth smiled. "You have my full attention, Mr. Kelly."

I took a deep breath. "I care a lot about Emily," I said. "And I—well, this probably seems a bit sudden, but these last few days have made me realize how much she means to me."

Dr. Wentworth's eyes narrowed. "Continue."

My throat felt tight. "I want to court her, sir. With your permission, of course."

Dr. Wentworth's expression grew thoughtful as he weighed my words. "Emily thinks highly of you, Mr. Kelly," he said slowly. "But my daughter is strong-willed and intelligent. She needs a man who respects and supports her. Emily will not tolerate being anything less than a full partner in your life. You will face judgment for her more eccentric choices. You will face challenges and scrutiny from our peers. Are you ready for that responsibility?"

"I am, sir. I want to support her in every way I can."

Dr. Wentworth nodded. "Very well; I, too, once made the decision to court a woman of higher standing. It was a challenge, but it was also the greatest decision of my life. Mutual respect and understanding are paramount. Emily cares for nothing as much as her autonomy. Honor that, and you will have earned my blessing."

I grinned. "Thank you, sir. I doubt if she'd stand for anything else."

"We can discuss the particulars when we are back in New York. If this relationship progresses, there will be financial questions. And we both know that Emily will have something to say about the terms of this courtship."

"I've already spoken with her about it. She favors the effort."

"Of course she does," he said. Dr. Wentworth paused to adjust my blankets. "It was wise of you to ask her before searching for me. My daughter does not like to have others speak for her."

"No, sir. She doesn't."

"Incidentally, her mother will be pleased. She has been harboring a strange feeling about the two of you."

"Really?"

"My wife's body may be weak, Mr. Kelly, but her mind is as sharp as it has ever been." Dr. Wentworth checked the wound on my arm, then rose to his feet. "Before I leave you, is there anything else on your mind?"

I knew I was pushing my luck with Dr. Wentworth, but now that we were talking, I didn't want to stop. "There is something else. You mentioned the financial element of this courtship, and that made me think of it. I've realized what I want to do with my life."

"You have, have you?"

"Yes, sir," I said, preparing to voice my desire aloud to him for the first time. "I want to become a detective. I want to help other people, like Mr. Harlowe helped us. And I want to stop people like Mr. Clarke."

"Ambition is the first step on the path to accomplishment," Dr. Wentworth said approvingly. "Given what I have seen, you would make a fine detective. When we return to New York, we can see what needs to be done for you to begin your studies."

I exhaled slowly, tension fading from my weary joints. Dr. Wentworth hadn't ridiculed my suggestion. He even thought I'd make a fine detective! "Thank you, sir," I said. "For everything."

He gave me a final reassuring smile. "Get some rest, son. You, more than anyone else, have earned it."

With that, he left the room. I closed my eyes and settled into my cozy bed sheets. Before long, I was nearly asleep. Unbidden images of Emily and a detective's uniform swirled in my mind, first as separate thoughts, then combined into a bizarre image of Emily wearing the detective's uniform. She was scolding me for losing evidence.

I had a smile on my face when I drifted off, my thoughts neatly transitioning into pleasant dreams.

TUESDAY MORNING DAWNED, and for the first time in several days, the new day brought with it the sun. The storm had subsided, leaving the *Olympic* to rock gently on calmer seas. She'd taken a beating plowing through Mr. Clarke's storm, but she'd proven herself more than a match for the Curse of the Sundered Wings. The ship's crew was still assessing the damage, but the only person to have lost their life in the chaos of Monday night was Mr. Clarke himself.

"I still can't believe there really was a curse." Emily sat by my bedside, the bruises on her face evidence of last night's events. She wore a soft, white cotton blouse with a high lace collar and delicate pin-tucks, its loosened sleeve accommodating the sling on her injured shoulder.

"I told you there might be. It just took the world almost ending for you to believe me," Oliver said. He was sitting on the edge of the bed opposite mine, smiling as he twirled his cap. "Is the doctor letting you out of here soon, Jimmy?"

"Quite soon, I think." I held up my forearm. "Dr. Widmer says this'll scar, but I won't have any loss of function."

Emily tucked a loose strand of her wavy hair back. "That's a relief. We're really going to be fine, aren't we?"

"We are. Better than fine. When we dock, we'll have to work out how best to begin our courtship, now that your father approves of it."

Emily beamed at me while Oliver shook his head. "This is bound to be frightfully mawkish," he griped.

A knock at the door announced Dr. Widmer's return. He entered the cramped room to give me a final once-over, prodding at the bandages on my arm to check that everything was tight. It seemed to be. Satisfied, he moved on to examine the other minor cuts and bruises that peppered my body.

"Everything is in order here, Mr. Kelly," he eventually pronounced. "Keep your bandages clean and change them twice a day. And don't be ashamed of your wounds—if you feel any pain or discomfort, please see a doctor on shore. We still don't know what sort of aftereffect there may be from holding those artifacts."

"I'll be staying with Dr. Wentworth, sir," I replied. "He won't let me die."

"He might, now that you've asked to court his daughter," Oliver said. "Father is wily."

"Too right," Dr. Widmer said, chuckling while he concluded his final checks. Then, satisfied with my condition, he pronounced me free to go. "The rest of you, clear off. Give Mr. Kelly a moment to prepare himself."

My friends left, and with one last, fond smile, so did Dr. Widmer. I swung my legs over the side of the bed; the cool floor felt strange under my bare feet. Standing can be an odd motion when one is accustomed to an extended period of lying down. After a quick change of clothes and a perfunctory wash at the basin, I was prepared to rejoin the rest of the world.

"You can come back in, now," I called out.

Emily and Oliver, who had been waiting by the door, rushed to my side. Emily's smile was bright with relief. Oliver clapped me on the back.

"Ready to leave this place?" Oliver asked. "They're saying we'll be in New York soon."

"More than ready," I said, a smile breaking across my face as I savored the prospect of fresh air. "Before we go, is Mr. Harlowe still here? I'd like to offer him my thanks."

"He is, but he's resting," Emily said. "He has a nasty concussion, but Dr. Widmer says he'll make a full recovery. They want him back in London as soon as he's fit."

"For what?" Oliver asked.

"To explain what happened here, of course. And I see that look on your face, James, but you needn't worry. I spoke with him earlier this morning and passed along our thanks. We part with him on good terms."

"Thank you," I said, wondering what my expression must have revealed for her to so accurately guess at my concern. "We couldn't have done it without him."

"He knows that."

As we left the room, we passed the padded cell in which Assistant Purser Haverford was confined. None of us had spoken with him since our encounter in the gymnasium. According to Dr. Widmer, he'd lost his mind, inconsolable at the loss of the Wing of Light. There were doctors in New York who were waiting to receive him, though it was questionable whether they could ever make him whole again. The powers offered by the Sundered Wings had proven to be highly addictive. I was eternally grateful that Emily and I had only touched them for a few seconds.

We climbed the narrow stairs to C-deck in a single-file line. The promenade was in poor shape. Its planks were littered with splintered wood and shattered glass. And yet, in the light of day, the damage didn't seem as bad as it had the night before. Nothing had been done that could not be repaired. Even the porcelain doll had been salvaged; it was propped up on a bench, supervising the cleanup.

"Look who it is!" Oliver said brightly. "My favorite steward!"

Alex Cunningham's sleeves were rolled up. Sweat soaked his hair as he worked to sweep up shattered glass. Upon hearing Oliver, he straightened up and studied us warily. "You're not here to draw me into some other unpleasant business, are you?" he asked with a trace of genuine concern.

I raised my hands in mock surrender. "Not today, Mr. Cunningham. Today, we're just here to help—or at least get out of your way."

Alex smiled even as he shook his head. "You lot have done enough, I'd say. Saved the ship, didn't you? But if you're feeling conscience-stricken, there's plenty of cleaning to be done."

Emily laughed. "Be careful, or we might take you up on that! But first, we need a bit of fresh air. It's been a long couple of days."

"I imagine it has. Go on, then. But if you see any more crazed murderers, do give me a shout. I want to know ahead of time if I need to run the other way."

We all laughed, the tension of the past days easing. We bid

farewell to Alex and stepped along the promenade to the aft staircase. We'd barely reached the landing before Dr. Wentworth, Mrs. Wentworth, and Captain Bartlett flagged us down. They didn't seem surprised to run into us there.

Captain Bartlett greeted us with open arms. "James, Emily, Oliver, I hope you're feeling better."

"Much better, thank you, sir," I said. "Dr. Widmer said I'm fit to leave the hospital, which is welcome news."

Dr. Wentworth smiled. "I am glad to hear it. Now, I know you are eager to get away, but Captain Bartlett has much to discuss with you, if we might have a moment of your time. He has been waiting patiently."

His tone left no room for debate. Captain Bartlett led us into the library, which had already been cleared of debris. I smiled when we sat in a familiar semi-circle of green armchairs. Sunlight streamed through the large windows, bathing my favorite room on the *Olympic* in a warm, golden light. We settled in as we prepared to recount our story.

"Let's hear it from the beginning," Captain Bartlett said. "We need to understand what happened."

Emily, Oliver, and I took turns recounting the events of our voyage. We described our initial partnership with Mr. Clarke, our suspicion of Mr. Blackstone, the unraveling of the Sphinx Society, our work with Mr. Harlowe, the discovery of the Sundered Wings, Assistant Purser Haverford's involvement, Mr. Clarke's sabotage of the wireless, and our final showdown with him on the boat deck. Captain Bartlett listened intently, occasionally nodding or asking a clarifying question.

When we finished, Captain Bartlett leaned back in his chair with a thoughtful expression. "These artifacts... they're unbelievable. Your entire story is unbelievable. It will be difficult to relay all of this to the authorities without sounding insane."

"I am still struggling to believe it myself," Emily admitted. "But we all saw what the Sundered Wings could do. They were real, sir."

"Mr. Clarke's influence over the storm was real as well," Oliver said. "Haverford said he used the Wing of Darkness to accelerate our journey, but... it was obvious that it drove him mad to do it. I think that's why he jumped."

Captain Bartlett nodded. "That storm was no ordinary one. It blew out of the east, hard and fast. We got an accurate position this morning when the skies cleared, and we're much closer to New York than we should be. Mr. Clarke succeeded in that regard."

Oliver crossed his arms. "He fooled us. We didn't figure him out until it was almost too late."

"And you are certain about his allegiances?"

"Yes."

"He was a German spy," I clarified. "He intended to use the Sundered Wings to aid his country in future conflicts. I don't know how much of his ravings were him and how much of them were the curse, but he was fanatical."

"My Chief Officer told me the same story when he explained how Mr. Clarke managed to steal the Wing of Light last night." Captain Bartlett shook his head in disbelief. "It is a wonder neither of them was shot in their exchange. I never imagined such treachery among my passengers. You three showed incredible bravery standing against him."

"What will you tell the authorities when we arrive?" Emily asked.

"The truth. Nothing less. I suspect Mrs. Henderson will be interviewed. Dinsmore will be charged for his involvement.

After all, such happenings are far too dangerous to ignore. Imagine if Mr. Clarke had succeeded?"

Dr. Wentworth nodded. "We shall endeavor to ensure the authorities understand the gravity of the situation. Why, it is a matter of public safety!"

Mrs. Wentworth, who had been listening quietly, finally decided to speak. "You have all been brave beyond your years," she said. "I would not have chosen such a weight for you to bear, but I am glad you all are safe; accept what praise comes your way with pride."

Captain Bartlett stood, signaling the end of our meeting. "We will be docking soon. You three have done a great service —not just for this ship, but for everyone on board. You have my thanks."

I could feel a blush rising on my cheeks. "It was the right thing to do, sir. You don't need to thank us for that."

"Posterity will huzzah for us," Oliver agreed sagely. He stretched his arms above his head. "Shall we head up top? I think we've earned a bit of fresh air."

Emily smiled. "After you."

WE EMERGED on the boat deck, grinning, pleased to find the warm sun awaiting our arrival. Stepping around the place we'd played deck quoits on Thursday afternoon, Oliver found a spot on the railing to lean against. He reached for his lighter. Then, evidently thinking better of it, he stowed it away. "It's hard to believe we're almost in New York," he said. "Feels like we've been at sea for a lifetime."

Emily joined him against the railing, her charcoal gray skirt blowing in the breeze. Her hair, untamed and glorious, danced like the flames of a torch. "It does, doesn't it? It'll be strange to go home."

"A part of me can't believe we made it," I admitted, stepping up to join my friends. "Or that the Sundered Wings are at the bottom of the Atlantic. At least they can't cause any more harm there."

"Too bad, that," Oliver said wistfully. "It would have been nice to save one as a souvenir."

I chuckled, but I wasn't sure I was amused. I hadn't told anyone about the voice. It felt too personal to share. "We don't even know what they really were, you know? I still have so many questions. Who really made them? How? And why?"

"Who knows?" Oliver shrugged. "Look, all I'm saying is the gold would have been nice to have. You might have saved the world, Jimmy, but you didn't save my bank ledger."

"Oliver! That isn't funny!" Emily punched her brother lightly on the shoulder. "James was trying to be serious!"

Oliver stumbled back as if she'd hit him with all her might. "What? I meant it as a compliment!"

Emily put her hand on her hip. "You have a funny way of showing appreciation, Oliver Franklin."

"Me? Do you know how hard I worked to save you from the dangers on this ship?"

"Excuse me?" Emily sputtered. "What about everything I did to save you?"

Oliver laughed. "Come on, Em. We wouldn't have been involved with this mess in the first place if you hadn't wanted to go on one of your moral crusades."

"Oh, no, don't you go twisting this around. The way I remember it, you're the one who wanted 'one last adventure' before medical school!"

"Which is a completely justifiable position!" Oliver retorted. "What if Johns Hopkins turns out to be boring?"

"Boring?" Emily repeated incredulously.

"He has a point," I said, not altogether unfairly. "It might very well turn out to be boring."

That did it. Emily whirled around to face me, her eyes twinkling with mirth. "You! Why didn't you stop us from getting involved?"

I couldn't help it. I laughed. Not because Oliver shouldn't be blamed for our involvement—I still think he should be—but because we'd survived. Despite everything, we were standing here together, which was worth celebrating. Another laugh bubbled up from my chest, erupting in a near-hysterical bark. Emily snorted, then dissolved into giggles. Oliver's shoulders shook as we clung to the railing, tear-streaked and giddy with relief. To this day, I can't explain those tears except to tell you they were the most cathartic tears I've ever shed. They were happy-to-be-alive tears.

The sun climbed ever higher, casting a divine glow over the ship. It illuminated the jagged edges and sweeping peaks of the distant New York skyline. Home was on the horizon. I wasn't sure what awaited me there, but I knew one thing: nothing would ever be the same again. How could it be, after all we'd been through?

I glanced at Emily, who wiped her tears away and beamed up at me. I grinned back. It dawned on me then, as sure as the sun rising in the sky, that I didn't want things to go back to the way they were before. For the first time in a long time, I was ready for my life to change. Excited for the future. To leave the past behind.

To move on.

AFTERWORD

I began writing this afterward on April 14th, 2024, at around 9:30 EST. It was a warm Sunday evening. For many, that date holds no real significance. For me, it carries the weight of history. It's impossible for me to think about Sunday, April 14th, without being transported back to the tragic loss of the RMS *Titanic*, a story that has captivated me for years.

That might seem strange to you. Perhaps it is. I don't know what initially drew me to the black hulls and towering funnels of ocean liners, but my interest spans decades. I was drawing pictures of *Titanic* in my school books years before James Cameron graced our screens with Jack and Rose. I consumed hours of grainy footage narrated by Bob Ballard just to glimpse the ship. My parents, supportive of my boyhood interest, humored me and bought me a fleet of picture books and VHS documentaries.

I was hooked. I've never stopped being hooked.

At some point, my interest in *Titanic* spread to her sister ships, *Olympic* and *Britannic*, and from there to the rest of the White Star liners, the Cunarders, the fabulous German liners, and even the various warships employed by nations in the Great War. Something about the age of steam captures my imagination. It's a foreign world, as fantastic and dangerous as any to be found in the pages of fantasy. As both a historian and an author of fiction, it's hard not to be inspired by it.

Indeed, as you now know, I couldn't resist that inspiration. I wanted to find a way to merge a pair of my passions—fantasy fiction and steamships—and this story was the culmination of that effort. I am honored to have had the pleasure of presenting it to you. Please understand that I did not use the setting of *Olympic* lightly. Despite the supernatural nature of the story I told, I did my best to present the ship as accurately as I could. She deserves nothing less.

The characters in *The Curse of the Sundered Wings* are entirely fictional. I debated using the names and likenesses of historical figures, like Captain Herbert Haddock, but ultimately decided against it. I wanted this story to stand as a pure work of fiction, complete with fictional heroes and heroines, unbound from the associations and comparisons that the use of real people would inevitably invite. James Kelly bears the names of two of my own immigrant ancestors, James Hill and Timothy Kelly, but he is not a historical figure. Nor are Emily, Oliver, Alex, or Mr. Clarke. Feel free to enjoy them as they are, not as they might (or should) have been.

Lastly, now that you've finished the novel, I cannot encourage you enough to seek out some of the "real stories" associated with the *Olympic*. They are every bit as fantastic, thrilling, tragic, heart-warming, chilling, and human as anything this writer's keyboard might conjure.

Thank you for joining me on this crazy voyage. I hope you enjoyed it as much as I enjoyed writing it for you!

Acknowledgments

First of all, thank you for reaching this point in the book! I appreciate all of my readers, and I hope to see you soon on social media (or out there in the world). I couldn't do this without your support, and I am so, so grateful for it. Please consider leaving me a friendly rating or review online. It means more than you know.

My beta readers stepped up big for this one. It isn't easy asking people to learn about steamships or read century-old dialogue for you! To Gabrielle, Lydia, and Brad—thank you. Thank you for your time, your expertise, your advice, and your kindness.

On that note, I would especially like to highlight the efforts of my editor, Melanie Porter, who has worked with me on all four of my novels. Thank you for taking the time to help me make this book the best version of itself.

About the Author

Born and raised in Ohio, M.P. Hill spends most of his time teaching social studies, gaming with his friends, traveling to historical sites, writing novels, and catching up on the never-ending backlog of books he would like to read.

Hill is on a quest to read 50 classic novels before the end of 2025. So far, *The Woman in White* has been his favorite of the bunch. He lives with his wife and cats, who never let things get too dull!

ALSO BY M.P. HILL

Crafters of Light

Shapeless

Clearing the Mist

Made in the USA
Monee, IL
30 October 2025

33271524R00208